Ain't No Messiah

Tales of the Blessed and Broken
Book 1

MARK TULLIUS

VINCERE
PRESS

Published by Vincere Press
65 Pine Ave., Ste. 806
Long Beach, CA 90802

Ain't No Messiah
Copyright © 2019 by Mark Tullius

Printed in the United States of America
First Edition
ISBN: 978-1-938475-91-7

Cover design by J. Campbell
Graphic Design by Florencio Ares aresjun@gmail.com

For those with the courage to question all they believe.

Also by Mark Tullius

Brightside
Try Not to Die: At Grandma's House #1
25 Perfect Days: Plus 5 More
Twisted Reunion
Somber Stroll
Unlocking the Cage
Untold Mayhem
Try Not to Die: In Brightside #2
Beyond Brightside
Try Not to Die: In the Pandemic #3
Try Not to Die: In the Wizard's Tower #4
TBI or CTE: What the Hell is Wrong with Me?
Try Not to Die: In the Wild West #5
Try Not to Die: At Ghostland #6
Try Not to Die: At Dethfest #7
Try Not to Die: Back at Grandma's House #8
Try Not to Die: On Slashtag #9
Try Not to Die: In a Dark Fairy Tale #10
Dethfest Confessions: The Devil's Playlist

Chapter One

Most my life I been saying I ain't no Messiah. All my life people been swearing to God I am. And now I'm here on this throne of flames, not knowing what to think, figuring it probably don't matter either way.

This cathedral spread out before me is unbelievable. It takes up the entire 47th floor, shiny oak pews and plush red carpet stretching to every corner, a massive glass pyramid above us, the adjustable tint letting in just the right light. Fifty-thousand square feet, the largest in the world, high above Las Vegas Boulevard, the epicenter of sin.

And even crazier still is that this is just one floor. The Church of His Son owns the entire complex. So not just this building, but also the six connected ones, the giant lake that spans the front, and the massive waterpark behind us.

There's not a soul present here besides a few friends and me, but it's already sold out for the next three years. I haven't seen my massive suite on the 46th floor, and I never will. This emptiness. This loneliness. This time to myself was my final request, the price Father paid for me to play along.

As much as I was against this place, I can't deny they did a tremendous job. The glass cross elevators adorning the front of each building are my favorite part, especially when they're set to red, a hint of flame flickering up. My sanctuary sits atop the highest cross, directly above where the triple-wide elevator deposits visitors. Tonight's mass, my very first live speech, won't be full capacity. The whole world will be watching, but in here there will only be people in the three pews before me. Only those whose dedication has proven they deserve to bear witness.

The glass that makes up the box surrounding the sanctuary is the same two-inch thick bulletproof material used in the walls. With so many people wanting me dead, it made little sense to make things easy for them. That's why we've got a lock on the glass door and the *Gone with the Wind* style staircase to separate the masses from their Messiah.

This sanctuary is twenty-by-twenty, just big enough to hold the throne, the altar, and the pulpit, all carved by Father. On the top of the pulpit, hidden beneath *The Lost Gospels*, he installed a small monitor I can use as a teleprompter so there's less of a chance I'll mess up my words. And if I ever need help with my lines when I'm looking up, Father stuck a bigger one on the back of the massive mega-screen hanging above the first pew. TV's been nothing but death and pain, sex and lies, all of which I've had my fill. I leave it all off and enjoy the silence, that's not really silence thanks to the faint shouts from down below. Jeremy said he couldn't hear them on my mic, but I know I'm not just imaging them.

Father didn't want the throne to swivel, said it cheapened his work of art, but I put my foot down, listed it as another demand. Sitting four feet from the edge would have paralyzed me with fear five months ago, but that's when things were different. Now I feel nothing looking at the empty skies, not a single helicopter in sight. Everyone from news crews to tourists are grounded until after my speech. There's no one around to film me popping this Percocet, downing it with the rest of this whiskey.

If I sit too long, the blood in my legs starts to clot and aches something fierce. Plus, I've spent too much of my life staying still, eyes locked on the uncertainty—and absurdity—of it all. It's time to show myself and see what's out there.

The black suit Father had custom tailored four months ago is now baggy, my appetite all but gone since the explosion I shouldn't have survived. But when this thing begins, I'll stand up tall, shoulders back, chest out. I'll look every bit as powerful as he wants you to believe. If I've learned anything, image is everything. It's all that matters. What people see is what they believe.

The window's cold on my forehead and palms, just two of the places the Almighty left his mark. The vote doesn't start for another hour, four more until it's over and I'll give my speech. The entire Strip has already been shut down, the streets packed with parked cars, crawling with people as far as I can see, phones and faces pointed this way. Directly below there's a small circle of red in front of the glass elevator, a staging and filming area for our special guests.

Armed guards behind gates hold back my most devout followers, those filling the sidewalks, trampling the shrubbery, and spilling into the lake hoping to be mass baptized. On the other side of the lake is a solid wall of vehicles, Metro and the National Guard working together to keep away everyone without a ten-thousand-dollar red wristband.

There's no question I can hear the crowd, their voice pulsing through my palm. That roar is all for me. People shaking their banners, a couple of them the size of rooftops, barely big enough to read. *Charles 3:16. Do It. Save Us. Burn in Hell.*

I turn from the window and limp to the pulpit I never asked for, but Father insisted on. He spent over a year working on it, twelve years waiting. Waiting for me to finally speak. To tell the world who I am and what I've done. That I'm here to judge the living *and* the dead.

Chapter Two

I was born mostly dead, my body purple, not a single breath or thump of my heart to be heard. Everyone figured I was already walking into Heaven, spying the Pearly Gates with closed eyes yet to see the mortal world. I guess that's where all this Messiah stuff started. Mother was the only one who believed I wasn't fully gone. She begged the Committee not to put me in the ground, but they'd made their decision.

Mother nearly tore off their skin trying to keep them from putting me in that tiny casket. Once they had restrained her, they started hammering nails. Father fell to his knees, looked to the darkening sky, and begged God to spare me. My parents had been trying to have a child for almost seven years. The Committee had told Mother she'd never conceive. I was a gift from Heaven, and God decided to take that gift back.

So Father offered a deal. He promised God I'd be a vessel for His will. I'd be His servant.

And that's when my cry ripped through the night.

Mother tore off the top of the casket and pulled me from the earth just as the sun sank.

At least, that's the way Father recounts it.

Just like all his other stories, it's a mix of fact and fancy and no one will ever know how much of each. They're simply tales to build my legend. He says belief is the only thing that matters, that we must do everything to preserve it, because without faith, there's no reason to live.

My parents had moved to the commune in the early 90s. Father couldn't hold a job and was tired of the city. Laura, Mother's sister, was convinced the radio waves were hurting Mother's chance to conceive. Laura was already living on the little plantation in South Carolina, just west of Charleston.

They packed up their station wagon and drove east, cutting themselves off from society, deciding to reconnect with the earth. Aunt Laura and the Friends of Solstice community greeted my parents at the gates with candles and song.

Father says it wasn't a cult, more like a bunch of hippies trying to prove the ideals of the 60s weren't dead. He didn't talk about it much and never mentioned the wine, weed, or magic mushrooms. In his story, he always pointed out the rules, how the Friends of Solstice only had a few of them.

No jealousy. No God. No politics. No violence.

Mother had broken the fourth by injuring a Committee member, even though he was the one who technically tried to bury me alive. The law was rule-breakers were either sentenced to the forest for a period or banished for good. Since Mother had to wean me, they allowed us to stay.

Father kept talking about God though. He began having dreams, visions in his mind's eye of a new plan for all of us. He said he'd been given a message by the Archangel Gabriel.

"God has chosen Joshua to bring forth his new kingdom on Earth."

Father told everyone I would lead the people. The Committee asked him to stop. Talking about God was forbidden. They said it brought too much division, too much suffering.

By the time I was two, Father was fed up with the hippie garbage. He knew there was an Almighty Being, and my heartbeat was his proof.

Father could no longer be silenced. He needed to spread the Word.

He even convinced a dozen others from the commune to follow us. I'm guessing they were high on dope, so it probably didn't take much effort. They packed up in the night and left Mother's sister behind, the clean break Father insisted we needed.

After a few days, they found a dilapidated house in Hartsville. The property was on five acres. It belonged to this little old lady, Mrs. Hester, who let us live there for next to nothing. Father said we were pilgrims on a journey to God. Mrs. Hester was lonely and dying of cancer. She passed a few weeks later, left the place to Father in her will, an open-and-shut case of Divine Intervention.

With Mrs. Hester's passing, the help of his followers, and a small loan, Father built our church, converting the attached garage into our sacristy. Our raised stage was a bunch of two-by-fours and plywood covered by a deep red carpet. More plywood painted white became the back of the stage with Mother's scarlet satin curtain hanging down the middle. Mother said it was to hide the opening, but it also made it more mysterious. There weren't any lights or windows inside that sliver of space we called the passage, where all the junk we couldn't throw out filled the right side. To the left was the door that led into our laundry room.

The altar, pulpit, and kneeler on stage, along with the piano right before it, took up almost all of the garage. Father tore out the massive garage door and expanded the walls lengthwise, made it flush with the front of our house. Stage Right the church shared our kitchen's blood-red stained-glass window and a plain one in the living room we always kept curtained. Stage Left were two sets of windows on the swamp side for natural light. To keep the cost down, Father covered the dirt driveway with green artificial grass painted pious white, a thick line of red down the middle. We had three rows of three folding chairs on either side of the line, with room for at least twice as many rows. Each of the chairs came with a cushion but I didn't get one because Father said kneeling was good for me and would make me stronger. An overhead fan was the last thing added, but all it did was push around the hot summer air.

My muddled memory is full of gaping holes, but occasionally there are sharp points like knives that stick out clearly. Earliest I can remember is when I was five, middle of summer. It was the Lord's Day, which meant it was my day. I was carrying my cross in my spot next to the altar. Father wanted me to carry a real wooden cross, but Mother said it was too heavy. She made one by wrapping brown canvas around cardboard tubes. The canvas was the same scratchy stuff she used for the pulpit's yellow banner, which read, "The Second Son," above a large red flame.

I paced in my spot with my shiny black shoes, two sizes too small. I was growing too fast. Father said he wasn't blowing an entire Lord's Day collection on clothing every month.

The canvas was rubbing my neck raw.

Finally, it was time to kneel. The solid oak piece was Father's very first creation, the wood so smooth, yet so hard, fit for the Son of God. The pain in my neck and feet moved to my knees. I folded my fingers and squeezed, could feel the congregation staring at me. I couldn't show any discomfort, that's what Father instructed. The flock needed to see strength. God's strength.

Our congregation had dwindled to a little over a half-dozen people. Most of the Friends of Solstice had gone back to the plantation. Our remaining followers were people from the neighborhood and a couple of homeless vagabonds who lived in our basement.

Old Man Thomas lived up the road. He liked to walk into town on Sundays and would stop by to get out of the sun. Usually he'd stumble about, talk a little too loud. This day was no different and his breath stung my eyes from five feet away.

The tips of my shoes pressed to the floor, my knees pinched together. I drove my shoulders back, my chest pushed out with elbows resting on the kneeler's ledge. My fingers pointed to the heavens. I was the picture of peace.

Father rose from his comfy chair, his black suit matching his wavy hair and watchful eyes. I snuck a peek and saw Mother in the front row smiling at both of us, her neck muscles standing out like strings on some strange instrument.

Father was a giant behind his pulpit, which was two small desks stacked on top of each other, hidden behind Mother's fiery banner. There was no microphone. Father wouldn't have needed it even if we'd been a thousand people deep. You could probably hear him in Florida when he felt the spirit.

"'Jesus, against his Father's wishes, drew his sword as he led his battalion of angels into the depths of hell, charging to take down the demons of darkness!'"

Father was reading from the first book of *The Lost Gospels*, the only one he'd written so far. He was simply the instrument transcribing the message, one that he claimed, "Finally infused the New Testament with the righteous passion of the Old."

Sweat dripped over my brow and into my eye, but I didn't blink. I tapped my shoe on the plywood, my toenail pushing back into swollen skin, my foot throbbing like a big fat bullfrog. I kept breathing through my nose, stared straight ahead, tried not to listen to what Father was saying. He was talking about how there were demons everywhere, trying to tempt and distract Jesus, just like my sweat, which was begging to be swiped.

Father said despite their best efforts, the good angels were overwhelmed by the demons, their wings burnt to a crisp, bodies flung into the lake of fire below. Jesus stood all alone in the darkness.

"'But he couldn't turn back. Jesus continued down the cliff's winding path. With each wet step, Jesus tried not to think of what he walked on, his feet sinking in the rotting corpses, sliding in their gore.'"

My hands ached as Father retold the story of the demon pinning Jesus to the rocks, his barbed tail shooting though Jesus' left hand, a black talon piercing the right, the blood of Christ bubbling on the bodies below.

Father said it would be the fate of anyone who didn't follow me. I was the only true path.

I pretended to listen as Father finished up his reading. I pretended to pray.

"We ask this in Joshua's name," Father said.

This was my cue to rise and throw off my cross. It landed with the lightest thud. The congregation smiled. They thought I was adorable. This only angered Father.

"Those who cannot repent shall all burn in hell! Whether they are family or friends, anyone who does not accept the path will be damned for eternity."

Father dabbed his hanky over his brow. Sweat ran like a river down my butt crack.

"All we can do is speak the truth and spread the word. That is our mission. Save as many as we can before it is time to be judged. Let them know that Jesus Christ has returned." He stretched his arms wide and turned to me. "Christ has died. Christ *is* risen. Christ *has* come again!"

Mother and most of the others said, "Amen."

I picked up my cross and stared straight ahead. I hated having to keep my chin up so high while everyone stared at me, knowing I was just a boy who'd done nothing special.

Father promised a new chapter the following Sunday and started us down the aisle, didn't even wait for Mother to get on the piano. Our tiny flock sang as we shuffled across the grass, out the door, up our porch and into the house. I went straight to the kitchen to get the basket of oatmeal raisin cookies Mother made every week, the one good thing to look forward to.

Usually, Father would head back out and talk with the people after a service, but when I turned to take the basket outside, he filled the doorway. Without a word, he whacked the basket out of my hands, cookies bouncing off my face, the basket landing on the linoleum.

The front door closed and Mother ran inside, stopping at the doorway just in time to see Father flip over the kitchen table, our Sunday best bowls and plates shattering.

"Charles, please."

"Eight people! Eight Goddamn people!"

"The weather's been nice. I'm sure some—"

"Just shut your mouth! If I wanted your opinion, I'd damn well ask for it."

Mother stood there with lowered eyes, then went to picking up the shards of glass. I knew better than to get in Father's way, so I stayed planted against the wall. I was hoping I'd slip right through the sheetrock when he turned his gaze to me.

"And what the hell was all that twitching and fidgeting?"

I stared at my shoes, at Mother's fingers collecting the sharp pieces.

"How in the world are people supposed to believe in anyone who can't even control his own fingers?"

I had been scratching a little. The canvas cross was so itchy.

"I mean what are we trying to do here? What are we trying to accomplish?"

I honestly didn't know.

"God's given us a roof over our heads, a place to worship and spread his good word, but it doesn't mean squat if no one hears it." Father took a deep breath and let it out, shook his head as he looked at me. "Now are you willing to play your part?"

Blood dripped from Mother's finger.

"Look at me when I speak to you."

"Yes."

"*Yes what?*"

"Yes, sir."

Father gripped a fistful of my hair, tilted my head back, his cold black eyes burrowing through me. "My patience is wearing thin."

I couldn't nod because he had a hold of my head. I just swallowed.

"It's time you prove your worth. Next week we're going into town. And you're going to inspire people to join our church."

† † †

"Why are we here?" I asked.

"Because these people need to hear the truth," Father said. I couldn't read but he made sure I knew what was on all the picket signs. His read, "REPENT OR BURN!"

We were setup across the street from the Hartsville Baptist Church. Mother sat at a little folding table straightening a stack of pamphlets. Each one had a picture of me as a baby with a little halo over my head.

Old Man Thomas was sleeping under the shade of a huge oak tree. He'd ridden with us into town so he could buy groceries. There were bags of liquor and deli meats beside him.

Father kicked his leg. "Get up, they're coming out."

Old Man Thomas groaned and staggered to his feet. I thought he was going to fall on me, but he burped and stood tall with his picket sign: "FAGS GO TO HELL!"

Father had stayed up all night making the signs. There were fifteen other ones in the station wagon, in case anyone passing by might want to join the cause.

I hoisted the cardboard cross over my shoulder. Father had insisted I wear a crown of thorns. Mother had secretly snipped off the pointy tips to protect my head. The sun was so bright, I could hardly see, but I could make out a truck rolling up. The teenagers inside were laughing. One of them threw a soda can at us. It clanged off the sidewalk and landed on the grass.

"They'll all pay," Father said, his eyes locked on the church.

The doors opened and the congregation poured out. The women were wearing lacy gloves and big hats. The men had on suits and ties. Everyone was fanning themselves or tugging on their shirts from the heat, but they were smiling. They were happy. Nothing like the flock walking out after our services, especially after one of Father's more fiery sermons, the kind where he spoke of what the demons did to our souls. The sermons that kept me awake most nights.

Two little black boys ripped off their ties and started chasing each other. Their mother grabbed them by their collars, pulled them in tight.

"We ain't out five seconds, and you two acting like fools."

"TURN AWAY FROM YOUR FALSE GODS AND FEAST YOUR EYES UPON YOUR SAVIOR!"

Father pointed at me, which was my cue to shuffle down the sidewalk with my cross. I moaned, kept my face down until I had to turn back. The people in their nice clothes were staring at us like we were lunatics.

"YOUR DAYS ARE NUMBERED UNLESS YOU EMBRACE THE SECOND COMING."

My foot hit a crack and I started to stumble, but I kept myself moving. I knew Father saw my mistake. I kept pacing, moaning, trying to make up for what I'd done.

We'd never actually performed something like this before. Father had handed out pamphlets on the street and we'd given talks outside the homeless shelter, but we'd never staged a spectacle in front of a church.

Mother just smiled and kept organizing her table. She was looking at the people, but she wasn't making eye contact, almost like she was staring right through them.

"REPENT OR BURN!" Father yelled.

Some of the congregation laughed; others shook their heads and went back to chatting with each other.

Old Man Thomas said, "Charles, I don't think niggers burn." He was trying to whisper, but he was too drunk for that.

Father's eyes widened. The congregation had heard what he'd said. "Dang it, Tom."

"What? I'm just saying their pigment don't feel the sun as much."

Father tried to go back to his speech. "TURN TOWARDS THE LIGHT—"

A young man stepped off the curb, his face all furious. "What did you say?" He headed right for us. Other men followed.

"Say it again!"

"I...I..." Thomas stammered. "I didn't..."

Mother had told Father we shouldn't bring Old Man Thomas along, but Father wanted bodies for our demonstration. No one else would come.

"We are simply offering a better path, a path of redemption," Father said. "Gentlemen, please, Brother Thomas didn't—"

"Fuck your *please*." The man stepped right up to Old Man Thomas, who was shaking and looking all around, probably for a place to run. "Call me that again, you racist piece of shit."

"I...wasn't calling... I'm...just...I'm drunk."

"That just exposes the real you." The guy bent down and pulled out a bottle of whisky from one of the grocery bags. He took his time unscrewing the cap. "Come on, let's see some more."

"Please, I'm—I didn't mean nothing."

"Oh, I think you did, and I want to hear you say it." The young man raised the bottle over Thomas's shiny head.

"Bernard, stop that!" An older woman in a purple dress forced her way through the men. "Now, just let it go. Whatever he said ain't worth it."

The woman reached for the bottle, but Bernard pulled it away. Whiskey sloshed out and splattered Old Man Thomas, as well the woman. She squealed. "Bernard!"

"Mama, I'm—"

"Look what you did to my dress."

"Give me back my booze," Thomas said. He lunged and stumbled into Bernard, who shoved Thomas back. Then everyone was pushing. Father, too. There were legs and fists and men the size of refrigerators, everyone bouncing around. I got hit in the back as I squeezed between some bellies. There was nothing but darkness in that pile, so I wedged myself through to the light. I tripped off the curb. I was about to fall, but I flung my right foot forward and kept my balance, both legs stretched out like I was about to do the splits.

I heard the screeching. Tires skidding across the pavement. I think there was a horn. Mother and people were screaming. Then everything fell silent. You couldn't hear a sneeze. All I saw was the truck, the reflection of my face on the grill, my lips all wide, just like my eyes. Then the thunderous crack, like I'd jumped off a skyscraper and landed on my back.

Clouds were above me, the hot pavement searing my arms and neck. Blood shot through my body in big, pulsing throbs. My eyes were closed, but I could tell people were standing over me, blocking out the glare of the sun. There was screaming and some guy moaning, "I didn't see him."

Fingers touched my neck, something heavy on my chest.

"What's going on?" Mother said, her voice taut as a guitar string about to break. "Is he breathing?"

"Tell us," Father said.

"I'm so sorry, mister," another guy said. "I swear, he came out of nowhere."

A voice by my chest said, "I don't hear anything."

"Oh, God!" Mother wailed like I'd pictured her doing in Father's story of my birth. I was kind of glad my eyes were closed so I couldn't see her in case she attacked with her nails. "Look what you did!"

It felt like my ribs were squishing into my lungs. My fingers scraped along the pavement. I couldn't move my left arm. His body was pinning it down, but with my right hand, I finally pushed his head. "Get...off..."

The head lifted and I opened my eyes, saw it was someone's gray-haired grandpa. Everyone was standing over me. I scooted back and got to my feet. They all said to sit down, but I didn't want to.

"I'm okay," I said.

Mother knelt in front of me, stared with this horrified look as if my face had been ripped off.

There was a car. I walked over, saw my reflection in the window. I still had eyes and a nose but now there was one hell of a dent across my forehead. My hair was matted with sweat. There was a little blood on my cheek. I looked down. My clothes were a bit ripped, but I didn't see anything too gruesome.

Father grabbed me and stood me beside him on the sidewalk. There was something strange in his eyes. He was...happy.

He raised my hand and spun me back to the crowd. They clearly didn't know what to make of me.

"Joshua lives!" Father yelled. "Your savior has returned!"

Two of the women made the sign of the cross. The others circled around, everyone staring at me with this confused reverence.

"Say something to them," Father whispered.

I didn't know what he wanted, but they were clearly waiting to hear my voice. "It's…all okay," I said.

I just meant my head and body, but they seemed to think I meant something more.

✝ ✝ ✝

I'm not going to lie and say the next week our church was packed, but there were more people, and less than a quarter of them homeless.

The first row was taken by Mr. and Mrs. Walker and their four little girls, each of them in a peach dress, their long curly hair pushed back over their shoulders. Mr. Walker owned the gas station at the edge of town. He also happened to be the one who'd hit me with his truck. When the collection plate went around, he dropped in a nice stack of bills.

Mr. and Mrs. Durrington, the wrinkled old couple that lived at the top of our hill, were seated behind the Walkers. They'd never actually attended one of our services, but word had spread and they wanted to make sure we weren't practicing voodoo. Mrs. Durrington wasn't a strong whisperer. She said, "Those voodoo folk sacrifice goats and all. I don't want no goat blood in this neighborhood."

Doc Hargrove and his black leather bag took up two seats in the third row. Doc had checked me out after the accident, didn't find a single fracture, just the dent in my skull and the bruise on my back. And when he asked witnesses what they'd seen, he almost called it a miracle. Almost. Oh, Father would've loved that, but Doc would only go so far as to say it was remarkable.

There were a couple other people I didn't know sitting in the last two rows Father had added. Everyone was looking at me as I paced around with my cardboard cross. Everyone except Mother. She sat up straight in her lily-white dress, focused only on Father. She didn't even glance in my direction. Ever since Mr. Walker slammed me with his truck, she hardly said a word. At first, I thought my near-death moment had frightened her, but I started to realize she wasn't worried for me; she was freaked out. If I so much as *tinked* a juice glass with a fork, she'd leap out of her seat. It was as if I'd done something wrong by not dying in the street.

Father had been keeping us busy, mowing the lawn, painting the church, printing up new pamphlets, baking goodies to sell after the service. He knew people were going to be curious and there'd be more butts in the seats. He wanted to make sure their first impression was a good one.

Father spent every night that week working on his sermons. He must have downed ten gallons of coffee. He'd pace and talk into this little handheld recorder and make Mother type it up each morning. He chucked most of it in the trash, but every so often he'd get this look like he found gold in a river. He'd mark those lines and have Mother type it up all over again.

We even had a little band, with Mother on piano, Father on guitar, and Old Man Thomas on harmonica. He was almost sober enough to make it through the whole service without nodding off.

Initially, Father had wanted me to sing, but after a brief audition, he let me know I was more of a listener. During the song, I stood next to my parents and stayed away from Old Man Thomas' foul breath as I hummed along. Father said it made me more of a mystery. He was actually being nice to me for the first time. Even when I screwed up, he didn't hit me. In order for the people to believe I'd survived the accident unscathed, he couldn't leave any new marks.

In some ways, getting hit by that truck was the best thing for my well-being.

After that first service, people were shaking my hand and saying things like, "I still can't believe it," and, "You sure are resilient, gotta give you that," but they kept angling their heads, trying to really look me over, hoping to find a scratch or nick. One guy even picked me up in a tight bear hug. Pretty sure he was trying to see if I had any broken ribs.

Mother stayed near the house, in polite conversation with a few people. It was obvious she just wanted to go inside and escape all this. I felt like a freak show with everyone prodding and poking. I didn't blame her for not wanting to watch.

Father, on the other hand, was in heaven. He spoke of the visions and dreams he'd had since the day I was born. He said, "When God delivered this child to Earth, he was as dead as a severed snake, but I fell to my knees and promised we'd be His vessels. And just like that, Joshua's cries rang out. God had answered our prayers. And He sent us this message: Nothing, not even a truck, can injure His Son. Nothing compares to the power of the Lord!"

Father was certain this was only the beginning. He was convinced the people would just keep pouring in. He even talked about having to build a real church to accommodate all the new members, but the next week we only had a couple more. The week after that saw a couple less. After a few months, we were down to just over a dozen.

Father's anger returned. His face was always red, but he still couldn't bring a hand to Mother or me. He'd get close and raise a fist high, but at the last second he'd pull up, punch the wall, or just fall to his knees, all that hate coursing through his veins.

"Why have you teased us, Lord, bringing us just a taste of your glory, only to rip it away?"

Sometimes he'd take the blame, but most times he put it square on my back. One Sunday night, after a long day stewing over an almost empty church, Father grabbed my hand and yanked me along.

"You haven't given the people the purity they deserve," he said. "You haven't repented and begged God to cleanse your soul."

Father opened the basement door and told the few homeless men to take my room. He shoved me down the stairs into the darkness. From the top of the stairs, he yelled, "I don't hear no prayer!"

So I prayed. I said The Lord's Prayer and a Hail Mary and some of the ones Father had written himself.

"Blessed God, I ask you to take your sword and slice off the infectious sins clinging to my mind and heart. Chop off the wickedness and rotten core of my body. Give me peace and purity. Make me perfection so that I can deliver your spirit."

Father carried down the hard, wooden kneeler. He expected me to use it, but when he went upstairs I'd sit on my butt and act like I was suffering. It's strange how your eyes adjust to the dark. That first night, I could hardly make out the stairs or walls. By the second night I saw spiders spinning webs and a whole line of ants devouring something the homeless guys had dropped. I couldn't make out the demons, but I knew they were there.

I heard things down in the basement, too. All the creaking whenever someone walked into a room, Mother's whispers late at night. She begged Father to let me upstairs and end this, but he refused. He said starvation purifies the mind. The smell of cookies, bread, and pies made mine crystal clear.

By the fourth day, Mother was sneaking me sandwiches.

"Now, don't leave no crumbs," she said. "Your father sees this, and it's both our behinds."

I devoured those sandwiches. I didn't even worry about the crumbs, figuring the ants deserved a meal, too. That night I slept like a baby until just before the sun popped up. My whole stomach was gurgling and clenching. I had to go to the bathroom something awful.

Father had given me a bucket, but since I was only getting a cup of water, it was just for piss. I didn't even have anything to wipe with. For a second I considered sneaking up and making a beeline for the bathroom, but I heard Father's big clomping footsteps. I didn't have a choice. I hovered over that bucket and tried to push as fast I could, but my legs kept shaking and I fell in it mid-shit.

I honestly didn't care if Father found out about Mother's sandwiches. I just wanted out of the damn basement. My fists were wet with that filth as I marched up those steps. I was full-ready for Father's verbal lashing, but he wasn't even there. He'd gone into town. Mother found me in the kitchen.

"Oh Joshua…" She started to touch me, but pulled back. "Come on, let's get you in the shower. We'll burn these clothes."

It took a good half hour to scrub off the stink. Mother made me chicken noodle soup. Father came home and found me on the couch.

"What are you doing? Did I tell you to come up?"

"No…"

"No, *what?*"

"No…sir."

"Charles, I let him up."

"*You what?*"

"He got sick. You left him down there with a bucket?"

I'd never heard Mother stand up to Father, and by the look on his face, it was clear this was uncharted territory. But when he saw my soiled jeans in a bag, even he couldn't defend his actions.

"Well, I was going to bring you up anyway," he said. "It's time we got you a real cross."

That afternoon we took a long walk out back, and Father hacked down a tree. Together we dragged the big log back to the house. He sanded it down a bit and nailed a second beam to it.

"We'll stain it later," he said. "This'll do for this next service."

That Sunday, I paced in my usual spot as that heavy thing nearly sent me to my knees with every step. I stumbled once, and Mother almost went for me, but Father waved her off. He was in an especially fiery mood. Hardly anyone had shown up. Not even Mr. Walker, who was without question the most consistent member, on account of he nearly killed me.

After the final prayer, we didn't even stick around to mingle with our members. We just got in the car and drove straight to the gas station, where Mr. Walker was sitting behind his bulletproof glass.

Father reached into that little slot where you pass the money and get your cigarettes or candy or what-have-you. Mr. Walker only had to step back a foot to escape. I stayed in the car with the window down.

"You think you can just not show up to service?" Father asked.

"The guy who works Sundays called in sick."

"I don't care if you ruptured your spleen, you show up to our church. That was the deal."

"Charles, that might have—"

"You hit my son with your truck!"

"And I have apologized and tried to repay you."

"Well, you're not even close."

"That's not fair. Your boy wasn't even hurt."

"Not hurt? You know…actually, he was banged up. We just didn't say anything. Been having all sorts of neck problems."

"Now, Charles—"

"And I'd hate to have to get a lawyer and take this little station away from you. I mean, it's a child we're talking about."

"There's no need for that."

"Plenty of witnesses. They'd be happy to vouch."

"No, come on. I promise I'll be there next week."

"You're going to do more than that, Gary. You're going to make sure our little church is filled to the brim."

"I can't bring my kids."

"You'll bring whoever I tell you to."

"My wife put her foot down. You scare people, Charles."

"*Scare people*? I share nothing but the Lord's message."

"Well, it frightens my children, and they had nightmares."

"I'm done talking. If that place isn't full come Sunday, you'll be speaking to my lawyer."

Mr. Walker looked around a little then nodded. Father got back in the car. On the drive home, he grumbled, "Frightening people? What do you think hell's gonna be? I'm saving people's souls." He turned to me. "You hear what I'm saying?"

I nodded.

"I'll use whatever tool I can to make sure God's message is heard."

"Well…"

"Well what?"

"It's just you…say God is all loving."

"So? He's also not to be disobeyed."

"Right…but maybe you could talk more about the love part. Just to remind everyone."

"Oh, so now you're telling me how to preach."

"No, sir. It's just…well, even sometimes I forget there's a good side, too."

"Yeah, well, that's because you're an idiot."

But despite what Father might have thought at the time, his next sermon was different. Oh, he still hammered on about all of God's wrath, but his face softened when he spoke about eternal paradise. He said your best day on Earth wouldn't be one-tenth as wonderful as your worst moment in Heaven. Then he told a story I'd never heard about a dolphin protecting her babies by throwing herself in front of a fisherman's spear. Father said that God holds nothing in higher esteem than self-sacrifice. That dolphin was the first animal allowed through the Pearly Gates and that all kinds of animals, especially pets we've lost, will be waiting for us in Heaven.

Some of the adults in attendance snickered a bit, but every child in that church was grinning from ear to ear. And there were a lot of children, too. Mr. Walker had somehow convinced his daughters' Girl Scout Troop to show up, their parents as well.

By the end of the service, after Mother sang *Amazing Grace*, there wasn't a dry eye in the place. And most everyone made a point to tell Father and me they'd be back next week. Half weren't lying either. The next service wasn't as packed, but there weren't many empty seats. Father even stuck to the fifty-fifty split of damnation and God's love, and the following week we were back to standing room only.

The collections plates were full, too. We weren't rich by any means, but Father said we had breathing room. The wick had been lit. Our flame would begin to shine bright.

Chapter Three

There were always kids at church, but hardly a one spoke to me. Most of them went to school at Westerlog Elementary. We'd drive by it when we went to the Piggly Wiggly for groceries. The boys were always running around like wild animals, swinging from the monkey bars and chasing the girls with carefree abandon, something I longed for.

"Maybe I should go here," I said one afternoon.

Father's head whipped to the right, the huge wave in his hair swaying with him. "You learn everything you need from *The Lost Gospels*. Last thing you need is some woman who can't get a husband trying to scramble the only message that matters."

"I could ask some of them to church."

"You don't worry about that. We're fine. Plus, I wouldn't leave you with those little demons in a million years. Word's out on you, son. One of them is gonna want to prove himself, liable to take your head off. We can't have that. And I don't even want to think what your mother would do."

I hadn't considered the whole head chopping off thing but it fit neatly into Father's stories. With no reason to not believe him, I apologized, swore I'd never ask it again.

Even though I might've been dumber than most everyone, I wasn't so dumb I didn't notice it. I saw the faces when I went to speak and before long I stopped speaking pretty much all together, except to Mother, who wasn't much of a talker herself.

Sometimes she'd talk about the weather.

"Getting hot."

"Yeah…"

"Hotter than yesterday."

"Yeah, I think so."

Other times she'd ask if my food was warm enough.

"I can put it on the stove."

"No, it's fine."

"You sure?"

"Yeah…"

Mostly she'd just sip her tea and stare at the wall. Even when she'd say something, she'd barely look at me. A few nights she just got up from the table and wandered off without saying a word.

During his service, Father would talk about the darkness we carry around in our souls. Most of the people thought he was talking about them, but I knew he was talking about Mother. She'd just sit on the couch, her eyes glazed, looking at nothing. It was like she was peering through the wall into some other world in some other dimension.

One morning she wouldn't get up. Father was waiting in the car. We were fixing to drive across town to hand out pamphlets, but she just wouldn't move.

"Mother, come on, he's waiting."

She shook her head, her eyes all watery.

Finally, Father came in. "What in the hell is the holdup?"

"I don't think she feels well."

"Well, she never does. Now get!" He pulled her by the arm, and she just flew right past him, doubled-over and heaved. I'd never seen that much puke in all my life. Then the blood came pouring out between her legs.

Father yelled at me, "We're going to the hospital."

Until this moment, Father viewed medical centers as the modern-day Tower of Babel, man's wicked desire to remove God from the equation of life and death. But there he was racing to the hospital, begging the nurses and doctors to fix his wife. She was almost green. Her eyes were slits, pupils jittering back and forth like she'd been taken by the Devil himself.

They wheeled her away and left Father and me with the other nervous people in the waiting room. A little kid crawled around picking up old Cheetos and shoving them between his lips.

"Go sit down," Father said. I thought he might join me, but he just kept pacing and peering down the hallway.

Mother had been emotionally bad for a while, but I'd never seen her sick. Even when Father got the flu, she never so much as sniffled. She was just one of those people with a good immune system. I think that's why Father was losing his mind.

Mother was his rock, and now she was dying.

"Sir, you need to step away from the desk," the nurse said.

"I want someone to tell me what's going on. Why can't someone tell me?"

"Sir, they're doing everything they can. So you just need to sit and try to remain calm. Think of your son," she said with a pointed look in my direction.

Father finally came over, plopped down next to me. He wiped at his cheek, and I knew things were worse than bad, because just as Mother never got sick, Father never cried.

The little boy on the ground held up a Cheeto, offered it to me. His mother said, "Wayne, get off the dirty floor. And don't stick that in your mouth!" Wayne was already chomping away. She grabbed his head, but he swallowed fast.

Father got up, started for the nurse, but changed course and headed straight into the restroom. The nurse called over the mother and Wayne. They disappeared through the doors. All that was left was the TV in the corner, a tool of the devil I'd only seen seconds of. A man and a woman talked behind a desk while their own TV played behind them. The small screen had big explosions and men with guns.

A toilet flushed and Father walked out of the bathroom. He took one look at me and said, "What's going on?"

I turned left then right, couldn't find an answer anywhere.

"You better not have been watching that."

"I'm just sitting."

Father had no patience for me and made sure I knew it. My right leg had a hard time staying still so he gave it a swat.

The nurse and doctor came out, their voices low and hushed when they spoke to Father.

"Oh my Lord." Father's hand flew over his mouth. "No. Are you serious?"

The nurse nodded with a smile.

"Is she going to be okay?"

The doctor said, "She'll need complete bed rest. No movement at all for the next three months."

Father pinched his bottom lip with his thumb and forefinger. "But…we're going to have a baby?"

I'd never seen Father's eyes so wet and wide.

"If you stick to the orders I'm giving. And you're going to need a full-time nurse to help with the medication and general care. Do you have insurance?"

"No…"

"Well…there are options. Nurse Amanda will provide them. I'll leave you two to discuss."

"Wait, Doctor. Can I see her?"

"In a few minutes. She's just finishing up some blood work."

"Thank you, Doc. Thank you!" Father threw his arms around the doctor. The nurse brought Father behind the desk into a little office. They walked in, Father not even turning back to see if I was still there.

† † †

The doctor wouldn't let us leave until the middle of the night. We drove home in the dark, just about the only car on the road. Mother kept her hand over her belly, gently stroking herself. She was six months pregnant, but hardly looked it. She was pretty much her frail self with a bit of a bulge. Father kept asking if she was okay, if the window being down was bothering her. I'd never seen him this nice. He reached out and held her hand.

When we got home, Father helped her from the car and into the wheelchair he'd gotten from the hospital. He rolled her to their room and made her a sandwich and some tomato soup. He told me to go to bed hungry.

The next day a nurse showed up with IV bags and a bunch of prescriptions. She showed Father how to replace the bags and move Mother to keep her from getting bedsores. I'd never thought a bed could hurt you.

After the nurse left, I sat outside my parents' room and listened to them talking.

"How are we going to pay for this?" Mother asked.

"We'll find a way. God will show us."

"But what if He doesn't? Our services don't bring in enough and we'll lose all the money we'd make from baking."

"Then we'll travel, move outside the area."

"Charles, I can't leave. The doctor said—"

"I KNOW WHAT THE DOCTOR SAID!"

It kind of made me happy to hear Father yell.

"Look," he said, sounding almost remorseful for his outburst, "we just need to grow our flock. We'll have more money. We can do it."

"But I can't be here alone."

"Well, we'll get Mrs. Durrington from up the road. She just sits around doing nothing anyway."

"I'm not putting this on Mrs. Durrington. Plus, she smokes a hundred cigarettes a day."

"We'll find someone else. What about your sister?"

"Absolutely not."

"She's family, and you know she'd do it."

"I said no. We're not having this conversation."

But it wasn't over.

Father and I were going to drive to Florence to drum up members. Mrs. Durrington stopped by to watch Mother, but the stench of that old woman sent Mother puking all over her blankets. Father tried to get a few other ladies from our church to keep watch over her, but the women all had families and kids and the scheduling was impossible.

We could only travel when someone was there to watch her, not that it made any difference. No one from the other cities had seen or heard about me getting hit by that truck. We just stood on the street with pamphlets and Father's words. People pushed past us. If they did take a pamphlet, it'd be on the ground within two steps. Father didn't want to waste them, so I picked up the ones that didn't have too much dirt or oil smeared on them.

One afternoon, I saw him eyeing a delivery truck rolling past us. I could tell he was thinking about throwing me in front of it. I ran up to a woman and handed her a pamphlet.

"I've returned from Heaven!" I said.

She smiled and took the brochure. She didn't even throw it away, at least not where we could see her. When we stopped for gas on the drive home, Father called Mrs. Durrington to remind her to check on Mother. Apparently, she already had, and she'd found her crumpled in the hallway. Mother had been trying to go to the bathroom and collapsed.

Father and I drove straight to the hospital, where the doctors had gotten Mother stabilized. For the first ten minutes, they couldn't even find a heartbeat. But then it started thumping. They'd saved the baby, but if something like this happened again, they warned, she'd lose the child—and maybe even her own life.

That night Father started getting his visions again, said he was going to have the strongest boys in the entire world. He dreamed we'd one day usher in God's return and that the Kingdom of Heaven would rise from the ashes of this wickedness.

"He'll be Cain, and you'll be Abel," Father said to me over breakfast.

I knew Abel was the one who died. "Why can't I be Cain?" I asked.

"Eat your eggs."

When Mother was finally released from the hospital, she arrived with a whole new stack of bills. Father put his foot down. The next day Mother's sister, my Aunt Laura, arrived.

I had been clearing rocks from the front yard that doubled as the church's parking lot when the tiny brown car zoomed up the driveway, kicking up a cloud of dirt. For a second I feared it was going to keep going and smash through the church, but it whipped to the right and parked up against the trees, a surprising disappointment.

The driver's door opened and a lady wearing a white blouse and blue jeans stepped out. Her blonde hair went past her shoulders and she had on the kind of red lipstick Mother said was for trollops and harlots. Her blue eyes locked on mine.

Without hesitation, she walked up and knelt, threw her arms around me. Her fingers were hot and sticky on the back of my neck. She smiled through the tears rolling down both cheeks. "Hello, Joshua."

When we'd left the commune, I was obviously too young to remember her voice or what she looked like, but there was something strangely familiar about her. She smelled like blueberries and that tangy scent of sweat.

Her hand held my cheek. "I'm so glad to see you. I never thought I'd… I'm your…" Her eyes caught something over my shoulder. The flash of fear said it was Father.

"Joshua, why don't you get your aunt's suitcase."

I said, "Yes, sir," but just stood there.

She smiled at Father, but not nearly as nice. "Hi, Charles."

He slapped the back of my head. "Now!"

For the next week or so, I probably spent thirty seconds alone with Aunt Laura. Every time we found ourselves in the same room, Father would pop in and whisk one of us away. He had me doing chores, like mowing the lawn or cutting firewood. He had Aunt Laura washing clothes, making lunches, washing Mother's feet.

Sometimes I'd hear Aunt Laura talking to Mother, or rather *trying* to. Mother never said a word. I didn't understand it. Mother hardly ever talked about her sister, but I got the feeling she really hated her, probably because Laura had a prettier face.

And she definitely didn't like the way Father laughed at Laura's jokes. Or all the times he touched Laura's arm, even though she always pulled it away.

When Father wasn't bugging her, Aunt Laura's icy blue eyes were always on me. She could be doing dishes or taking a sip of her tea, and it was like I was the only thing that existed on this earth. It was sort of nice, but really weird, too. It was as if she was peering into my head, trying silently to tell me something with that penetrating gaze.

Father had always said Laura was nuts, and mean, too. He said she'd been locked away at the commune for hurting people. I didn't see how that was possible. She was always smiling in our house, even as she was cleaning Mother's bedpan.

Although she couldn't bake anything worth selling, Laura was a decent cook when it came to pancakes and eggs. She drizzled almost everything with butter or syrup and was always giving me seconds and thirds, until Father saw I was putting on some weight.

"No one's going to believe in a fat messiah."

It bothered her when he called me that, not "fat," but "messiah." Her eyes would lower and she'd look so sad every time Father said it.

There was something about her, like she was holding onto all these secrets and she just wanted to let them out. It was as if they were killing her.

I almost asked her a few times. I wanted to know so badly.

One morning I was awoken by a sharp scream. Father said Mother had a nightmare and flopped off the side of the bed.

When we finally got her to the car, I thought she was gonna die. It was still almost two months before she was due, but at the hospital the doctors said they had to take the baby out right then or risk losing them both.

Father held her hand as they wheeled her into surgery. It was just Aunt Laura and me in the waiting room, alone except for the nurse at the front desk.

Aunt Laura put her arm around my shoulder, pulled me into her with a little squeeze. "She's going to be okay."

I started crying. I didn't actually think Mother was going to die or that the baby wasn't going to be alright; I just felt like something inside me broke. I'd always been told to keep it together, to stay strong, to project what the followers needed to see. But in Aunt Laura's arms, I was just a little kid, and I was free to do anything. So I kept crying.

"Oh, sweetheart, come here." She kissed my head and whispered, "Can I tell you something?"

"What?"

"I think we should run away together. The two of us."

And the tears stopped rolling, my breath clumped in my throat. "What do you mean?"

"Let's get in the car and drive. We can live anywhere you want. It'll just be us, like we're meant to be."

Her eyes were wild, a turbulent sea, the deepest blue you'd drown in and be happy about it, content with the fate. "Don't you recognize me, sweetie?"

All those feelings of familiarity.

"You know who I am, don't you?"

"No…"

"You know it's true, Joshua. Don't lie to your mother."

Her fingers dug into my shoulders as she pulled me closer. Her breath reeked of onions. "You know I'm your mother. You can feel it."

"Get away! You're hurting me!"

"Maureen couldn't have a child. They needed me. So I gave birth to you. But now they have their own, so you and I can be together."

"Let go!"

I ripped free and tore off down the hallway. The nurse said I couldn't go in there, but I burst right through the doors. I heard Mother grunting and yelling. I followed the sound until I saw her legs in stirrups. Everything was dripping blood. Father had her hand. Her knuckles were white. It looked like she was crushing his fingers.

Through the surgical mask, he said, "Breathe."

Mother's roar sounded like she was being torn apart.

The doctor said, "Almost, keep going."

He pulled out this purple blob. Its face was all mushed and caked with goop. I'd have bet every nickel in a bank that the creature was dead or retarded, but when the doctor slapped its little butt, the creature cried. Seeing that angry little face tickled Mother something silly. She and Father took the child and gushed.

I found myself drawing closer. "Is it okay?"

"Of course he is," Father said.

Speaking to my parents, the doctor said, "He's premature. We're going to have to put him in incubation."

I stepped next to the bed and held out my hand. Mother helped him give a tiny wave.

"I'm sorry, but I need to take him," the nurse said. She carried him straight out the room, Mother's eyes already closing.

Father said, "You did good."

She gave a little nod.

"Come on," Father said. "Let's let her get some rest." He put his hand on my back and guided me out of the room.

"Is he really going to be alright?" I asked.

"He'll be fine."

"What's his name?"

"Paul."

"I like that."

What I didn't like was seeing Aunt Laura at the waiting room doors. She was arguing with the orderly and nurse.

"I don't give a shit!" Aunt Lara yelled. "She's my sister, and I'm going back!"

"What is going on?" Father said.

I put on the brakes. "Don't. Let's just go back. She's crazy."

"Crazy? Wait…what happened?"

"Nothing."

"Don't tell me nothing." His voice cut right through me. "What did she say?"

"Please, let's go check on Paul."

Father's eyes searched mine until he had his answer. He stormed down the hall.

"I want that woman arrested!"

"Arrested? How dare you! You can't keep me from my son!"

"She attacked my family."

"I DID NO SUCH THING! I GAVE YOU A CHILD—"

The orderly dragged her away. The nurse ran to a phone to call for more security.

"JOSHUA!"

Memories can be deceiving or sometimes not even there, one of the joys of head trauma. There isn't much I remember about Paul's first few years, just that he was usually inside with Mother and I was outside, limited to the backyard because Father forbade me to leave the property alone.

Certain days' memories are clear as a saint's conscience, the opening day of The Church of His Son School being a big one. It was eight o'clock sharp and I was a statue in front of the door, staring at Mother's hand on the knob, the pale blue veins snaking up her forearm.

Her other hand was holding Paul's. Even though he was too young to officially start school, we were dressed in the same black pants and white shirts buttoned to the top. Her precious little Paulie looked almost nothing like me, softer and more delicate all the way around, his shiny brown mane still thin and manageable. Not the matted blond mess of mine Mother tore through every Sunday, telling me it was my own fault for not combing it during the week.

Footsteps hit the end of the driveway. I turned and saw the oldest Walker girl running for us. Mother grabbed the back of my head and made me face the front. She was looking at the girl, her eyebrows pushed together in the middle, her hawk face ready to snap.

Nearly out of breath, in the quietest voice, the girl said, "I'm so sorry I'm late. My daddy's car wouldn't work."

"We don't make excuses, Patricia."

"Most everyone calls me Patty."

"Is that your given name?"

"No, ma'am."

"Good then, Patricia. I don't know how it was at your old school, but we have rules here. I will only go over each one once, so all of you listen up."

Mother looked down at the four of us. Sounding like Father, she said, "You will speak when spoken to. You will listen and learn. Do you understand?"

After we each said yes, Mother opened the door and flicked on the fluorescent light, pointed to the rectangular table in the back corner that we used for Sunday's pamphlets and collection basket. Now it held four yellow notepads. She had assigned our places.

My seat faced the cross. Patricia was to my left, her long curly hair swept over her shoulder, covering the peach dress just like in church. David next to her with his perfectly parted hair, his top two shirt buttons undone. Directly across from me, was Paul's chair, but he wasn't in it. He was waiting for Mother to sit so he could stand beside her.

Mother took her spot to my right, beside the boarded-up window. She'd hung a green blackboard over it on which there were three numbers, a bunch of words beside them.

"You may call me Miss Maureen or Teacher, even Ma'am, but that's it. These are your notebooks, in which you'll write down your lessons." She handed each of us two pencils, starting with Paul and ending with me. "If you lose or break one, you will have to replace it. Take care of your supplies or they will be taken away."

Mother went on to say some other things but I was staring at my pencil, the first one I'd ever been trusted with.

She put her hand on top of mine. "Pay attention."

I put my hands on my lap and promised I would.

Mother pointed at the board. "Now, who can tell me what this says?"

David put his hand up, then Patricia. Even Paul looked at it like he had a chance, but I kept my hand by my side. I knew all my letters, but that was about it, words like dog and god were the only ones I spelled right. I couldn't even spell my own name, got away with signing J because Mother was the one doing the grading.

Mother called on David and he sat up a little straighter, cleared his throat. His tone was smart and smug, and it sounded practiced, as if he spoke that way all the time. "Number One: What is our purpose? Number Two: Who is the Second Coming of Christ? Number Three: Who will He save?"

She asked who knew one of the answers. All three of them raised their hands so I did, too. She called Paul first.

Paul gave a big smile because he knew he'd be right and he was barely four. With a sweet little lisp that always made Mother smile, he said, "We're here to spread the good word, let everyone know Christ has returned."

Mother smiled her approval, and then pointed, told me to answer the second question, but I was thinking about the third one and said, "Anyone who believes."

David laughed and so did Paul. Mother pointed behind me at the table on the other side of the aisle that we'd put in for the bakery display, an hour of smelling fresh cookies ensuring a sellout after every mass. "Go," she said. "School is no place for jokes."

"I wasn't joking."

"The Messiah should have his own space. Get over there."

I pushed back my chair and got up.

"And take your things."

I picked up the notebook and pencils.

Mother's eyes said she was done, staying on me for a second then up to the heavens with a shake of her head. She used her slow voice when she wanted my attention. "Joshua, grab a chair and sit down at that table. Now."

I wanted to turn my back on them and face the wall, but I knew Mother would yell. She never did that before Paul, but like I said, things had changed. I sat down, barely able to see the blackboard, not that it mattered.

The rest of the day, I didn't say a word and Mother never asked me to. It seemed like forever and all I had to show for it was a page I'd covered in crosses. Long ones, short ones, fat ones, thin ones. Not a single one with a man nailed to it.

The egg timer dinged and Mother put down her book. "Pencils on the desk, notebooks closed. Everyone rise for dismissal."

I stood with the rest of them and got nervous when Mother called my name. "Yes, ma'am?"

"Every day at the close of class you will lead us in prayer. Understand?"

All of a sudden I was back on stage, my heart thudding so hard I could barely swallow. "Which one?"

"The True Nicene."

I just looked at her. She must've known I couldn't say it.

So I didn't look dumb, Mother spoke to the others. "Joshua will say 'Christ has died, Christ is risen, Christ has come again,' and you will say 'Amen.'"

I stalled. "Can you say it once more?"

The look on Mother's face made sure I'd never ask again. That look wasn't annoyance or frustration or even fear. If I suspected it before, I was certain now: that woman did not like me.

Paul said, "I can do it."

"Someone has to," Mother said.

Paul did it perfectly and we all responded.

Mother spoke to the class, but looked right at me. "That wasn't so hard now, was it?"

✝ ✝ ✝

Paul didn't spend much time outside, and never without an adult, but Mother said she'd make an exception because he'd proved himself in class. Plus, now that half her day was being taken up with school, she had less time in the kitchen, and couldn't get all the baking done with Paul underfoot.

I promised I'd watch him. He promised he wouldn't do anything dumb. We changed into our cords and white t-shirts, barefoot since neither of us had shoes we could afford to ruin.

Paul was too tiny to climb trees and most likely he'd tell on me if I did, so I took him over to the swamp side of the church where there were always interesting rocks. I was looking for rocks with just the right weight. Paul only wanted ones that were shiny.

I went past the pines where the ground got squishy, snapping off branches I could reach, not about to let one stab us in the eye or rip a shirt.

Paul sat down on a fallen pine Father would sell as firewood. "You like school?"

I kept on walking. Maybe I wasn't the smartest guy, but I knew he was a parrot.

He didn't budge, looked like he might cry. "Hold on a sec."

I did, but just because the swamp was a stone's throw away and we were real close to the side of the church we were never allowed in ever since I asked Mother in class what F-U-C-K spelled.

Paul pulled pine needles from his hair. "You mad at me?"

I walked past him and headed toward the porch, breaking off branches and casting them down.

He followed. "Why you mad?"

"You know everything I know."

Paul kept right behind me. "I could never know that much."

I emerged from the trees and crossed the driveway, wouldn't even look at the church. "I'm not all-knowing."

"You're calling Father a liar."

"Go inside you little baby."

Paul did the thing with his lower lip, sucking as he chewed on it. "I'm not a baby."

Father's station wagon wasn't in the driveway and Mother was busy baking. I knew I shouldn't do it, that I wasn't being very Son-of-God-like, but I stuck my foot out behind him, gave his chest a little shove, laughed as he crashed on the grass. "Then why you taking a nap?"

Paul popped up with a scream, his tiny face all scrunched up like a rabid weasel.

I ran past the porch steps, Paul in hot pursuit. Ahead lay the hill of grass that stretched to the thick wall of trees we were forbidden to cross. Around the corner was the rusty burn barrel on a mound of dirt, not far from the faded brown barn, another place we weren't allowed.

I stayed close to the house, my arms and legs pumping, my feet barely touching the grass. When I was running, I wasn't the Messiah. I was just running and I was good at it, especially compared to a four-year-old.

Paul came tearing around the corner, not far behind. I slowed a bit as I came upon Ms. Hester's rusty red Plymouth parked at the back of the house. Mother drove it only when she had to, never sure if it would start.

I checked over my shoulder and saw Paul about five feet away. I veered toward the car, spun around as I passed it and threw open the front door. Paul hit it full speed with a loud clunk then a cry, called me a jerk.

I kept running, the plan to get in the back door and lock it, make Paul walk back to the front, teach not him to be such a goodie-two-shoes. I rounded the next corner, headed for the back door, four strides away when I saw the dog, a massive black beast, its head lowered, onyx eyes on mine.

All at once, everything stopped. My first thought was to keep going; I could make the back door, but I wasn't by myself. Over the sound of my pounding heart and rushing blood, I made out Paul shouting I was a cheater.

I stood tall and made my voice deep as Father's. "Down!"

The dog, which was nearly as tall as me, kept growling, but didn't move.

Father shouted my name from somewhere, and I knew that Paul was still running, but all my focus was on the dog, my eyes on his, willing him to obey. I put both hands in the air then brought them down. Louder than I shouted anything in my life, I said, "Now!"

The dog quit growling, lowered its butt on the long grass.

Paul came around the corner. "You cheater. You…oh, ohhhh!"

The beast charged Paul, its front paws flinging grass, its front teeth bared. Paul was turning tail, but he'd never make it.

I don't remember leaping, but I'll never forget the collision, a train slamming into my chest, the air pounded out of me.

My shoulder sank into the muddy grass, the side of my head smacking down, knocking my teeth together. I tried to get up, but I was pinned. I rolled onto my back. Warm saliva dripped from above into my mouth.

Paul screamed and when the dog looked up, I grabbed fur and flesh and took hold of his chain collar.

It twisted, trying to bite at my hands, the snarl in his throat shaking my fingers.

The loudest whack filled my ears. The dog yelped and so did I, its claws shredding my shirt, sinking into my skin.

The collar ripped free and I covered my face. Snap and my forearm was stuck in a vice, tightening, tightening, a row of nails puncturing the flesh.

Father shouted, "Shame!"

Another thunderous smack sent the dog scrambling on my stomach, pulling on my forearm. I screamed and pushed my arm and the dog's head into the air as a piece of wood broke in two across its snout. The dog hobbled away, left Father holding half the broom like a sword, Archangel Michael before the descent.

I was trying to figure out if I was okay when Father threw down the broom. He jerked me to my feet and there was the sound of something breaking, a lightning bolt of pain shooting from Father's fingers wrapped around my collarbone. "What the hell were you thinking?"

I couldn't think. My left hand was bloody from clutching my stomach, two gaping holes pierced each side of my right forearm, a fire spreading across my shoulder.

Father sent Paul inside and let go of me. "Stop crying."

I hadn't known I was crying, but I didn't care. "It hurts."

"Then that's what you get for being so stupid. Do you have any idea what he would have done to you?"

The area between my neck and shoulder was warm and swollen.

Father batted my hand off it. "He would have torn off your face and then what? We'd lose everything."

It was hard to speak with my teeth clenched, but I managed to say sorry.

Father looked me over. "Jesus, Joshua. You pissed yourself."

My brown cords were wet, but the top half was blood. I said, "The dog."

"Just go. Have your mother take care of you after she takes photos. Better send for Doc Hargrove, too."

Chapter Four

It was October and I was 10, the past year spent raking leaves, gathering wood, praying for the sins of the world. Although, that last part, I had no way of knowing if I was doing it right. Father seemed pretty damn sure I wasn't.

But I wasn't even pretending to pray this day, with Mother locked in her bedroom and Father delivering cookies, cakes, and his gospel to anyone who'd listen. Paul and I were out on the porch, a safe distance from the demon dog tied up in the backyard, Father's answer to the hell-spawn who regularly desecrated our church.

I unbuttoned my dress shirt and set it on the rail above my shoes and socks. There was no letting my brother out of my sight for even a second, so I said, "Come on."

Paul got off the steps, leaving his shirt on because he never got dirty. "Mother said to stay on the porch."

We both had a pile of rocks next to the stairs. I snatched the burnt orange one off the top of his and chucked it, the rock sailing so perfect all the way to the tree line, smacking the top of the tallest one.

"What'd you do that for?"

"It's a rock."

The way Paul sounded, he was going to cry any second. "It's mine."

I headed for the tree, the grass cool beneath my feet. "Relax, I'll get it, you crybaby."

Paul leapt on my back and slid off, grabbed hold of my bad forearm and pinched me hard.

"Ow, damn you!" I batted him away. "Better not do that again."

"I'm not a crybaby!"

Last thing I wanted was to see Mother, so I said, "Alright, I'm sorry." I hurried across the yard, over to the tree. The rock was by the trunk. I tossed it to him and told him to leave me alone.

He asked what I was doing when I was two branches up, the bark digging into the bottom of my feet.

I said, "Ain't you the smart one."

Paul said something about Mother, but I was done listening. I climbed branch after branch and would've kept going, but Paul wasn't stopping. When I looked down at him, I couldn't speak. I clutched both branches, all ten toes curling bark.

"You're up too high," Paul said.

There was still half a tree above me, sunlight slanting through the needles. It got better and brighter, the higher I climbed, the trunk getting narrow enough that I could wrap one arm around it, branches becoming thin as my feet.

This was my ascension to heaven. I had nothing to fear. My heart returned to normal, my hands stopped shaking. My left shoulder ached and my feet were cut up, but it didn't matter. I'd made it to the top.

Father said the ache from my break was God punishing me. He said whenever it hurt, I should think about what I was doing and I'd see that I shouldn't be.

But being up there couldn't be wrong. After all, I was closer to heaven and to God, right? The branches came together like a seat, my own green cloud, so close to the sun sitting in the pale blue sky.

It was quiet, the only thing I could hear was myself. Just me and God.

Seemed like if I was ever going to talk to Him, this would've been the place to do it. It was just the two of us, Him all ears.

But I wasn't up there to pray. I was at the top of the world, seeing things a whole new way. The end of our roof to the right, then swampland as far as I could see that direction. Over to my left there were trees and more trees, two roofs and a small clearing of grass spaced between.

The wind blew and I held on, my cloud swaying away. I turned toward the hill and found myself even with its top, the Durrington's faded green house on this side of it. And just beyond that, on the other side, the top of a giant white cross sticking straight into the sky.

A blue station wagon drove over the hill. Father wasn't supposed to be home until dark, but he was halfway down the block before I got moving. As the car crunched onto the driveway, I was still too high to jump. I slid down the bare trunk, my t-shirt bunching up around my chest, the bark tearing into my stomach, the tender skin of my inner arms, the side of my face. My left hand smacked off a branch as I leapt and landed on my feet.

The station wagon pulled up to the porch. My skin was on fire, tiny drops of blood dotting the scratches. My pinky pointed the wrong way, the capital I now an L.

The car door opened and shut. Father faced the house and shouted, "Boys!"

I used the bottom of my shirt to wipe off the blood then tucked it into my pants. I couldn't look at my finger, my vision going black, my ears buzzing. I put my good hand on the tree to keep from falling.

I couldn't help thinking I was paying for my sins when I accidentally banged the crooked finger against my thigh. The pain focused me, and I grabbed hold of the finger and jerked it into place, my teeth digging into my bottom lip, biting back the scream wanting to erupt.

Paul gave Father a huge hug. I swallowed the tears and jogged over.

Paul pressed his face to the station wagon's window. "Is that what I think?"

"It's not for you, so calm down. And go open the door for us." Father lowered the tailgate and slid the giant cardboard box onto it. "Joshua, you grab that side. We'll lift on three."

My hand hurt so bad I wanted to cry, but I couldn't afford Father really looking at me, asking what the hell happened. I put my cheek where the box said *Twenty-Seven Inch RCA* and did my best to get my hand under it.

Father picked up his side, the edge of the box crushing my fingers. "You got it?"

Afraid of what might come out of my mouth, I picked up my end. The box was the heaviest thing I'd ever carried and pulled on my fingers every step. I couldn't see Father, but he never sounded more serious when he said I better not drop it.

Paul stood in the middle of the living room, looking all around. "Where's it going?"

I kept my bloody cheek squished against the box, lifted it high to keep my side even with Father's. I didn't know what an RCA was or why Paul was so excited about it. I just knew I had to put it down, my hands all sweaty, my finger a throbbing mess.

Father backed up to the hallway. "My bedroom."

"She's in there," Paul said, leaving out that Mother had been there since Father had left. Paul was her dutiful little servant, the only one allowed to see her.

The box dropped an inch or so on Father's side and he grunted it back up. "Do what I said, boy."

Paul opened the door I'd never been past. The room was dark except for the slivers of light sliding under the drapes. It smelled like a midnight garden, the only room in the house not reeking of fresh-baked bread.

Father told Paul to get the lights.

From her chair over in the darkest corner, Mother said, "Leave them off."

The box was shaking so Father propped it on his thigh, most of the weight sliding down on me and my finger. He said, "You'll want to see this."

Mother remained turned toward the drapes. "I can see just fine."

"I've got good news," Father said. "We sold them all. Cormack's said they could take double what we gave them."

Mother said, "Wonderful," in such a way that we all knew she didn't mean it.

Father told me to put the box down on the bed. I did and pulled my face away, a wet schlop as the blood stayed behind on the cardboard.

Mother turned my way and I was sure she could see my face, even in the dark. "So what is it?"

We weren't allowed to raise our voice inside, but that didn't stop Paul. "A TV!"

I backed up. Television was evil. Father warned the congregation every week. It would be humanity's downfall.

Father patted the top of the box. "Robbie's brother gave us credit."

With the same voice she usually saved for me, Mother said, "Why all of a sudden?"

"How can I preach about the devil if I don't know him in all his forms?"

Mother didn't say anything, just looked back at her curtained window.

Father sounded a lot more like himself when he said, "You want it or not?"

She didn't answer right away. Then so soft I could barely hear, Mother said, "Set it on the dresser."

Father fixed half-frozen pizza for dinner, the clumpy cheese and chewy pepperoni about as appetizing as raw fish. I finished two pieces and stared at the remaining nine soggy squares on the plate in the middle of the table. All the leftovers had run out the day before and I was still hungry, but I but didn't ask for another slice, not about to bring any attention my way.

Paul sat to my right, Mother to my left. Father was across from me, the red stained-glass window that we shared with the church directly behind him. He hadn't said a word since we sat. Not even the prayer.

No one was talking, and we acted like everything was normal. Like no one saw the purple Mother's make-up couldn't hide.

She sat to my left, close enough to nudge my foot if I said something stupid, but I wasn't worried about her seeing the side of my face. She no longer looked at me unless she had to.

Mother wasn't looking at her precious little Paul, either. She studied her plate, picked at the pizza, forced a small bite here and there.

Paul looked at Father, but only when Father wasn't looking. "When do we get to see it?"

"You don't," Father said.

Mother flicked her eyes toward me. "Did you tell him to ask that?"

"No, ma'am."

"It's not fair," Paul said. Then Father looked at him sharply and Paul said sorry.

Mother turned to Father. "What did you expect?"

Father got a little loud. "I expect to be listened to and not questioned."

I kept quiet, focused on both hands lying in my lap, my swollen finger throbbing worse than ever.

"We're going to end this right here," Father said. "That machine is for research by myself or your mother. It is not for children. It is not for *you*."

We both said yes sir because there was nothing else we could say.

Father finally noticed me. "Jesus, Joshua. What'd you go and do to yourself?"

I turned toward Mother a little so he couldn't see my cheek. "Scraped it over in the trees when I was raking. I'm okay."

Father shook his head and grabbed another pizza square. "Think about what you're doing, son. You have to use your head."

"Yes, sir."

Everyone went back to not talking. Mother waited until Father cleared his plate before she said, "I won't be feeding the dog again." She slammed her fist on the table, her face twisting. "It grabbed hold of my leg!"

Father held up his hand. "Calm down, woman. You won't have to do it again."

Mother took a deep breath and blew it out. "So it's you or Joshua. Paulie's not going near that beast."

Father stared at her, worked his mouth, his nostrils going. "Fine. Joshua will do it when I'm not here."

I hoped I'd heard wrong. "Feed the dog?"

"It's simple," Father said, "no problem at all."

"He bit me!"

"Lower your voice," Father said, the argument over.

"All you do is fill up his cup and take it out to him. But hold it high so he doesn't jump on you."

I nodded.

"And tell him to stop if he does. Remember, you have nothing to be afraid of."

"Okay."

Father shook his head. "Not like a girl. Do it loud. Dogs are no different than people," he said. "They won't listen unless you make them."

† † †

The next four nights, I made sure to be somewhere else when it was time to feed Azrael. I didn't need to practice just so Father could point out all the ways I was doing it wrong. I didn't want him there to save me. Maybe

I wanted to put it to the test, see if Father was telling the truth. If I really had nothing to fear.

But then it was Monday and Father was gone, the backyard all mine. We were on the front porch when I told Paul to go inside.

"I need to bear witness," he said.

I picked up the white cup filled with food. "Watch from a window. You're not coming."

The screen door banged shut behind him. I went down the steps and headed around the house. I was just to Mother's car when Azrael let out one deep bark, nearly enough to stop me.

I kept walking because I had nothing to worry about. I was the Messiah.

Azrael waited five feet away, his rope pulled tight, the chain collar sunk into the thick fur around his neck. His mouth was open, tongue out, those razor-sharp teeth protruding. The same as those that ate the flesh of Jezebel. The demon had tasted my blood.

Neither one of us moved, my eyes on his, his on mine. Those weren't the eyes of a stupid animal. They called me to come close, willed me to slip, become fodder for destruction.

The blue food bowl was across the yard alongside Father's shed. It didn't make sense walking all that way when the dog could eat off the grass. I was about to dump the cup, but our bedroom curtain shot up, Paul's wide-eyed face staring out. He was supposed to look up to me. I couldn't be a coward so I raised the cup over my head, the dog's eyes following, the tension in his legs telling me I better put it higher.

My free hand slipped into my pocket and pulled out Father's Swiss army knife. I flicked out the blade with my fingernail, swore I'd slam it into his eye if he tried to bite me again. Under my breath, I said, "Down. Down. Down."

Azrael stayed right where he was. The tiny knife didn't scare him.

I took a step toward him. Azrael leapt for the cup, the rope holding tight. Just as loud as Father, I shouted, "Down!"

He dropped to the ground and stayed on his belly. I treated it like it was nothing and walked to his bowl, dumped the food right in. My insides were shaking.

I turned around expecting to be knocked over, but the dog was still down, his eyes on the bowl. "It's okay," I said. "Eat."

Once I backed away, Azrael crept forward and ate with ravenous intensity, his bushy tail smacking my jeans. In mere moments, he looked up from the empty bowl.

I lowered the cup so he could see inside. "I don't have any more."

His teeth clamped onto it an inch from my fingers and he ripped it away. He shook it back and forth three times then tossed it to the side.

I stuck out my hand and prayed I was right. Father would flip if I had to explain another attack and his knife stuck in his guard dog's eye. Azrael nuzzled his face against my hand and rubbed his massive shoulder against my leg. "Are you a good boy?"

Azrael opened his mouth, his tongue darting over my palm. His tail swished back and forth. He was a good boy, just sad and alone, no one to love him.

I folded the blade away and put it in my pocket, sat on the grass. Azrael rubbed his head against mine, kept it there. I wrapped my arm around him, pulled him even closer, his thick fur not much different than the tangled mess on my head. I called him a good boy and he got excited, pushed me over.

My shoulders hit the ground and playtime was over, Azrael's face just inches from mine. My right hand grabbed hold of his collar, my left went after my knife. He dropped even closer, opened his mouth, and licked my face.

Afraid to move fast because I might spook him, but just as worried he might want another taste of me, I told him to get off and guided him with both hands around his collar. Back on my knees I realized I was choking him, that metal links were already digging into his neck without my fat fingers stuck between the collar and his fur.

The collar was easy to figure out and still tight once I loosened it a rung. I gave Azrael one more hug and told him his new name was Blackie.

✝ ✝ ✝

I spent nearly every night down on my knees, all alone in the church for quiet time. That was my atonement, when I prayed for the world, just as Mother and Father insisted. That night was no different.

I knelt in darkness, quiet time no excuse to waste electricity. It wasn't totally dark thanks to the dull red glow from the kitchen and the full moon shining through the door I'd propped open, my eyes locked on that rectangle of light.

According to Father, quiet time meant sixty minutes of praying. That's what I was supposed to be doing instead of crying about my aching knees and staring at the doorway. But the longest I'd ever prayed was three minutes, not seeing the point in talking to someone who never talked back.

I felt the 7:40 train before its rumble obliterated all sound, covering the crunch of leaves or the slithering of an unknown predator. That got me talking to God, asking him to watch over us. Don't let a demon get me or my brother.

Demons were real. I had a book with their pictures and understood they could come in any form. That's why the church's windows were permanently boarded up. Like Father said, who else would hate us enough to keep breaking them?

The train faded and the silence returned. Then the frogs and the birds, all the night noises stirred up again. I went back to telling myself there was nothing to worry about. Even with Father on the road, I wasn't scared. I had Blackie out back, my first friend, another eighteen minutes until I could sneak him the piece of roast I'd wrapped up in my napkin.

A deep, long growl rose from the darkness. Blackie barked once. Then came a splash from the swamp. A yelp. More splashing, then nothing.

I couldn't run outside to check. I needed help, so I stumbled through the passage, ran into the kitchen screaming Mother's name.

She was in her bedroom, back in the corner chair, outlined by the soft glow coming from the TV. Paul sat between her feet, his head on her lap. "What is it?" she asked.

I stayed in the doorway. "Something hurt Azrael," I said. "Something from the swamp."

Mother didn't bother looking at me, too busy stroking Paul's hair, making the curls perfect. "That rope doesn't reach the water, and gators don't come this high."

"I heard it."

"So when your Father gets home, you can tell him what you did."

"What'd I do?"

"You were out playing with him. What did you think would happen?"

Paul kept looking at the ceiling instead of at me standing there like an idiot. "I didn't do anything," I said. "I didn't touch the rope."

Mother checked the clock. "Go finish your prayers and ask for forgiveness."

It was two days later and I still wasn't talking to the tattletale. That's why Paul was halfway up my tree, higher than I'd been when I slipped.

"Stop being stupid and get down," I said. "She'll lose it if she sees you."

Paul had both arms around the trunk, his brown shirt snagging on the bark. "Forgive me."

I had, but I wasn't saying it. He believed he was going to hell if I didn't say some magical words. "You're ruining that shirt."

Paul reached up like he was going to climb higher.

I shouted for him to get down.

"You're crazy," he said. Paul hugged the tree. "Mother will come."

"You're the one in the tree."

Everything got quiet, both of us listening for a door. A gust of wind blew through the trees, Paul swaying, his arms wrapped around tight. "Say it first. Say you forgive me."

Not saying it was too much work. "Fine. Get your butt down here before she comes out."

Paul started shaking. He was too high to be doing that, his bones more delicate than mine.

"I said I forgive you. Come on, Paul."

"I can't."

The screen door slammed shut and Mother screamed down the stairs. One slipper flew off, but she kept running, bright orange curlers twisted in her hair. "My baby! Hold on!"

"He'll be okay," I said.

Paul started crying.

"Does that sound okay?" she said.

I told Paul there was a branch below to his left. "Just do it real slow."

As if I might've lied, Mother said, "It's there, Paulie. You can do it."

Paul didn't move so I got underneath him. "I won't let anything happen to you."

Mother shoved me out of the way and spread her arms wide. "Come on, honey, you can do it."

With Mother right below him, Paul climbed down. Mother grabbed him when he came close enough and squeezed him tight. She called him honey again, a name she never used for me. "Why did you go up there?" she asked. "You're smarter than that."

I prayed Paul knew how to lie.

"It looked like fun," he said.

Mother said okay, and I thought that was it. Then she grabbed Paul's chin so he couldn't turn away from her. "Looked?"

He nodded, his curls barely moving thanks to her grip.

"Why'd you go up the tree? You saw Joshua do it?"

Paul's eyes were scared. They didn't want to say yes, but they snaked toward me while his head stayed put.

I wanted to say it like Father would, but it was more like a whisper when I said, "I go up there to pray."

Mother let go of his chin and looked down at me, her disgust no different than Father's. The hand by her side was twitching. "I told you no climbing."

That hand was coming no matter what I said, so I yelled, "I hate you!"

The complete absence of hesitation is what surprised me. Her palm smacked my cheek and her wrist smashed my nose, dropped me to my knees.

The Messiah's blood sprinkled the dirt.

† † †

I was eleven and the back of the church was an oven. Mother even let me undo my top button, the last thing she had said after telling us to read in silence.

Our notebooks were open, but no one was reading. Usually sharp like a hawk, Mother was suffering and had her eyes clenched shut, fingers kneading her forehead.

Not much had changed in the last two years. Paul, Patricia, and David still sat where they'd always been. Sarah, a quiet little mouse the same age as Paul, sat in my old seat.

I had the back table to myself, no one around to see me mark the wrong answer or mumble something stupid. No one near enough to make fun of my crooked nose, my messed up hair, my stupid drawings.

The timer went off and all eyes went down to our books. Mother groaned when she got up. Halfway to the curtain, she told Paul, "See everyone out."

Paul led a prayer and got us out of there. I closed the door behind me and watched our classmates kicking dirt halfway down the driveway. Sarah in her blue dress, brown hair tight in a bun, was struggling to keep up with the other two.

I took off my dress shirt and laid it across the counter of the baked goods stand we built for Mother that summer. Paul took off both of his shirts and laid them next to mine.

I slipped off my dress shoes and turned to Paul who was picking something off the grass.

He came up with a purple flower and his gentle smile. "For Mother."

I said how nice, but only because he was so sensitive.

He handed it to me, his eyes soft, but searching. "You should give it to her."

I set the flower on top of my shirt. It'd just make her ask me what I'd done wrong. "When she feels better."

Paul ran his fingers through his curls. "Can't you make them go away?"

He meant her headaches. He always asked about them, and I always said no. I shook my head.

"You ever really try?"

"What do you think?"

"Just seems like you should be able to."

I pushed past Paul and bumped his shoulder pretty hard. "Yeah, no kidding."

Paul followed as I walked across the four sets of parking spaces Father had already cleared for Mother's customers. "Don't get mad," he said.

"I ain't."

"Yeah you are."

I stopped him with one glance. "I'm getting there."

His upper lip quivered and his eyes were getting ready to spill.

"You've got to cut that crap out. You're not going to hell."

"You forgive me?"

I said I did and he went back to being himself, skipped over to the thick white rope tied around the tree I got my nose broke over. "See, was that so hard?"

Mother had given the order to rip out that glorious tree the day of the incident. It'd been nearly a year but Father had barely started on it, said it'd be down by the next weekend.

Paul stepped back toward me until that rope was all stretched out, a good forty feet or so. He gave it a few twirls. "Come skip it for me."

I was looking at the sad stack of pines piled on the ground that'd become someone else's firewood, the only way we were able to ever afford meat. "I got a better idea."

He dropped the rope. "Where you going?"

I changed direction so he wouldn't follow, as the side of the church was strictly forbidden ever since Blackie was snatched.

"What are you doing?"

"Why, you going to tell on me again?" I didn't wait for his answer, and walked past the wall with the boarded-up windows that'd been painted white at least five times. FAKE MESSIAH covered up but ever-present there underneath.

Father camouflaged the bear traps with twigs and leaves, easy for me to spot, but not a demon doing work under the cover of night. One of these days, Father said, we'd catch us a nonbeliever. He said he wanted to hear who they'd be praying to with one hundred pounds of pressure crushing their leg. The safest form of vengeance, he argued, was hurting others before they could hurt you.

Father always kept the shed locked, but the shovel and ax he left leaning against the wall for easy access. We weren't supposed to touch them, especially without him home, but the bright red handle of the ax just begged to be held.

The ax was solid, the blade freshly sharpened. I liked the way it felt, five pounds swinging by my leg as I walked back to the front.

Paul said, "You're going to get busted."

"He'll be glad. It took him all last Saturday to cut down those three."

Paul looked at the tree that was ten times taller than him. "You want to do this one?"

"It's next. I bet he could get a whole pew out of it."

"You should put it back."

"You telling me you don't want to try it?"

His eyes got so big, so saucer-like it was almost comical. "Can I?"

"Just got to be careful. No telling Mother."

Paul promised he wouldn't.

That didn't mean much. "Swear it on me."

He'd be in deep trouble if he was heard saying that so he checked over his shoulder then turned back. "I swear on you that I will not tell."

I'd helped Father bring down enough trees to have an idea how long they took. He'd already taken a big chunk of the one side, but I guessed it'd still take him at least twenty good swings. I figured it'd take me and Paul each about double that. I told Paul, "We'll switch every five swings, after I work on it for a bit."

Paul ran back to the rope and wrapped it around his waist. He'd seen me help Father and knew what to do. "This right?"

"Yeah, but don't tie it. Wrap it once and hold it, back up to the driveway."

Paul wrapped it around himself, then bent down and wiped his hands on the grass, even though they'd be just as dirty five seconds later. He backed up and stretched the rope tight.

I leaned back and twisted my body, the ax all the way behind me. I thought of Mother and Father and Paul and everyone else who was counting on me to save them, how I'd done nothing but mess things up.

I whipped around, the ax biting deep. I yanked it out, did it again, a big triangle of wood falling at my feet. I swung again and again, got into a rhythm.

A thud for the sinners. A thud for the saints. A thud for the disbelievers. The ones that pointed. And sneered. And laughed. The ones who called me names.

Paul was shouting but I could barely hear him. "Holy cow!"

I kept attacking the tree, didn't even notice my bad shoulder.

"When's it my turn?" Paul yelled.

I had the rhythm, making music like Mother but so much mightier. I kept whacking away and shouted, "Stay there! Keep the tension!"

"It's my turn. My turn—"

The earsplitting crack was like lightning, but I must've yelled just as loud. "Run! Run!"

The tree began to topple, gaining speed. Paul skidded to a stop, the falling tree blocking the sun and casting him in darkness.

I dropped the ax and ran for my brother, trying to outrun the tree. Paul was frozen, his entire body in the shadow of death.

The whoosh rushed on us, pine needles pushing down every inch of my body as I left my feet and soared through the air, pulled Paul beneath me. We smacked the ground hard, a tremendous blast of white pain ripping through my right side, the devil's fire burning through my body.

Everything was black, so much pressure like a truck had parked on my back. Paul grunted underneath, sounded like he couldn't breathe. I pushed off the grass into a new world of pain. The skin on my back tore further, the hole inside me growing wider. I reached under the right side of my chest, a slick branch protruded from the front of my shirt and pierced the ground.

There was no time to worry about myself. Paul wasn't moving.

Biting down, I pushed up high as I could, taking weight off Paul, digging my hand underneath me and rolling him toward the rays of light. I tried to call for help, but nothing came out. The tree sank further down, my

face smashed against the grass, the shallowest breath in and out of my nose.
I couldn't see Paul, couldn't breathe, wished I could tell him I was sorry.

53

Chapter Five

It'd been about a year since we survived the tree. Father was furious at first, with the hospital bills and all, but not once I recovered. That branch had somehow missed my heart, lungs, and everything important. The odds of me surviving were like one hundred to one. Father said I was undeniable. Once a month he paraded me around town, shouting that I was the Messiah, letting people pay to touch my deep purple puncture wounds.

The scars are pretty nasty, front and back, but I didn't care because they're usually covered up. This day I couldn't bear to wear a shirt. It was so hot and muggy, it was almost like that branch had pierced my heart and the Almighty sent me the wrong direction. Hell couldn't be much worse than our backyard, the air like quicksand, so hot the swamp could boil. And my job was to lug around a wheelbarrow full of boulders all the way from the front yard to the very back. Over and over. All weekend long.

When I turned the corner of the shed, Paul was right where I'd left him, lying on our three-rock tall wall, Mother's old yellow towel beneath him, reading *The Lost Gospels*.

Paul was only seven but sounded just like Father when he got to reciting. I could break his body in half without even trying, but his voice had that boom, so different from the little sissy one Father had effectively slapped out of him. He also inherited Father's slippery tongue and wasn't afraid to use it. That was Paul's gift to share with the world. And ever since the tree, there was no doubt in Paul's brilliant young mind that Father was correct. He swore he'd praise my name until the day he died.

I was breathing like a bull by the time I got to the wall. Paul didn't bother looking at me, so I didn't bother warning him, just tipped over the whole load inches from his head.

He shot up. "What the heck did you do that for?"

I kicked one of the smaller rocks out of my way and took a seat on the wall facing the swamp. A beautiful orange and black spider the size of a snail wasn't but an inch from my shoe. "Maybe I did it because I'm tired. You get the next load and I'll stack 'em."

"It's not my job. You heard what Father said."

The spider made the wrong move and I squished it with my heel. "Father says a lot of things."

"What's that supposed to mean?"

"You're the smart one. You can figure it out."

"Tell me."

I couldn't trust Paul to keep his mouth shut so I said, "Never mind." I picked up a palm-sized rock and side-armed it through the trees. A loud splash came thru the darkness.

He asked, "You trying to stir up trouble?"

I picked up another rock and weighed it in my hand. "What if I am?"

"You want me to tell?"

"You want to go in the swamp next?"

Paul got to his feet on the safer side of the wall. "You wouldn't dare."

I threw that rock as far as I could, heard it thunk off a tree and splash down. "You're the one backing up."

Paul would never admit to being frightened. He adopted his almighty voice and said, "The Devil's down there. The Devil is everywhere. You just have to open your eyes."

I found the biggest boulder I could lift and raised it over my head. "Ever consider that I'm not scared of no Devil?" I started for the swamp, the dark, deadly place I'd never visited. "I got the whole world in my hands and all my hands have ever done is mess things up. The Devil ain't gonna make things worse."

Paul said, "Don't do it."

I almost said okay because I was scared, but I needed to prove something. To myself more than him.

Something whipped through the woods off to the left, made me stop moving.

Paul heard it, too, and whispered, "Don't be stupid."

I veered toward the noise, pretending my destination all along had been the steel pole with the faded red flag marking the edge of our land. I dropped the boulder and felt the vibration of the thud all the way to my knees. Loud enough for Paul to hear, I said, "The wheelbarrow can't get any closer and I know you can't carry them."

Halfway back for another rock, I heard the laugh. It was a girl's, long, loud, and full of life.

Paul said, "Where you going?"

I pushed the thin trees to the side and continued past the marker, stepping off our property for the first time without Father. "Didn't you hear that?"

"You can't leave."

"I know the rules." But I didn't care and continued through the trees.

The voice laughed again. It was a girl and she sounded happy. "Go! Go! Go!"

I walked a little faster. Paul hurried behind and whispered, "Joshua, what are you doing?"

I didn't bother answering him. I walked out of the forest where two boys raced bikes on a dirt track. I'd only seen one other bike before, and that'd been when David brought his by after his birthday. He'd wobbled all the way down our driveway and sure didn't move like this.

These boys were flying, whooping and hollering as they went over small jumps and banked past bushes. But it was the angel by the back of the mobile home cheering for Jeremy that had my attention. Even from fifty feet away, I could see she was beautiful. Dark brown hair hanging past her bare shoulders, a bright pink shirt, and tight blue jean shorts I'd never seen on a female.

The race track was a circle and the boys were headed toward me, neck and neck. The path was about ten feet away so I stayed where I was, watched their legs pump up and down.

The bigger boy pulled out in front by a few feet, had an angry sneer on his face. The smaller guy with the long hair the same color as the girl kept his eyes on the road, pedaling hard. They were just about to pass when Paul ran up beside me, wiping at his arms.

The big guy with the short black hair and eyes set back like a gorilla glanced over and nearly crashed. The girl jumped up and down and shouted when the long hair boy passed her. He jumped off his bike, raised his hands high.

The bigger kid threw his bike down. "No way," he said. "That's bullshit!"

Jeremy said, "It was fair and square, Frank."

Frank pointed right at me. "That queerbait distracted me."

Everyone was staring. The girl waved.

Jeremy said, "You're the Messiah kid, right?"

Father said everyone knew or would one day so I better hurry up and embrace it. All I could do was nod.

Frank yelled, "Go put on your shirt, faggot!"

I had no idea how to respond. I almost said sorry, but before I could, Paul took off running.

There was no question where Paul was going so I went after him, dodging trees, splashing through the muck, calling his name, begging him to stop. I made it to the rock wall as Paul hit the back porch, mud flying off his shoes. I yelled one last time. "Stop!"

Paul threw open the door and disappeared inside, slamming it behind him.

I'd just reached the bottom stair when Mother screamed, "What do you think you're doing?"

It was strange to hear her yell at Paul, but that's what she was doing, both her hands on his arms, pinning him still. She turned him around so he could see the mud splattered across her kitchen. "What's gotten into you?"

Paul's face was all screwed up into a jumbled mess. He was past hysterical, unable to cry, a low mewling worse than anything he could've said.

"It's my fault," I said. "I'll clean it."

Mother didn't question me, just pulled Paul close. "What'd Joshua do?"

Paul couldn't lie to her so I jumped in. "Nothing. I was teasing him. Sorry, Paul."

She turned Paul so he faced her. "Is that true?"

I backed up toward the door when Paul shook his head.

Mother froze me with her stare. "What did you do?"

"We were just working on the wall."

"You stay right there." She turned to Paul. "What'd he do, honey?"

Paul leaned close to her ear so I couldn't hear. Mother's eyes got huge. She shouted, "Charles!"

I would've sworn time stopped if the clock hadn't kept ticking, the only sound in the world. Mother waited another second before yelling for Father again.

Father shouted back, "I'm busy. You handle it."

In the loudest voice I'd heard her use with him, she said, "No, you deal with him! He's your son."

Mother carried Paul to the back sink, not saying sorry when his shoe wiped mud all over my shoulder. With nothing but hate in her eyes, she said, "What are you waiting for?"

Part of me was waiting for Father to walk over and set her straight, tell her that wasn't how she talked to people, but he wasn't coming.

I knocked on the office none of us ever entered. He didn't bother opening the door, just told me to go to the basement, don't be expecting any supper.

Late that night, heavy footsteps thudded down the hallway. Dust floated down on me in the darkness. There was no question where he was headed, no time for me to do anything but sit there, hands on my knees.

The door flew open and bounced off the wall. Father said, "Get your ass up here right now."

I walked upstairs, but slower than usual because if I was the Messiah like he said, I should only have to listen to myself.

Father had on his black jacket, the shoulder and elbows the faded gray that dusted his hair. He shook his head and pointed to his room. "Get in there."

I started to walk, thought how Father wasn't that much bigger than me anymore. His belly was growing from all the cookies he ate, but I was only about a head shorter.

He screamed in my ear. "Right now!"

I hated myself for hurrying into the only room that didn't smell like a bakery. The lights were off, the bedspread pulled tight, the fan blowing cool air and the smell of her gardenias.

Father pointed at the wooden chair next to Mother's empty one. "Sit your ass down."

I took my time.

"Now or get out of this house."

I wasn't even a teenager and knew nothing of the real world. I didn't have a choice.

The TV took up the top of the dresser next to the window filled with white flowers. Its wide black screen reflected an obedient little boy in a big body, my perfect posture, sitting like he taught me.

Father put a disc into the gray machine next to the TV. "I've made a huge mistake," he said. "I realize that now."

He'd made so many, I wasn't about to guess to which he was referring.

"What'd those boys call you today?"

He already knew so I went ahead and told him.

"And what did you say?"

"Nothing."

"That's your response? Someone calls you a vile abomination condemned to hell and you say nothing?"

"I'm not one."

"That's better, but you didn't tell them that."

"Paul ran away and I chased after him."

His eyes cast judgment before his mouth. "A coward."

"The other two seemed nice."

"Seemed?" Father raised his voice, made like he was about to slap me. "You've got to stop being so blind and see people for what they are. Stop being so damn naïve."

"I'm sorry."

"How are you supposed to judge the living and the dead when everyone 'seems nice?' People aren't nice, that's just what they show you. Look for the worst in them and you'll find more than you ever wanted to see."

"Okay."

"Your brother won't always be there to watch over you. He'll help you on your path, but he can't make you do the right thing. You're old enough to know better by now."

"I know."

"I'm not so sure that you do." Father picked up his notebook and turned it so I could see his scribbles. "You know what's in here?"

"Your stories."

"They're your stories. They're the truth."

I had yet to hear Father say anything that felt true, but I kept quiet.

"The things I write down in here are the things you'll tell the world. I know you have a hard time finding the right words sometimes so that's where I come in. But you have to trust me. You have to believe me. Believe in yourself."

"I do."

"You don't sound it." Father eased himself into Mother's chair. Even in the dim light I could see the gray fanning out from his temples. In profile Father appeared defeated and dejected.

After a long pause, I asked, "How do you know it's true?"

"Some things you just know. Just like I know what you are, even if you don't. It doesn't stop my faith one little bit. You are the Messiah. You will save the world."

"Okay."

Father leaned back, ran his hands through his thinning hair, and turned on his church voice. "You have no idea what these nonbelievers will do. They're demons wanting to sabotage you. They laugh at our church, at me being your mother's errand boy. A goddamn delivery man."

He wasn't about to stop so I stayed quiet.

"Look for the worst in people, for that's how you shall judge them. Anyone can be nice for a day, a minute, a moment. It's what they try to hide. The things they know are wrong, but they do them anyway. That's how to judge."

I nodded, looked at him like he always told me to.

"It's a fine line. You must walk among your fellow man, yet you must always remain above them. Be the example for them all to see, the beauty they desire, the strength they need."

When I didn't respond right away, Father said, "Are you even listening?"

"Yes, sir."

He spread his arms. "All of this. All my work. It's for nothing if you don't take your place and start acting like it. We're down to seven families, Joshua. That doesn't even pay for the electricity. But that's fine, I'll keep driving around the country trying to spread the word so you can ruin it by sneaking off and throwing this all away. You think I want to be yelling at you, having this conversation?"

I wasn't so sure but I said no anyway.

His contemptuous gaze was on my hands as if I sickened him so much he couldn't stand to look me in the eyes. "I've tried to protect you and your feelings."

He walked to the TV and punched a button. The screen lit up and was suddenly filled with the image of a man and a woman, tangled together, sheets barely covering them. I hadn't seen television since my last stay in the hospital, and even then I only got a few minutes before Father spoke to the nurses and had the box of temptation taken from the room. It amazed me, witnessing such lifelike drama coming from such a small screen.

"I warned your mother not to baby you. I worried you wouldn't be able to handle the real world. You wouldn't be able to deal with what you saw."

Father's voice ramped up with every sentence. "But I can't do that anymore. You think that you're a man? You watch this. You watch and see what you're doing. Your sins, your refusal to be the Messiah, to follow the rules; look at the evil you're sanctioning. See the world we live in thanks to you."

I wanted to say that that was all I ever wanted. Especially if it was like the place I imagined, where people could do whatever they pleased if it didn't hurt anyone else. But all I did was look at him and keep my mouth shut.

I'm not sure how long she'd been there, but Mother was in the doorway, yellow dishrag in her hands. She said, "Charles, I don't think…"

Father silenced her with one finger. "I know what you think."

Mother shook her head and walked away, the first time in so long I didn't want her to.

"Pay attention," Father said. He hit a button on the machine and dialed up the volume. "Tell me you think you're setting a good example, you're showing people how to live."

The screen flashed to another scene: a beautiful morning, blue skies, white clouds. Buildings so high they didn't look real. "Is this a movie?"

Father backed up to the bed. "Watch it."

How could I not? It was incredible. It's what I'd been missing my whole life, a glimpse of the real world, an escape from mine.

A collage of images passed by, one after another, the city so huge, one hundred times Hartsville. The smallest buildings were ten times the size of anything I'd ever seen, but it was the two massive ones I was stuck on. The way they stretched past the clouds and into the heavens, a testament to what man could achieve.

This went on for a minute, showing me a world so much bigger than I could have imagined.

The image got shaky, screams as black smoke gushed out the hole ripped through the top of the first structure. An airplane headed for the second tower. I started to point but it was too late, the plane hit where I couldn't see, a gigantic fireball blowing out the other side.

"Were there people on there?"

"What do you think?"

The angles were changing, zooming in and out, the fire, the smoke, people hanging out windows. People leaping from the flames. A couple holding hands.

"The animals that did this," Father said, wiping his forehead and clearing his throat. "The cowards behind this, they don't believe in you."

One of the towers collapsed straight down in an explosion of gray dust.

Bloodied bodies being carried away, people running, crying, everyone gray. Who decided who lived and who died? I hadn't chosen.

"There they are." Father pointed to the nineteen dark faces on the TV, most of them bearded. "The heathens responsible for so much death. Men who say you're not real."

The screen was back to carnage. Twisted metal, covered bodies, faces of the victims.

"Your actions do have consequences for others." Father's throat caught and he had to clear it. "Think about this the next time you sin. Think about what you're doing, what you're condoning."

A tear rolled down Father's cheek, the first seen since Paul. It only made him madder. "Damn all non-believers to hell, have no mercy on their souls. Pray for the innocent people that died." Father grabbed my head and forced it back to the TV. It was a big white building with five sides, one of which was blown to hell from some sort of explosion. "Do something for once, make this world a better place." Father stomped away, slammed the door behind him. "Do something!"

Chapter Six

The day had been a long one, and I was sitting at my table half asleep, doodling dead people in my notebook, thanking God that Mother never called on me. The dead people were riding waves, being blasted into buildings, sucked out to sea. So much life wiped out by an uncontrollable force of nature.

Sometimes I didn't know when the disaster in the footage I was watching had taken place, but I knew this tsunami had just happened. Over the last year, we'd nearly caught up on all major disasters, so Father was always amped up when something big came in. I had to pay attention during my atonement because Father always quizzed me on the content. Unlike the tests we took in school that Mother never handed me back, Father didn't tolerate wrong answers. I took in every heartbreaking moment, all the deaths I was responsible for. All because these people wouldn't believe in me; because I failed to give them a reason.

I wish I had kept track of just how many people I'd seen perish. Children holding machine guns half as big as their bodies. Fires in factories. Mass graves. Workers picking up dead kids by their legs and stuffing them in black bags. Explosions tearing buildings in half. Fires in apartments. Bodies on a dirt road, rotting into puddles, flattened by vehicles. Fires scorching out families. White kids my size hunting down classmates. Children crying, starving, bleeding, covered in flies. Death and decay. Destruction and debris.

But there was something else I was paying attention to. Hartsville was nothing, a tiny little town compared to all the places I'd now seen from around the world. Gigantic cities where you're surrounded by strangers, just another bit of the blur. Not like here where my entire world was a house and a church, and everyone for miles had heard my name.

I drew another dozen dead and looked up to pretend I was listening. This last part of the day always took forever, Paul pausing after every word, each one said precisely, just like Father, all so Warren and Tamara could write it down.

The siblings had joined the church after the tree incident, and both were stuck with me at the back table, but I hadn't said more than a couple words to either one. Warren, who sat to my right, was a year below Paul. He held his pencil in his fist and pressed his block letters down so hard sometimes they went through the paper. All I really knew about him was he liked not having to take the half-hour bus ride to school each day, and he wished his daddy to hell for leaving them.

Tamara, who was on the other side of Warren, just turned thirteen like me, only she thought she knew it all instead of nothing. When Mother wasn't around, Tamara talked to anyone who'd listen, but only about the real world, how what we had wasn't it. She swore she wouldn't be with us long, but this was the second year I'd heard her saying that same thing.

Mother and her favorite four were at her table, Paul sharing Mother's updated *Lost Gospels* because Father had only printed four for the school. Paul sat upright at the end of the table, his eyes closed because he had this part memorized. He savored each sentence. "'Jesus looked down at the carnage, broken wings and bits of bone floating in the lake. All the demons were dead. Jesus didn't bother looking up. There'd be more. This was hell.'"

The story went on, the confrontation with the doubting Thomas who had transformed into his real form, a wretched demon. "'Jesus rammed his sword through Thomas's throat, removing his head with a flick of his wrist.'"

Mother was staring at me, shaking her head. Not one quick shake like she'd just made a mistake. She kept shaking it super slow, back and forth like she couldn't believe how stupid she'd been.

Maybe it was the lack of sleep from the nightmares, but I didn't look away. Paul preached about Jesus fighting to the cell James was kept. I could barely follow. All my attention on Mother, the scream building in my chest, bubbling in my throat. I didn't care we were in church. I wanted to yell that not everything was my fault.

The phone rang and Mother was on her feet. She told Paul to continue and then hurried inside. Her shadow was a dark shape on the other side of the red window when she said hello.

I tried to hear what she was saying, but Paul was talking too loud.

The phone slammed down and Mother said, "Damn it. What next?"

Paul stopped talking, everything silent except Mother stomping about the kitchen muttering something about a piece of crap. Her shape filled the window when she shouted, "Finish the lesson. I'm getting your father."

Paul kept reading. By the time the screen door banged shut, Paul was at the part where the grand demon three times the size of Jesus flew on the path and blocked his way.

Tamara said, "Can you please slow down?"

Paul said sorry, he got excited.

David said, "Don't you want to go?"

Paul looked to me so I gave him a nod to finish. He hurried through the confrontation, Jesus cutting down the demon in four strokes, saving James from the falling body.

David shook his head and mumbled, "Yeah right."

Paul said, "Is something wrong?"

David leaned close to Patricia and whispered something that made her giggle.

Paul sounded just like Mother when he said, "What did you say?"

When David turned to Paul, I could see the thin moustache I wanted to tear off. He said, "My ass, four swings."

Paul pointed at the book in front of David. "You're calling this a lie?"

"I'm saying no way he cut it down in four swings."

David was seven years older and at least fifty pounds heavier than Paul, but Paul didn't seem to notice when he pointed to the first-row pew where he and Mother sat every Sunday. "Where do you think that came from?"

"That doesn't mean anything."

Paul's cheeks were getting red. "How about the pictures?"

"It shows a fallen tree. There's no video, no proof of him cutting it down."

"I was there. I would've been squished if Joshua hadn't saved me."

"You're his brother. You have to say it."

I didn't like where this was headed so I said, "Class is over."

Paul looked at me like I'd said the wrong thing, but he went along with it and told everyone to rise. When Paul said the closing prayer, David stood silent. Paul asked him, "Are you a non-believer?"

"I didn't say that. I'm just saying I bet he can't do it again." David turned to look at me. "Not with four strokes. Not with someone around to watch."

I thought maybe now there was a chance I could do it in ten or fifteen, but four was obviously out of the question. I never understood why Father had to exaggerate, but so it'd been written, so it'd been done. Four swings was the official story and neither Paul nor I could refute it so I said, "Don't you ever call my Father a liar."

Everyone turned toward me all wide-eyed. David didn't say anything and I gave him plenty of time. He was an inch or two taller, but that was about it, no question which of us was stronger.

I knew without a doubt that if he said one word I was going to hurt him. I knew what God did to those who didn't believe. Why should it be any different for me? Hurt first. What's good enough for my father, was good enough for me.

David said, "This is dumb." He snatched his book off the table and left the room.

It was Paul's turn to take control. "That's enough," he said. "Everyone out."

When we got outside, I told Paul I could use some help clearing graffiti, but he ran up the porch. "After Mother gets home." The screen door slammed shut behind him.

I shook out my size twelve tennis sneakers I'd worn the last year. They looked like sandals because I'd cut open the front so my toes could stick out. Mother had permitted it since Paul would probably never grow into them.

I didn't want Paul with me anyhow; I wanted to be alone. I was thinking how good it would feel to climb another tree. There was a tall one by the driveway that would be perfect. I thought it'd be funny if I happened to slip from way up there right when Mother and Father were pulling in. For my face to explode all over their windshield.

I looked up at the blue sky for the answer that'd never be there, the voice I'd never hear. Then over our rooftop there was a flash of red and yellow. A giant butterfly kite flying through the air, the most glorious thing I'd ever seen.

The wind whipped past me, the butterfly soaring higher. If I was ever going to have a sign, I figured this had to be it. My shoes were all muddy, each step a wet squelch, but I had to get closer.

The barn door was cracked open, but the sun shining the wrong way, keeping the inside hidden in shadow. I wanted to see in there, but not right then because the butterfly was back, lifting into the air, swaying lower and lower, dipping below the tips of the pines, then up again, one loop then two, flashing its beautiful red wings for all to see.

Right past the barn was the thick line of trees and sturdy rock wall we were never to cross. I paid it no mind and had taken a dozen steps when something swooshed through the branches above. I figured it had to be some kind of bird and continued on. After a few more trees, I caught glimpses of grass. There was another swoosh, something speeding through the leaves and smacking the ground a few feet to my right.

It looked like the shortest arrow until I pulled it out of the muck and saw it could go all the way through me. There were four tiny nails jutting out from the razor-sharp arrowhead.

I heard the softest giggle and had to get closer. I stayed behind the thickest trees until I reached the edge. The butterfly kite was less than a rock's throw away, the string attached to it now visible. It was the same girl as last time holding the spool. I'd only seen her that once but I remembered that laugh. That was her smile.

Her white shorts and matching shirt were so tight that in the bright light it was nearly like she was naked. She was beaming bright, looking up at the kite the way Mother looked at Paul.

A gust of wind blew her long brown hair behind. There was a soft twang and then a rip as the middle of the butterfly shot out its back, the body crashing straight down.

The girl fell to her knees and sobbed.

The arrow whistled down and I jumped back, covered my head with both arms. It struck the ground where I'd been standing, pieces of kite stuck on the nails.

The archer was on the porch, standing proud, bow in one hand, arrow in the other. Frank, the one who had called me a faggot.

The girl picked up the broken butterfly and clutched it to her chest, her face pure anguish. "Why?" she cried. "Why?"

I did something I'd never done before and spoke up. Spoke up as loud as I could. "Why'd you go and do that for?"

The guy who looked like a poorly-disguised demon turned toward me. "What the hell you doing?"

The girl stood, the battered butterfly forgotten by her feet. She wiped tears off her cheeks and turned to him. "I don't think he knew."

The other boy, Jeremy, with hair past his shoulders, was over by the garage. He had a huge silver camera up on his shoulder, just like the Fremonts brought for the baptism. He shouted, "Cut!"

The ugly guy yelled that I ruined it. Jeremy headed over and said, "Relax, Frank. I got the shot."

"Yeah, and this idiot yelling."

Jeremy kept coming, his camera aimed at my shoes dripping with mud, my toes poking through them. "I'm adding music to the whole thing," he said. "Don't worry about it."

"That shot was perfect." Frank looked at me and said, "You got any idea how many times it took?"

"At least three."

"Are you fucking with me?"

I didn't like the way he was gripping the bow, how his forearm muscle bulged. I did the same with the arrow, felt it about to snap.

Jeremy stopped a few feet in front of me and turned to his friend. "Go on home and let me take care of it."

"He's the homo who made me lose that race. What the hell you doing sneaking around?"

"I'm not a homo."

"I said leave him alone. He's my neighbor."

"Are you serious?" Frank threw the bow onto the grass and dropped his arrow onto the porch. "Fine. You two can suck each other off for all I care."

Jeremy bent over and pulled the arrow from the ground, spread out the punctured piece of kite. He left his camera on it for a second or two before turning it off and holding it at his side. "Sorry about that. Frank can be a real dick sometimes."

"That's okay."

He stuck out his hand and introduced himself and his sister. I started to say my name, but he stopped me. "I know who you are. Everyone around here does."

"That's what I've been told."

Danielle walked up beside him and gave a little wave, her shirt doing nothing to hide her chest bouncing, no thick bra keeping everything in place. "I wasn't really crying, but thanks."

I looked down and said I was sorry.

Jeremy tapped the camera. "So what do you think? Should be pretty tight, right?"

I had no idea what he was talking about and didn't think I could play it off. "What?"

"The video. It's for my art class. I'm calling this piece Life."

"We don't do that. Art."

Both Jeremy and Danielle nodded, but neither looked surprised. Jeremy asked, "You guys learn about everything or just religion?"

"I guess everything, but I don't know for sure."

Jeremy brought the camera up to his shoulder, his voice all deep and rich. "So is it true the things they say about you? Are you the Second Coming of Christ?"

I'm not sure how long I stood there, that red dot blinking, Danielle watching right next to her brother. He was looking for a one-word answer and my not knowing would take thousands.

Jeremy said, "So what's it going to be?"

Her eyes were on me and I had to say something. "Everyone says I am."

"You don't sound so sure."

My sad little face was reflected in the camera's black circle, my dented forehead, crooked nose, uncombed hair.

He said, "That just seems like something you'd either know or don't know. Can't imagine Clark Kent ever doubting he was Superman."

"Who?"

Jeremy lowered the camera. "Are you fucking serious? Superman? You never heard of him?"

I shook my head and tried not to hear Danielle's giggle, the way it sounded aimed at me.

He went back to filming. "What about Spiderman?"

Shake.

"Batman?"

Shake.

"The Hulk? How about Terminator? Gladiator? Lord of the Rings?"

Danielle had stopped laughing, her smile no longer there. I finally asked Jeremy, "Can you turn that off?"

"Got to answer the question first. Are you or aren't you Him?"

Danielle said, "Say no comment." Her eyes matched the sky with a softness that said I could trust her. "Just say it."

Jeremy told her to keep quiet.

I said, "No comment."

Jeremy turned off the camera. "Fair enough." Then he kicked Danielle in her butt hard enough to make her jump. "Remember what I said."

Danielle lowered her head. "Sorry."

Jeremy handed her the camera. "Go put this in my room. Mess with it and I'll break your jaw, make sure you never get a boyfriend."

Danielle ran up the steps and disappeared into the house. Part of me wanted her to come back, the other part was fine never looking stupid in front of her again.

"Sorry if I upset you," Jeremy said. "Just acting you know. I'm gonna be a big-time producer one day."

"Producer? What's that?"

Jeremy clapped me on the shoulder. "Holy shit, you got some catching up to do."

Danielle burst out the door and down the steps, stayed half a step behind Jeremy.

He asked, "So what you want to do, Josh?"

No one had ever called me that but I liked it. I shrugged my shoulders.

"You sure don't talk much, do you?"

"Only when I need to. My parents have a thing about that."

"Man, what it sounds like you need is some TV. I'd say we'd watch some, but my mom's in there stinking up the place."

Danielle started back toward the door. "She won't care. She'll want to meet you."

Jeremy ordered her down. "You ain't bugging her."

"Maybe I should go," I said.

"Nah, man, don't worry about my mom. She don't give a shit what we do as long as we stay out of her hair."

Jeremy's blue bike was lying on the gravel driveway. I pointed at it and said, "Is that hard to do?"

"Riding a bike?" He shook his head. "Nah, not at all. You've never been on one?"

"Unh-unh."

"Danielle, get him yours."

She ran off to the garage and Jeremy got on his. "Ain't every day you get to meet Christ, and teach him how to ride a bike."

He was showing me which lever did the brakes when Danielle came rolling around the corner on the hot pink bike, hands forward, her boobs hanging down.

Jeremy must've thought I was staring at the color. "Hers is better to learn on. Trust me."

"I do."

Danielle stepped off her bike and held it still for me. "Get on," she said.

I swung my leg over the big banana seat. I put my left foot up on the pedal and kept my weight on the right just like Jeremy.

He showed me how to balance with both feet off the ground. I tried again and again with no success.

Danielle put her hands on my hips and steadied me, the kindest hands I ever felt. Her perfume smelled like peaches and her voice was just as sweet. "Try to relax."

"Ah, isn't that cute," Jeremy said. "Now, let's ride." He slammed his foot down on the pedal and took off down the driveway.

I wanted nothing more than to stay right where I was, leave her hands on me, but I had to follow. I pushed down hard on the pedal and held the handles tight.

I started to tip, but Danielle corrected me, running alongside as I pushed down and down, faster and faster.

The faster I went, the easier it got, the bike nearly standing up on its own even after Danielle let go with a final push. She cheered, "You're doing it."

And I was, pedaling the pain right out of my knees, the wind blowing my hair, mud splattering my back.

Jeremy barely had to turn his head to see me. "Good job, man. We're headed left."

Left was a small dirt road leading to town. If anyone from church spotted me I'd be a dead man. My legs were on fire, but I kept pedaling like a maniac and swung past Jeremy as we headed for the top of the hill where the road became concrete.

He sounded kind of nervous when he shouted, "Get on this side!"

I swerved onto his side of the yellow line I hadn't noticed before. I matched his every stroke.

"Better slow down," he said.

But I wasn't slowing down. The freedom was incredible.

The hill was steeper than I thought it'd be, and I was already flying. My feet flew off the pedals. I struggled to get them back on, pinched the seat between my thighs.

I pulled on the brake levers, but nothing happened.

Jeremy shouted, "Fuck, it's all clogged!"

I held on tight, squeezing the brakes, my arms shaking, sidewalk and houses whizzing by. There was a green light at the bottom of the hill where our road met a street going across it. Our street ended at the T, where there was a lush lawn in front of a massive white building with the huge cross on top of it.

Jeremy kept yelling, "Bail! Bail!" In a blink, I was at the intersection, holding the handles tighter, praying to God like never before. The light that had been green turned red and the cars waiting on Main Street started moving. There was no deciding, nothing to do but hold on tight.

All sound was gone, time like molasses, a red pick-up missing me by a few feet. My front tire hit the curb, the fastest stop I'd ever felt. Both thighs smacked the handlebars when I flew off and I somehow brought my hands to my head a split second before I smashed into the massive black billboard with two lines of white letters:

Your Life Will Be Better

If You Believe

Everything went dark, then someone said, "Oh shit. Oh fucking shit. He's dead."

I opened my eyes, my face in the mud. "Who?"

Jeremy knelt beside me. "Man, are you okay?"

I pushed myself up and wiped the dirt from my face, felt kind of sick seeing the blood on my hand.

"Maybe you should stay down. You hit that thing like a fucking cannonball."

I moved my head side to side to make sure everything was working, and then got to my feet. The world was spinning and I went back down. I was seeing double but I didn't tell him and said, "I'm alright."

Jeremy helped me sit so I faced the sign, the fallen letters by my feet. Maybe he could tell my vision was all screwed up because he read it for me:

You Better

Believe

Dead serious, Jeremy asked, "You sure you ain't Him?"

Chapter Seven

It was November, over two years since the bike ride, and I was old enough to be a sophomore at Hartsville High. That's where Jeremy and Frank went. Danielle, too.

I knew all about their school from its newspaper, even had my nose re-broken by a rolled-up edition a few days after the collision. Father hadn't been happy about the article written by Jeremy Ludlow. A giant photograph of the splintered billboard with the remaining letters, the headline below read, *'Self-proclaimed Second Coming of Christ has Something to Say. Who's Going to Listen?'*

Father had been furious until the following Sunday when he had to put the school tables outside and add more chairs because our church had never been so full. Just like the other occasions where I didn't die, our fold instantly grew. We even held on to some of them, even though I nearly passed out both times I was asked to speak.

Not much had changed with the school, except a couple faces. Patricia had a baby and it looked way too much like David's for him to deny it. He'd gone off and was working at his uncle's mechanic shop.

Sarah and Paul sat at the ends of their table, Warren and Tamara in the middle. Beth's desk was a TV tray off to the side, but I couldn't see much of her with Ashley blocking my view. The entire week Ashley had been with us, I'd been trying not to stare. Although she'd just turned 14, the tall blonde was mature like me, our bodies not much different than an adult's.

The way I was hunched over, I could peek under my left armpit and see the lower half of Ashley's leg. It wasn't all thin and shiny like the girls in the magazines Jeremy lent me, but I'd already imagined my hands wrapping around it, pulling myself into her. She and Danielle were the reasons I had to wash my own sheets.

The kitchen timer went off. Mother said, "Break. Be back in ten minutes."

I pretended like I was still reading while everyone left. It looked like a nice day out there, but it was easier to stay at my desk, turn to the back of my book and pull out the page with all the crosses on it.

On the other side of the wall, Paul and Mother switched out the cooking trays, and talked about the soap operas coming up at lunch.

I drew crosses and swords, the ends sharp, dripping with demon blood. The next sword turned into a penis, the tip stretching to the sky and poking through the clouds.

Someone cleared their throat and I flipped the paper over, went back to making crosses. I glanced at the doorway and saw Beth, black skirt, black shirt, black fingernails.

"Can I ask you something?" she said.

We hadn't talked since a hello her first day. I hadn't even noticed, but her skirt was just to her knees. "Sure."

Beth walked up to my desk, set her hands on the top. "Paul said you're not going to get Ashley?"

I went back to my drawing, finished off the tip of a cross. "Correct."

"Because of me?"

It was too hard looking at her face because of all the hurt. Her fingernails weren't any better, all ragged and chipped. I said, "I never liked doing it."

"Well, I want you to."

I shook my head so she knew I was serious. "Sorry. I can't."

Her black fingernails tapped the top of my desk three times. "No," she said. "You don't get it. If you don't do it, I'm telling your mother what you did to me."

Mother's timer signaled another batch of baked goods and the start of lunch. Usually I stayed inside the church while everyone else hung out by the bake stand. This time I followed them. Paul distracted Mother on the front porch while I slipped inside the house. Even in a hurry, I ran my finger along the shiny shotgun resting on the mantel, the one they'd fought over because that money had been meant for groceries.

Paul coughed an extra loud warning and I made it to the laundry room before they hit the kitchen. I took a deep breath and entered the sweltering darkness of the passage. If I put my hands out I'd be able to run my fingers along the walls, but I hated touching things in the dark, always waiting for the demon to bite, to jump, to chop off my head. I stopped and took another breath, told myself to fucking chill. In two more breaths, my eyes adjusted, the satin curtain to the right, a folding chair in front of it. The metal was warm, the curtain resting on my knees, the soft glow behind it helping my heart regulate.

The church door opened, then closed. The lights blinked off.

Everything was black except a sliver of light under the door to the house. I nearly asked Ashley to put the lights back on, but she was already walking my way, footsteps headed down the aisle, climbing onto the stage and stopping at the kneeler.

I forced myself to take a breath, knew I wouldn't be able to talk like Father if I didn't. The chair on the other side of the curtain slid closer, a creak of the metal settling in when she sat on it.

Using Father's voice, I asked, "Are you okay?"

The voice came from so close, I nearly jumped. "Yes, Father."

Ashley had spoken only once in class, her voice so soft and sweet, one word running over the next like honey. "I'm on my knees."

Had she seen my drawing? Did she know why half the time in class my right hand was busy in my pocket? Was I going straight to hell for thinking that?

Already this was a bigger thing than I wanted. I wanted to tell Ashley it was a joke I couldn't pull on her, just tell the other kids I did. I'd wasted time not saying anything, and there was no telling how long Paul would keep Mother out of the kitchen where she might hear.

I welcomed Ashley and told her to relax. "Consider this a talk with a trusted friend. Tell me anything you like and our savior will hear."

The heat from the kitchen was amplified in the passage. The sweat dripped off my forehead like Mother had stuffed me in her oven.

She said, "Anything?"

What I was doing wasn't right, but I couldn't stop. "Yes. Whatever your heart desires."

"There's an awful lot I desire."

"Such as?"

"I want to be close to Christ. As close as I can."

That was a prepared answer, but the way she'd said it made me wonder. "Go on."

"I want to be filled with Christ's love."

Every time she spoke, the passage grew hotter, less air to breathe. "You are."

Her voice went down to a whisper, got rougher, huskier than it'd been. "I want him to lay his hands on me."

My legs trembled, caused the curtain to ripple. My voice cracked when I said, "That sounds like a good thing."

"I want Christ inside me."

My raging hard-on was pointing to heaven, pushing on my zipper. I was going to hell.

She asked, "Are you there?"

"I'm here. Just not used to such enthusiasm."

"I'm not just saying it. I want it to happen."

I wiped my hands on my pants and silently screamed at myself. What was I doing?

She said, "Don't you believe me?"

"Of course I do."

Everything became quiet. Warren was saying something out front, the birds chirping, Mother marching around inside. "Listen," she said. There was nothing, then something wet like a cat lapping milk. Her voice was different, like she'd lost control of it. "You hear that?"

My swallow became a gulp.

She whispered, "Stand up."

I did as I was told. The satin curtain brushed the front of my face.

"Give me your hand."

The curtain enclosed my hand, pulled me forward and down. Into something warm and wet, back out again just as quick. She let go of my wrist and the curtain pushed forward, a hand on each of my thighs. "Take them off," she said.

My pants and underwear fell to the ground, my whole body shivered.

Her breath was warm though the curtain. "Don't be afraid."

The satin wrapped around me and I almost came, buried both hands in the material by my face. "Oh, Jesus," was all I could say.

Her grip grew harder like she was trying to cut off my blood, then she moved the slightest bit up and down.

It felt incredible but she was too slow, my hips rising, up on my toes. A gust of warm wind against my head, three soft nibbles through the satin.

There was no stopping at that point, some other part of me calling the shots. I bucked my hips forward and pulled on the curtain as I unleashed my demon seed. The curtain tore free and I crashed back into the chair.

Mother shouted, "What's all that noise?" The laundry room door opened and she gasped, screamed my name.

I pulled the curtain onto my lap. "I fell."

Mother rushed forward and knocked my legs to the side. Beth was running, already out the door. "Jezebel!" Mother screamed. "Out of this church, you dirty creature!"

Looking down at me, she warned, "Not one word. So help me God, not one word."

✝ ✝ ✝

It was five days later and I was on my ninety-seventh set of pushups, stretched across the blanket on the basement floor in just a sweaty pair of underwear. I broke my record with fifty-three pushups and wrote it in my diary. Maybe I wasn't good at a lot of things, but these numbers proved I wasn't hopeless.

Jeremy first suggested I do them a couple months before. The increase in my numbers was hard to believe. He said his real dad could do hundreds of them, said it helped to kill time.

My arms and chest, shoulders and stomach were all taking shape, getting harder, becoming a man's. I wasn't there yet, but at least part of me was.

I sat back against the wall and took a few sips of water. It was only 10 o'clock and Paul wouldn't be back with a new glass until he brought lunch.

As to be expected, my presence was no longer needed in the classroom. Paul brought me that news along with my books and activities. If I had questions, I could ask them at night.

I wasn't expecting visitors but it sounded like someone was coming. I hurried over to my kneeler and faced the door just in time to see it open. Father kept his hand on the doorknob but wouldn't look at me. "Get dressed." He walked away and said, "The barn needs cleaning. Now you have time for it."

It took me all of a week working every day to get just the outside of the barn in decent shape. It had been completely overgrown with only glimpses of faded red siding among the vines and branches, a haven for spiders and every form of insect.

Since it was a Saturday morning, a couple minutes past eight, I just did a quick glance toward the corner. Jeremy had been a no show for a long time. I guessed he'd moved on.

I set down my cardboard box of cleaning supplies in front of the barn. I rubbed my hands together, the sting of callouses and blisters rubbing together, countless punctures from all the thorns.

The barn was void of growth, its rotten skin laid bare. The inside of the windows were still black, but the outside spotless. The opening between the two doors a dusty darkness, no hands having touched it since I could remember.

All my life this was where the demons lived. I took out my flashlight and crossed myself with it, shined it inside. The light sparkled off cobwebs draping the entire place. I kicked at the door, knocked it down on the third try.

With the door on the ground, I barely needed the flashlight. I kept it in front of my feet, making my way through the maze of waterlogged boxes, surrounded by the stench of decay. I stopped where the daylight died and looked to my right at the wall full of rusty equipment.

Something slithered behind me and I spun around, flashed my light. Boxes upon boxes, stacked high and tilting over, everything rotting but in much better shape than old lady Hester, their previous owner.

It slithered again. I zeroed in on a flash of black darting behind a box by the wooden loft ladder.

I turned my light to the end of the barn and a square of reflected light, the window to the backdoor. Hoping nothing would leap out, I headed for the door, shoving boxes out of my way with my leg, keeping both hands in front of my face to wave off webs.

The door opened an inch before the latch stopped it. The padlock was small and my flashlight metal. It opened on the third strike.

It was difficult breathing in the cloud of dust I'd created. I yanked the door open and walked forward, felt the web tear on my fingers, a black and red spider the size of a tennis ball less than an inch from my face.

I jumped back and tripped over a box, stuck out my hand to stop my fall.

The sound like a bed sheet ripped in half, pain shooting through my left palm, up my arm, slamming into my brain. I screamed *fuck* so loud it was all I could hear until the faint pitter-patter dribble on the ground beside me.

Enough light came through the door that I could see everything: the boxes I'd flattened, the long wooden handle of the three-pronged rake.

I screamed again and didn't stop. Six inches of rusted steel was sticking through my hand, blood oozing out the fleshy volcano, dripping into the pool below.

Black spots blurred my vision and my voice sounded fuzzy. I raised that hand and the rake came with it, a river of blood running down the forearm I couldn't feel.

I woke on the backseat of the station wagon, my head on Paul's lap, my hand a mind-numbing pulse of pain. Paul's face hung above me, the whitest I'd seen it. He shushed me and said, "Mother."

She turned around in the front seat holding my hand up high, putting pressure on both sides of the towel wrapped around it. "It's okay, honey. Look at your brother."

Mother never called me that so I kept looking at the sopping red towel, the matted hair on my forearm laying the wrong way. Every time my heart beat, the spike went through my hand again. *Jesus fucking Christ, just stop it. Please.* My prayer over and over.

Paul turned my cheek so he was all I could see, a brilliant blue sky behind him. "You'll be okay."

Father took a hard turn to the right, Mother telling him to be careful as I slid across the seat. There was no question he was talking to me when he said, "What the hell were you thinking?"

I didn't like the sound I was making, but it kept getting louder. My chest tight, breath catching when I tried to say sorry.

"There you go," Mother said, "close your eyes. We'll be there in a minute."

Three days of bedrest was all I could do, hand elevated above my heart, ice bags every hour and pain pills that made it so I could barely think straight.

I waited for school to start before I got dressed to go outside. Every time my hand dipped lower than my shoulder, the dull thump magnified by ten. I took another red pill. The pain wouldn't stop me.

At the barn, I turned on the hose with my good hand, used my bandaged one to hold the flashlight to my shoulder. It didn't matter the back door was open, anything could be hiding there.

I stepped inside and gagged on the stale air. I went around in circles, spraying off each window, knocking down the webs. The smell was alive, pulling on my guts, making me throw them up in the corner. I used to be a baby about that sort of thing, but it was my third time in the last two days. I put my stream on it and blasted it into the mess I'd be shoveling onto the grass.

Father came back that night, grinning ear to ear. All four of us were at the table, my elbow allowed to rest on it, bandaged hand up in the air.

"Everyone's asking about you, Joshua. The story's out there catching fire. They see it's a sign."

I couldn't remember the last time I'd made him happy so I kept quiet even though there was something I wanted to ask.

"And your Mother tells me you're already back at the barn. Way to go. Shows how tough you are."

Even with the new overhead fan, I was sweating. "Maybe after I'm done with barn I could go to school."

"We already discussed that. You can learn in your room."

"No, a real school. I could walk there."

Father set down his drink. "What is our rule?"

"I know, but I'll have to leave some day. How am I supposed to tell people what to do if I don't know anything?"

"If you ever listened to me, you would never ask that question."

Jeremy, Frank, and common sense would have pointed out all the holes in Father's reasoning, but I couldn't figure anything out.

"He doesn't look right, Charles. Joshua, do you hear me?"

I didn't know if it was day or night, a fire burning through my body, it's flames licking at my brain. All the lights were off in the bedroom, a touch on my fingertip making me yell.

"Jesus, Joshua," Doc Hargrove said. "Are these the same bandages from the hospital?"

Mother said, "Why do you think I kept asking if you were keeping it clean?"

"They just got a little wet."

"They showed you what to do," Mother said. "I told you to pay attention."

I didn't remember much from the hospital, just the pure pain of them scraping the wound clean.

Doc gagged as he undid the dressing. "Better bring him a bucket and a towel to bite on. I'll need both of you to hold him down."

The next day came and went, melted into the next, ice baths, medicine, water to sip. It was a few days later when Father came to my room, asked if I could walk.

I was still lightheaded but managed to do it, using my good hand to help along the hall.

Father pointed to the chair and hit play on the VCR. "This is what you're missing."

Little kids being led away from the playground, images of all the ones that didn't make it. The scars, the deaths, the tragedies. In the words of my father, all of it my fault.

It was Saturday morning and my fever was gone. I was hard at work in the barn when I heard the knock on its back door. I was surprised Paul would be up so early and out of the house. Not in the mood for his games, I said, "Go around."

From the other side of the door, Jeremy said, "If you say so."

I checked over my shoulder to make sure no one could see him then told him to open the door.

He stood there holding a small gray camera, acting like everything was normal. He nodded at my hand that rested on my shoulder. "Read about that. How's it feeling?"

"Where'd you read that?"

The *Herring* had a little piece. At least it was only your hand. What the hell were you doing, trying to crucify yourself?"

"Ha-ha."

Jeremy looked at my eyes, studied me a second. "What they got you on? Vicodin?"

"Percocet."

"You going to use them all?"

"They make me want to puke."

"What you need to do is smoke a bowl."

"Of what?"

Jeremy stepped past me into the barn and looked around. "Wow, pretty fucking cool. Too bad it smells like something crawled out of Satan's vagina."

"Should have smelled it last week."

"So how about the pills? Want to get rid of some?"

I said sure and took out the little bottle, counted out ten pills for myself, gave him the rest. "You've been busy."

"Frank's dad got the internet. I just about live there now."

He walked along the wall, picking up stuff, putting it down. "It's incredible, best thing ever invented. You should see all the stuff Frank saved on there."

"Pictures?"

"Yeah, and videos, anything you could imagine." Jeremy went over to the pile of crap pushed to the front. He stopped when he came to the crate of colored bottles. "They even got animals. All kinds of crazy shit."

"Animals?"

"Yeah, donkeys and dogs, horses and snakes."

"Snakes?"

He examined a purple bottle. "Yeah, it's supposed to be just the tip, but this one chick had gotten herself way too wet and that snake just slipped out of her grasp and went on up. The whole thing. And then she started screaming like crazy, get it out, get it out."

"Wow."

He pointed to the crate. "How about these?"

"What about them?"

"Want to get rid of them?"

I'd already broken a bunch with the hose and planned on breaking the rest, but the way he asked sounded like Paul when he was being sneaky. "Why, they worth something?"

"Maybe. Probably not much, but I'll split it with you."

The bottles were probably older than Father and all kinds of colors, each one of them empty. I said he had a deal and shook his free hand, checked over my shoulder to make sure no one was coming.

"You got to stop that," Jeremy said like he was talking to a little kid. "Stop worrying about them so much. You should be able to do what you want."

"What can I do? He'll kick me out."

"There's always the Army."

"They just take anyone?"

"As long as you don't tell them you're a fag."

"I ain't one."

Jeremy pushed something away from the wall with his foot then kicked the small, dark package at me. "You haven't got it figured out yet, have you?

You really think they'll disown you? Throw away the whole church? Those books he's been writing, all of it wouldn't mean a thing."

I kicked the package back hard because I felt like an idiot. The rotten paper wrapping ripped halfway off, the book stopping at his feet. "What is that?"

Jeremy picked it off the muddy floorboard along with a crumpled ribbon. "Someone's present."

I cracked the door for more light and asked him to unwrap it, seeing as how I only had the one hand. "Whose do you think it is?"

Jeremy slipped his camera into his pocket and tore off the rest of the paper, held up the waterlogged book. "Yours now."

I stood next to him as he flipped through the pages. "Any idea what it's about?"

"Looks like Viking stuff." He tossed it to me. "Too bad it's ruined."

I set the book on the windowsill so I could read it later. From the other side of the barn, Jeremy said, "Oh shit. Check this out."

He held up a canvas sack that was soaking wet and had all sorts of stuff sticking to it. "We can patch up these holes and make a badass punching bag."

"For punching?"

"Come on, man, what'd I tell you about that?"

I nodded. Think first.

"For boxing. My old man taught me some things."

"They can't see it."

Jeremy turned and looked at the ladder. "Up there."

"I won't be able to clean it any time soon."

"I'll do it."

"You serious?"

"Yeah, when your old man ain't around. I'll be careful."

I sensed a condition. "I don't know—"

"In exchange for one thing."

"What?"

"You do some interviews."

"No way."

"Just pretend ones so I can practice. I want to get out of this place, and no station's going to hire some hick with no experience."

"Pretend?"

"Yeah, I won't even really record. This is what your father should have had you doing from the start. Getting comfortable talking in front of one person, deal with your anxiety. Just put up your arms and say 'I'm the Messiah. Bow down and worship me.' You'd have a ton of followers in no time."

"What if I don't want them?"

"Then we keep it all pretend like I just explained. Come on, man, want me to put the bag up or not?"

The loft was bigger than I'd imagined, with plenty of room for the mud-filled sack he had roped over the rafters. Jeremy had placed two folding chairs, a lantern, and some other junk all along the edge so it looked like I hadn't gotten started up there yet.

The hole in my hand had finally closed up, but I still couldn't make a fist. We'd just finished up our first lesson and it'd been invigorating, even with just my left hand. "This is pretty cool."

Besides being faster and the much better boxer, Jeremy never showed off or tried rubbing it in. Before his dad got put away, he used to do tough man contests and taught Jeremy all kinds of tricks. Jeremy was just happy to pass on the lessons.

He brought out his tiny Go Pro. "Now it's your turn."

My mouth went dry, but I couldn't say no. "So only pretend, right?"

Jeremy turned the camera on me, no red light flashing. "What's your name?"

I froze.

"Come on, man, you got to play along."

I wanted to help him. "It's hard."

"Do it for the chicks. Pretend a bunch of beautiful women are going to be watching this." Jeremy grinned like he had a great idea. "Do this, and when I'm famous, I'll fly you out to Hollywood and introduce you to all the supermodels. You better learn how to talk in public between now and then."

The red light went on. Jeremy twirled his finger.

I cleared my throat. "Hey, I'm Joshua."

"Say Josh. Sounds way cooler."

I tried again. "Hey, I'm Josh."

He twirled his finger.

I said that was all I had.

Jeremy ignored me. "Can you please tell us what happens to those who don't believe in you?"

I shook my head, didn't care whether the camera was running.

"You gotta say something. Not unless want to stay a virgin your whole life."

"I don't know how to answer."

"Like your dad would."

I started to say okay, but Jeremy cut me off. "Then do it again but say what you really think."

Chapter Eight

It was the last Friday of March, nine o'clock on the dot. Lights had been out for an hour, our bedroom as black as the moonless night. The creak of Mother's rocking chair and a couple crickets filled the silence. Then two quacks, three quacks, one quack, two. There was a break and the pattern repeated.

From up above, Paul whispered. "You hear that?"

I shushed him and rolled out of bed.

Paul's curls poked over the railing. "Why are you dressed?"

I had on my best white shirt and my black pants, the only pair that fit. "Never mind me."

"You can't go anywhere."

"If I'm the Messiah, I can do whatever the hell I want."

Paul just stared.

In the meanest whisper I could manage, I said, "Now lay your ass back in bed."

He did what I said but didn't keep quiet. "I'm telling."

I put my hands on the railing. "Oh yeah? I'll tell him about the shows you watch."

"You wouldn't."

"You really want to try me?"

Paul didn't say a word, kept his eyes on the ceiling.

I felt sorry, but just for a second, then stuffed my pillows under the sheets. The window slid up so silent. I didn't bother saying goodbye before I slipped out.

Darkness consumed everything except the sliver of light behind the barn. Jeremy was by the back door, his flashlight showing off his blue jeans and black t-shirt with a word on it I didn't recognize.

I said, "I didn't know what to wear."

"It's cool. Just undo the buttons and don't tuck it in."

I started to do that and he said, "Better yet, just leave it here. Your tank top's fine."

"You sure?"

"Yeah, man. You're a fucking stud. Show off those guns."

Jeremy knew about a thousand times more than I did, so I took his word for it and tried not to feel foolish in the white tank top digging into my chest.

He grabbed my shirt and hung it on a nail. "You ready for this?"

I nodded, afraid of what I'd sound like, and followed Jeremy out the door and through the woods, careful where I stepped. "How far is it?"

"Other side of town. Frank should be here any minute."

I stopped next to a large pine. "Frank?"

Jeremy shined the light on me. "I told him you're cool."

It'd been years since the butterfly incident, but I said, "I don't know. Maybe I should stay here."

"Dude, I'm trying to get you laid."

"I know."

"Then come on." Jeremy kept walking. "Her daddy's a big ole bible thumper and she's down to fuck the shit out of you."

I'd been telling myself it was too good to be true, no one wanted to be with me. Not if I wasn't hiding my crooked nose, pimpled face, and punctured body behind a curtain. I followed him, figured it was worth a shot.

Jeremy's house was to our left, Danielle sitting on the porch steps, a jean skirt that showed all her legs, a tube top that didn't hide much when she waved. "Please, Jeremy," she said. "Can I ask him?"

"There's no room." Jeremy pointed toward the gray pick-up idling at the end of the driveway, the passenger door open. "Go on," Jeremy told me. "Get in."

Danielle said, "I'm not scared to ride in the back."

The back sounded way better than riding inside with Frank, and of course I wanted her to go. "I'll jump in the back. I don't mind."

Like I hadn't even spoken, Jeremy told her, "You'll fucking stay here like I told you to. Take care of Mom." He headed down the driveway and said to me, "Come on, last thing you want is to bring along a little cockblock."

Jeremy opened the passenger door and pointed for me to go first. Frank was bigger than since I'd seen him with the bow and took up half the front seat. He'd shaved his head, but he still had the same sunken eyes and permanent sneer. He was dressed like Jeremy, only his shirt had skulls all over it. He took one glance as I got in. "Nice shirt."

I said thanks. Jeremy scooted in next to me so all three of us were touching no matter how I tried to turn.

Frank jerked his shoulder so it was in front of mine. "This is so fucking gay."

Jeremy took a big whiff and said, "Damn, Frank, whatcha been into?"

Frank nodded toward the glove box. "Help yourself."

Jeremy opened it and brought out a small bottle and a colorful pamphlet. He unscrewed the cap and took a swig, grimacing as he held it in front of me.

I couldn't have grabbed it if I wanted, my right hand glued to the dashboard, my left gripping my knee. Father didn't drive like Frank. "Maybe in a bit."

Jeremy took another swig, shook the pamphlet. "Can't believe you really did it."

"Take it," Frank said. "They need photographers. I asked."

I asked Jeremy what it was and he turned the pamphlet over. *Become a Marine.* I asked Frank, "You're really doing that?"

"Hell yeah. Gonna get me some of them fucking towelheads, show them how the fuck we do things over here."

"What about your parents?"

"What about them?"

"They're letting you go?"

"Ain't got a choice. You turn eighteen, you don't belong to them anymore."

Jeremy said, "Just someone else." He took another swig then handed me the bottle. "Go ahead."

It looked like he'd sucked a lemon with no sugar. "What is it?"

Frank asked if he should turn around. "I can take you back to your mommy."

It smelled awful, like the time I'd left uneaten mush under my bed two days. I took a swig, set my throat on fire, warmed my belly.

"Nice job, rookie," Frank said. He turned down another road. "Hey, there's something I've wanted to ask you, because I know this pussy here hasn't. If you're Jesus, where the hell's our universal peace?"

"What's that?"

Frank sounded like Mother when he said, "Wow."

"The Millennium," Jeremy said. "The golden era of peace that's proclaimed to begin at Jesus Christ's Second Coming."

Frank said, "That proves it right there. No offense, but you ain't no fucking Jesus. You didn't stop Iraq, Afghanistan, Syria, or any of that shit. There's no thousand years of peace."

Thanks to Father I was quite aware that all that shit was my fault. The little girl getting blown up by the landmine, her father clutching half of her to his chest. I didn't say a word.

Jeremy jumped in, asked Frank about his recruiter. I focused on the world outside that I so rarely saw. The deep, dark pasture flying past. The occasional car here and there, the headlights blinding.

A few blocks past the brightly-lit Exxon, we turned onto a dark street with smaller houses on either side. Frank rolled down the windows as the truck crept along. "Told you it was going to be a bunch of assholes with their hip hop shit. I fucking swear."

Jeremy told him to chill. We followed the low *boom, boom, boom* to a brown house on the left, a large white For Sale sign square in the middle of the lawn. "Bingo."

Frank drove us to the back of the property where four other cars were parked along the chain-link fence. Jeremy nodded at the pink one and said, "Check it out. She showed."

We all got out of the truck and headed over to a section of fence that was leaning back. Frank took hold of the corner and peeled it back even more. "Ladies first."

I went after Jeremy, walking where he did, sidestepping the rotten peaches. Some of the branches were pretty low and I had to duck down. I asked, "Is the front door broken?"

From right behind me, closer than I liked, Frank said, "Yeah, that's it."

Jeremy said, "Just try to enjoy."

When we got to the back steps, Jeremy stepped aside. Frank didn't bother knocking, just walked on in like he belonged. He said, "Let's grab a fucking beer."

We followed him in and found ourselves in a kitchen, way nicer than mine with all its tile and woodwork, but with absolutely nothing in it, not even a stove. No table, no chairs, just a guy and girl hugging in the corner, oblivious to the pounding music.

The dining room was the same, just another empty space, three guys my age circled up, each holding a red cup. Frank and Jeremy said what's up to them as we walked into the living room. Nine folding chairs were spread around, a large silver barrel with ice on top and a stack of red cups directly in the middle.

I hadn't realized I'd been clenching my fists until Jeremy handed me three cups and poured the foamy brown liquid from a small hose attachment. Frank took first pick and joined his buddies in the dining room. The cold cup felt great against the dull throb of my hand.

Jeremy bumped my cup with his, sent beer splashing over my hand and onto the floor. He said, "Here's to good friends and you saving the world."

We each took a big gulp, but my throat wasn't ready for how cold it was. I shook off my brain freeze and followed Jeremy into the hallway, turned left toward the music. There was a guy and two girls hanging around a card table, a large radio on top of it. I didn't look at the guy at all, and just real quick at each girl and the colorful bottles in their hands.

Suddenly I felt self-conscious in a way that I never had before, a complete fool in my wife-beater and Sunday school slacks.

Jeremy walked over to the skinny blonde wearing jeans and a thin white t-shirt over a blue bra, a smoking cigarette in her long fingers. "Josh, this is Maryanne." He kissed her cheek and smacked her butt. He pointed to the pudgy brunette in a black leather skirt and red halter top straining to rein in her giant tits. "And this is Kara."

I said hi, did my best not to stare at her shirt, her nipples pushing out the fabric, the roll of skin bunched at the top of her skirt. They said hi back, and then we all stood there. I finished my beer so I wouldn't stand out as the one not talking. Jeremy asked if they'd been there long.

Maryanne said, "About an hour."

Kara held up her bottle, some kind of purple juice sloshing at the bottom. "Long enough for four of these."

Jeremy handed me his beer. "You've got some catching up to do." He turned to Kara and said, "Why don't you show Josh the rest of the house. We're gonna get a smoke."

Kara took hold of my bad hand and squeezed. "Come on, let's go where it's quieter." She led me down the hall, all that leather barely containing her butt wiggling back and forth.

I took another drink. We passed a bathroom on the left and entered the room at the end, a dingy white mattress on the floor shoved against the wall.

Jeremy had taught me a lot, but there wasn't anything he could do for me now. I had to speak. "Is this your house?"

Kara laughed, but it lasted too long and sounded like a horse. "Take a load off."

There wasn't a sheet. I sat down on the corner that was the least yellow, ignored the puff of dust.

Kara slid down next to me, her skirt brushing my shoulder and bunching up against my thigh. She smelled like roses. "So," she said, and wrapped her hand around my bicep. Her breath warmed my face. "You're the Messiah."

Most times I'd want to say no way, I ain't Him. Jeremy had told me that most people thought I was a joke, and that Father was off his rocker. But I was going to get laid, so I said, "Some people swear by it."

Kara took a drink and licked her pink lips sparkling with glitter. She missed a drop that landed on her chest and disappeared between her tits.

I tried drinking but had a hard time not spilling with her on my arm. She let it go, her chubby little hand dropping onto my thigh, her sausage-link fingers giving a squeeze. "So what do you do for fun?"

"Afraid I don't get much of that."

She ran her hand up and down my thigh. "Ohh, poor baby."

The music changed to something upbeat. I finished my beer and set down the cup, afraid to open my mouth and put my foot in it.

Her hand tapped my leg to the beat, some song about fireworks. "What do you listen to?"

"You mean like my parents?"

Kara had just chugged the rest of her bottle, and most of it sprayed out on me when she laughed. She said sorry and wiped my face with her hand. "Music? Who do you like?"

On a couple of my atonement videos there were segments on Marilyn Manson and Slipknot, but I'd never heard their music, just knew they were evil. "I don't know any bands."

"You're serious?"

"My parents are pretty strict."

"Shit, I'll say." Kara used my shoulder to stand. She swayed in tune. "You like this music?"

I sat for a second and listened. Although I might have exaggerated, I said, "It's way better than my brother."

Kara held out her hand. "Let's dance."

I didn't want to say no, but I shook my head. Getting up with a hard-on wasn't happening.

She looked at me like I'd called her fat. "You don't want to dance with me?"

Part of me wanted to have her body pressed against mine, but the bigger part was petrified. "I don't know how."

Kara sighed. She was already out the door when she said, "I need another drink."

I sat and listened to the rest of the song. Halfway through the next one, Jeremy and his girl showed up.

"Where's Kara?"

"Getting a drink?"

Jeremy stepped in and handed me two of the four full beers he was holding. "You cool?"

I nodded because this was the coolest I'd ever been. They took off and I got to sipping, telling my heart to stop thudding.

Halfway through the second beer, some guy with a scruffy beard appeared in the doorway and said, "This room's couples only."

I almost said Kara was coming back, but I kind of knew she wasn't. I started to get up then plopped back down, surprised I was so dizzy. I tried again, getting on my knees first and using the wall. "I need a drink anyhow."

The beard guy left before I got to him. "Good for you."

There were a handful of people in the hallway. I put my shoulder to the wall for balance and kept saying excuse me. The living room was packed with probably as many people as our biggest service. I didn't really look at their faces, didn't want them looking at me. Kara wasn't with them. Neither was Jeremy.

I stumbled into the kitchen, walked right through the puddle of puke by the fridge hole. One of Frank's buddies was pissing in the sink, which made me realize I couldn't hold mine much longer. I barely made it out the back door, my zipper down and dick out by the time I hit the grass. A girl I hadn't noticed said, "Eww, how gross."

The fresh air felt great, made me think I'd be okay. I went back inside the house, tried to steer clear of all the people on my way to the back room. The door was closed.

I grabbed the handle, but it wouldn't turn. A hard shove with my shoulder and I was in the room, the lights out.

Some guy from inside said, "What the fuck?"

I ran my hand along the wall until it hit the switch.

The guy with the radio had his hand over his eyes, his mouth inches from Kara's puffy nipples.

I slammed the door, but heard her say, "Told you he's lame."

This time I didn't say sorry when my shoulder smacked someone. I needed another beer and got in line. I should have paid better attention when Jeremy was doing it, because only foam came out for me. Some smartass behind me said, "Who's this clown?"

I spun around, searched for the voice. The smallest guy in line looked away, his tough guy act all gone. Maybe I was a little mad about Kara, and there was no denying I was already drunk, but I wanted to prove at least I'd listened to what Jeremy had taught me about being a man.

I waited until the punk looked forward again. "What'd you say?"

"It wasn't about you," he said. "That guy back there."

I didn't look, knew he was lying. I also knew it was a bad idea to get any drunker so I tossed my cup at his feet, waited three full seconds to see if he'd dare look me in the eyes or say a fucking word.

I tottered over to the far corner, put my back to the wall. Everyone else knew each other, probably all disbelievers, not one of them bothering to risk a glance my way. There was a ruckus from the kitchen and four new guys came in and cut in line for the keg. Two of them had baseball bats, one of them wore a black tank top. A couple people said something about the wrecking crew. Frank gave them each a high five. "What's up, fuckers? Put some real music on."

The thinnest one got out his phone and headed to the radio. "Consider it done."

This was a stupid idea and I wanted to go home. I tapped Frank on his shoulder and he just stared at my hand, told me to go bug Jeremy.

The music shut off. Some people booed but they were quickly blocked out by furious guitars and a piercing scream, my heart racing along. Someone yelled, "FUCKIN' SLAYER!!!" and a couple guys threw devil horns in the air. All the females retreated to the kitchen and hallway, most the guys backing up to the living room wall.

The music playing at breakneck speed, Frank and the four new guys ran around the keg, throwing their arms, kicking red cups and plastic chairs, throwing themselves at each other.

More and more guys joined the circle and soon there were ten. I was getting dizzy watching them and found myself splattered with beer from all the cups flying.

A chair bounced off my leg. The big guy in the black tee had thrown it. He went around once, wouldn't look at me.

I stepped to the edge of the circle.

The second time around he was laughing.

Third time around I launched my shoulder right in his fucking jaw and put him on his back.

Nothing stopped, the bodies flying past me, jumping over their friend. Frank got in a cheap shot and nearly knocked me over, shouted, "Come on, you big snatch!"

I rushed after him, knocked a skinny guy out of my way. Before I could catch Frank, the circle broke apart, guys scattering to each of the walls, punching and kicking, letting loose with the bats.

There was no time to think and I went into attack mode, took on the closest wall. My shoe went through the plaster on my third kick, my right fist on my first punch. Windows shattered, lights ripped from fixtures, holes in every wall, the band called Slayer screaming about the angel of death.

Everything became a hate-filled blur as I threw my body upon the wall, picked myself up and did it again, picturing Father, Frank, and every other motherfucker who ever laughed at me.

A man-sized section of plaster was busted, several holes shining through to the other room. It was defying the Son of God. It had to be punished.

I backed up into somebody but didn't pay them any mind, all my focus on the wall. I ran full speed and lowered my shoulder, a loud crack as I blasted through to the other side. I dusted off my hands and noticed I was bleeding from somewhere. I looked up where the wall had been and saw the red light blinking in Jeremy's hand. Louder than I'd ever gotten, I yelled, "No! Turn it off!"

Someone shouted, "Cops! It's the cops!"

Everything went quiet, the music silenced, heavy breathing. Someone whispered, "You better be fucking around."

There was a loud bang on the front door. "Open up, it's the police!"

Everyone ran for the back door, Jeremy pulling my arm, my feet barely keeping up. My eyes weren't ready for the dark and I fell down the steps. I bounced off the grass and scrambled back up, people running by me, Jeremy nowhere to be seen.

I couldn't remember what the truck looked like or where it was parked, but I knew better than to get clogged up in the pile of people bunched up at the opening in the chain-link. I ran for the far corner, figured I could jump the fence, didn't see the branch until the last second, no time to stop or duck down.

I woke to a hard slap on my cheek, Father kneeling over me. "What the hell did you do?"

The porch light stung my eyes. It was entirely true when I said, "I don't know." Last I remembered was the tree.

Father looked behind him. "Call Hargrove."

"It's midnight," Mother said.

"If that's not stitched, it'll scar for sure."

"I can smell him from here."

"The phone. Now!"

Chapter Nine

It was a warm August night, Mother's window wide open, the first half of atonement finished. I turned off the DVD player, thirty minutes of white hazmat suits and brown bodies. One tiny virus, all my fault.

Mother was bagging peanut brittle on the couch. She didn't bother looking up.

I walked through the kitchen, past all the delicious things I couldn't eat because that was our profit. I opened the door to the passage and closed it without moving. The crinkle of plastic bags, a bowl being set down on the coffee table. Mother sighed, her footsteps headed away. The TV snapped on. Friday night was *The Amazing Race* since Father was out on deliveries and wouldn't be back until the next night.

I went through the passage, let the new curtain brush my face, take me back to Beth.

Paul was waiting at the piano. "So what do you want to hear?"

It didn't matter what Paul played or why he was there. They said it'd help me pray. I said they were right, never letting on I knew he was their spy.

Whether or not she was my mother, Paul was my brother. I said, "The usual, but with just one change."

He'd gone through a growth spurt over the last few months and was only a few inches shorter than me, but still half my size. And there was no denying he was their child, the best of them blended into their shiny star. He stretched his long fingers and said, "What's that?"

"If you hear Mother coming, switch to *How Great Thou Art.*"

"Why?"

"'Cause I'm gonna be outside."

"You'll get us both in trouble."

I walked over to the piano. "All you got to do is play the song."

Paul looked at the kitchen window. "She'll know."

"She's in her room. I'll come right back when I hear the song. You just say I went outside to check out a noise."

"I can't lie."

"Stop being such a homo."

Paul arched up like a cat. "Don't you ever call me that."

"Then don't act like one."

"She'll tell Father."

"You know she ain't coming. Not with you keeping an eye on me."

Paul didn't say he would or wouldn't. He just started playing the piano, beautiful, but entirely way too soft and slow for my liking. I knew now what real music was, and this wasn't it.

I slipped out the church's front door and into the moonlit night. Mother's curtains were closed, but I kept low until I passed her window, the commercial for Church's Chicken reminding me of my hunger.

Father had made sure I knew there were people out there who wanted to hurt me. People who wanted me dead. I read it for myself in the mail he passed on. The ones spending forty-nine cents to share their hate.

I ran to the barn, telling myself there were no demons lurking in the trees. I reached under the overturned wheelbarrow and pulled out my lantern, turning it on low once I was inside, the door cracked so I could hear Paul. The barn was close to immaculate, all the junk gone, burned or hauled off, except the three large boxes at the base of the ladder.

Up in the loft, I set the lantern on my table, and opened the window, the rock 'n roll music nearly as loud as Paul's piano. It was coming from Jeremy's, his going away party. He was leaving for college in Texas, determined to become one of the top movie producers of all time. He said he'd be back for the holidays, but there was no way to know if I'd ever see him again.

I pulled the sheet of black plastic off the heavy bag and cardboard box. I took out the Marine pamphlet Jeremy left in my hidey hole after a month of me begging. It showed how much money I'd make if I joined. I'd look the like guy on the cover, a person who commanded respect.

Beneath the pamphlet lay the waterlogged book with the iron cross on the cover. I turned to the first page, where I always went. The one line of cursive spread out all blotchy blue was obviously not Father's even though it read, *Lessons from your father.*

I'd forgotten all about the Norse book and only saw the inscription because of the letter. Along with all the hate mail I was forced to read, Father screwed up once and let by a nice one. The guy said he lived with my aunt Laura and that we shared the same father. He asked why I wouldn't write back. He promised he wasn't lying. He included a photograph of him holding that same book, one Jeremy said he couldn't find online. His wide shoulders, rectangle face, and dingy blond hair made it that much harder to deny we were related.

I threw everything back in the box and tossed the rope over the beam. I gave it two enormous tugs and tied it off, swung my arms back and forth and leaned side to side, warming up like Jeremy said to. He also said to always wrap my wrists and knuckles, but I didn't need protecting. The first strike was half speed to wake my body, my right hand the hammer behind it. A person responsible for so much pain and suffering could surely handle some himself.

I let my hands go. One, two, my fists sinking into the bag. Mother's sour face, Father's glare. One, two, faster and faster. All the letters I never received. All the letters I did. A flurry of fists striking harder and harder. Jeremy, my link to the real world, gone. I was back to no friends.

Skin peeled back, my knuckles bleeding, the sting of each shot, the blotches left behind. Images of evil feeding the fire, spilling the blood of Christ across the canvas.

Paul stopped mid-song, switched to my warning. I pulled the rope free and the bag thumped to the ground. I cut the light, slid down the ladder, ran like the devil was hot on my heels. The last ten feet I slowed down, took two deep breaths, and wiped my forehead.

Mother stood next to the piano. "Where were you?"

I took my place at my kneeler, used the time to steady my breath. "Thought I heard someone sneaking around out there."

She looked down at my hands that were dripping on the oak. "To your room. Now!"

That was fine. I got up and headed for the front door. Someone from the party howled. Someone else howled back and shouted, "Fuck yeah!" I pretended like I didn't hear it and kept walking.

Mother sounded tired. "You're breaking his heart. You know that, don't you?"

† † †

It was the following year, less than two months shy of my eighteenth birthday. That's why I was in Father's office at three o'clock on a Saturday.

Father got up from his desk and held his head high, kept his shoulders pulled back. Even with his glasses on, I could see his eyes trying so hard not to show fear. But he knew the time was coming and he was terrified that I was going to screw it up. Those eyes were trying to be excited for a future where I was accepted as the Messiah, a future where nothing else mattered.

"Rise, Joshua."

I got up but not fast enough.

He ran a hand through his hair that'd gone all gray. "Do it right."

I sat back down, glad there wasn't a camera. Then I got up the right way, chin raised, eyes to God, hands at my sides as if I could fly to Him like a rocket. When I looked at Father, I saw the glimmer of hope that I could do it. That I wouldn't be the world's biggest disappointment.

"Good. Now show me how you'll stand."

That's what I was doing, but it must've looked wrong. I drew my shoulders back a bit more and stood as tall as I could.

Father held out his arms, as if he was addressing the world, not some sorry kid with no clue. "Try this."

My arms didn't want to do it, but I made them. They stayed up there a second then went back down to my sides.

Father said, "What's the matter?"

I put my hands back up like his. "Nothing."

"Now deliver your speech. Say it like you've prepared."

My arms went down. "Here?"

"Why not?" He pointed at my feet. "There's your pulpit. I'm your crowd."

The thought of all those eyes looking at me made me want to puke. I had to show them they hadn't wasted their lives believing. That it wasn't just a father's stupid dream.

Father wasn't far from raising his voice when he said, "You can do it."

It took all I had to open my mouth. "Can I do this next week?"

"You don't know it yet?"

The speech was over a page long, but I did know the whole thing. It was that some of the words I couldn't bring myself to say. I looked Father in his eyes and said, "Next week I will."

Father snatched a paper off his desk. "Read my copy."

All that practice speaking in front of Jeremy had helped, but this wasn't the same. If I tried to read the speech, Father would know for sure there was a problem. "Please, next week."

Father let the paper fall to his desk. "That's fine. How about we call it a day?"

I tried not to sound excited when I said okay.

"Good. I want to show you something."

"What?"

He squeezed past me and opened the door, shoved me into the hallway. "You'll see."

Part of me worried he might finally go for the shotgun, and another part wanted him to, but he continued to the back door. The weather was perfect, a beautiful day. The barn looked like it'd been resurrected, every inch sanded down, Mother's bright red curtains hanging perfectly in each window.

Father headed toward it. "We'll be getting the paint on Monday."

I didn't say I knew, but we all did thanks to the shouting match they'd had when Mother found the bank statement. She said he was out of his mind. He said she lacked faith. She laughed and called him a fool. The crack of the slap, end of discussion.

"There's no rush on it, but sooner is better," Father said. "All prettied up by the end of the month will be fine."

My shoulders were still tender from finishing up the inside, but I kept my mouth shut and nodded.

The smell of fresh paint hit me ten feet from the door. Father got to it first and stepped inside, flipped on the light Carl had installed.

Directly beneath a sparkling cross-shaped chandelier, on the freshly scrubbed floor was a huge lump covered with the same black tarp that'd hidden my punching bag. The chair I kept in front of the ladder was over in the corner.

Father took it all in. "A fresh start. A new beginning."

I got what he was saying. The place was spotless, all that white so bright with the sun shining off the chandelier.

Father clapped me on my back for what felt like the first time. "You did a nice job."

I said thanks as I tried to guess what was under the canvas.

"Go ahead," he said. "Take it off."

I yanked on the tarp and tossed it to the side. It was a giant oval tub that must've been made from two trees. The bowl was big enough for a body.

He asked what I thought. It was the truth when I said, "It's beautiful. It's really something else."

"Took me half of the year to make it."

"It looks it."

"I've got another surprise I'm working on. It'll go right there facing the bowl."

"What?"

Father's eyes got excited. "Your very own pulpit. You're going to love it."

All those people looking at me, expecting me to do something I could never promise. The blood drained from my head, my hearing got fuzzy. I held on to the bowl, pretending to admire it, while trying to keep my shit together.

"This place will be packed. Just the congregation alone will fill it, but with the bake-off, oh, it's going to be a glorious day!" Father looked up. "I'm glad we have the loft."

I couldn't speak.

"There's really quite a lot of room up there."

I nodded, looked down at my hands, turned them over so my scarred knuckles didn't show.

"How'd you like to live up there?"

Instead of under their roof. A room of my own. "Are you serious?"

"It might be best for all of us if you had your own space."

That stopped whatever it was I was going to say next. I hadn't considered that I was the problem.

Father took hold of my hands and made me face him. Standing eye-to-eye, he pressed his fingers into my knuckles and squeezed tight. "And there'll be no more of that."

He was still squeezing, but I held still, acted like it didn't hurt. Punching the bag wasn't hurting anyone, but that argument would get me nowhere so I casually said, "Yes, sir."

"Good." Father dropped my hands and looked about the room, his gaze stopping at the baptismal tub. "This is going to be something special, Joshua. You just have to believe."

It was impossible to look in those eyes, the little bit of hope hanging on. "I'm trying."

Father shook his head. "That's not good enough. You're not a boy anymore."

"I know that, but—"

Father shushed me with one finger. "You hear that?"

Only thing I heard was my inner self screaming that I never wanted any of this shit. All I wanted was to be left alone. Then I heard the piano, a sweet girl singing to hold it against me.

Father stormed out the door and toward the church. I followed a few feet back, the confrontation sure to be ugly.

The door banged open and the music stopped. Paul closed his mouth, the look of pure happiness gone just like that.

Mother was resting against my kneeler watching the whole thing. Father walked up to the edge of the stage and looked right at her. "What in the world is going on?"

"Now, Charles."

I was glad to be behind Father so I couldn't see his eyes. He barked, "No. Get inside."

"It's not hurting—"

"Now!"

There were five feet between them, but Mother still flinched.

Paul told her it was fine. Father said it wasn't and ordered Mother to leave.

She spun around and went past the curtain, slammed the door shut.

"I'm sorry," Paul said.

Father stayed where he was at the foot of the stage. "Get over here."

Paul was slow to get up. "I said sorry."

Father grabbed hold of Paul's arm and dragged him down. Paul yelped and wriggled free, backed into the pew.

Spit flew off Father's lips. "How dare you play that filth in the Lord's house. Britney Spears is a whore."

"How do you know who she is?"

Father's fingers flexed, curled up into the tightest ball. Usually they would stretch out wide again, but his hand wasn't opening. It was staying a fist just like his other one. He took a step toward Paul. "Why, you little shit."

"It's music," Paul said. "What's the big freaking deal?"

Everyone knew freaking meant fucking. Father leapt like a lion, snatched Paul up and spun him around, one arm around Paul's throat, the other squeezing his head.

Paul was making noises, pulling at Father's arm.

I told them to stop but neither of them listened, both faces growing dark as Father squeezed harder. "You little shit," he said. "Goddamn little shit."

Paul swatted at Father's face, knocked off his glasses, and slipped away. Father snatched hold of his collar, the rip long and loud.

My body was trembling, but my voice had never been stronger when I shouted, "Enough! Let him go!"

Father was breathing so hard he could barely speak. "You don't tell me what to do."

Paul jerked out of his torn shirt and stood beside me, rubbing his throat. I told him to go to our room.

"He's not going anywhere."

I pushed Paul toward the door and stood in Father's way. "You touch him and see what I have to say about being the Messiah."

"You'll be out on the street without a penny. And don't even think about the Marines. They would never take you."

It was later that night, way after the front room lights blinked off. Not one word had been spoken in the four or five hours of lying in bed, listening to Paul roll back and forth, back and forth. But I'd been doing a lot of thinking about what I'd been dreaming about since that first time on the bike.

I made up my mind, then whispered like a little kid. "I'm leaving."

The top bunk creaked as Paul popped his head over the edge, his curls all I could see.

"I'm leaving," I said. "For good."

"When?"

"Another five minutes. Maybe ten."

Paul stuck his head over the side a little more, spoke softer. "Where?"

"You gonna tell?"

His curls shook back and forth.

"Georgia. We have relatives out there. If that don't work, somewhere else. Just not here."

"You aren't scared?"

Shit. I was beyond scared. Maybe I didn't know a lot about the world, but I knew it was evil. I knew it was full of murder and rape, war and death, fire and floods, death everywhere. Cults on every corner, murderers never getting caught. That was the world I'd be entering, but I didn't care.

"Father says I got nothing to worry about. Not a thing in the world I should be scared of."

Paul hung his head, didn't say a word. I hated him right then for making me ask. I had no business bringing anyone along, especially a twelve-year-old, but I said, "You can come with me if you want. Might not be a bad idea."

His tongue windshield wiped his bottom lip back and forth. "What about Mother?"

"What about her?"

"She'll miss us."

"She'll miss you."

"I can't do that to her."

I told him to write her a note. "Tell her you're sorry."

"You write one already?"

There wasn't much sense in sugarcoating it. "I got nothing to say to her. To either of them." The clock said nearly nine. I told Paul I needed to know. "You coming or not?"

Paul turned his head toward the window and I could make out the top of his nose, the tips of his lashes. He looked back at me and said, "What would you do if you were me?"

"I'm the wrong guy to ask."

"You're the only guy to ask."

He deserved the truth so I said, "I wouldn't stick around." I gave that some time to settle in. "But that's something you gotta figure out on your own. Just figure it out quick."

Paul said, "I'm in."

"You sure?"

"Yeah. As sure as I'm gonna get."

I got out of bed without a sound and watched Paul creep down like a cat. We went to the drawers and got dressed in blue jeans and t-shirts.

Paul put on his shoes and socks. "What should I take?"

I hadn't thought it through that far, which should've been a sign that the timing was off, but I acted like a know-it-all. "Couple sets of clothes, and whatever will fit in the biggest bag you can carry.

Paul pulled his bag from under the bed and filled it with clothes. "What else?"

"Anything you want to see again. Money, if you got any."

He glanced over his shoulder then studied his hands. "Can you turn around?"

With all that black behind the window, I could see everything in the reflection. Paul pulling something from under the mattress and stuffing it to the bottom of his bag. Digging something else out of his sock drawer and shoving it in his pocket. Him whispering he was ready.

He wasn't even close to being prepared, a boy with no idea what the world had in store for him. A boy with soft eyes who only knew the world from books and bad television shows. He wasn't ready at all. But neither was I, and I couldn't leave him. "What about the note?"

"It won't help any," Paul said. "She'll think what she wants."

I ripped a piece of paper from my notepad and handed him the pen. "Just tell her you're sorry. You're coming to keep me out of trouble, document my journey."

Halfway through the first line, Paul's shoulders started to hitch, the tears right behind. I shushed him while he finished. I said we'd be okay.

He wiped off both cheeks, kissed the bottom of the letter like it was Mother's forehead.

"You sure about this?" I asked. "I would never blame you for staying."

Paul laid the letter on the middle of the floor. "I want to go."

"Then you got to understand something. I ain't no Messiah. Not no more. The second we're out of here, I'm just some dumb hick. That's what people are going to say and we're going to let them."

His perfect little curls bobbed up and down. "I understand."

Instead of giving him a hug and saying I loved him, I stood there like a dick, arms crossed. "I need to hear you say it."

Paul pushed past me and headed for the door, sounding broken when he said, "I got it."

Chapter Ten

It's getting late, the sun directly over the mountains to the west. If I squint and look to the right of the MGM, I can just make out the tiny patch of green, the shadow of the mountain starting to swallow it.

That's where I just came from, saying a final goodbye. Saying I'm sorry.

No, this shit isn't what I wanted. None of this. The billion plus followers, the millions of dollars. It's just numbers. I would trade it all.

I empty my glass and fill it back up, promise myself I won't get too trashed. I flinch at movement on top of the Monte Carlo. I wait for the gun, for the sniper that will finally do it, use a special bullet that'll punch through this glass and erase my brain. There's several guys up there, but they're just pushing something off the edge. A huge white banner drops the length of the building. Charles 3:16 bigger than I've ever seen.

I turn my back to the window, head to the pulpit. This book right here was Father's gift to Lily. I never read it until now, figured there wasn't much point since I'd heard every one of those stories from Father's very lips. All except the last chapter. The final passage. The last word.

I hate to admit it, but his bible's not half bad. If it weren't about me, maybe I'd even buy one. At least that way I wouldn't have to think about the inscription every time I see the damned thing.

The book goes on the altar next to the tiny black box with the red button so I can use both hands for the pulpit's monitor. The screen comes to life, the Almighty Charles Campbell standing outside the entrance, a phone number, big and bold at the bottom, four lines of fine print below it.

Father looks fabulous thanks to his fake tan, private trainer, and enough money to gloss over every flaw, but I've got the TV muted because I can't listen to what he's saying. The red message flashing across the screen gives me a pretty good idea. Voting Now Open. Shit is in motion. Action is what Jeremy'd say, but only if he wanted you to know he was filming.

Father smiles like everything's grand, that nothing was sacrificed for this once-in-a-lifetime opportunity. For him, this is bigger than big.

There ain't a day that goes by that I don't wonder what my life would've been like if I'd listened to Father and been content with my life. If I had a little faith and just believed. Maybe things would be different, but I kind of got the feeling it wouldn't have mattered. We'd all end up in the same place.

Forty-seven floors up, the entire world waiting and watching. I'll vote before it's over, so at least I can have a say, no matter how insignificant.

My legs can't hold me up like they used to, so I head back to my throne and pick up the bonus edition *Lost Gospels*. Lily got this one for her third birthday. In Father's eyes, it's never too early to learn about the fiery depths of hell, how God's just waiting to push in every son of a bitch that doesn't believe.

He hadn't cut any corners on this copy, issue number one, bound in black leather. I just sold it for $920,000 which already cleared my bank. Close to a million for a book that's in perfect condition except for two pages.

There's only one page that's been altered and that's the first one. There are two lines of typeset at the top, the rest of the page filled with Father's perfect penmanship, the curves so tight, the loops so little. Eight lines of the stuff, but all it really says is how great I am, how lucky she was to have me as her father. He even signed it. Love Grandpa.

With a quick rip, one page becomes two. I don't care if it could have earned me another hundred thousand if I left it in. No one else gets to see it.

I light the blood red candle from the altar, the flick of the lighter flaring pain up my fingers, my forearm, and the constant ache at the back of my brain.

The smell of cinnamon and burnt memories fill my box. The paper's gone, another thing of the past, the bible ready to be shipped off. Maybe I'm not the Messiah, but I'm a man of my word so I take another pill and down it with some Jack. I force myself up and take the bible with me into the main church, holding onto the railing to get down the staircase.

At the bottom, I walk over to the elevator and push the button for my sleeve mic. "Troy, it's coming down. See the courier gets it immediately."

Troy says he will, which means he will. He was there when they carried me out of the rubble. He's a true believer.

Chapter Eleven

Paul said it was dark. He'd never been out this time of night.

If I'd shown even the least bit of fear, Paul would've turned tail and jumped back through the window. But I whispered it was ok and told him to follow.

The lights were off in Mother and Father's room. I buttoned up my denim jacket, tiptoed toward the barn, and waved for Paul. I wondered what he saw when he looked at the barn's open mouth; was he worried there were demons within? Men that killed wives. Wives that killed babies. Young boys with machine guns shooting anything that moved. That was the world I was leading him into.

We walked to the corner past the barn. I didn't really believe anyone was listening, but before we scaled the wall, I asked God to watch over us.

I pulled my lantern out from my hidey hole. I turned it on and handed it to Paul, the light barely half of what it used to be.

Paul said, "What's that?"

He was talking about the two pieces of paper that'd been below the lantern. I unfolded them and got close beside him. "Jeremy said they were in case I ever grew some balls."

"Maps?"

First one included a half page of instructions underneath a small map. "Yeah, this one's to Georgia." The other one was a black and white overhead photo featuring a blue squiggle highlighted with yellow marker. "And this one's to the bus stop."

"Is that the top of our house?"

I thought he would've been more impressed. "Pretty crazy huh?"

"Anyone could do that with their smartphone," he said, talking like he'd actually ever held one.

"We're wasting the batteries." I pointed him toward the trees. "We head straight through there."

Paul didn't move.

"It's the safest way," I said. "You got to trust me."

Paul said he did and led the way, listening to my directions as I guided him through the trees along the back of Jeremy's property. The lights were off inside the house, no last glimpse of Danielle. We came out on the road and headed up the hill.

Since the lantern was almost dead, we turned it off and put it in my bag. The light from the moon and a few street lights at the top of the hill were enough to see where we were going. I said, "Ok. Rule number one, stay behind me to the right, always watching our back, and I'll keep look out. There are people out here that'll run you over and just keep on going. It happens all the time."

We got to the top of the hill and looked down. Paul said, "I forget it's so small."

I'd only been to town a few more times than Paul, but Jeremy's pictures and papers had put everything in perspective. I marched us down, told him to act like we belonged, both of us glad no one was driving around.

Paul pointed out the church's electronic billboard that Father always complained about; the one we paid for since it was my head that broke their old one. I didn't care to look, so Paul read it. "An open mind is a dangerous thing: Your brain might fall out."

Sounding dead serious, he whispered, "Should we break it?"

It was nice knowing I wasn't the only one with stupid ideas, but that wasn't the kind of guidance I needed. I ignored him and took us down Main Street. The map said the address we wanted was 107, but it was just a small liquor store, a bench with a roof over it, dark on the sidewalk.

Paul asked, "What's wrong?"

The only two vehicles in the parking lot were the dirty brown Camaro and a big red Ford Bronco with no roof, just the front windshield. "I don't see the buses."

Paul pointed at the liquor store where at least twenty signs were posted in the windows, half of which were blinking on and off. I read the handwritten one on the door. "Bus Tickets Sold Here."

We went inside, the automatic door closing behind us. The round-faced man standing behind the counter said, "Gotta leave those by the door."

The only things we were holding were our bags so we set them down and the door reopened.

The man put both his hands on the counter, smoke from his cigarette rising in front of his face. "You boys retards?"

I said, "No, sir."

He shook his head and pointed next to the door. "Right there."

Paul piled his bag on top of mine. "Look at all the stuff they got."

The store had three aisles filled with everything you'd ever need, and a bunch of stuff I'd never seen.

Paul said, "All that food."

Neither one of us had had dinner so I told him, "Go ahead and grab some. Batteries, too."

The white door at the end of the aisles banged open. Out came a man with a dirty gray beard sporting a red flannel shirt and a lawnmower driving across his hat. He crumpled up a paper towel and tossed it in the trashcan, took the stool at the end of the counter, across from the worker puffing away on his cigarette.

Paul went down the aisle and I approached the man behind the counter, keeping clear of the cloud of smoke. "Excuse me, sir. I'd like to buy bus tickets."

"Where you headed?"

I told him and he grabbed the brown folder. He flipped it open, ran his yellow fingernail down the page.

"Joshua, look at this." Paul stood in front of a machine with blue and red stuff swirling behind the small windows. "It's frozen. They got cherry."

The counter guy said, "What time you looking at? Got 8:20, 11:20, 2:20."

"11:20 tonight?"

"Jesus, kid."

The guy on the stool put his cup to his lips and spit out something dark. "Relax, Bud."

Bud took a long drag and blew it out at me. "First one anywhere runs through here at seven in the morning, last one at six."

"We can't wait that long."

He shrugged his shoulders. "Guess you're shit out of luck."

The guy with the beard finished his drink and crushed the can on the counter. "Might can catch one over in Columbia. Run through there all day."

"Where's that?"

Bud hawked up a loogie and spit it in the trashcan. "Save your breath, Dusty."

Dusty waved Bud off. "You ain't from around here, are you?"

"No, sir."

He threw a thumb over his shoulder. "'Bout seventy miles that way."

Paul ran up beside me, arms crossed to hold his pile, a giant plastic cup in each hand. "Got you blue raspberry."

I said fine. I wondered how long it would take to walk that far.

He put everything on the counter then picked up the bag of bread. Heavenly Host Cinnamon Raisin. "They got Pumpernickel and Sourdough, too."

Bud ran items across the counter, red numbers popping up on the little screen with each beep.

Paul waited until Bud got to the bread. "I helped make that."

Like he couldn't care less, the guy said, "That so?"

"Yes, sir. Best bread in the region."

Bud squinted at the register. "$33.47."

Paul pulled a wad of cash out of his pocket. The stack was twice as big as mine and nearly filled his hand. He peeled off two twenties and handed them over.

"Mother give that to you?"

"I earned it."

Bud took another drag from his cigarette, held it in for a while, blew it out on us when he handed Paul his change. "So whatcha boys waiting for?"

Dusty spit a brown wad into the cup. "Easy on 'em, Bud. Seem like good kids."

"That better've been your last beer."

Dusty turned to us. "So you guys need to get to Columbia?"

"That's what it's looking like," I said.

"I live right by there. Could drop you off if you like."

I thought I must've heard wrong. "Really? You wouldn't mind?"

"Not at all. Christian thing to do."

I stuffed the food in our bags while Dusty got off his stool and walked over to glass doors with all the bottles behind them. From the bottom shelf, he pulled out a long red and white box and told Bud, "Put this on my tab, will ya."

"A whole case?"

He smiled so big his beard split, showed off a mouthful of yellow teeth. "Tomorrow's the Lord's day, gotta load up tonight."

"Well, that's a lot of loading up to do."

Dusty headed out the door. "You know I'm good for it."

The door closed on whatever Bud said, but Dusty paid it no mind. "Where to after Columbia?"

"Georgia."

Dusty walked to the passenger side of the truck and set the case on the seat. "What's there?"

"Family."

I tossed our bags behind the back row, nodded for Paul to get in, then walked around to the other side and got in behind Dusty. Paul didn't look so sure, handing me both drinks so he could lock his hands on the bottom of his seat. He let out a squeak when the engine turned over, that roar ten times louder than Father's.

Dusty looked over his shoulder to back out of the parking lot. "Ain't got no seat belts so just hold on tight."

I hadn't used one in Frank's truck, so I figured it was no big deal. Paul's arms were steel poles, his eyes riveted straight ahead.

Dusty turned left onto Main and drove us away from the church, our home, our world. I snuggled into my jacket and positioned Paul's Slurpee between my feet, my hair whipping.

Up ahead, a big green sign for Columbia pointed toward a loop. Dusty took it too fast, the tires squealing. We started tipping over, just a tiny bit more and we'd have been airborne, but then the wheels dropped back down and shot forward. Dusty pumped his fist in the air and shouted, "Hot damn!"

The wind whipped around us. Paul leaned forward, his eyes on the instrument panel. I read his lips. "Fifty-five. Sixty-five. Seventy."

There were headlights coming at us not five yards away, nothing but a narrow strip of grass between the lanes. On our side most the lights were behind us, a couple of red ones up ahead. We were moving faster than I thought possible, my arms now clenched as tight as Paul's. No seat belt, bodies flying through windshields. I'd seen that a bunch. That and tons of motorcycle accidents. Paul had no idea how far a body could fly, how easily parts could come off, yet he was scrunched down in his seat praying the Lord's Prayer.

God seemed pretty real right then and I was talking to him, too, but only in my head. *Protect us, protect us, protect us.*

We passed a sign that said Columbia was 60 miles away, and I knew we'd never make it. Even in the dark I could see Paul was as white as a sheet of paper, his arms shaking. I kicked his shoe and said, "Breathe."

Paul looked seconds away from all out panic, like the time I held him down and swore I'd send him to hell if he couldn't get free in five minutes. Eyes all big, he said, "I can't."

Dusty checked his rearview, shouting so we could hear. "Everything okay?"

Paul sat up a little and nodded.

Dusty got over to the right lane and dropped his speed. Two cars passed by and disappeared into the night. We had the highway to ourselves when Dusty put on his blinker and got off at the rest stop.

All ten of the parking stalls were empty. Dusty took the one at the far end, a stone's throw away from a dark river.

He killed the engine and turned toward Paul. "Might want to throw some water on your face."

Paul looked at the river then leaned over to me. "I'm not going down there."

Dusty laughed and got out of the truck. "Come on. I gotta take a piss anyhow."

Paul looked like he was still thinking about puking. I pointed at the bathroom. "Let's go."

Dusty started walking. "Probably best if one of you stays with your bags."

I felt dumb for not thinking about that. "Hurry up, Paul. I'll go after."

Paul got out and headed after Dusty. They were inside the restroom when I heard something splash. It was too dark to see past the trees, the water's slow ripple hiding the demons.

It wasn't long before Dusty came out. Loud enough for me to hear, he said, "Hey, Bud, your brother ain't doing so good."

I jumped out of the truck and headed his way. "What's wrong?"

Dusty walked right past me. Like it was no big deal, he said, "He wanted you."

I was just about to the bathroom when the truck started. I didn't think anything of it until Paul staggered out, hand to his nose, blood slipping through his fingers. "My money!"

Tires peeled out and the chase began. I was running faster than I ever had, flying over the grass, the sidewalk, the concrete.

Dusty had a head start, pulling away with our bags and more than half my money. I almost gave up then saw the rock on the road, the moonlight sparkling on it, a sign I couldn't miss. It was smooth and solid, fit perfect in the palm of my hand.

I chucked it hard, never thought I'd hit Dusty, but the thud was too wet to be anything else. He dropped out of sight as the truck weaved to the right and jumped the curb, plowed through the fence. I thought for sure he was going in the river, but then the red lights flashed on and the truck slowed to a stop.

Figuring my best chance against a grown man was not letting him recover all the way, I ran for the truck. I stopped next to his door, grabbed the handle. I couldn't see him, and pictured him lying on the seat, coiled up to kick the door into me.

Paul was getting close so I threw open the door with my fists ready. Dusty was in there, his lower half slumped below the wheel, his belly caught up against it. His head was back, eyes open, staring at the roof, but not seeing a thing. There was a dark puddle on the seat where his butt should have been, and it was getting bigger, the blood dripping off the back of his head.

Plop. Plop. Plop.

Paul stopped by the back bumper. "What happened?"

This wasn't something he needed to see. I said, "Reach in the back and grab me the rope. I saw some under our bags."

The puddle of blood kept growing, filled the indention and spilled over the seat.

Paul nudged my shoulder with the rope. "Now what?"

I took the rope without taking my eyes off Dusty's. "The biggest rock you can carry."

He whispered, "What did we do?"

I turned to Paul, his battered face barely holding back tears. "It wasn't you," I said. "I'm the one who judged him."

"It's my fault," Paul said.

"No, I sent a wicked man to hell. Now go, get the rock."

† † †

It was seven the next morning and I was half asleep in the back of the taxi, Paul curled up beside me, his head resting on my shoulder, bouncing every time we hit a bump. It seemed like we'd been in the cab forever. The last hour had been endless green fields, beautiful shrubs, and enormous oak trees shading the street. Every mile we put between us and that damned rest stop, I felt better, breathed easier.

Nolan, the cabbie we'd been with for the last hour, slowed down and put on his left turn signal. We sat there and waited for the long line of cars coming the other way. The *tic, tic, tic* of the blinker brought back the drips on Dusty's seat. I'd spilled a man's blood. The proof was on my pants and shirt now tucked inside my backpack.

After a truck with a horse trailer went by, we turned onto a wide street with ranch houses on either side. Three blocks down, Nolan pulled to the curb and said, "We're here."

The house looked so peaceful, like it could have been the picture on a magazine cover. But then I saw the mailbox, all black with red letters. HENDRICKS.

Nolan caught my eye in the mirror. "There a problem? This is what you told me."

Vincent Granger was the name I was looking for, same one Mother used to have. That's how he signed his letter, and what was printed in big black letters on the corner of the envelope.

I nudged Paul with my elbow and told him to wake up. He brought his hand to his nose and groaned.

Icing his nose probably would've helped with the swelling, but once I got Dusty's truck on the road, there was no stopping until we ran out of gas. Both of Paul's eyes were black and blue, his nose leaning too much to the left. "You'll be fine," I said. "Go ahead and get out."

Nolan said, "Ninety-four-fifty."

This was the first time I'd stayed up all night and I wasn't thinking clearly. "What's that?"

"What you owe me." He pointed at the numbers to his right. "Read the damn meter."

I hadn't known what a meter was. "That's a lot of money."

Nolan had both hands on the steering wheel, gripping it hard. "You saying I cheated you?"

I handed him $100 in fives and tens. "It took me two months to make that."

"Get a better job."

Great advice, but I didn't have the first idea how I'd go about it. Seemed all I knew how to do was cut down trees and kneel still for hours. I got out of the car, grabbed my bag and went to Nolan's window for my change.

He drove away with a huff, left me in the middle of the street.

Paul said, "You know what you're going to say?"

"To who?"

"To whoever opens the door."

I walked up to the porch and knocked on the screen door, not thinking the people inside might still be sleeping. If Paul hadn't been beside me, I might've run when I heard the footsteps.

It was hard to see much through the screen door, but I could make out the shape of a lady. Sounding more curious than irritated, she said, "Can I help you?"

"Is Vincent here?"

The woman made a small noise. I was about to ask again, but then she said, "Joshua?"

The screen opened before I answered. It was Laura, her eyes just as blue as they'd been twelve years before. She had on a pale-yellow dress, her braided hair hanging down her back, a bright white dish towel clutched in her hand.

Laura reached up and wrapped her arms so tight around me, a warmth I barely remembered. "Oh my God, you're so big." She put her cheek against mine and said, "I'm so glad you're here."

I didn't know how to tell her how much I needed her right then. How I needed her touch. How I didn't want her to stop.

Laura gave me a final squeeze then stood back. She held both my hands and said, "Let me look at you."

Her smile looked so genuine, yet out of place on a face so much like Mother's. Same sloped nose and pointed chin, crow's feet around the eyes, and straight teeth.

This was one of the first times I didn't mind having all the attention, but I clapped my brother on his shoulder and said, "This is Paul."

The smile all but disappeared from her face. "Oh, the miracle child."

Paul looked confused. He didn't know the story of me calling her crazy and ruining his entrance to the world. It was never talked of in our house and I'd been so young, who knows what I had made up over time. But none of that mattered when Laura noticed Paul's face. "Oh my God, what happened? Are you okay?"

Paul wasn't a very good liar so I said, "A guy tried to rob us."

"You stopped him?"

"We got our money back."

"Do you want some ice, sweetie?"

Paul shook his head. "I'm okay."

I didn't want her asking any more questions, and I was grateful to point out the thin wisps of smoke creeping up behind her.

Laura said, "Oh shit," and ran inside, called over her shoulder for us to come in. The living room was twice the size of ours, and was decorated with stuffed wildlife; two deer and a wildcat adorned the walls. The kitchen was much nicer, too, everything brighter and more airy with yellows and whites. Laura pulled a tray of muffins out of the oven and dumped them into the sink, fanned the smoke toward the open window. "Goddamn it!"

The smoke tickled my throat and I stifled a cough.

Laura kept on fanning and said, "Have a seat, boys. Just not the one with the armrests."

There were only four chairs at the pine table. The one with the armrests was closest to the back porch. I took the seat across from it, Paul to my right by the window.

Laura brought a box from the cupboard and washed out a glass bowl. She shook her head when she looked at the clock then back at the stove where three things were cooking.

Paul asked, "Can I do that for you?"

Laura stopped for a second. "You know how to bake?"

"Yes, ma'am." Paul got up like he belonged there. "Mind if I take a peek in the pantry?"

Laura showed him where it was then tended the stuff on the stove. She took the seat to my left, her smile back, her warm, soft hand on mine. "You're so handsome."

With all my scars and depressions, topped with no sleep, she was obviously lying. I mumbled thanks and watched Paul work his magic with the mixing bowl, pouring the batter into the tray.

Laura opened the oven door and punched in numbers on the screen when Paul asked her to set the timer. She said, "That was so sweet of you."

Paul said he was glad to help and they both returned to the table.

"How'd you boys get here?" It sounded like there was a little bit of sorrow when she said, "Maureen's not here, is she?"

"She's at home."

Laura looked out the window. There was no mistaking the fear when she asked, "How about Charles?"

I shook my head. "We kind of ran away."

It looked like she'd been hit with something heavy. "How kind of?"

"Not kind of at all," Paul said.

"They have any idea where you were headed?"

"None," I said. "I don't even know."

She got up to pour a cup of coffee and set it in front of the special chair. After bringing each of us a water, she asked, "So did you finally figure out they were both crazy?"

That wasn't easy to hear, but the truth never was. None of us said anything, her words just hanging in the air. Everything they told me. Everything they made me believe dismissed in one sentence.

I asked, "Is Vincent sleeping?"

Laura's smile disappeared. "I'm afraid he did what you did. Last month."

"I'm sorry."

"Not your fault. Said there was something he had to do."

"Where?"

"California. Out by Los Angeles."

The taxi had wiped out most of my money. I sipped the water and worried how much it'd cost to get there.

Laura said, "So you got his letters?"

"Only one. Seemed like a pretty nice guy."

Her face looked ready to break. "Vince is a good boy."

She didn't look ready to answer my questions so I switched to small talk about her house. I didn't remember a word she said, my mind craving sleep and the sizzling bacon. Heavy footsteps approaching the back door pulled me out of the daze. Laura hurried to the stove and said, "That's Jim."

The door opened but I couldn't see from where I was sitting. A rough voice barked, "Ronnie up?"

"Didn't you hear him last night? He got in after three."

A sink ran on the porch. "That isn't what I asked."

Laura brought a plate stacked with bacon, eggs, and pancakes to the table and set it in front of the coffee. "Far as I know, he's still asleep."

The water turned off and Jim walked in, blue jeans and a green flannel, gray hair in the places he wasn't bald. He went straight to the fridge. "You can lose the attitude."

"Sorry, I just worry about him getting pulled over again."

"Drop it, Laura. He's my boy." Jim brought out a tall glass of orange juice and headed for the table, noticed us for the first time. "Who do we have here?"

Laura told him our names. "These are my nephews."

He sat at the head of the table, didn't offer to shake hands. "You two are brothers?"

I didn't know what the whole truth was so I said what felt truest. "We are."

Jim took a bite of bacon, crunched it up while studying us. "I don't see it." He spurted a puddle of ketchup on his plate, took his knife and cut his egg, the runny yolk oozing out. As if I'd have the answer, Jim asked me, "So why'd I never hear of you before?"

Laura sat down. "You know I don't talk to her."

Jim looked at us and smacked on another strip of bacon. "So what's the special occasion?"

The timer rang and Laura got up to turn it off. She took out the muffins and set them on the stove. "They just left their home."

I didn't care for Jim's grin. I explained, "It was in everyone's best interest."

"I'm sure it was," he said. "Now what? What are your big plans? You going to go strike it rich in California like Vince? Make your millions?"

Laura said, "They're just boys. They don't have it all figured out just yet. I was thinking—"

"'Boys is right," Jim said. "How old are you?" he asked Paul.

"Older than my age."

Jim shook his head and told Laura, "I know what you're thinking."

She said, "I try not to ask for much."

Jim continued to examine us while he finished off his eggs.

Laura said, "We have the guest room. They'd be out of the way."

Jim stared at me. "You expect me to feed you, put a roof over your head? What's in it for me?"

I told him I was a real hard worker.

"What can you do?"

"Pretty much whatever needs being done."

He turned to Paul. "How 'bout you?"

"I can help out in the kitchen."

Jim laughed. "What kind of boy wants to work in the kitchen?"

Sounding just as sure as Father, Paul said, "The kind that could make you five hundred dollars a month if you let him."

"Be straight with me, boy."

Paul pointed to the tray. "Try one of those muffins. Be careful they're hot."

Laura asked Jim if he'd like one. Jim kept his eyes on Paul as he used the tip of his tongue to push out his cheek. He took the muffin from her and asked, "You watch him make it? How do I know he didn't slip something in it?"

I was starving and offered to eat one.

Jim said he was joking and broke it in half, the steam passing over his leathery face. He took a bite and we waited, but not long. "You can make five hundred selling these things?"

"Did back home. That and bread."

The other half disappeared in two bites. A guy about my age entered the kitchen without a word, walked straight to the fridge. He had the same build as Jim, the same asshole smirk. He had on blue jeans and a tight black shirt, barbwire tattooed halfway around his arm.

Jim took a swig of coffee and cleared his throat. "You got a place to stay as long as you do what you say."

"Thank you, sir," Paul said. "You won't be disappointed."

Jim said he wanted another muffin and waited for Laura to get it. "Make it six hundred and I'll give you Ronnie's room.

The fridge slammed shut. The guy looked at Paul and said, "Shit."

Jim sort of smiled. "What, you're not ready to move out?"

"Not so some little homo can move in."

Laura said, "Ronnie!"

"Relax. I'm just fucking with him."

Paul smiled to show no harm done.

Jim got up from the table. "How about you get busy?" he said to Paul. "The boys break for lunch at eleven. I'll need about three dozen of these. We'll have each of them take some home, see what people think."

Ronnie walked up to the table. The other three chairs were empty, but he pointed right at me. "Now how about you get your sorry ass out of my chair."

Chapter Twelve

We'd lived with Laura for close to a month, still two more to go before I turned eighteen. I was out back dripping sweat on the boulder between my feet, telling myself it wasn't that big. Everything hurt, especially my hand, but this was my last one.

Everyone else was already inside for lunch, but I was used to it. If I took too long, someone would go back for seconds before I got my firsts, and I'd be stuck with peanut butter and jelly.

Lining both sides of the driveway with boulders were Paul's idea, what he called a touch of class. It would've been easier if I could've used the wheelbarrow, but Ronnie said it was his.

I bent down, wedged my hands between the boulder and dirt. My low back was a belt of bright pain, my palm stinging as an edge dug deep. I drove forward, one step then another, finally close enough to smell the sloppy joe's. Brad's favorite. He was the ranch hand three years older than me. I could see him through the window, sitting in the seat I usually did, his shirt tight enough to show off his abs.

I dropped the boulder with a thud and shoved it into place. Ronnie was in the kitchen, too, but I couldn't see him when he said, "The shit was sick. You really gotta see it."

Brad said, "That's what I heard."

My palm had opened in a slow leak I wiped on my jeans and headed toward the back of the house.

Ronnie said, "Yeah, they had a chain looped around this guy's neck then let the car creep one inch at a time. Tore his head right off, but it took a while."

Paul sounded like a girl. "Ewww. That's sick."

"My favorite's the machete."

I stomped the dirt from my boots and stepped inside. Ronnie was still going on all excited. "Yeah, the knife was like this fucking long."

Laura said, "Ronnie."

"Can I tell the damn story?"

I turned on the sink, the dirt and blood swirled down the drain, looked like Dusty's mouth when I pushed him under. Laura set her empty plate on the counter, gave me a quick pat on the back before leaving the room. Paul was at the stove, all his attention on the table, his face back to normal.

Louder than he'd already been talking, Ronnie said, "So the knife was like this fucking long."

Paul put a plate of tater tots and a sloppy joe at the table where Laura had been sitting. I thought it was meant for me, but when I went to sit down, he took the seat for himself and pointed at the stove. "There's plenty if you want to help yourself."

"So these four ISIS fucks got this guy pinned down on the sand. Then the dude with the machete started going *thwack, thwack, thwack*," Ronnie said, bringing his forearm down on each beat. "You could hear everything. Every sound he was making. He was gurgling and screaming."

I took what was left of the food, which was never much. Paul was turning into quite the cook so I didn't blame them, but it would have been nice to leave enough for the guy doing the hardest work.

Jim's chair was the only one empty, but no one sat there, even with him out of town. I leaned back against the stove and took a bite of my sloppy joe.

Brad asked Ronnie, "You'll be around tonight?"

"After work," Ronnie said. "Bring a twelve pack."

Brad got up from the table and gave Paul's arm a friendly shove. "Good grub, Paulie."

Paul acted like it was no big deal, but his eyes gave it away. "Glad you liked it."

Brad washed off his plate at the sink and headed for the back door. Paul eyes followed him.

I took my spot without a word and finished off the sandwich. I was trying not to wonder about the picture I found when I was putting away our clothes.

If it hadn't been so smooth and folded up so many times, I might've thought it was trash and thrown it away. But I made the mistake of opening it up and spreading it flat. It had four sets of washers and dryers, the prices and descriptions lined down the side. On the bottom was the word Target and a bunch of small print.

Then I turned it over. Young men and boys standing around in their underwear, the blond boy in the middle looking an awful lot like Brad, maybe a little younger and not as good-looking.

The back door closed and Paul took a bite, waited a few seconds before he said, "Hey, Ronnie, would you care if I watch it with you guys?"

Ronnie finished his juice. Like it was the God's honest truth, he said, "I don't give a shit."

I told Paul, "You don't want to watch that stuff."

Ronnie said, "How do you know?"

"I do."

Ronnie crossed his arms and sat back, looked like he'd already won whatever we were going to talk about. "You're all-knowing?"

"He's my brother."

"So you know everything he wants?"

"I know watching that stuff isn't good for you."

Ronnie was looking pretty smug. "Why?"

"It don't do you any good."

"It teaches about death."

I gave up on him and turned to Paul. "Some of those things you can't unsee."

Ronnie said, "You don't know everything."

"That's true." I would have let it go if it wasn't for his smile. "But I bet it's a hell of a lot more than you."

Ronnie sat up and grabbed the table. "Oh yeah?"

Paul kicked my foot. "Don't."

I pushed him away, kept my eyes right on Ronnie. "Probably."

Ronnie got to his feet. "You sure as shit ain't no messiah. You got that? Not in this house."

I looked at Paul who was studying his plate. "I never said I was."

Trying to look all tough, Ronnie puffed out his chest. "Well, you ain't, so stop fucking acting like it."

From the other room, Laura said, "Boys."

I was tired of taking his shit and stood to show him I wasn't scared. "Or what?"

"You're gonna threaten me in my own house?"

I kept my cool. "I just asked a question."

"My house. I ask the questions. You think you can whup me?"

Laura stepped into the doorway. "What's going on?"

I kept my eyes on Ronnie. "I ain't scared of the devil. I ain't scared of you."

Ronnie said, "Fuck you, altar fag."

"Fuck you!"

Laura screamed. "That's enough!"

Ronnie pointed at me. "This asshole started it."

"No, I didn't."

Laura pointed at my chair. "Sit down, Joshua."

"But—"

"I said sit!"

Ronnie's grin got bigger when I obeyed. "Good boy."

Laura told him to go outside. Ronnie took off with a smile. "Yeah, sure thing."

"You, too, Paulie," she said, her hand on his shoulder the same way she held mine. That was how she handled her nephews, a tiny touch to show she cared.

The cut on my palm was still bleeding, a line of red stained the seat.

Laura sat in her chair and took hold of my good hand. "Please look at me."

It took me a moment, but I did. I mainly saw Mother in her, the same iron toughness that had been dinged up and tarnished.

She said she was sorry for yelling, and I told her it was fine.

"You need to understand some things," she said. "Jim's not a bad man, but he's doing me a favor by letting you stay here."

"Me?"

"Paul's doing what he said and then some."

"I'm a good worker. Better than any of those guys."

"I know that, but it doesn't mean a thing if you can't back down to Ronnie."

"He's a jerk."

"But do you understand?"

I nodded.

"Good. I like having you here." She smiled.

"Thanks."

"So what was all this about?"

"He just wanted to fight."

"I heard him say messiah."

I'd never talked about the church. "Paul must've told him."

"Don't be mad. That was a big part of your life. Both of your lives."

Backstabbing Judas was what I wanted to call Paul right then so I kept my mouth shut.

"How do you feel about all that?" She waited long enough to know I wasn't planning on answering then said, "Do you miss it?"

I said, "Not at all," which was mostly true.

It was ten o'clock Friday night, and I had the living room all to myself. Jim's poker games ensured he wouldn't get home before two in the morning and Laura had disappeared after dinner to the front porch.

Paul usually joined me for movie night, but he was back in Ronnie's room chuckling it up. I didn't give a shit because I didn't have to let him pick the movie or listen to him bitch about my choice. It might have been *Thor* that'd just finished, or maybe *Captain America*, or *X-Men*. That's all I'd watch when given a say. Those movies provided a nice break from real violence with enough action to hold my interest. They taught me a lot about life, different places and cultures, how people act. It was also nice to think maybe I wasn't the only person who had trouble not dying. Did make me jealous however that I didn't have any cool super powers.

Instead of starting the next movie, I went out on the porch. The swinging stopped.

Laura sat still on the swing, stared into the backyard's darkness. I asked if she was okay.

The tears down both cheeks said she wasn't. She took a drink and set the glass between her feet. "Just get sad sometimes," she said.

It was getting awkward so I turned to go. Sounding like she wanted a real answer, Laura asked, "Why'd you finally decide to leave?"

"It was the right thing to do."

"God, you sound just like him sometimes."

We'd never once talked about him, but I figured she meant Vince. Laura picked up a brown photo album and held it out to me.

I leaned against the railing and opened it. The blue-eyed, dirty blond boy looked about six in the first photo, Laura just as I remembered her. I turned the pages and the years flew by. A young boy was always smiling, especially in the ones with Laura squeezing him into a hug.

Every event was captured. Birthdays, school plays, him reading books. The only photos of me were taken right after accidents, but I could see the resemblance. Only Vince looked happy. Normal.

The farther I got in the book, the faster Vince grew. A few more pages and there was no denying our relation, his wide shoulders and tree trunk legs the same as mine. There were also a lot less smiles.

Laura slurred a little when she said, "Oh, yes, such a fun age."

I cleared my throat. "His letter said we were brothers."

It took her a moment. "I figured as much."

"Why would he write that?"

Although she could have been, she wasn't mean like Mother when she said, "Why do you think he would?"

"I can't see any reason why he'd lie. And he had the same book."

A smile crept out. "Oh, you found it."

"You put it there?"

"Why don't you sit down, sweetie."

"I think I better stand."

"I had promised I'd pass the present on to you when you were old enough to read."

"But why hide it in the barn?"

"Charles would've burned it if I gave it to him, so I had to leave it up to fate."

"What does it mean?" I lowered my voice, tried not to let it break. "What'd you tell me when I was little?"

"Vince found my journal," Laura said. "He knows everything."

"But he's not here. You tell me."

Tears ran down her cheeks and she hugged me to her chest. "I'm sorry, Joshua. I'm so very sorry."

"For what?"

"This is my life," she said. "This is all I have."

I told her it was okay and patted her back. "Don't cry."

She couldn't stop. "I swore on everything holy, on your very life that I'd never tell a soul."

"But you said Vince knows. What can it hurt telling me?"

"It's why he ran away."

"I'm not him."

That ended the hug. Laura studied me then said, "Help me up. And bring the bottle." We walked to the stables where it was just us, the horses, and the whiskey. She said not to say a word or she'd most likely stop.

"When it comes to the official account of your birth, Charles got some of it right. You were born purple and quiet. Maureen went temporarily insane."

"So the gospel's true?"

"I didn't get it at the time, why she was so upset. I was the one who'd been carrying you for nine months. I was the one who pushed you out."

She held up a finger to keep me quiet. "Vincent was born just minutes after you, but over in the shed they'd set up for small surgeries. Kelly was tiny and your father wasn't. They had to tear her open."

I could see the blood with my eyes open, my imagination conditioned for darkness.

Laura must've seen the question coming. "No, not Charles. You saw the photos."

"You can't expect me not—"

"I do." Laura drank what was left in her glass. "Charles convinced Maureen they couldn't get pregnant. He talked her into letting him have a stab at me."

"So he is my father?"

She ignored me. "Things were different back then and Maureen wanted a kid, or at least said she did to make him happy."

I didn't want to hear more, but couldn't walk away.

"Charles and I worked on it for a while, neither of us with anyone else part of our unwritten contract. By the time we hit ten times, I was beginning to think Charles wasn't even trying, that maybe he was praying we'd never conceive, that he could just fuck me forever. That's when my roommate, Kelly, brought this bearded traveler back from town, told the Committee he was an old friend.

"Kelly had tired of most of the men in the commune and often had guy friends stopping by. Those nights would get loud and her bed was just a thin wall from mine. I'd walk the fields, look at the stars, wonder what the hell I was doing with my life."

Laura asked me to mix her a drink. "I got back to the room a couple minutes past eleven, pretty high and all ready to sleep, glad they weren't making a peep. I lie down, close my eyes, start to nod off. Then a hand pinches my nose shut and covered my mouth, tied off my right hand with the strips of bedsheet he'd already tied to the pole."

I should have known better than to come here. My hearing grew fuzzy, like my brain might switch off. My whole life a lie.

"He said all he needed was one shot, that you'd be a gift from the gods, but he was greedy like Charles."

The pain and anger burning in her eyes, an inheritance I could not deny.

"You and Vince were each left a book. Kelly and I each a warning to deliver it. Nothing else was given, not even a name, Kelly and me deciding the police would only make things worse."

I was rarely grateful for Father, but he sounded so much better than a rapist. "How could you know for sure I'm not Charles's?"

"Not tonight, Joshua. And not tomorrow. I love you, but you're my nephew. It's the only way this works."

Paul had stuck yellow stickers to each of the rocks he'd handpicked for the wall. The wheelbarrow was still sitting unused in the garage, right where

Ronnie said it better be in case he ever went looking for it. I played along. I was their mule. The boulders were my cross. Shit was the same as it ever was.

The boulder at my feet was an eighty-pound monster with flecks of red. It was after eleven, the sun was blazing overhead and I'd probably dripped a pound of sweat by the time I carried that behemoth to the driveway. Paul and Brad were in the far corner where I was headed. Brad was on his knees applying mortar, Paul a few feet in front of him, sitting on the low wall I'd spent the last week hauling.

Brad set down his trowel and grabbed the beer bottles from Paul. I nodded at Brad and he nodded back when he walked by. I pretended I was watching where I was going, but my eyes were really on Paul whose eyes were on Brad. I stepped in front of Paul and blocked his view, dropped the boulder.

Instead of acknowledging my efforts, Paul said, "Isn't it beautiful?"

I brushed my hands on my jeans, flinched a little when my scar rubbed the ridge. "Where'd you send him off to?"

Paul nodded at the table in the back where Ronnie was waiting. "He said they wanted some cold ones."

"What do you think Jim would say?"

"Last time I checked, he wasn't here and won't be until tomorrow."

I shook my head.

"What?"

"Nothing."

Paul got off the wall and handed me the glass of lemonade beside him. "Here."

I wouldn't grab it. "Go take it to your friends."

"What's your problem?"

I looked at him then the wall. "Where the hell you want me to start?"

"The wall? That's what it is?"

"You think it's easy?" I pushed at the boulder with my foot, couldn't budge it. "They're fucking heavy."

"You're good at it."

"Don't mean I like it."

Paul chewed on his bottom lip. "And it's my fault?"

"It was your idea."

Real slow, he said, "They don't like you. Ronnie wants you gone."

"He's an asshole."

"He's Jim's son. If you weren't doing the wall, you still think we'd be here?"

"You'd leave, too?"

"You don't even try to get along with them."

"You mean I don't kiss his ass."

Paul pouted. "I don't."

"Yeah you do. Both of theirs. Ronnie and your little boyfriend."

Paul got in my face. "Take that back!"

"What?"

"He's not my boyfriend."

"You're always trying to hang out with him."

"What's wrong with trying to make friends?"

"They're not your friends."

"Well, they're sure as hell not yours."

I took a deep breath and blew it out. Ronnie was watching us. I turned back to Paul. "I don't like you hanging out with them."

"That's fine."

"You won't anymore?"

"All I said was that's fine. You can think what you want."

"What's that mean?"

Paul held out the glass again. "You want it or not?"

My throat was parched, but I wouldn't take it. I meant to push away his hand, but I caught the top of the glass and sent it crashing to the ground.

Ronnie got up from the table. "You breaking shit over there?"

"Yeah, you want to see?"

Under his breath, Paul told me to stop it. Then he turned to Ronnie and said, "It was an accident. My fault."

"Nah, Paulie. I seen it. He knocked it out of your hand."

I said, "It's a stupid glass."

Ronnie walked over, Brad right beside him. "That was my Momma's."

I picked up the largest shard of glass, held it in my hand. "I'll buy her a new one."

Paul said, "She's dead."

"You're a fucking dick," Ronnie said, "you know that?"

I wasn't sorry, but I mumbled I was.

"You think you're so tough." Ronnie made a fist and cracked his knuckles. "You go around thinking you're all hot shit, holier than thou. Thinking you're the goddamn Messiah."

"No, I don't!"

They all took a step back, Ronnie shutting his mouth long enough for me to say, "You're the one who thinks he's so tough."

"Tougher than you'll ever be."

I nudged the boulder with my shoe. "I bet I can throw this farther than you can carry it."

He looked at it and hesitated. "Yeah right."

I wasn't so sure I could win the bet, but I could see he was just as nervous. "Come on. Let's put some money on it."

"I got nothing to prove to you."

"Twenty bucks. What's twenty bucks?"

"You even got that much? Let me see it."

Everything I owned was in my pocket in case someone like Dusty showed up and tried to take advantage of me. I pulled out a twenty.

"It's a stupid bet," he said.

"Tell you what. You and my brother. Unless you're chicken."

Ronnie said I was on, he wasn't no goddamn chicken.

I moved to the side. "Ladies first."

Ronnie pushed past me and squatted down behind the boulder, his face super serious like the football picture in the living room. The picture where he had forty less pounds wrapped around his waist. He grunted and got the rock off the ground on the first try. He made it three steps before it thumped to the floor.

Brad said, "Will you look at that."

Ronnie dusted his hands off. "Would've been better if it hadn't slipped."

I got into position, hands under the boulder. "Of course." I was no longer tired. I wasn't thirsty. I was a better man than him and I was going to prove it.

"Come on already," Ronnie said.

In one clean move, I snatched the boulder to my chest and got my legs under me.

Ronnie chanted, "Drop it, drop it."

I glanced at him and imagined what the boulder would do to his head. As hard as I could, I heaved that rock, watched it tumble twice, thudding down where it'd been by no more than a foot.

"What you so excited about?" Brad asked. "Paulie, you got that shit no problem."

Paul said, "I don't want to get all dirty."

"We'll it's too late for that," Ronnie said.

"Come on, Paulie, that's one step, maybe two. Easy as pie."

Paul walked over to the boulder and stared at it. He looked to Brad. "Which way should I pick it up?"

I said, "You seen me do it enough times to know."

"Yeah," Brad said, "just pick it up."

Paul gave me a dirty look and bent down, his legs spread wide. The boulder didn't budge.

Ronnie asked if he was fucking serious.

"Hold on, hold on." Paul brushed off his hands. "I can do it."

Ronnie said, "So do it."

Paul got down and wriggled his hands beneath the boulder. He had Father's look of determination, but Mother's hands, and he gave up on the count of five.

"Come on, Paulie," Brad said, "don't be such a pussy."

Paul wrapped his arms around the boulder and let out a yell as it came off the ground, his spine curved like it was going to crack. He got it up to his waist before it crashed down.

I told Ronnie to pay me.

"Hell no," Ronnie said. "This little girl couldn't even move it."

"Don't matter. That wasn't the bet. Pay me."

"I already told you no. Just cuz my dad's fucking your aunt don't mean I got to take your shit."

I stepped toward Ronnie. "So do something about it."

"Try me," he said, no surprise he'd choose words over action.

Paul jumped between us, looked right at me, and shouted just like Father. "Stop it!"

I pushed Paul out of the way, stared down Ronnie. "Maybe I don't know much, but there's one thing I'm sure of. You're a spineless little bitch."

"Grab your shit and get the fuck out of here," Ronnie said. "This is my house."

I took a step forward, said that was fine.

Paul lashed out at me, his palm connecting with the side of my face, the loudest crack.

My hands were around his neck, lifting him up, then slamming him down. I crouched over him, kept half his throat closed with my left hand. "And fuck you, too, you little faggot. Guess who's gonna call Father and tell him you're over here blowing cowboys."

His anger flashed to rage, both hands around my wrist, nails digging in and taking flesh. My right fist came down on the side of his head and all movement ceased.

I hadn't meant to hit him that hard, but I had to make him stop. Ronnie and Brad took a step back, neither one risking a word. Paul groaned which relieved me a bit.

"You better get the fuck out of here," Ronnie said. "I'll call the cops."

I stepped forward, got in his face and said, "I bet you would." I punched Ronnie in the gut and he dropped to the ground with a loud *oomph*. When I went to kick him, an arm wrapped around my throat and started squeezing, Brad's breath hot on my ear.

Paul held his head and cried, "Stop it! Stop it!"

We were long past stopping. I pulled Brad's arm straight then down and I shot my shoulder into his elbow, the snap almost as loud as his scream.

Paul got to his feet and pulled Brad toward the house, yelling for help.

Ronnie stayed on the ground and clutched his stomach. When I picked up the boulder, he said, "What the fuck you doing?"

"Say I'm the Messiah."

Ronnie scooted back on the grass. "What?"

I took a step and stomped on his foot so he couldn't get away. The boulder was getting heavy. Through gritted teeth, I said, "The Messiah. Say. I'm. Him."

Ronnie didn't need convincing. He said it like he meant it.

I turned and threw the boulder into the wall, knocked down the entire section. I said, "You best remember that."

Chapter Thirteen

Three days later, a little after nine o'clock in the evening, I was dropped off at the university's front gates. It said something across the arch, but it looked like Latin, and I had a hard enough time with English.

The trip from Georgia to Texas hadn't been easy. Buses and trains, a whole lot of walking, a blur of cars flying by, a few drivers willing to pick me up. I'd gotten a couple hours of sleep here and there, with my arms in a death grip around my duffle bag, but I was running on adrenaline.

The campus was beautiful, green grass and huge trees, just like the pictures Jeremy had shown me. Five giant brick buildings flanked each side, kids my age strolling around, a couple with backpacks, none like my sorry sack full of ratty clothes. They were having fun, talking, laughing, no threat of violence. Most had phones in their hands.

Jeremy's dorm was fourth on the right, the massive front door propped open with a rolled-up newspaper.

Room 13A was at the last door on the left. The door was closed so I knocked.

A guy in a brightly colored Grateful Dead shirt opened the door holding a controller, and he didn't look happy about being interrupted. "Yeah?"

I looked past him but couldn't see anyone else in the room. "Does Jeremy live here?"

"Used to."

He started to close the door, but I'd come too far for that and blocked it with my foot. Maybe I wasn't the Messiah, but I also was no longer someone to mess with. I said, "Do you know where he lives now?"

The guy huffed, but still answered. "He's on the third floor."

I pulled out my foot, went up the stairs. Fourteen rooms, only two with their door open. I had to ask three people about Jeremy before I found someone that asked, "Is that the camera guy?"

I nodded and she pointed to his room.

I knocked on the door. A girl inside said, "Fuck. Oh fuck me." She kept going then stopped mid-fuck a second before the door opened.

Jeremy's hair was past his shoulders, a bit of pudge sticking over his shorts. "Goddamn, Josh!" He slapped my shoulder and brought me inside, tossed my bag by the door. "How the fuck are you, you big son of a bitch?"

The room held a bed and a desk, with a mountain of clothes between them. I said, "I'm good."

Jeremy sat down at the desk where there was an empty 2-liter bottle of Coke, three slices of cold pepperoni pizza, and an enormous computer monitor, its screen filled with muted porn. "So what the hell are you doing here? You really fucking did it!"

"I had to."

"Danielle wrote you got out. Said you and your brother."

"Yeah, talk about mistakes."

Jeremy noticed the clock and said, "Oh shit. I got to get going." He picked up a pair of jeans from the top of the pile and slipped them on over his shorts. "Want to go to a party?"

What I wanted to do was curl up on his bed and turn off the lights, but I said, "Sure. I guess."

Jeremy grabbed the black t-shirt lying on his desk. "It'll be cool," he said. "I'm going to be working it, but you can hang out. We'll catch up after."

I mumbled yeah, all my attention on the computer screen. In a room not much bigger than the one we were standing in, a naked man and woman were doing things I'd only dreamed of, showing the things magazines only hinted at. The movies I had watched at Laura's had it all wrong with their gentle, sappy romance.

"Nice, huh?"

These people weren't trying to make babies. These two looked like they were trying to hurt each other and loving every minute of it. "Is this a disc?"

"Nah, all downloaded. I've got over ninety gigs."

I had no idea what a gig was but it sounded like a lot. "You ever leave your room?"

"Research, man. I worked on this most of the summer. You got any idea how popular this shit is?" His fingers flew across the keyboard, ending with one tap at the end. "Watch this."

I'd rather have continued watching the sex, but suddenly it was gone, replaced by a white page with words all over, half of them highlighted in dark blue: *Drunk College Sex.*

He must've seen I wasn't getting it because he pointed at the numbers below it. "Twenty-two million results." He clicked another button and it went to a screen full of miniature videos, each with an apparently drunk girl doing something naughty. Jeremy clicked on the first video. Ten minutes long, over five-hundred-thousand hits. "There is money to be made."

I was paying attention, but not to what he was saying. The new video had me mesmerized. Jeremy put the sound on so we could hear the guy slamming into the chick bent over the couch, his foot pinning her head to the cushion, his hand smacking her ass red. I asked, "Are they acting?"

"Every one of us is acting. Especially if a camera's on."

All the times I'd thought of being with his sister, Danielle, it'd never been like this. "Do they make a lot of money? Do they know each other?"

Jeremy put on his shoes. "Those two? Nah. This is supposed to be real college kids, but you know that's bullshit. Unless this same chick goes to different schools all over the country. I've got her in at least a dozen different scenes."

Jeremy pointed at the screen. "But it's what you want to get close to. Look at the quality of it. The girls look nice, but keep it real, that's what people want. Fuck, this could be me, squint my eyes a bit or get a nice point of view, and all of a sudden I'm balls deep."

"Balls deep?"

"I'll let you figure that one out on your own."

"So all those other sites are like this? They all have movies like this?"

"A lot of them are pay sites, but man there's enough free stuff out there to keep you busy the rest of your life."

The guy kept plugging away and the girl kept springing back, yelling at him to give it to her. "I wouldn't mind trying."

"You wouldn't want to. There's some sick shit on here."

"You don't worry about your neighbors hearing it?"

He thumbed the wall. "This one's a skank, every night someone different. And the dude across the hall's an asshole, so fuck him. Everybody does their own thing. Ain't a big deal."

Jeremy slicked back his hair and sprayed some cologne. "Come here," he said. "You need this more than I do."

I declined because I wasn't ready to get up with a boner. My eyes were glued. I couldn't believe he wasn't watching it.

Jeremy stepped over and sprayed me three times for good luck. He grabbed a black pouch off the desk and opened the door. "Got to go, dude."

The party was five blocks away and we were both breathing heavy when we got there. Jeremy said, "Let me do the talking."

A big guy wearing a red and black jersey with #72 on it stood in front of the door, the windows rattling from the bass, glimpses of guys and girls all over each other inside. The guy took a swig from his Budweiser can and looked at me just long enough to let me know we weren't going to get along. He asked Jeremy, "Who's this jerk-off?"

Jeremy patted my shoulder. "This is my boy, Josh. He's gonna help me out tonight."

As if trying to impress us, the guy crushed the can on his thigh and tossed it on the pile in the corner. "How? Holding your little dick?"

"With filming stuff."

He nodded at Jeremy's pouch. "You got another camera in there?"

"Come on, Wyatt. He just came all the way from South Carolina. No one will even know he's here."

Wyatt looked at me then back at Jeremy. "Twenty bucks."

Jeremy asked if he was serious.

"I don't got to let him in at all."

Jeremy turned to me. "I don't have any cash."

I had less than a hundred left, but there was no way I was finding my way back to Jeremy's room on my own. I pulled out the money. Four hours of hard labor to walk past a man no better than me.

Wyatt opened the door, stopped Jeremy with a finger to his chest. "Keep an eye out for my sister. Let me know if she gets out of line."

Jeremy agreed and went inside, waved me along.

The music was pounding, pulsing through my shoes, people everywhere, the floor slick. "First things first," Jeremy yelled as he led me into a side room with a keg. "Come on, let's get something to drink."

I remembered what happened the last time and said no thanks.

He filled two red cups and handed me one. "It's a party."

I took the cup, glad to have something to do with my hands. "Maybe just one."

Jeremy pounded his and threw the empty away. He took out his camera and headed to the dance floor. His camera crept left to right, took in the bodies upon bodies, so much skin, hands on hips, tits shaking, everyone having a good time.

The camera stopped at the curvy blonde in a checkered blouse and tight shorts grinding on a jock's thigh. The blouse was unbuttoned, her huge boobs swinging in a red sports bra, her skin so smooth and shiny, glistening with sweat.

The girl looked up and I looked away, finished my beer. Jeremy moved around to the right, but I went back to the girl. She smiled and I held up my cup and pretended to drink.

She kept watching me, her smile even bigger. While she shook back and forth, she held up her cup, let me see it was empty.

I pushed past everyone to get out of the room and made my way to the keg. Jeremy found me there with my back to the wall, halfway through my third beer. He had me follow him upstairs.

A couple people were in the hallway, and a skinny guy was passed out in the corner, surrounded by bottle caps and red cups, like they'd run out of chalk for the crime scene. Jeremy stepped inside the first room to film a group of guys circled around a table, taking turns trying to flip a quarter into a cup, everyone else drinking from their mug whenever a person made it.

Someone ran up behind us and smacked Jeremy's butt.

Jeremy spun around and turned the camera on the curvy blonde from the dance floor. "Easy, girl. What's up, Riley? You cool?"

She came right up to me, her baseball cap level with my chest, not seeming to notice she'd just spilled her drink on her bare feet that were black all around the edges. "You're new."

Jeremy saved me. "This is Josh. He's going to be the next heavyweight champ of the world. The Great White Hope."

Riley's cheeks were the same red as her hat and so big there's no way she'd get past Mrs. Durrington without a squeeze. Sounding like she believed him, she said, "That's awesome. Where do you train? Vegas?"

Jeremy stepped back, the camera taking it all in. "He doesn't like to talk business. Maybe you can show him around."

"Love to." Riley grabbed my hand, put my other one on her waist to lead me down the hall, the first female I'd felt since Kara. She stopped at the doorway with a desk in it, a tray of small cups on top. She handed me two of the cups filled with yellow Jell-O and ate two by herself. "Go ahead," she said. "They're yummy."

It'd been a while since I'd eaten anything and thought I'd feel better with something in my stomach. I wanted to touch her again, have her hand on me, so I downed them both and told her she was right.

Riley laughed and gave me two more, said to stay close. She peeked her head into a red-lit room but backed out when someone said, "We're busy."

At the end of the hall was a large trashcan filled with a dark punch and pieces of fruit floating in it. Riley dunked two cups, careful to get us each an orange slice.

I'd finished half of mine when the guy she'd been dancing with walked up to me and asked, "Who the hell are you?"

"Wyatt said I was cool."

"Well, then he lied."

"You heard him," Riley said. "Wyatt cleared him."

"We'll see." The guy took off, said 'dirty ho' loud enough for us to hear.

Riley just smiled and took my hand. "Don't worry about him. He's just mad cuz he thought he was gonna get some."

I took another drink because I had nothing to say.

Riley moved in closer. "Know what? You are fine." She put her hand on my chest and ran it down my stomach, wrapped her fingers around my belt.

I couldn't believe her hand was so close, especially with people around, but I didn't complain.

She started down the stairs, pulled me by the belt. "Come on, we need to dance."

I put on the brakes. I wanted her against me, but dancing was out of the question.

"It's easy." Without even looking back, she stuck out a finger, flicked me twice to verify I was rock hard. "You just got to stand there."

No amount of embarrassment was stopping me. I followed like a little puppy, my drink finished by the time we hit the dance floor. She guided me to the back wall, and put my hands on her ass, started grinding against me. She pulled me down and slipped her tongue in my mouth. It was obvious I didn't know what I was doing, so she went to my neck and started to lick.

Someone shouted Riley and she grabbed my hand, dragged me to the stairs. I asked what was wrong but she just shook her head, acted like everything was cool as she filled up our drinks at the trashcan. My balance wasn't what it should be so I put my back to the wall and held on to the railing.

Riley pulled me into a room where two guys were standing in front of the television, white guitars strapped around their neck, music blaring.

"They're good," I said. "Where's their singer?'"

Riley laughed. "Want to give it a shot?"

My mouth watered and I shook my head no. "I don't feel so good."

She went back to rubbing my chest. "Shit, you feel wonderful. Just need to relax a little."

I couldn't think, just let her pull me along until we were inside the red-light room.

She eased me on the couch and undid my buckle.

I tried to ask what she was doing, but she leaned in and kissed me, freed my top button. She wrapped her hand around my dick while undoing her shorts. "Feel me," she said, taking my hand until I felt wetness.

My finger slipped inside her, no curtain getting in the way, a closeness I'd never felt. The most incredible flood of feelings washed over me, an animal taking its new form. How could it be wrong? Charles would say I was sinning, doing something so awful it could land me in hell. I put in another finger and moved my hand faster, figured it couldn't be worse than killing a man.

Riley bucked her hips and jerked her hand, bit down on my shoulder but not hard enough to hurt. From the hallway, someone shouted, "Jeremy, where the fuck is she?"

I kept my hand where it was and turned to see Jeremy with his camera back up from the doorway. "Who?"

Wyatt walked up to him. "Who the fuck you think? I heard she's—" He looked in the room and saw me. "You motherfucker!"

"Hold on, Wyatt."

Wyatt shouted, "She's seventeen!" and sent Jeremy flying.

Riley jumped up and pounded Wyatt's chest with her fists, her shorts puddled at her ankles. "You're such an asshole!"

Wyatt shoved Riley out of the way and turned toward me. "You're fucking dead."

I put my dick away, buttoned my pants. "Don't think so."

From the hallway, Jeremy said, "Keep it cool."

"Fuck him. Go get the brothers. They'll want to see this."

I got up, not sure what I could say.

Jeremy stood in the doorway, camera rolling. "Leave him alone, Wyatt. We'll take off right now."

"Fuck that shit."

The room was spinning, but all my attention focused on Wyatt. Jeremy said, "Be first," and I listened. I threw the hardest left hook I could, caught the side of Wyatt's head, and knocked him onto the couch.

The crowd of people in the doorway hooted and hollered, screamed at Wyatt to get up, but he was out cold. One of them said, "Holy shit, who's this dude?"

I stared at them, at every guy that could come after me. I used Father's voice and shouted, "I'm the motherfucking Messiah!"

Everyone got quiet, then started laughing, a couple of them cheered. We squeezed into the hallway and I was surrounded by guys wearing black and red, many the same size as Wyatt or bigger.

I looked for the first guy I was going to cast judgment upon, promised myself I'd hurt at least one. A guy with glasses stepped up to be their spokesman, agreed Wyatt had it coming, but he was still a brother and I had to leave. I said that's all I wanted to do and thanked them for asking so nicely.

Finally, some respect.

† † †

It was two days later and I was on another bus, the sun sinking into the desert. I wanted to close my eyes, but if I did I'd fall asleep. I couldn't risk missing my stop at the end of the line and returning to the start.

The night after the party, I passed out in a park to celebrate my eighteenth birthday. The next night out wasn't much better on a bench in the bus station, arms wrapped around my bag. I needed a bed.

I should've known I couldn't stay with Jeremy, even if the fight hadn't happened. When he told me I better split he said it wasn't my fault, what the fuck did I know. But I could tell he was pissed.

The buildings flew by, all the stuff I'd been missing. The streets were filled with cars on either side. Drivers, young and old, some singing, some talking, most with a phone to their face.

The size of some cities and all the stuff they had amazed me, the bright lights mesmerizing. We passed a sign that said thirty miles to Albuquerque. There was no one sitting next to me so I slipped off my shoes, sank down across both seats. I asked myself what the hell I was going to do, and nearly cried because I had no damn idea.

I had forty-eight dollars and fifty-seven cents in my pocket. I'd been living on seven dollars a day thanks to the dollar menu and the stack of refillable plastic cups in my bag. I was never the best at math, but I knew it didn't give me long to get a job or find Vince.

The plan for the military had been blown to bits earlier that morning. The Marine recruiter laughed. The Army recruiter said it was impossible. My size. My injuries. No GED. No chance in hell they'd accept me.

A girl's voice said, "Hey," but I kept my eyes closed. She said it again.

I slipped on my shoes hoping that might've been what she wanted. I leaned back and told myself to ignore her if she spoke again.

"You were on the news," she said.

It was the girl directly across the aisle, and there was no question she was talking to me. She wore black boots and tight jeans, a jet-black shirt to match her hair which bobbed at the bottom of her neck. "I knew I'd seen you."

My heart stopped, my mouth dried. All I could think of was Uncle Jim's favorite show, "America's Most Wanted." They must've found Dusty, traced me to his murder.

"You're him, right?"

"I think you got the wrong guy."

She wagged her finger at me. "It's not nice to tell a lie. Isn't that a sin?"

I told her I was no one and wondered if anyone else was listening. "Why would I be on the news?"

"Yeah," she said, her smile growing. "You're even wearing the same clothes."

I shook my head.

"Where're you from?"

"Not around here."

She leaned in. "Say it. 'I'm the motherfucking Messiah.' I want to hear it without the bleep."

All those phones filming, me not even thinking about it. I just told her sorry, hoped she'd drop it.

She dug a phone from her pocket. "Your dad saw the video, too, put out a reward." She pointed it at me and there was a flash and a click.

"Erase that."

She smiled and took another one. "Why? You're not bad looking. No need to be shy."

I held up my hand to cover my face. "Please don't."

She put her phone away. "I'm just screwing with you. I made up the reward part."

"Oh."

"So what's your name?"

There was no point in lying so I told her.

She said her name was Naomi. "Where are you headed?"

"Good question."

"Tell me."

"I meant I don't really know."

"You're just cruising along, headed wherever? Just going with the flow?"

"Yeah, but mostly west." I pulled out the crumpled map from my pocket. "I got this."

She sat there for a second. "Wow, that is pretty cool. Just travelling the land, spreading the Good Word and all that."

"Not quite."

"So does that mean you don't have any plans?"

"Pretty much."

Naomi rubbed her hands together and squealed. "Now you do. You're taking me to the fair."

"The fair?"

"The church by my house. Everyone's going to be there."

"I'm not too big on churches."

"You don't have to pray or anything. It'll be fun."

"I better not."

"Give me one good reason," she said.

"Everyone will be there."

"Relax. We'll have a good time."

"Thanks, but I need to keep moving."

Naomi thought she was so cute sitting with her feet curled beneath her, head tilted to the side. "Are you going to make me call your daddy?" She went back to her phone. Before I knew what she was doing, Naomi turned around, leaned over and snapped our photo. "Me and the hashtag Messiah. Imagine how many likes I would get posting this."

I didn't think she would, but couldn't take that chance. "Fine. I'll take you."

We got off three stops later. I held my bag in my left hand so she could hold my right. She said we weren't moving until I did.

Naomi had a grip on me that felt like she thought I might run, which is exactly what I wanted to do. I could hear the screams and shouts from three blocks away, the bright lights beckoning in the darkening sky.

I hadn't realized I'd stopped walking until she tugged my arm. "Come on," she said. "This is going to be fun."

I seriously doubted it. People were hanging upside down, swinging so fast I couldn't see them, their screams piercing my brain.

My chest started getting a little tight, my head even foggier than it'd been. I shook it away and looked for an excuse. "What about my bag?"

She walked me to where the fence and church came together. "Set it down over there."

"It's all my stuff."

"It's a church."

I figured she knew better than I did, so I put it down and leaned a discarded piece of cardboard over it.

She said, "That'll stop 'em."

"Who?"

She headed for the ticket booth. "You're funny."

The wrinkled old lady behind the desk held out her hand, said it was five dollars each. Naomi laughed when I asked if that got us food.

"No, but there's all kinds here. We'll get some after the rides."

I couldn't believe what I was seeing, so many people all in one place. So many people having a good time. Men and women, boys and girls, holding hands, laughing.

Naomi pulled me along through the aisle, booths with food all around us. I held onto her in case she let go. Everything smelled delicious, but the prices killed my appetite. Five, six, seven dollars. She stopped at the longest line at the end of the aisle. "You old enough to buy a beer?"

I wasn't sure but told her no.

"You look it. Go get one."

"I don't have a lot of money."

"Don't be a cheapskate."

I waited my turn and asked for a beer, my six bucks all they cared about.

When I handed Naomi the drink, she turned and walked a few stalls down. In two large gulps, she finished half the cup.

A woman from behind me said, "Naomi?"

Naomi pushed the cup back in my hand. "Oh, hi, Miss Jackson."

"Who's your friend?"

The woman looked like an over-ripe pear in a purple dress, her lower half all big and squishy. I tried to shake her hand, but she kept her arms crossed. "How old are you?"

With the beer in my hand, I wasn't sure how to answer. Naomi answered for me. "Old enough."

Miss Jackson shook her head. "Your aunt's here. I suggest you go find her."

The lady walked away in a huff. I asked Naomi who she was.

"My biology teacher from last year. I hate that bitch."

The next ten minutes was spent with Naomi dragging me from booth to booth, pointing to the prizes she wanted me to win. Pennies slid off plates, balls banged off rims, rings bounced off poles, and twenty dollars later all I'd won was a tiny teddy bear. "I told you I never played this stuff."

"You weren't lying. No big deal. They're just stupid games." Naomi tugged my arm and spilled some of her second beer on my pants. "Let's go on the rides."

There was nothing I wanted to go on. Everything was too fast, too loud, too bright. Then I saw it, a massive multicolored pole reaching into the sky, a man with a sledgehammer sitting on a stool beside it. "What's that one?"

She looked where I was pointing. "What's it look like? Hit it as hard as you can."

I let go of Naomi's hand and walked up to the fence. I asked the old man in the baseball cap, "How do I win?"

He pointed at the pole, the lower three-quarters of it a bright yellow. Sounding like he was reading it off a card, he said, "Orange is a small toy. Green a large. Ring the bell and the hundred dollars is yours. Three tries for five dollars, highest hit counts."

"A hundred dollars?"

He pulled a bill from his pocket and set it on his stool, used his cap to weigh it down. With his thin fingers he slicked down a few stringy clumps of oily hair. "Real as it gets."

Naomi squeezed my arm. "You're going to do it. I just know it."

I didn't believe in fate, but I had a good feeling and paid the man. The hammer was heavier than it looked. I put it over my shoulder and stepped into the spray-painted square in front of the target.

From back by the fence, Naomi said something stupid about swinging it hard, and the old man sighed like I was wasting his time. I concentrated on the little black circle and brought the hammer high. Mid-swing, Naomi yelled, "Don't miss it," and that's exactly what I did, the hammer slamming into the asphalt, the vibration stinging so sharply I had to drop it.

People behind me were laughing. So was Naomi. She said, "What did I tell you?"

Embarrassed, I wanted to run, but I couldn't do that. I picked up the hammer and turned around, looked at her the way Father did when he wanted Mother to listen. "Can you shut up for one minute?"

Everyone got quiet and I got into my stance, focused on the black button until it became a small log ready to be split. I raised the hammer high and brought it crashing down, the wrath of God.

The bell rang before I could look up, then boom after boom, the electronic backdrop flashing lights and colors. The God of Thunder had returned.

People were cheering behind me, hooting, whistling, some saying I got lucky. Naomi jumped on my side and yelled in my ear.

I shook her off and went up to the old man looking up at the lightning.

"Oh, sorry about that. Just never seen anyone hit it."

"Never?"

"Been doing this twelve years."

It sounded like it was new to all the people huddled around behind us. Everyone tried to get a peek at the guy that was going to walk away with a hundred dollars.

The old man picked up the bill and stuffed it in his pocket. "This one's not real." He nodded behind me and said, "My boss will take care of you."

He didn't look like the kind of person who'd have a boss, but the guy he was looking at didn't look like a boss with his braided red hair and bushy beard that swished back and forth over his blue polo. The man walked past the growing line and stared up at the display, stroking his beard as he waited for the thunder to pass. "Amazing."

We shook hands and he introduced himself as Owen and said, "I run this place." Another round of thunder boomed overhead, lightning flashed. "Absolutely amazing."

Owen admired the line that'd grown to twenty deep, and then disappeared behind the pole. A switch flipped and the backdrop went black. The old man yelled, "Batter up. Who's next to win big money?"

Owen came back and looked out at the crowd. He pulled a large wad of money from his pocket. "You think you could do it again?"

"Probably."

He counted off five twenties and put them in my hand. "You wouldn't be looking for a job now would you?"

I thought there was no way he could know, and then I realized how I looked. "Sort of."

"What do you say about coming along with us? Hit this thing once or twice a night to show people it can be done."

"Are you serious?"

"Always am. The job's yours if you want it. I'll pay you fifty bucks on top of the normal wage. If you can ring it again."

I had no idea what normal wage was, but fifty alone would be worth it. "When can I start?"

"Right now. I'll put Abe on cleaning crew."

"There's just one thing I need."

Owen narrowed his eyes. "What's that?"

"The girl in jeans behind me. That's a beer she's holding."

"No big deal," Owen said. "Just tell her to keep it quiet. Don't make a fool of herself."

"No, I want her gone."

Chapter Fourteen

The following June we had a three-week stint in Phoenix, the furthest west our rotation would take us. It was our final night there, and it was a hot one, still a hundred degrees at ten o'clock.

I was on my stool, the hammer leaning against my legs, counting the minutes 'til it was over. A field of dirt spread around me, filled with tough guys in tank tops and women in sweatpants with JUICY stretched across their asses. The smell of greasy carnival food was making me queasy. Even with my earplugs in, my head was pounding, the way it did every night since Owen squeezed me between the Zipper and the rattling roller coaster that continually screeched above.

That noise didn't sound right, metal on metal for just a split second, not enough to worry about according to Zeke. But there wasn't much Zeke worried about. He was sixty-two with three kids he couldn't talk to, grandchildren he'd never met. What did he care?

I looked straight up at the reason I'd only been on the ride once. The curve was just too high, too fast, too sharp. Maybe it might have felt okay over water, but not with the zipper cages rolling right at me. It'd been a good thing I'd had an empty stomach.

Two ladies that looked about Laura's age walked up, both of them carrying the 44 oz. blue and white Beer Bomber. There was nothing special about either one, not much to tell them apart except a couple wrinkles, a few pounds, a little leather. I saw women like them every night and wasn't surprised when they ignored the gate and my personal space.

But I was still pleasant. "How are you ladies doing tonight?"

The one with more leather put her hand on my forearm. "Well, aren't you sweet?"

The heavier one's fake smile threatened to crack her caked-on makeup. Her hand went on my bicep and gave it a squeeze. "I'll say."

I was used to the attention, but that didn't mean I liked it. I held out the hammer. "Did either of you want to give it a shot?"

The first one raised her hand and jumped up and down, her boobs flopping all around like half-filled water balloons. "I do, I do."

Her friend dug out her phone and took aim. "Smile."

I held up my hand to block out my face. "Sorry, no pictures."

"Oh, come on." Spit flew onto my cheek when she leaned in and said, "What if I tell you a secret?"

"Still no pictures. That's my rule."

The roller coaster roared over us, the metal grinding. Her fleshy fingers stuck to my arm. "We'll see about that." Her tongue flicked inside my ear.

I pulled away and said no.

It didn't take much to make her ugly. "Can you blame him?" Loud enough for everyone else to hear, she said, "Would you want people knowing you're a carnie?"

They walked away, the joke on her. I didn't give a shit if people knew I was a carnie. I made a hundred bucks a night to take money and hand out toys. I even had my own little six-by-eight room with a cot and a stack of plastic containers for my clothes.

There hadn't been a paying customer in close to ten minutes, and I'd rung the bell a few hours back. Two times a night was the usual, sometimes three, but it only made sense to do it when the lines nearby were long.

The line for the Rattler snaked all the way to the beer booth. That's when I saw an incredible blonde in light blue jeans hugging her bubble butt, a Beer Bomber in each hand as she made her way to the end of the Zipper line.

She walked up to a monster of a man, huge black stripes tattooed down each arm, tapering to a point at his middle knuckle. He was looking right at me, mad-dogging was what Eddie called it, seeming not to notice her body pressed against him and raising up on her toes to kiss his cheek.

The girl turned to see what he was looking at. It looked like she was asking him what was wrong, but with that screeching overhead, I couldn't make it out.

He shook her off and kept staring.

I held out the hammer and talked slow so he could read my lips. "Do you want to play?"

He pushed his drink to her and started my way, chest puffed out and arms flexed as if someone pulled a string to inflate him. With a voice even deeper than I imagined, he said, "What'd you say?"

"Do you want to play?"

He stopped on the other side of the fence, his girl by his side. "I don't want to play your stupid game."

"You keep looking over here. Maybe you want to try it and show everyone how strong you are."

"You're the faggot checking out my bitch."

Even I knew that didn't make much sense but I left it alone. "I'm trying to figure out what's tattooed on your arms. You got 'em so people will look, right?"

He flexed even harder than he had been. Like I was supposed to be scared, he said, "Mess with the bull."

I didn't get it.

He put both arms straight down. "Horns," he said. "They're fucking horns."

His girlfriend leaned in close and said, "Relax, hun."

"I'm not letting some punk kid—"

"It's not worth it. Come on, we should get back in line."

He shot her a nasty look.

Instead of letting it blow over, I said, "Do you want to play?"

"Are you a fucking wise guy?"

"No, just a dumb carnie. You want to play or not? Show her what those muscles can do."

"Please, baby," she said. "Let's just go."

He ignored her. "Maybe if my shoulder wasn't all jacked up."

I'd come a long way with reading people. "Tell you what," I said. "It's on me. Three free shots."

Bull didn't say anything, but I knew he was considering it.

I pulled out a hundred-dollar bill. "I'll even throw in one of my own."

At least twenty people had circled around. I held out the hammer like it didn't weigh a thing. "Three tries. What can it hurt?"

He snatched the hammer. "Alright, but I'm not paying for this. Two hundred if I hit the bell."

I gave him my word and he spread his feet wide on either side of the button like he'd done it before. He shook out one massive arm then the other. His arms were bigger than mine, and I wondered if I'd made a mistake, maybe I'd met my match. One hundred dollars was no big deal with all that I'd saved, but I was a little worried about how I'd handle the gloating.

The hammer rose high and crashed down, but the mallet only hit half the black circle, the silver disc barely reaching the orange.

Again, the hammer went back up and down, striking the dead center of the target. The disc soared toward the top and stopped at eighty-nine, the very last segment before the red.

Somehow I knew I'd just seen Bull's best. "Come on," I said. "One more try."

Bull dropped the sledgehammer and made a face while he swung his arm in a big circle. "Told you my shoulder's all fucked up."

I got the blonde's attention and pointed at the row of tiny teddy bears. "Any color you want."

She said red and he said she didn't need that stupid shit.

I tossed her the bear anyway then picked up the hammer. Most everyone in line for the Rattler was watching, a bunch from the Zipper as well. Sounding as casual as possible, I wound up my shoulder like he had, and said, "Mine's pretty sore, too, but I'll give it a try."

He walked away and called after the blonde who was still at the fence. "Stacy, hurry the hell up."

Stacy didn't move, her blue eyes all over me. Waking the Thunder God was never a sure thing, so I took my time and slowed my breathing. I forgot about the crowd, the roller coaster screeching above.

In one quick movement, I brought the hammer crashing down on the button, Thor's explosion lighting the night. I turned to face the cheering crowd. Even Stacy was clapping, clearly impressed.

I smiled at her and said it was nothing. The line was long enough and I couldn't take the noise, so I turned off the machine. I went back to my stool and shouted, "Three tries for five bucks. Who wants to win a hundred dollars?"

Bull was back, pulling Stacy by her arm. "That shit's fixed. That's bullshit."

I said, "Care to tell me how?"

"You do something, press a button. I don't know." He looked around and said, "Might not even be you. Probably one of your toothless buddies."

I stepped up to him. "Don't call me a cheater.

"Come on, Bull," Stacy said. Even though he was twice her size, she managed to pull him away. "It's not worth it."

I turned to the line of customers, spent the next five minutes taking money. I'd nearly forgotten about Bull when I heard someone yelling from over by the Zipper.

It was Bull and he was on phone. He moved it away from his mouth and shouted to me, "What time you get off?"

I'd been threatened before, but never by anyone his size. I figured I could handle myself and a little practice would be good for me. "We close at eleven. I'll meet you up front."

He smiled at me then spoke to the phone. "Hear that. Eleven, out front."

Bull was putting the phone in his pocket when Stacy hit his arm. "Call him back. You don't need to hurt anyone."

I turned back to my customers, figuring that anyone that had to have a friend at the fight was too much of a pussy to even show up. A few minutes later I heard him yelling retard every time he zoomed by.

The fourth time, I saw a flash of his face, a demon behind the screen. He disappeared as the Zipper whipped them around and back up. They were zooming back down when there came a loud twang of metal snapping and shrieking screams as the last two cars of the coaster shot over the edge, turning in the air, smashing into one of the Zipper's cages.

The coaster cars and the cage smashed to the ground twenty feet away. Everyone started screaming, pointing at the pile of mangled metal. Another cage dangled from above, blood streaming out, a woman screaming for help.

I ran to the bottom of the Zipper and climbed the ladder. At the top, I lay down on my belly and scooted forward until my chest and arms were over the edge. Bull's and Stacy's cage was barely hanging on by a twisted piece of metal a few feet below. I slid forward, secured both feet below a rung, and then lowered my hand until it was at the opening to their cage.

Stacy was hysterical. "Oh, my God! Help us!"

Bull was barely breathing, his hands locked on the seat, his legs nearly severed where the cage collapsed. I told Stacy to slide her legs from under the bar.

She started to listen until Bull grabbed her arm. "Don't move. The whole thing's gonna go."

I told her to concentrate on me. "I will not let you fall. I will not drop you. Give me your hand."

Stacy got up, reached through the opening, and took my hand.

Bull said, "Don't do it. No, no, don't do it."

I shouted at her to move and she clambered up my body and onto the beam. There was nothing I could do for Bull, and I started backing up, but he snatched hold of my wrist, begging me to help.

Bull was going down with or without me. I shook him off and backed out of the cage a split second before it broke off and slammed onto the concrete, silencing his screams.

† † †

It was a year and three days since the rescue video hit the headlines. A year and two days since Father called looking for me. It was exactly one year to the day that I moved to Flagstaff and started working for Eddie's older brother, Rick.

Rick had his own moving company and we were on the last job of the day. We were in the living room, holding up the couch, both of us pretending like we didn't care how long it took Terry to make up her mind.

Terry was a twenty-two-year-old college senior in a blue and yellow football jersey. She said she was a cheerleader and I believed her, her full lips painted red, her long brunette hair just like I imagined Danielle's.

She stood a few steps behind Rick and looked right at me. "Where would you put it?"

I looked to Rick to bail me out, but he gave me a look that said, "What the fuck." Then he let me sweat another second and said, "That depends on what you plan on using it for."

Terry shared her perfect smile, her eyes on me. "So maybe away from the window until I put blinds up."

Rick was done helping me out. It was a two-bedroom apartment so there weren't a whole lot of places to put the couch. I nodded at the wall behind her. "How about up against there?"

Terry said sure and moved over to my side, not leaving me much space to lower the couch. She smelled like flowers, her hand so soft on my back when she told me great choice.

I didn't know what to say so I followed Rick out the front door.

Terry caught up to me and asked, "Are you trying out for the team? I know a lot of guys get summer jobs."

"Team?"

"You know, football."

I told her I never played and left her at the bottom of the ramp. When I got to the back of the van, Rick slapped my arm and whispered, "What the hell's wrong with you?"

"What did I do?"

"You for real? This chick's digging you and you won't even talk to her."

"She's just being nice."

"Yeah, to your dumb ass." Rick came closer. "I'm going to send her in here. You talk to her."

"What about?"

Rick picked up the computer chair and walked down the ramp. Terry came up a few seconds later, pointing over her shoulder. "He said you could use me."

Jeremy would've said something dirty, but I stuck to business, not sure how many words I'd get out before she realized I could be a little slow. "What would you like next?"

She sounded disappointed when she said, "Oh." Terry took a second and picked out the loveseat beside her, the biggest piece left. "I guess this."

The box her hand was all taped up, PHIL'S SHIT scrawled across the side in black marker. I nodded at it. "Important stuff in that one?"

She shrugged her shoulders. "I wish I knew."

Other boxes had Phil's name on it, but none were taped. "Don't you want to open it?"

She shook her head. "You look hard enough for anything and you'll find it."

"That's what I was taught to do."

I'd made it so neither of us had anything to say. I bent down and lifted the end of the loveseat, and then positioned myself underneath it.

"Aren't you going to wait for your partner?"

"Nah, this is nothing." I proved it wasn't and walked it inside.

Rick hurried out of the bedroom we'd already finished. "Damn, girl. What a slave driver."

"I told him to wait."

Rick just stood there, hands in his pocket. "This guy don't have a pause button."

That's pretty much how it went for the next ten minutes. Rick keeping her smiling, me quiet. When we were done, Terry caught up with us in the driveway and handed Rick the money. Then she added a twenty to it and glanced over at me. "And this is for being so great."

"Sorry," Rick said. "Can't take it."

I was owed two weeks of back pay, but Terry was the one who asked why not.

"I got a better idea," Rick said.

"Oh yeah? What's that?"

"You use that to buy my boy Josh a few drinks. He's still new to this place and doesn't get out much."

She turned on that perfect smile, the one too good for a dumbass like me. "I'd love to," she said. "I'm meeting my friends over at Hardy's tonight. You should come."

I mumbled something about maybe. Rick pushed me toward the passenger side and said, "He'll be there."

Once both our doors were closed, Rick said, "Holy shit, am I going to have to hold your dick while you're fucking her? That ain't my thing, homie."

"I'm not going."

"Man, if I was built like you, there wouldn't be a woman in this town I hadn't touched. I don't know what the hell it is, but these girls out here just eat up the whole redneck deal."

Rick put the money in his pocket and caught me looking. He brought it back out and said, "That's right. It's pay day."

"Yeah, my rent's almost due. Is there any way to catch up?"

He counted out a hundred and fifty dollars. "Gonna have to be patient. I need all the checks to clear and…"

I took the money. I'd heard that line before. We almost always got paid cash.

Rick started the van. "I still think you're a moron for passing up something like that."

"She's got a boyfriend."

"Who cares? If she doesn't, why should you?"

I took out my stash and added the money to it. "I don't know."

"Your loss." Rick looked over as I stuffed my money back in my pocket. "What'd I tell you about that? Walking around with all your money isn't a smart thing to be doing."

I patted my pocket. "It's not that much. I've got most of it under my mattress just like you said."

"You still have that ID I got for you?"

"Of course."

"Alright, you and me are going out. I'll get you ready for your big date tonight."

When I worked the carnival, I drew nearly every night, so it never made sense to splurge on a TV. Now I was averaging about ten movies a week, playing catch up with the rest of the world. "I was going to watch the second part of *Star Wars*."

"Priorities. You ever want to be able to talk to women? *Star Wars* ain't going teach you that. Shit, it'll probably do the opposite."

I thought of Jeremy, how he said he'd have models for me one day, that I better learn how to talk to women by then. If someone wanted to help me I should let them, and to be honest, staying home in my studio apartment every single night was getting a little lonely. "Where we gonna go?"

Rick said I'd see.

The sign said, Girls, Girls, Girls, but I still asked, "What's this place?"

"You crack me the fuck up." He got out of the van and said, "Go ahead and leave your jacket in here. I'll lock it up."

I only had a wife beater on underneath so I told him I was okay. I had my ID out before we got to the guard at the door, a pencil-thin Hispanic holding a metal detector.

Rick told me to chill and put it away. He patted the guard on his back. "What's up, Enrique? How the girls looking?"

Enrique did so-so with his hand. "Go see for yourself."

"Big man's with me."

Enrique opened the door for us and said, "Enjoy."

My heart thumped with the music, my eyes adjusted to the darkness, the air conditioning sending a chill down my spine. The place was smaller than my church, a stage with twelve chairs horseshoed around it, a bouncer with a shaved head standing beside a black curtain.

Rick headed for the stage, whistled at the brunette with a dragon tattooed down her leg, wearing nothing but the thinnest pair of panties. She was dancing for the only guy at the stage, an older man in a white button down, his power tie hanging loose.

The woman looked over her shoulder at Rick who sat at the rail like it was nothing. She bent over and reappeared between her spread legs with a smile, one hand pulling her dimpled butt cheek to the side, her other finger just below her panties wiggling him forward.

I took a seat two tables back, thought back to Riley and how wet she'd been, how much she'd wanted it. How that naughtiness was nothing compared to this place with people paying for sex.

The dancer turned around and played with her tits, lifting one then the other. The whole time shaking her ass at the old man holding the dollar.

Rick noticed I wasn't next to him. "Get over here. They won't hurt you."

There was no way I was moving. Rick left the stage and called me a pussy. "Give me two twenties."

He was the boss so I handed it over and watched him walk to the booth in the corner. The guy in the booth slipped off his headphones and slapped hands with Rick. They exchanged a few words before Rick headed to the bar.

The DJ called for Destiny to head to the stage as the song wound down. Rick came back as the DJ told everyone to clap for Misty who was on her knees picking up the stray dollar bills and her bikini top.

"Looks like you got a yardstick up your ass." Rick set a stack of ones on the table and handed me one of the beer bottles. "Need to chill, homie."

I hadn't touched a drop since the dorm, but I took a drink and said I was fine.

"I'm driving. You ain't got shit to worry about."

The DJ came on again. "Destiny, you're up."

The black curtain below the VIP sign swished open and a dark-haired beauty walked out with a business man messing with his belt. The woman adjusted her top that looked like it could pop off and walked on the stage. I pretended not to see her and read the back of my beer bottle.

The new song was slow and classy. Rick nudged my foot and said, "Pretty nice, right?"

If I didn't look I'd be a faggot. She was beautiful, pretty enough to be in porn, moving so slow, her hands running over her body. "Yeah."

"Throw some ones at her."

I took another drink. "I'm exhausted. I'm not getting up."

"It's nice, makes them feel good. You want her to think you think she's ugly?"

She stood at the edge of the stage staring right at me, her hand gliding across her breasts. I picked up the ones. "How much is this?"

"What do you think?"

I didn't care Rick thought I was stupid. I didn't want to look back up like a pervert.

Rick stood with a huff that sounded a lot like Father's. "I got to take a piss. I'll grab some more beers from the bar."

"I need to piss, too."

"You stay here to pay the waitress when she comes. I got a bottle coming." He pointed up at the stage and said, "And stop being so rude."

The girl on stage was dancing directly in front of me. She licked her lips, sucked the tip of her finger and circled each nipple, making them rock hard.

I turned back to my beer and busied myself peeling the paper off the bottle. When I felt the hand on my shoulder, I thought it was Rick's. Then it came up and stroked my cheek, went down my chest. I turned my head to see who it was, but her lips stopped me with a kiss, her hand traveling down my stomach.

Her breath was a peppermint ashtray. All raspy, she said, "I'm Misty. What's your name, baby?"

There was no sign of Rick so I would have to talk for myself.

"I love your body," she said. "Didn't you like my dance?"

"I didn't really watch."

"You can make it up to me. Get a lap dance."

"I'm with a friend."

Her hand slipped under my shirt and stopped at my nipple. She squeezed it hard and said, "Does he dance for you?"

An older lady in a vest dropped off drinks and said, "Would you care to buy the lady a drink?"

I didn't want to be rude. Misty ordered champagne. The waitress left when Rick walked over and said, "Whoa, whoa, whoa. We're waiting on someone."

Misty got up and said, "Whatever, asshole."

Rick sat down and mixed our drinks. "The one time you don't want to be choosy. Did you see her grill? Bitch's been chewing rocks."

"This place was your idea."

Destiny put her top back on, came down from the stage and headed over. "Rick, baby, who's your friend?"

I adjusted my jeans as Rick told her my name. I couldn't believe when she sat down on my lap, wiggling her butt until I was lined up just right.

"I'm Destiny." She leaned back and rested her head on my shoulder so she could look up at me, her hair so soft, sweet vanilla flowing over my arm. She ground into me some more, but a little softer. "Ohhh," she moaned. "You feel nice."

Rick pushed me my drink and said he'd be back. "You two have some fun."

I tried to stop him but he just kept walking. Destiny reached behind and took hold of me through my pants. "Why don't we go back and get to know each other better?"

I took a drink, wondered how I could get up with my dick standing straight up. "I'm okay."

Destiny squeezed harder. "A big boy like you would be so fun." She put her mouth to my ear. "First one's on me."

I pushed my demons aside and said, "Why not."

Destiny waved over the waitress. "We're headed to the back." She looked at me and said, "What do you want to do, champagne? That's okay, right, baby?"

I figured it couldn't cost that much. "No problem."

She spun around and kissed my cheek. "Oh, goody. Get all your stuff out of your pockets and leave your jacket here. Don't want anything getting in the way."

I took the keys out of my pants and put them in my jacket. While I finished my drink, debating whether or not I was making the right decision, Destiny slid her hand down the front of her skirt and moved it in tiny circles. "You going to make me wait all day?"

That decided it. I slipped off my jacket and draped it over the chair. She pulled me toward the black curtain like I was her little dog.

The bouncer held open the curtain for us. Inside the dark room there were three little cubicles, each with a loveseat, everything black. She sat me in the last one, spread my thighs as far apart as they could go. "Relax," she said. She rubbed her hands up and down. "Relax, baby."

I sank into the couch as much as I could, but my dick kept twitching like it was running out of air.

Destiny took off her top and eased her skirt and panties over her hips, dropped them to the floor. With one arm around my neck, she stood on the couch, her body brushing my cheek. She grabbed the back of my head and pushed against me then slid down, her stomach, then tits, everything so warm, so close.

The song was slower than the others had been, or I wouldn't have lasted. Destiny ground back and forth, whispered all kinds of dirty things in my ear, her foul breath the only thing keeping me from blowing my load.

When the song ended, Destiny pressed against me, her tongue flicking my ear. "Want me to keep going?"

There was no possible way I could have said no, even if she'd admitted she was a no-good demon trying to take my soul. Destiny kept dancing, moving on me like we were one. She stopped when the song wound down. I figured the DJ had just grown tired of it and decided to play something new.

Destiny dropped onto her knees. Her mouth pressed against my pants, warm bursts on my thigh. Higher, then higher, nearly to my balls when the song changed.

The next song seemed shorter, but I was so caught up in Destiny I didn't care. When she stood, I asked what was wrong.

Destiny slid on her panties and skirt. "I need to pay the house first. Then I'll be right back."

"Okay."

Even in the dark I could tell she was looking at me like I was an idiot. She said, "I need you to pay me first."

I apologized and got out my money. "How much?"

She didn't sound so sexy when she said, "Four hundred."

I laughed because she had to be joking.

She held out her hand. "My money."

"You barely even danced."

"That was ten dances plus the bottle."

"What bottle?"

"It's at the table. And if you don't believe me about the dances go ask the DJ."

"I will."

"After you pay me."

"Are you serious?"

"Yes, I'm fucking serious." She stuck her head out of the curtain. "Larry! Larry! Get over here."

"You said twenty dollars."

"A dance."

Larry was the bald bouncer. He threw back the curtain, shined his flashlight in my face and said, "What's the problem?"

Destiny crossed her arms. "This asshole says he's not going to pay me."

"Not four hundred dollars She didn't do anything."

"This isn't some whore house," Larry said. "Pay her. Now."

"You're going to judge me?"

"What?"

I got up from the couch and said, "I'm leaving." I had a hundred dollars in my hand. It bounced off her chest.

She picked it up. "Where's the rest?"

Larry stepped over so he blocked the way. "Need me to call the other bouncers?"

I warned him not to.

He did it anyway. Next thing you know, I've got his head in my hands and I'm bashing it into the wall, letting him crumple to the carpet.

Destiny screamed for help and I ran to my table the waitress was wiping down. My jacket wasn't there. I asked her where it was.

She shrugged. "Maybe your friend took it with him."

Destiny ran out from the curtain and screamed. "He robbed me!"

The music was cut and the bouncer by the DJ booth got off his stool. Destiny screamed again. "Call the police! Call 911!"

Rick was nowhere to be seen; the bouncers were running at me. I broke for the door that said Emergency Exit and found myself on the side of the building. The alarm shrieked and I took off running.

It took me ten minutes to find a cab, another ten back to my apartment. The door was wide open. I ran up the steps and prayed Rick was in there.

The mattress was flipped against the wall, my porno magazines still there, my bag of twenty-six hundred dollars missing. All that I had.

I tried Rick's number, but it just kept ringing. I thought of the police but they were out of the question.

For all I knew, I was wanted for murder. I'd been watching those crime shows and knew I must've left a shitload of evidence with Dusty. And it wasn't just me I had to worry about. If I got busted so would Paul, and I swore I couldn't let that happen. Even if those bones just happened to float up one day, who knows what they could find out. And then there was the assault and robbery local cops would start investigating. The bouncer's word against mine, and my word wouldn't mean shit.

I closed the door and put the mattress back, sat down on it. No one at the strip club knew anything about me, except my first name and what I looked like. Only problem was I looked like just about the biggest white guy in town, my scars not helping any.

What I wanted to do was track down Rick and get back my money, but that wasn't likely. I'd never been to his place, no idea where it could be. All I had was a number he'd never answer.

After I changed my clothes, I counted fifty-four bucks in my pocket. I filled my duffle bag with everything I could, and then went to the neighbors and sold everything else for eighty-six more, told them I had to hurry home to Alabama.

Chapter Fifteen

I'd been living in Vegas for fifteen months, keeping a low profile and using Charles as my last name, positive that'd elude Father's search. The only time I ever left my studio apartment was for the gym or work. The bar was off the strip but we got packed, tough guys in fighting shirts that promised pain, girls with tight tops showing off their chests.

It was Tuesday, about one in the morning, and the local rush was over. I'd already restocked so I leaned against the back of the bar and tried to ignore Jules's ass.

Jules was the brunette bartender bent over the counter, giving the guys in front of her a great view, me an even better one. Her shirt was tight enough to see she didn't wear a bra, her leather skirt as short as they made them, no panties as usual.

I tried not to stare, but she wanted me to. It was just looking.

Jules had an incredible body, an ass just waiting to be smacked, a face prettier than any porn star's. And on that subject, I was becoming all-knowing, first time that'd ever happened in my life. The one habit I was having a hard time trying to shake.

If I'm not the Messiah, I'm burning for sure. And if I am Him, I've got some explaining to do. But right then it didn't matter because Jules was slowly swaying back and forth as she laughed at a lame joke.

The guys left with their beers. Jules tossed their tip into the nearly full jar then whirled around with a sly smile. "Caught you again."

I wouldn't turn red. She loved seeing that. "You know I'm here."

Like it was no big deal, she said, "You think about what I said? Amanda is off tomorrow. We'll be in bed all day."

"You really asked her?"

Jules looked at me like I was the crazy one. "She *told* you she wanted you to join us."

"I don't know."

"What, do you think I'm ugly?"

"Are you kidding?"

Jules bit her bottom lip and gave me a look that I'd think about for days. "I know you like my ass. What is it?"

I wasn't sure what it was and didn't want to say what it might've been. I was scared. It was wrong. Dirty. It was her girlfriend. I could damn the entire world. A million things I could've said, but then I got lucky and two women walked up to the bar. I nodded and said, "Customers."

"We'll talk about it." Jules turned around, rested her elbows on the bar, arched her back even more for me. "What can I get for you ladies? First round's on me."

I could only see the one to Jules's right. A tall blonde with strong features, like she could take a punch if she had to. Her top was two red triangles barely holding back her mounds of silicone. I figured she was being funny when she ordered a White Russian with her thick accent.

The one I couldn't see said, "Double cherry Grey Goose sour."

Jules said, "Yummy," and grabbed two glasses from the rack.

The woman had a thin tribal tattoo circling her arm and tits as big as the blonde. Her hair was the darkest black and she still had it short, close to her ear.

There was no way it could've been her but when I said, "Beth," she looked right at me.

"Joshua? Oh my God," she squealed. "It's the Messiah!" She jumped up and reached across the counter, wrapped me in a huge hug that smelled like sugar-coated strawberries. "So good to see you. You work here?"

I broke off the hug. "Until I figure out what I want to do. Not sure if I plan on staying."

She said cool and wrapped her arm around her friend's waist, broke her away from whatever she was saying to Jules. "Sasha, you've got to meet the Messiah."

Jules mouthed 'messiah' and I said, "Long story."

In that same Russian accent, Sasha said, "Get over here and give me a real hug."

Jules smiled at me. "Yeah, take your break, Messiah."

"You sure?"

"You better get over there before I do."

I went around the bar and put out my hand, but Sasha slipped inside and guided it around her back, and onto her ass. Her hug even tighter than Beth's.

Beth scooted in between, all three of us connected. "Nice try, slut."

Sasha slapped Beth's ass then slid back on to her stool. "Can't blame me for trying."

Beth took both drinks from the counter. "Just for that I'm taking yours."

She nodded at the dark booths lining the far wall and told her to bring the next round.

Watching Beth lead the way was something special, her low-cut jeans showing me she felt the same way Jules did about panties. She slid into the tiny booth and handed me the White Russian. Her foot worked its way around my leg. "So how long you been bouncing here?"

The lights were low, but I could see her eyes, same blue as before, but dazzling, a shimmer of glass hiding most of the pain. "I'm a barback."

"Get the fuck out of here!" Beth whacked my shoulder. "I mean, Jesus Christ, look at you. You're a giant."

I didn't want to go into why I couldn't get a Sheriff's card or explain the number of professional MMA fighters on the hiring list. "It's a cool job for now. I don't mind working hard."

Beth's hand settled on my thigh and squeezed. "Oh, it's so good to see you."

"You're one of the only people I'd ever want to see again. Are you just out visiting?"

She shook her head and downed half her drink, licked the drop off her bottom lip. "I ran away the day we had our thing. Been here ever since."

"Wow, you were so young."

"So what about your dad? The whole religion thing?"

I wanted to say I didn't know, but I used my computer for more than just porn. "They got a new building, and from the pictures, it looks like a good deal of believers to go with it." It was a little embarrassing, but I admitted, "They're doing much better without me, but he still swears I'll return."

"Will you?"

It was so easy to smile at her. "And leave this?"

"How about your brother? He ever come out?"

"Out here? No, he left with me, but stayed in Georgia. I'm not sure when he went back home, but he's there now, sitting in my old spot, the right hand of Father."

Beth said, "Not what I meant, but that's cool. Glad he's doing good."

Sasha set three large drinks on the table and rubbed her butt on me until I scooted over. She was soaked in Jasmine, her tit pressed against my arm, her hand on my thigh. "So where you two know each other?"

Beth nuzzled up against me and took a drink while her other hand played with my pocket, her fingers slowly sliding in and out. "We were at the same school for a bit. It's where I learned how to be a lady."

Sasha was in the middle of a drink when she burst out laughing, spraying liquid across the table. "Hope you got your money back."

I'd talked enough about home. "So what about you guys? How do you know each other?"

Beth said, "Work."

It wasn't long before Jules comes over with the third round. It must've been obvious that I was already buzzed because Jules told me not to worry. "I clocked you out."

Sasha said, "Oh goodie." Her hand on my thigh crept up to my crotch and bumped into Beth's.

Beth shook her head. "Hands on the table."

"You're no fun."

"You got a man."

"That fat piece of shit. I just live there, I don't fuck him."

With the hand not protecting my package, Beth flashed her an OK. "Yeah right."

Sasha got close to my ear, her breath so warm, those tits squished on my arm. "I'll rock your fucking world."

Beth grabbed my dick and squeezed. "We've got some unfinished business."

"Fine," Sasha said. "He wouldn't know what to do with me."

Some pretty boy with spiked hair and a soft face came up to the table, a beer in hand. Slurring his words, he said, "Hey, beautiful, can I buy you a beer?"

Sasha held up her drink. "I'm fine, thanks."

"Come on. My friends really want to talk to you."

Sasha didn't bother looking his way. "I said no thanks."

"I think you'll want to talk to my friend. He knows you."

"You got trouble hearing?"

Beth held down my leg and said it was fine.

He set his beer down hard on table, didn't seem to notice it splash on his hand. "Why you so angry? We just wanted you to come back to the hotel. We got money."

Sasha turned on him. "What'd you say?"

"My boy said you know what you're doing, best he ever had."

"Who the hell said this?"

He pointed to the guys gathered by the mirrored column, none of them over two hundred pounds. The one in glasses smiled and waved.

"I don't know that little faggot. Probably confused me with your mother."

Beth laughed and the guy turned red. He looked at me and said, "Should I just talk to you? You her pimp?"

Sasha was out of the booth before I could grab her. She threw her drink in his face. The ice cubes bounced off our table and Beth kept me back, said to trust her.

If the guy could see what was coming, he probably would've covered up or said sorry, but he just stood there and laughed, used his shirt to dab his eyes. "Crazy bitch."

The glass was cocked over Sasha's shoulder like a baseball bat. She swung and let go of it a split second before it shattered on the side of his head.

Beth pushed me out of the booth. "Get her."

The guy dropped to a knee, but Sasha kept kicking him, screaming. "I look like I need a pimp, motherfucker?"

Before I could get there, a fist connected with the side of Sasha's face, knocking her to the ground. The coward who did it never saw me coming. I smashed in the side of his head, sent him to the floor.

The spiky-haired guy was back on his feet, his fists balled, his face all bloody. I told him not to do it, but he did it anyway. My punch landed first, square in his mouth and he joined his friend on the floor.

The other three guys were frozen, all eyes on me. I commanded, "Get these assholes out of here and never come back."

They obeyed.

† † †

It was a Tuesday in June, a hundred and fifteen degrees outside, but nice and cool inside my Lexus that was worth more than all three of my parents' cars combined. This car was only two years old and looked like new, but Jules wanted a new one and was okay with me paying ten thousand up front. She knew I'd be good with taking over payments.

I'd only had the car a week and Beth hadn't seen it yet. The sun had just gone down and my windows had a heavy tint, but I stayed scrunched low in the front seat, completely still so I didn't rub the new work on my back. I'd just finished my fourth session on the piece, proof I'd never be the man Father promised.

The gate to Beth's apartment complex was directly across the street. The place was beautiful, but in our eight months together, I'd only been in it twice.

The gate slid to the side and Beth's ruby red convertible eased out of the driveway. I waited for her to disappear around the corner before I flipped a U-turn and hurried after her, keeping a half block between us. It was my first time following anyone, but I'd watched enough movies to know how it was done.

Beth headed uptown and eventually pulled into the back of a shopping center. I idled across the street, saw her knock on the door of the last building before someone let her in. I drove around to the front of the complex,

178

MASSAGE painted big and red above the pitch-black windows, a flashing neon sign saying they were open.

It was two hours later and Beth's car was right where it had been. I drove around to the front. All the other businesses were closed, only three cars in the lot.

The temperature was still over a hundred, but I was freezing, keeping the AC on for the dozen roses. The flowers were only part of the surprise, the necklace in my pocket hopefully enough to get me laid more than once a week.

I shut off the car and stepped into the night, the heat like a pillow pressed against my face, making it difficult to breathe. I limped across the lot, my calf bruised from all the ankle locks we'd drilled the day before in jiu jitsu. There were no hours on the door, just the Open sign, but it didn't budge when I tried to push it. I put my hand up to knock and heard a loud buzz, the click of the lock being released.

The waiting room was nice, comfy white chairs and a deep red carpet. The big Samoan in the black security shirt sat in front of the only door. He pointed to the small window.

An attractive blonde smiled at me. "I don't think I've seen you before. First time with us?"

Her room was just big enough for her and her stool, no filing cabinets or desks. "Yeah."

"It's a hundred for half hour, one-fifty for the full."

I didn't want to look cheap and a hundred bucks is what I averaged every night on just tips. She took the hundred and nodded toward the door. "Go ahead."

"I need it to be Beth though."

"I don't know names."

"Brunette and real pretty." I pointed at my neck and said, "Hair down to here."

The girl said, "Sure, no problem, brunette."

"But don't tell her it's me, I want to surprise her."

"Go on, we'll take good care of you."

The Samoan stepped off his stool and we were eye to eye. We nodded at each other and he opened the door. On the other side was a hall of white carpet, red curtained doorways on either side.

The receptionist came around the corner and led me down the hall with her hand on my back. She brought it up to my shoulders and felt my arm. "Such big muscles. Are you a Marine? Police officer?"

"They would never take me."

When we get to a side hallway she asked, "Would you like a shower first?"

The showers were open where anyone could see. Even if I didn't have a thing about getting naked in front of others, I couldn't get my tattoo wet. "I already did."

"Great." She pointed to the second door on the right. "After you."

The room had two glowing candles but no overhead light, a long table with a wall mirror beside it. She went to the back of the room and opened the bamboo dresser. "Your shoes and clothes go in here." She pointed at the top shelf. "Extra towels right here."

I said okay and waited for her to close the door before taking off my shirt, being super careful not to let the fabric scrape my back. After I put my shoes and shirt away, I turned my back to the mirror. The thick black outline of a massive Iron Cross, MESSIAH engraved in the metal. It was like looking at someone else's body, the skin would never be blank again. Beth was going to love it. It'd been her idea.

The lady had said clothes in the dresser so I supposed that meant pants, too. I set the necklace box beside the tissue holder then laid face down on the table and covered my butt with a towel. I turned my head to the wall even though my neck still hurt to turn that way. The cut below my left eye was nearly healed, the skin a fading purple, a reminder not to train with Robinson. It's how he fought so it's how he trained. MMA wasn't for the weak.

The door opened and closed, soft footsteps beside me, the tip of a finger trailing up my hamstring. It took all I had not to face her. I wanted to see what she'd say about the latest addition, if she'd see her initials, B.C. at the bottom of the cross. She'd thought of that one, Before Christ, when she'd knelt before me.

The hand rested on my leg, just below the towel. "Oh, that's fresh," the voice said. "It should be covered."

She had brown hair and big tits held back by a string bikini, sheer lingerie over it. I pushed her hand off and turned on my side. "You're not Beth."

The young woman gave my leg a gentle squeeze and said, "She's busy."

Everything clicked. The towel fell to the floor when I got to my feet.

She took a step back and bumped into the wall, her eyes all glassy like Beth's after a long day. "Hey, just relax."

"Show me where she is. Now."

She put her hands up. "You're crazy."

"I'm her boyfriend."

She reached for the white robe hanging on the wall but I grabbed it first and threw it to the floor. "Now!"

She hurried out the room and took me to the hallway with the shower. There was only one door and it was closed. "In there."

I told her don't move then banged on the door.

A voice shouted, "I'm busy!"

I slammed my shoulder into the door. The wood splintered around the lock and I tumbled into the small room, stopped a few feet from the gray desk that Beth was bent over, an Asian man with no shirt standing behind her, holding her hips.

Beth covered her face. "What the fuck?"

It was more than obvious, but I shouted, "What are you doing?"

The man leaned down to his right and pulled out a silver handgun, the barrel so black. "Shut your mouth!"

It was the first time I'd had a gun pointed at me. All my strength now useless.

"You stay right there." He got back behind Beth, his other hand on her neck, smashing her chest against the desk. "In fact, why don't you get on down. Get down on your knees."

I took a step back and said, "I'm leaving."

He cocked the gun and let out a low grunt as he pushed forward.

Beth closed her eyes. "Don't be dumb."

Something cracked the back of my head and I dropped to my knees, my face inches away from her hands holding the edge of the desk, her knuckles white.

She said, "It's work."

† † †

The following New Year's Eve I spent alone with my movies. The one after that I was working Vegas's hottest spot, thanks to Kyle, one of the pro fighters I trained with. There I was, twenty-four-years-old and averaging three hundred dollars a night telling people what they could do and where they could go. A job not too different from Father's, although he would've been happy to make that much in a week.

That night I was stationed on the fifth floor, my back to the wall because I'd seen my share of sucker punches. The elevators were to my right, the glass-enclosed VIP booths fifty feet in front of me, the hallway to the VIP bathrooms behind me. The rest of the level was spread along the balcony to my left, groups of idiots surrounding tiny tables with overpriced bottles, a four-foot high railing the only thing keeping the morons from falling to their death on the dance floor below.

The elevator opened and Kyle stepped out, same black suit and earpiece as me. A mass of flesh herded past us and he disappeared back inside without so much as a nod, neither of us talking since I put his boy, Robinson, in the hospital. I didn't want to hurt him, but Robinson was the one who took the sparring to the next level.

The last ones off the elevator was a group of five girls wearing just enough not to get arrested. The leader of the pack, a chunky blonde in a see-through brown dress with no bra, grabbed hold of her friend's hand and ran toward the balcony, screaming over the throbbing music. "Hell yeah! Vegas, Baby!"

Her friends huddled around her with their backs to the railing, everyone trying to fit in the picture, the massive jumbotron countdown clock high above the dance floor displaying 11:29. They squeezed together and kept their painted smiles until the clock ticked over to the 30-minute mark, massive flames shooting out from the screen in all directions, a wave of heat covering the club, everyone losing their fucking mind.

I wiped off my forehead while the girls made their way to the crowded table where a bachelorette party was in full swing, groups of guys hovering nearby, ready to swoop.

Kyle and the elevator were back. I clenched my fists when the first guy walked out, a stocky Asian guy that looked like Beth's boss. It wasn't him, but he was still out there. Beth had texted me not to do anything stupid, said I should be glad they let me live.

Shayne, the biggest and blackest man I ever knew, filled the doorway that led to the two VIP boxes. His eyebrows were arched, his angry brown eyes on me. Just like Kyle, he wasn't ever going to let Robinson's accident go.

The walls to the VIP boxes were glass so everyone could see who had coughed up thirty thousand for a five-hour party. There were only three couples in the room to the right and none of the women were anything special by Vegas standards. No one who knew anything would ever say that out loud. Lucas, the muscular guy in blue jeans and green button down taking up the couch was not someone to be messed with.

The real party was going on next door in the smaller room packed with people. The main players were the two white guys in suits who looked straight off Wall Street with their Cristal magnums and fancy watches.

Tammy, a tight little brunette, her black outfit barely covering her up, was working that side, taking tips down the front of her leather pants, between her tits, wherever they wanted. She must've seen the way I was looking at her because when she walked by to fill the drink order, she said, "I've got three fucking kids and no man."

The elevator dropped off more drunken idiots screaming, "Fucking Vegasssss!"

Another wave of hot air rolled over the club, morons screaming as 11:40 ignited.

A bleached blonde in a sheer white mini-dress slid close to me. "Hey, Josh. Whatcha know about those guys?"

"Tall one's Michael, the small one is his brother, Benji. Both seem like douchebags."

"Thanks, hon." She straightened my suit and asked, "Got an extra wristband for me?"

"Sorry, Lannie, you know my rule."

She left her hand on my belt buckle. "How come you're no fun?"

If she had a couple hours I could've explained how the world was turning to shit and no one seemed to care. How Father was pointing out the signs of the Second Coming and he was starting to look right. But Lannie was a whore and two hours with her would run a thousand.

Time was money and Lannie was done wasting it on me. In less than a minute she was past Shayne, introduced to the Wall Street guys and sipping from their bottles.

On the other side of the wall Lucas and his friends were hugging the women goodbye. Zach, whose red shoes matched the flames tattooed on his neck, walked them to the elevator, a chubby one in black trying to hold his hand. He loaded them all in the elevator before slipping Kyle some cash.

Zach strolled over and nudged my arm, pointed at the other VIP room. "You know those guys? Seen 'em before?"

"First time."

"I don't like 'em. You know we're cool and won't start no shit, but I'm just saying."

"I hear you."

Zach hung out beside me, his scowl never fading. The elevator opened and Kyle ushered out eight beautiful young women, and pointed them to Zach. One by one, they kissed him on the cheek and wished him a happy new year. The last one hugged him tight and thrust her tongue down his throat, breaking it off so they could continue in the VIP suite.

I hadn't noticed the woman standing on the other side of me, her back to the wall, shoulder to the column. She was scrolling through her phone, her hair hiding her face.

I pointed at the bachelorette party and said, "Aren't you with them?"

She looked where I was pointing. Two guys to each girl, drinking and dancing, groping and grinding, camera phones flashing every second. "Yeah, afraid so."

"Where's the lucky guy?"

"If I had to guess, I'd say doing the same thing, but a whole lot worse."

The clock hit 11:45 and exploded, the shout so loud. She said some stuff I couldn't hear. I think her name was Heather.

A bright light hit me, Shayne with his flashlight. Michael, the older of the brothers, headed my way with Lannie.

Heather said, "What's his problem?"

I'd hurt someone that tried to hurt me, but his friends didn't see it that way. Robinson had kept tagging me with cheap shots, sneaking in elbows even though we weren't supposed to. I slapped a crucifix on him and didn't ease off the gas, snapping his neck, making it so he'd never fight again. It hadn't been premeditated, but one of the fastest times I'd ever cast judgment. Heather didn't need to hear any of that and it was too loud so I said, "Long story."

Lannie led Michael by his hand, his eyes on her ass. I stepped to the side before they got to me, but he still stopped, waited until I met his eyes. Spit flew off Michael's lips when he said, "There a problem?"

"Not at all. Go right ahead."

He said, "Good," and licked the drool from the corner of his mouth, tripped a little on the carpet.

The clock exploded into 11:50. A group of girls squeezed out of the elevator, yelling ten minutes, their hands in the air. The balcony had to be close to capacity, a swarm of people as far as I could see. It was two girls per guy in Lucas's room and more entertaining to watch than when the wives had been with them. The Wall Street room was packed, full of females except for Benji, the younger brother, who was hunched over in the corner. Girls were pointing at him and making a face.

I wasn't supposed to leave my post so I flashed Shayne then the window. He waved me off, but didn't move so I went up to him and said, "That scumbag just pissed in there."

The scumbag in question saw me pointing and puffed out his chest. "What?" He held up his hand.

I thought about breaking his arm, but I needed the job.

Shayne said, "I got this."

I headed back to my post where the bride had her arms wrapped around Heather. Heather eased her off and said, "I'm fine."

If I hadn't known what day it was I wouldn't have understood her when she mumbled, "It's New Years'."

Heather pointed at the table. "So go enjoy it with your friends."

The girl grabbed Heather's hand and knocked the phone out. "Come on."

Heather pushed her away and bent down to get the phone. The bride wasn't listening so I stepped in front of her. "I'm sure she'll be over in a minute."

The bride smiled, wobbled back and forth. "Like my shirt?"

It'd been a plain white shirt, but it looked like they'd used the marker stuffed between her tits to write down different tasks. Kiss the Bartender. Get a Condom from a Guy. Have a Guy Buy You a Shot. Spank Someone – Hard. Number four had three checks beside it. Grab a Bouncer's Dick.

I said how nice but didn't mean it, the words barely out of my mouth when she grabbed hold of mine through my pants.

Heather hit her hand off and said, "Cindy, leave me alone."

Three hundred seconds to go. 11:55 exploded in a burst of fire and everyone screamed. Cindy stumbled back to her group that had moved to the packed balcony. Fist in the air, she shouted, "Whoo-hoo, Vegas!"

I kept my eyes on the crowd because things were amping up, the heat becoming unbearable. Several of women were flashing their tits at the crowd below, guys shooting their hands in for free gropes.

Heather was still beside me. I asked, "You okay?"

"Yeah."

"You don't sound it."

She was staring at Cindy, bent over the railing, an older guy holding her ass, laughing as he posed for the camera. "That's my sister."

"She's just drunk."

There were people everywhere, standing room only in VIP. Shayne wasn't at the door. He was drinking with Tammy and the brothers, surrounded by girls holding up bottles and snapping selfies.

Benji caught me staring. He held up his bottle and said it big and slow so I didn't need to hear. "Happy New Year, motherfucker."

The music pulsed louder and faster. Another blast of heat. 11:56.

Everyone counted down, found a friend or some stranger to cuddle up with. Fire burst every minute, sweat trickling down my brow, my armpits soaked.

At 11:59, the blasts came every ten seconds, bigger each time, a fiery hell. It got down to three and Heather placed her sweaty palm on mine, gave me a soft squeeze.

I hugged Heather as the new year exploded, purple and pink balloons pouring down all around us. "Happy New Year. Hope the next one's better."

She said, "I don't want to spend it by myself."

"You get used to it."

There were too many people in the VIP, no one at the door to stop others from rushing in. Two girls on Lucas's side were pressed against the glass mouthing for help.

Michael had his hand down the back of Tammy's pants, his head back in laughter. She jerked away and turned to face him and the wad of bills he held as an apology.

I was nearly to the door when Tammy put her hands by her side and let Michael stuff the bills down her top. He kept his hand there and pulled her close. She spun away and her top tore off, the bills falling to the ground.

Shayne finally saw what was happening and grabbed Michael from behind, but Benji had the giant bottle in the air. I tried to shout but the words barely left my mouth when the bottle collided with Shayne's head, dropping him, glass and champagne spraying all over the room.

Girls screamed and ran past me, Tammy covered herself in the corner. I flew across the room, felt his face break under my fist. I braced for the blow from Michael, but it never came, Lucas dragging him away by a handful of hair.

I appreciated the help, especially with Shayne unconscious, but Michael's screams scared me. He tried getting to his feet, but they just skittered off the floor with Lucas pulling too fast. Once they were on the balcony, Lucas changed directions, let Michael bounce off his chest and onto the floor.

Michael got up like Lucas was telling him to, but Lucas had the look of someone who already has his mind set. His eyes flashed the same anger that shines in my family.

I shouted, "Stop!" but Lucas was already moving. He stepped in close and blasted Michael sumo style, caving in his chest and knocking him into the railing, the smack sounding like something broke.

I grabbed hold of Michael's wrist and said it'd be okay, but Lucas came barreling into us and knocked him over the railing. Michael's fingers dug into my forearm and he screamed something I couldn't hear as he hung below. I sat back as far as I could, yelled for people to help. It felt like my arm was ripping off but I was more concerned he'd take me with him.

Lucas leaned over, our heads only a foot apart. He reached out and grabbed hold of Michael's right arm. "I got this, Messiah! You did good!"

Lucas had never called me Messiah before, never said more than two words. His grip on the suit sleeve wasn't reassuring.

My armpit felt like it'd tear in two and my grip was slipping, but I couldn't let go.

"I got him!"

I had no choice but to trust Lucas. His lie only lasted two seconds without me, Michael's eyes as wide as his mouth as he plummeted down.

Lucas pulled me back before Michael smashed below and he wrapped me up in a hug and headed for the elevators. Keeping one arm around my neck, our heads connected, Lucas spoke like Father, like he could not be ignored. "You go downstairs and tell them how we both tried saving this poor man's life."

His other hand came back, shoved a wad of bills into my pocket. "That's enough to take a little trip."

"What? Where to?"

"You'll figure it out, just don't come back for a bit." Once I was in the elevator, Lucas turned me around so we were eye to eye. "You're a good man. Do the right thing."

Chapter Sixteen

The New Year's Eve shift had me scheduled from six to six, but the casino cut me loose after I gave my statement. They told me to try and forget about it, it was an accident. They knew it wasn't my fault. It sounded like Lucas had already talked with them.

With traffic all fucked up, it took an hour to make it home. Most of my neighbors in the complex were probably asleep but that wasn't an option for me. Adrenaline dumps seem to take longer for me, my body teetering between fight or flight. And I knew when I did finally sleep, I'd have Michael's wide-mouthed scream haunting my dreams.

Besides the great-paying job, there was nothing keeping me in Vegas. It took thirty minutes to pack all my stuff and load it in the car. I left behind the emptiness and temptation, the illusion of greatness built on all that despair, and made my way west.

It was just past eight when I got off the 101 Freeway at Laurel Canyon. My phone said there were just four Vincent Grangers in the entire county, and only one my age. The address was a corner house with a wooden sign out front. GSG. Granger Security Group.

A shiny black town car sat in the driveway with its trunk up. I parked across the street and watched a guy built like a linebacker in a dark blue suit march out of the house with a black suitcase.

I got out of the car, my body aching from the four-hour drive, my ribs feeling like they'd been cracked with a bat from leaning over the railing. The guy didn't notice me crossing the street, his back to me when he slammed the trunk shut.

"Excuse me, are you Vincent?"

The guy spun around into a combat stance, but played it off with a smile that cut through his neatly trimmed beard. "No, I'm Erik. Vince is the boss."

"Well at least I got the right place."

"At unfortunately the wrong time," a deep voice said from behind me.

The guy was my age, my height, decked out in a slick gray suit, black briefcase in hand. He looked too much like me not to be him, but I still asked, "Vince?"

"Laura said you were on your way seven years ago. What took so long?"

The energy drinks had worn off and I was exhausted, had a hard time coming up with a reason. "Distractions."

"You never thought to call?"

"Didn't know the number."

Vince shook his head. "Well, maybe it was for the best. So what're you running from?"

I tensed up without meaning to, worried I'd made the news. I left out the part about getting punked out of town and just said, "Vegas."

Looking like he knew I was hiding something, Vince said, "Understood."

I wanted to explain I wasn't a coward. I wasn't scared Lucas would beat me in a fight, but I knew how he'd play the game. There'd be vengeance and it'd be brutal. I'd heard enough stories and saw a couple in the club. Lucas was the new kind of Untouchable, no charges ever sticking. But all of that still made me feel like a chickenshit so I pointed at the sign and asked, "What do you do?"

"We specialize in finding missing kids and offer private protection."

"That's impressive."

He held his briefcase out to Erik. "Would you mind?"

Erik set the briefcase on the back seat and waited by the open door. Vince turned to me and said, "I'm happy you're here and I am glad to finally meet you, but I've got a plane to catch."

I stepped aside and asked when he was getting back.

"Honestly have no idea." He looked me over and asked, "You got somewhere to stay?"

"Not yet?"

"There's a kitchen and bedroom you're more than welcome to until I get back."

Lucas had given me $2,400, more than enough to cover the $500 deposit I'd lose for not giving notice on my apartment. "I have money."

"Relax man, I didn't say you didn't. If you want to pay rent, go for it, but it's just a number already worked into my business."

"Sorry, that's really nice of you."

"We keep two cars in the back and someone will be in the office during the week from eight to five. As long as you can keep it down during those hours, everything will be cool."

I promised I'd stay out of the way. Vince looked me dead in the eyes and said, "Don't fuck it up though. I've seen what you can do to a wall."

"You saw that?"

"That and the other one. You've become quite the mini-celebrity." Vince adjusted his shirt sleeve and said, "And one more favor. Give Laura a call. She can use it."

I nodded. "Can you tell me anything about our dad?"

"Not without sounding crazy."

"Crazy as calling yourself the Messiah?"

"Close. Tell you what, help yourself to any of the books in my study. It'll make our next conversation that much better."

I'd never read a whole book in my life and didn't plan on starting now but I said okay.

Even though both his hands were free, Vince kept them to himself, didn't shake my hand or clasp my shoulder before walking to the back seat. He slid inside, but kept hold of the handle, turned toward me. "Make yourself at home. When Erik comes back he'll show you around."

"Thanks, I really appreciate it."

Vince steadied his wolf eyes on me. "I'm going to find him."

"Our dad?"

"I've got a message to pass on from my mother and Laura."

Vince was done talking so Erik closed the door and gave me the firm handshake my own brother wouldn't. He said we'd go over the rules when he returned.

I'd been living rent free for over a year, no word from Vince or sign indicating when he was coming back. Cindy, their gray-haired secretary, was in the office every day, and Erik every other, but we rarely crossed paths thanks to me getting off work at six in the morning.

The beater blue car wasn't supposed to be in the driveway, but this was the second time Jeremy had done it in the week he'd been with us. I never should have offered him a place to crash but I felt awful after asking how things were when I had bumped into him outside the supermarket. For the first time I'd ever seen, Jeremy burst into tears, said his car was doubling as his home since he'd lost his apartment.

Jeremy slept on an air mattress in the study, but when I opened the door he was on the recliner, working on his laptop. Beside him on the TV tray sat a bottle of Smirnoff and the camera I forbid him to use on me. No photographs. No video. Ever.

He'd apologized about releasing the Motherfucking Messiah video, said he only did it to get back at the assholes who'd roughed him up the second I split. When I asked about the other one with the wall, he said he'd forgotten all about that one. It was just something he had done a long time ago to get views. He'd been disappointed it didn't get very many.

The ice tinked in his glass when he held it up. "Morning."

"You just get home?"

He shook his head. "Rolled in around four." He turned the screen so I could see the skinny blonde's cheek pushing out, her lips wrapped around a huge penis. "Just doing some editing."

"I hate to be a dick, but can you move your car. Erik's orders."

He huffed and finished his drink, set it and the laptop on the tray. "Sure thing."

I almost asked if he was okay to drive but that wasn't something you ask when the sun's barely rising. Plus, I didn't want him in a worse mood since I had more to tell him. I dug the folded papers out of my coveralls and held them out. "Here, man."

Instead of grabbing the papers, he said, "What's that?"

I'd been working at the factory for the last nine months and making good money. "An application. Freddie, my manager, said it's a for sure thing if you could even do half the work I can."

Jeremy waved me off. "I got a job."

It felt a little weird being the one in the driver's seat, but I finally felt I was right about something. "How was tonight?"

"Fine. Five fabulous hours of filthy buttfucking." He nodded at the computer. "Plus, all the basics."

"And you made how much?"

"A hundred bucks plus I get a percentage of the net."

"Which means close to nothing."

"How are you going to judge me? You're not even paying to stay here."

"I'm not judging. But I do have the money to rent a place like this if I had to. Vince could come back any day and then we're both out."

Jeremy lowered his eyes.

"Come on, man." I touched his chest with the papers. "You'll make three hundred a shift starting out. Not many opportunities like this."

Jeremy took it. "It's all fucking crumpled."

"It's not a problem. Like I said, Freddie already gave you the thumbs up. That's just a formality. You start tonight."

My normal shift started at eight, but we arrived a half hour early to get Jeremy set up in the system and pick up his own pair of blue coveralls. He didn't seem too excited, even when I reminded him they were free.

Jeremy only had two rules for this shift. Watch what I was doing. Don't touch a fucking thing.

Co-workers like Freddie, a manager who said fuck every other word, made me think Jeremy might fit in. I introduced him to a couple of the guys at shift change and showed him where the breakroom and bathrooms were located, the cameras up above that kept an eye on every inch of the building.

He said it was too fucking cold. I told him he'd get used to it. Twice he leaned against the stack of red barrels and both times I reminded him of Freddie's warning. He said he wasn't doing anything. I said maybe so but I needed him to stop talking for a minute because I had to pay attention to what I was doing.

What I was doing was a direct violation of the OSHA guidelines, but Sanchez and Werneck assured me everyone did it. And Freddie turned a blind eye because it increased productivity.

Thanks to the kinds of chemicals we used, regulations required gloves to always be worn, but mine were off so I could unscrew the caps and get a better grip on the 50-pound barrels. I had four on the hand truck, two red stacked next to two blue, another violation no one observed. The machines were spaced a dozen yards from one another and my job was to stop at every one, top off the hydrochloric acid and water levels. A simple job and decent workout, the way I stayed strong without hitting the gym.

"Those are too heavy for me," Jeremy said, shouting so I could hear him over the machinery.

I carefully stacked the nearly empty blue barrel, didn't attach the safety strap, another ridiculous rule that sucked up time. "You'll get used to it. Same with all the noise." I leaned the hand truck back and pushed forward. "Plus, it's not like you need to move four at once. Freddie will say one at a time until you prove yourself."

Jeremy nodded, stood beside the barrels when I set them down at the next station. While topping off the acid, I reminded him how important it was not to breathe in, especially if he wasn't wearing the respirator that made it too hard to work. "And remember, red barrel, you step in red square."

He said he wasn't stupid, that was the third time I'd told him.

I wanted to ask if he was exaggerating but didn't want to let on I was afraid all my concussions were catching up to me. There was just enough liquid left in the red barrel for one more station. I told him to take it from me, he could do the next one.

The barrel's opening was a few inches below Jeremy's nose, but I didn't warn him, partly because he'd get all defensive and partly because he was the kind of guy that had to learn the hard way.

I took the blue barrel and topped off the water. I started telling Jeremy what this machine did but stopped when I realized he was no longer behind me.

Jeremy stood beside the next station, the tank's lid off because I was cutting corners. I shouted stop because he was starting to tip over the red barrel but standing on the blue square. He didn't hear so I dropped my barrel and ran at Jeremy, liquid spilling from his. I heard the reaction and sprang from my feet, shoving Jeremy away just as the acid erupted. I put up my left hand to block my face, the right one out to brace for the collision.

I got to my knees and crawled a few feet before everything began to burn, a thousand fire ants eating at my left hand and the right side of my face. I ripped off my goggles and swiped at my cheek with my good hand, but only made things worse.

Someone grabbed my arms and pulled me to the side, told me to stop screaming, it'd be okay. Panicked voices yelled about the wash and more hands were on me, dragging me away from the station, holding my arms so I couldn't tear at my face.

Seven days in the hospital, two burnt hands and a face forever disfigured, both butt checks sore from the skin grafts.

But I was a hero. I'd saved my best friend from certain death, kept him from bruising more than his ego.

Jeremy was grateful, brought me home from the hospital in my car because he thought I'd fit better. On a couple of turns, bottles clinked under my seat. I couldn't check to see what they were if I wanted to, my hands useless bundles of gauze for the next three days.

It was a Sunday, a slick red rental car in the driveway. My throat was still a bit raw and it hurt to talk, but I asked if it was someone from the firm. Jeremy shrugged it off and helped me out of the car and to my bedroom. He knew the pain medicine was kicking my ass and it had been impossible to get decent sleep in the hospital.

Once I was in bed, Jeremy asked if there was anything else I needed. The burn was creeping back in the spots where skin had been. I said, "Just my medicine and water if you don't mind."

He came back a minute later, handed me a cup of purple pain juice. "I've been thinking how I could repay you."

I waved him off with my cotton ball of a right hand. "Don't be ridiculous."

He waited for me to finish the medicine and wash it down with the water. "You talk to the hospital yet?"

"About what?"

"The bill."

"I got insurance."

"You better hope it's pretty good because with most you have to pay like twenty percent. And your stay ain't gonna be cheap."

"Worker's comp will cover it."

Jeremy paused. "Well, I'm not so sure they will. Freddie got fired and his replacement kept bringing up all the broken regulations, saying shit like gross negligence, willful misconduct, intentional violations. Everything was recorded."

I had close to twenty grand saved up in my stash, another five thousand in the bank, but all I wanted to do was close my eyes and dream it all away. "I'll manage."

"Yeah, for sure, but it just doesn't seem right your dad is profiting off this and not you. And when will you be able to work again?"

"I'm a quick healer."

"You honestly don't care if he makes money off you and you lose everything? You liked watching those videos?"

Jeremy had played me over a dozen different ones filmed during the past week, Father praising my name. News stations were picking up the story. The security camera clip the police had confiscated had gone viral. Same with the hospital photo of my face, the red palm print on my cheek that looked like I'd been bitch slapped by the hand of God.

I admitted, "I don't like seeing any of it."

"Then let me run all your social media. You'll be fucking huge, get all kinds of sponsors."

"I'm not doing it!"

"Relax, it's not saying you're the Messiah. It'd just be a place for your fans to—"

"I said no! No cameras!"

Jeremy turned and left the room.

I started to ask him to close the door when a figure filled the doorway, my vision too blurry to make out who it was. The figure came closer, revealed himself as the man once known as Father, the almighty Charles Campbell.

He stood in his crisp black three-piece suit, his hand on my shoulder to keep me in bed. His forehead was a maze of wrinkles, but the gray was all gone and he looked revitalized, like he'd been zapped with electricity. His smile was that of a proud papa. Last time I'd seen one that big I'd been impaled by a tree.

I asked what he was doing there, but my mouth was all mushy, the words taking too long.

He bent down and gave me half a hug, so unexpected I couldn't resist. "Oh, Joshua. Thank the Lord you're okay."

It was hard to breathe with him all over me. I pushed him away with my hands, the sting making it so I could hardly think.

"Your mother's sick. Your saving grace is a sign. You need to come home."

I didn't care if it crushed him and kind of hoped it did. "I'm not a believer."

He didn't even flinch, just said that was alright. "You rest up. Everything is going to be okay."

Chapter Seventeen

Jeremy and Paul working together one last time. Funny how stuff works out. The odds of all of us being back together for this one point in life. Our fucking finale.

Paul's perfect face and the empty lobby fill the screen, him and Jeremy the only people in it. I still don't have the volume on because I don't want to hear a word he says. I don't want to think about what he's promising, who he's praising, how there's no better way to unveil our sacred inner-city than with the Second Son of God finally being baptized or buried, depending on the vote. Plus, I've gotten used to the quiet, the soft chant of three-sixteen humming through the glass.

Christ has died, Christ is risen. Christ must die again.

Catchy. I even find myself singing along.

All that's left of the sun is the mountain's golden-rayed halo. I'm sure some would say it's beautiful, but it's of no concern. It's 6:10, twenty minutes before the polls close. The pain's not bad, but I wash down another pill, flip to the private feed streaming from our camera two blocks down, the perfect angle to capture all forty-seven stories. I wave my hand back and forth, pretend the tiny figure on the screen is Lily waving back.

Everyone down there just went nuts, thought the wave was meant for them. I feel foolish for a second, but I'm not the one worshipping the dummy who couldn't reach junior high. I put my hands by my sides although what I want to do is flip all these motherfuckers off. Father would most certainly frown on that type of behavior though. It's too early to cast any kind of judgment.

The light show won't begin until the sun has set, our one shot to ingrain this moment in everyone's mind. Jeremy waited his entire life to produce this masterpiece, a film half the world would witness. I told him I didn't need to see it ahead of time. I trust him completely.

I hadn't noticed it before, but the slightest hint of electric red flame is licking the bottom two stories, the forty-four stories above smoldering black, all except the cross outlined blood red. The closer we get to beginning, the less nervous I am, the more right this all feels. Jeremy's video is all prerecorded, nothing for me to do but watch, but I will fulfill my part of the deal. I'm ready to address the masses. I want the world to hear what I say.

Jeremy originally suggested we sell the special, said we could make millions. I refused and insisted it be free. No one should have to pay to hear another man's thoughts. Plus, now everyone will know this hasn't been altered, condensed, or censored. I can only imagine what version the mainstream would deliver if we'd sold it.

Back on Channel One, Paul is standing inside the front doors, head bowed in prayer. The camera leaves Paul and heads outside. Troy is watching over the red carpet, my special guests seated in front of him.

Jeremy walks past Paul and pans through the crowd, everyone pushing and screaming for their fifteen seconds. Over the earpiece, Jeremy says, "You ready to do this?"

The word flows naturally, no delay with my scrambled brain, speaking straight from the heart. "Absolutely."

"Then turn to channel two," Jeremy said. "Let the show begin."

I do it and turn up the volume, the rumble of the crowd nearly as loud as the assholes chanting three-sixteen. The screen looks the same until the flames start rising, creeping up the front of the building, burning brighter as they ascend, the clear cross sparkling into a blinding white, the pyramid blacked out except for my box.

I radio Troy. "Let's bring everyone up."

"Affirmative."

Jeremy says, "Back to Channel One."

He'd walked to the edge of the lake and turned around so he could capture all seven buildings, each of them with the white diamond cross, the fire flickering behind it. The electricity running through the crosses is nothing compared to the frenzied screams, the mass of flesh, my people chanting Charles 3:16. The people had spoken. I don't need to look at the next channel to know what they're saying.

Not even Jeremy can see channel 3, live results from the vote. There are two columns, a staggering blue yes on the left, a tiny speck of a red no on the right. Ninety-seven percent of the votes siding with Father's most famous passage.

It's pretty much been official since it got under way.

I knew it'd be lopsided, but nothing like this. It makes sense though. It's not just believers who think I must die. Every religion, every liberal, anyone out there whose power I threaten. The country's in chaos, the world a fucking mess, but it's nice to see everyone taking the time to give their figurative two cents at the cost of ninety-nine real ones.

This next screen is where it gets interesting, where I see how much those two cents are adding up to. The fine print is the reason why the dollar amount on the right is so much higher than the one on the left. I learned from Jeremy the smart way to make money: let people pay for something they want. I let people vote as many times as they liked. I figured it'd tip the odds against me since I couldn't picture someone liking me enough to vote over and over. I can't wait for all the haters to see their bill, realize they should've read the fine print, each repeated call costing twice that of the previous.

It's hard for me to even say what the dollar amount is, only partly because it's got all those zeroes. In another fifteen minutes, I'll be one of the richest men in the world. And I've got nothing but a world wishing me dead.

Chapter Eighteen

The lights were low, nothing in the room but a woman in white standing in front of a brown cabinet, a closed door beside her. Everything was fuzzy, no way to know if I was still stuck in the dream I couldn't pull out of, snippets of being surrounded by people, a voice telling everyone, "Make way for the Messiah."

The woman in white had dark brown hair halfway down her back and a snug nurse's outfit with the short skirt, not like the prison getups they wore at county. I figured there must've been a complication, a reaction to the medicine. When I cleared my throat to ask where I was, the woman jumped, fiddled with the black handbag on top of the cabinet before turning around.

The nurse looked so familiar, her face and lips delicate like Jeremy's used to be. "Danielle?" It had to be a dream, but I still asked, "Is this real?"

She eased onto the bed, scooted back so only a thin white sheet separated our hips. "Hey there. I didn't think you'd recognize me."

"Of course I would."

Danielle rested her hand on my bare chest, the warmth radiating from her fingers. "Ahhhh," she said, drawing it out. "You're still so sweet."

The grogginess was wearing off, but I wanted proof it wasn't a dream. "When did you move to LA?"

"Shush, honey, you just rest." Her hand moved from my chest, along the better side of my face, felt the dent in my forehead.

I asked, "What they have me on? We gotta it cut down. It's hard to think."

"It's whatever the doctor prescribed." Danielle's hand went back to my chest. "We all just want you to feel better."

"Well, I feel sick."

"Close your eyes and rest." Her hand inched down my stomach. "Get your strength back."

The upper half of me felt like puking, but my lower half had jumped to attention and was ready for action. Trying not to be obvious, I moved my bundled hand over my belly button, covered the opening where my sweatpants and underwear had risen off my flesh.

Danielle's hand that wasn't on me took hold of my arm and set it by my side. The voice of an angel, the girl always offering help, said, "Don't worry." Her hand kept creeping past my waistband, wrapped around me and gave a tight squeeze. "You've got absolutely nothing in the world to be embarrassed about. Especially not this."

I peeked and watched her pull my sweats down and stand me straight up. Back to believing it had to be a dream but still worried someone would walk in, I nodded at the door behind her.

She started with the slowest stroke, up then down. Up then down. "It's okay," she whispered. "It's locked."

With Beth it had always been straight sex just like the pornos, but never like this. I wanted so much to touch Danielle, but just covered my face because my hands were useless.

Danielle stopped everything. "No. I need to see you."

I slid my hands to each side of my head, pressed them into the pillow. Danielle said that was better and picked up where she'd stopped, asked if it was okay.

This was only the second time she'd laid her hands on me. What she was doing now made up for all the times we'd never touched. I grunted, "Fuck yeah."

She smiled. "Good. I want to watch you cum."

As incredible as it felt slow, I couldn't hold back and pumped my hips, blasted a batch of sperm all over my stomach and the sheet, a moat around her grip.

Danielle shushed me and said, "Just hold still," gave me three slow pumps, milking out the last drops. She cupped my seed, careful not to drop it, and backed up to the foot of the bed.

I was ready to close my eyes, afraid she was going to gobble it down like the skanks in the movies, but instead she wiped it off on a white hand towel. I said, "Holy shit. That was amazing."

She came back with the towel and cleaned me up, dabbed the sheet. "You feel a little better."

"Much."

Danielle slid my sweats back up and gave me one last squeeze. "Good, that's real good." She grabbed her purse and set the hand towel inside, told me to get some rest.

With her hand on the doorknob, she said, "And Joshua, please don't ever tell anyone about this. I could lose everything."

I could barely keep my eyes open, but I promised I wouldn't tell a soul.

✝ ✝ ✝

The creak of the door woke me, my name called out by another voice I hadn't heard in forever. "So, the prodigal son returns."

Paul had grown quite a bit in the seven years since we'd squared off. It was like looking at a younger version of Father, black suit, combed hair, dark eyes. Paul's nose was the exception, still leaning left thanks to Dusty.

There were so many things I could've said, but I kept replaying the words I'd last spat at him.

From the footboard, Paul asked, "Is it okay if I sit down?"

I said sure, propped myself up on my elbows.

Paul sat in the folding chair beside the bed on the wrong side of my face. The way he was sizing me up didn't match his tone of voice. "How you feeling?"

It felt like I was in the Twilight Zone because I was looking out the door at our old hallway, the photo Father took when they pulled the branch out of me hanging on the wall. "Where am I?"

Paul looked shocked. "Really?"

This room was smaller than the one we'd shared as kids but smelled just like it.

"This used to be Father's office."

I wanted to cry, yell, scream, but all that came out was a whimper. "Why am I here?"

Paul waited until I looked at him, another trick from Father's playbook. He'd also adopted the scary stare that said not to test him. "Trust me, I didn't vote for it."

"Why'd Jeremy let him take me? This is kidnapping."

Paul shushed me. "Relax. They both did what they thought was best for you."

I slammed my hand on the mattress, welcomed the pain. "What about my job, my car? Where's all my fucking money?"

"I'm sure Father will take care of everything. Things aren't like before." He looked at me like I was nothing. "We're about to skyrocket, with or without you."

"Then why am I here?"

"Because you're the Messiah, like it or not."

"Don't even start with that shit."

"Then why are you here? How many times do you have to survive near death to see that for some reason you're special?"

I knew he wasn't looking for an answer, but I'd given a lot of thought to that one. "Probably three or four more. Depends on how severe."

He shook his head. "You'll never change."

"Into what? What do you want me to become?"

"This is pointless."

"I don't want to be here."

"It's not all bad," he said like it was a fact. "Now is it?"

My mind flashed a memory of Danielle and the hand job. "You hired her?"

"Would you rather have had someone else?"

"Is he here?"

"Father? No, he's at the church, but will be back soon."

"So what now? What do you want?"

"Will you see Mother?"

"If she wants to see me, she can come in here."

Paul shook his head. "No, she can't."

I'd forgotten Father had said she was sick, probably because I knew better than to believe anything he said.

"How bad is she?"

"Come on." Paul got up, his voice back to the little kid, Mother's precious angel. "Let me help you."

When he reached for my forearm, I pulled it back, told him I could do it myself. I swung my legs off the bed and followed him into the hallway. Instead of turning right, I went left, shouldered open my bedroom door. The bottom bunk remained, the rest of the room transformed into an office. The stack of Stephen King books beside the desk, the green chalkboard with Charles 3:16 written in white.

Paul asked what I was doing.

"You don't mind sharing the room with him?"

He said, "That's Father's room. I've got a place in town."

I didn't bother closing the door. "They let you leave?"

"They knew they could trust me." He grabbed the knob. "That I would never abandon them again."

The hallway smelled like Lysol, just like the offices, old and new. "What about the bakery?"

"That's over."

"You don't miss it?"

We both knew I was stalling. Paul opened the door and said, "I'm meant for much bigger things than that."

The TV was on and facing the bed. My old friend that'd shown me what I was guilty of. All the death, dismemberment, disease.

This was the source of the Lysol, but in here it placed second to a riper smell of decay. It wasn't the geraniums in the window box because there was nothing but dirt and some weeds. The closer I got to the bed, the more obvious what it was. Mother so thin, pale matchsticks poking out of her hospital gown, tubes running in and out of her.

Her eyes never left the screen, some game show with contestants guessing prices, the sound so low I couldn't make anything out. I was nearly to the bed when Paul closed the door, made her look over.

The eyes that had chastised, criticized, and always been filled with despair, were now cloudy. She opened her mouth, her cracked lips making me look away. "Oh, Joshua." She paused for a breath. "I can't believe you came," she said, her voice barely above a whisper.

"You wanted me to?"

The strongest face I'd ever known cracked then crumbled. So much pain in those eyes. "I'm so sorry!"

It didn't make sense, but I came closer, stood beside the bed. I shushed her the way she used to do with me before she got mean. "Everything's okay."

She kept saying sorry over and over, tears flowing down her cheeks. "We left you no choice."

I wondered if apologies were something everyone did before they died. I'd never seen anyone that knew one hundred percent that their life was nearly over. Dusty never saw it coming. Bull knew he was fucked up but was still praying for a miracle. Same with the banker Lucas dropped. But with Mother, there was no denying anything. Even I was smart enough to know there wasn't a cure for her kind of sick.

Doing my best to keep her calm, I got down on my knees, made it so we were practically face-to-face. I must've winced because Mother cried even harder, started choking. I yelled for Paul to help, but all he did was come in and increase her IV drip. There was nothing else we could do he said. He suggested I pray with her.

Mother had it together by the time Paul closed the door behind him. I asked her if she wanted me to say a prayer. "I'll do it if you think it'll help."

"No." Her hand shook when she raised it, purple and black bruises up and down her forearm. She placed her palm on the palm print on my face. "How much did she tell you?"

Danielle?"

"No, but you stay away from that family."

"I'm a grown man."

"I'm sorry." Her hand went back to the bed. She took an extra breath to recover, the simple movement taxing her. "What'd Laura say? How much do you know?"

It seemed like a strange time to start crying, but my tears were falling. "I think I know it all. And then I think I know nothing."

"I never should've allowed it," she said. "It's what I get."

"Is there anything you want to tell me?"

"That I'm sorry I didn't treat you better. That I didn't treat you like my son."

Even if it wasn't completely true, I said, "It's not your fault."

She didn't deny it, almost seemed to lighten upon hearing it. "He would've left me. I gave him you so he wouldn't. I gave him a Messiah to consume our lives." Mother held up her finger while she caught her breath. "Joshua. If you are him. If you are the Messiah, there is only one thing I will ask."

I hated that I'd become a tiny little boy anxious to please, but I said, "Anything," and actually meant it.

She had to look away when she asked, "Can you forgive me?"

"As the Messiah?"

She brought her eyes back. "No, honey, I need to be forgiven by you."

I used my teeth to take off the tape on my left hand and unravel the gauze. I undid my right and took Mother's hand between both of mine, new flesh on old. I said, "I forgive you for any and all wrongdoing. I hold you accountable for nothing."

The smallest smile crept from her lips and she whispered thank you. She locked eyes so I knew she was serious. "And one more thing if you are him, if you are the Messiah."

"If I can I will."

"Send that awful man to hell. Make him burn. For me. For you. For Paulie. For all the people listening to his lies. For all the ones he's going to destroy."

Paul was waiting in the hallway, not five feet from the door. I walked past him and headed for the kitchen. He followed and said, "What'd she say?"

"Anything you didn't overhear wasn't meant for you."

Paul's gasp was as fake as the rest of his act. From the church on the other side of the wall, Father said, "Joshua, please come here."

I had something to say to him and it had nothing to do with him finally saying please. I told Paul to open the laundry door because of my hands. He did what I asked, but when I was walking by he said, "I hope you will pray for her."

The passage was so small I had to walk sideways. I went through the curtain, stepped to the side so Paul could join Father down on his knees in the first pew, a cushion taking all the fun out of it.

Father asked, "Will you pray with us?"

I stayed where I was, hand on the pulpit. "And what are you praying for?"

"Your mother, of course."

What I said was the truth, but I didn't say it to make him happy. "I am praying for her."

Neither of them said a word but I knew what they were thinking. I said, "You think I want her to die. Maybe I'm judging her."

Paul shook his head and Father took a few seconds getting to his feet, said I couldn't be farther from the truth.

"So my praying's no good then? I don't know how to fucking pray?"

Paul eased back in the pew, only a couple feet from where we'd all fought our last night together. Father said something but I wasn't stopping. "Am I not doing it loud enough? Am I not calling Him by the right name?"

Father stood as tall as he could but still came up short. He tried making up for it with his booming voice. "How dare you!"

I did dare because life had thrown every fucked up thing it could at me and I was still going. "If there's a god and he gave one shit about me, she'd be walking right now. And she'd be gathering all her shit and getting the fuck out of here, away from you two!"

Father said, "You can't—"

I shouted, "No!" I couldn't see my eyes but they must've read murder. Both of theirs most definitely read fear. "You wasted her life on a lie, forced your failures on her. Don't ever tell me different."

"My church is not a failure!" Father pulled out his phone, pressed a button and shoved the screen at me. "Nearly three hundred thousand followers, a hundred thousand podcast subscribers, a packed church, and one of Amazon's top books on religion."

"And you can't afford a hospital."

"This is what she wanted!"

I snatched the phone out of his hand and threw it through the stained-glass window, the pain in my palm clearing my mind.

Father chewed his tongue, looked like he'd draw blood. "You're going to pay for that."

"Give me my money and I'll happily pay you and get the hell out of here."

"I don't have your money."

I couldn't speak for a second, had to swallow first. "Then where is it? How could you have left all my money?"

"I didn't know anything about any money."

"You kidnapped me!"

Father became calm. "Are you going to report me? I'm sure Willie will be happy to come arrest me for rescuing my son."

"From what?"

"Yourself."

"I'll call the state police."

"Why don't you sleep on it? You can tell everything to Officer Harrows at tomorrow's service."

"This is bullshit."

"We'll ask him which one has a higher conviction rate: rescuing an injured loved one or destroying religious artifacts."

"I said I'd pay for it."

"They have laws against that now, probably label it a hate crime."

I tried not getting all flustered. "You can't have a hate crime against yourself."

Paul said, "Suicide."

I snapped, "Stay out of this."

Father said, "Stop it! The point is, you're not going to say a word. You're also not about to abandon your mother."

I wasn't going to win the battle, especially when I couldn't think straight. "I'll stay as long as she needs me, but not a day longer in this house. It's not good for anyone."

Prepared as always, Father didn't miss a beat. "Paul's already placed an air mattress in the barn. We'll talk about an apartment depending on how things go."

"What does that mean?"

"It means we need to see if you're going to play ball."

"I want my car. And I want my money."

"Your car will be here in two days. If you want money, you're going to have to earn it."

† † †

It was six weeks later, five weeks since Mother died gasping for air. I was in the small sauna of a sacristy. The Church of His Son was on the outskirts of town and had to be over a hundred years old, well before air conditioning was invented.

Danielle raised the narrow window, but the outside air did nothing to keep the sweat from rolling down my forehead. She grabbed a stack of pamphlets from the counter and waved me down, dabbed the drops with her handkerchief. "You're going to be brilliant."

"I just don't want to embarrass you." I tried not to lie to Danielle and added, "Or myself."

"Well, I'll be in here, so no worries there."

Even if Father hadn't forbidden me from being seen with any females, Danielle had said she wouldn't let anyone catch her inside the building. It was a small town and rumors spread quick.

I figured it was her mother she was worried about, the reason Danielle only stayed a couple of nights in the barn with me.

I kissed her forehead and thanked her for encouraging me to do this.

She smiled and said, "Of course. I wouldn't miss it."

I know I already asked her a few times but the cloak was super bulky and kept shifting on me. "Do I look okay?"

Danielle pinched the heavy black material from each of my shoulders, lifted it up and let it fall. She smoothed out the front and told me to spin around, her hand running down the flames embroidered on the back. "Honestly?"

"Of course."

"It's kind of badass. It's almost like you're the leader of a motorcycle gang."

I thanked Danielle and asked her to turn on the computer monitor so I wouldn't get my sweaty prints on it.

Some of what Father and Paul had been preaching had filtered through the heavy curtains separating our room from their stage but I hadn't been paying attention. With the TV on I saw we had less than five minutes before what Father was promoting as my glorious return. I was staring at the crowd, every seat taken, a line of people standing on either side of the outside aisles. Four hundred plus.

Danielle jammed her finger at the bottom of the screen. "Holy shit, Josh. Look how many viewers."

All those zeros couldn't be real, but I guessed Father hadn't been exaggerating. My voice cracked when I said, "Let's see how many come back next week."

Danielle's eyes were glued to the ticking number. "But even if it were a quarter..." Her voice trailed off.

The camera shifted from the crowd to Father behind the pulpit, a metal monster with the flaming Second Son embossed on the front, one of Jeremy's newly-installed floor lights sparkling off it.

Danielle said, "Almost time. You ready?"

I wasn't so sure, but pretended I was. She kissed my forehead and wished me good luck. I said thanks and took my place in front of the curtain, rolled the satin between my fingers, wondered where Beth was. If maybe she was watching on TV.

Father had always read the sermon, saving the readings for Paul and trusted readers. But today was special. He said, "This is a historic mass, the glorious return of the Messiah."

The thundering applause rippled the curtain. Father waited until it died down. "And today he will read a section from his first audiobook single 'The Descent into Darkness.' Ladies and gentlemen, I give you Joshua, the Second Son."

Danielle patted my back and said, "That's your cue."

I walked past the curtain careful not to mess up my hair. Jeremy was crouched at the edge of the hallway, all professional in his black suit, his camera zooming in for my close up, getting the palm side. Father instructed to always take advantage of stigmata.

I hadn't been happy Jeremy was working for the church, but he'd said he didn't really have a choice, it was the best move for both of us, really the only one we had. And even though I didn't totally believe him about my stash, I chalked it up to another misfortune, the shitty luck of the Messiah.

Instead of knocking Jeremy over with a knee, I smiled at him and glided on stage, another blast of cheers, a wave of people rising in my peripheral. While I took my place, Father got on the mic about putting away cell phones, threatened ushers would confiscate all electronic devices. He reminded them where they could buy the recording.

My hearing grew fuzzy and I feared the worst, but focused on my breathing, kept my eyes on the prize, the two pieces of tape stuck to the carpet directly in front of the cross.

I faced the cross, made sure each strip of tape was barely visible past my big toe, then raised my arms in a T, keeping my back to the congregation.

The overhead lights flicked off and one of Jeremy's switched on, my arms casting the perfect silhouette.

A red flickering light outlined the blackened cross and the speakers crackled. My prerecorded voice boomed from above, behind, all around. "This is a reading from *The Lost Gospels*."

As much as I hated my voice, I'd let Jeremy convince me it was perfect, the right bit of roughness for the dark tale. I'd been doing daily recordings for Paul, mainly stupid spiritual sayings and other things that'd been said much better by thousands of others. But they needed content and it was already written, so all I had to do was show up and record. We were down to it only taking five or six takes per minute-long segment, Jeremy insisting we could lower the number.

This recording described Jesus's descent into hell. I held my arms perfectly still, kept my invisible crown of thorns reaching for Heaven, my butt and legs unclenched so I wouldn't faint and fall flat on my face. There was too much riding on this. If I could do my bit I'd be getting my own furnished apartment.

They hadn't let me hear the final cut because they knew I'd want changes, maybe scrap the whole thing, but what I was hearing sounded pretty good, especially with the sound effects and music Jeremy laid underneath.

"A demon twice his size, landed before Jesus, knocking him to his knees." My voice deepened dark as night just like Jeremy taught me. "It said, 'I am Astaroth. You do well to bow before me.'"

While in the story, Jesus said never and rose to his feet, I was thinking how most men would've already lowered their arms or been shaking like a leaf. I'd been practicing though and was determined to show everyone that I was not most men.

"Astaroth grabbed Jesus by his throat and pinned him to the rocks. The grand demon came closer and snorted a spray of pus and bile, pestilence and disease. His voice was a river of razorblades and he had the breath of a thousand dead babies. 'Are you lost, little boy?'

"Jesus did not tremble, he did not shake. He remembered who he was and wiped the filth from his face. He looked the demon in the squirming balls of maggots it had for eyes. 'I have come for my brothers. For those that should not be here.'"

My shoulders began to tingle so I focused on my breath and the story. "The demon laughed and took Jesus like a rag doll, rushed him to the center of hell, the lake of fire licking their feet. In front of them was the man Jesus had searched for, a man he'd walked the earth with.

"Jesus shouted, 'James, you should not be here.'

"But James was, suspended in the air, dangling by his intestines, the heat melting his skin, demons on either side.

"James screamed, 'No, I believe,' but it was too late, the demons too strong.

"The demons dug their talons deep in the flesh of James's forearms and pinned his arms back. And when the demons reached toward his eyes, James yelled, 'No, no, for I will not be able to see.'

"The demons laughed as they plucked out the eyes that could not see and ripped off the ears which could not hear."

Both my shoulders were burning, the slightest shake as I drew in strength. I'd recorded the story so many times, I knew there couldn't be much left.

"Astaroth tired of the show and flew them away, Jesus watching as James's intestines slowly stretched, inch by inch for all eternity, praying for the drop that would never come, the end that would never be."

Father stood and walked toward the pulpit. Under his breath, he whispered, "Great job, son."

I didn't want his praise and hated how good it felt. I lowered my arms when Father said, "This is the word of the Lord. Bow your heads and pray."

Father said, "Thank you, brothers and sisters, for joining us on this glorious day and praising His name. As we can see from today's reading, it is not enough to attend church and say we believe. James was a good man, a friend of Jesus, almost like a brother. But he also had his doubts and that is all it takes."

He cleared his throat which reminded me I'd missed my cue to leave. I headed for the sacristy and stepped past the curtain as Father continued his talk.

"For those of you who have enjoyed the story and would like to hear the rest of the tale, you can now purchase the audiobook on all retail sites and we'll soon have a version up on YouTube."

Danielle jumped into my arms, wrapped herself around me. "You were incredible!" She pointed at the monitor and said, "Look."

The congregation was standing although Father hadn't asked them to. Danielle said, "The views have nearly doubled."

I still couldn't believe I had made it. To think all those people were cheering for me was too much. I pulled up the bottom of my cloak and asked Danielle to help me disrobe and grab me some water.

The ceremony ended five minutes later and a few minutes after that Father parted the curtain, led in an older white guy in a tan suit, a smile too perfect to trust. Father put his arm around the man's shoulder and walked him in front of me, Danielle by my side.

I knew the guy was important because Jeremy was right there, capturing the whole handshaking, and Father never got that close to anyone.

Father turned to Danielle. "Please wait outside for us."

Danielle looked to me and I was thinking of what to say when Jeremy chimed in. "Yeah, you better go check on Mom."

Danielle made a point to bump his shoulder on her way out. "You're such a jerk."

Father, the king of redirection, raised his voice and clapped my back. "Joshua, it is my absolute pleasure to introduce you to the honorable Senator Burkhart. Senator Burkhart, this is my son, Joshua Campbell, the Messiah."

The old man squeezed my hand harder than I'd expected. "I'm honored to meet you, Joshua. I believe you just might be the man who saves the world."

Father probably knew I couldn't respond so he said, "No just might about it. Joshua is the Second Coming. He'll help you achieve every one of your goals. In fact, why don't you let Joshua and Jeremy take you out tonight. You can see how we treat our friends this far south. They'll pick you up from your hotel at seven."

Chapter Nineteen

If the Church of His Son had been a publicly traded organization, all of Wall Street would have been buying. Our trajectory was ridiculous, the increase in social media followers and book sales over the last three months climbing a steep slope. Every Sunday service was packed to capacity, and the ones that I participated in guaranteed our meeting hall would be filled with the spillover watching on a big screen.

Jeremy had been the one to suggest the TVs, both the massive one in the meeting hall and the even bigger one hanging above the cross. He said all the hip Los Angeles churches were doing it, turning their services into multimedia events, pumping up congregations and putting them in the mood to give.

The screen was black, difficult to see from my chair on the side that used to be Paul's, unless I leaned forward. Father stood behind the pulpit, winding down his sermon. He'd been preaching the importance of vengeance, why everyone should fear sinning and be prepared to pay the consequences. The Messiah was meant to cast judgment, knock down evil doers, and dispatch them to hell.

The thundering applause told me that Father was finished. The blank screen blinked to life, a loud crack like lightning as the title flashed across the screen: *Struck by the Hand of God.*

The music kicked in, heavier than anything I'd heard in church. The footage was eight years old, my giant head taking up the entire frame, a close up of my face before most of the damage. Sweat flew from my forehead, my eyes narrowed, everything twisted into a scary mask of rage. The camera pulled back and showed me punching the canvas heavy bag without a shirt on, a deep purple blossom where the branch had torn through.

The video had been before any real training and my form was embarrassing, but still probably better than any of the weaklings watching. And how I wished I could move like that again. The video slowed and zoomed in close for each thud, my bloody knuckles leaving their mark with every strike. The film sped up with the music to match, the black and red strobe effect added between each blast making me wonder if anyone watching might have a seizure and stroke out.

On the next punch, the image on the screen froze then tore in two, each half dissolving to reveal me a year later standing in the dorm's hallway, paused so no one could see me swaying. The music built as the video went to the bully's face, the rage turning his face into a demon's. The standoff came to life, my fist connecting with his mouth, knocking him off his feet, blood and spit flying slow motion.

The next scene I'd yet to watch, but Jeremy assured me it had come out great. We'd discussed if we should share the clip, but Father said it was the clearest message we could send. Case was closed, he told us, no need to worry about any lawsuits.

It had happened only three weeks before, Paul and I exiting the back of the church after meeting with Father. Jeremy had been filming all day; this clip starting with the opening of that door. Jeremy had been in front of us to the left, capturing Paul's smile and my scowl as we headed for our cars. The camera jerked to the left and caught a man in blue jeans and a white T-shirt burst out of the bushes and sprint for us, something that looked like a machete in his right hand.

Paul stood his ground and held out his hand, commanded the man to stop. His words had no effect, but I was already rushing the guy. The guy looked confused by my attack and took too long raising the blade, my fist cracking his jaw, snapping back his head, laying him out on the concrete. A dark red puddle formed his halo.

The music faded as the screen turned black, flaming red letters materializing on the screen, *Fear the Hand of God*, burning bright before the video ended with another crack of lightning.

The congregation exploded with applause. Father quieted them by raising his arms. "This, this is the strength that we need. We are not weaklings that pray for protection. We take what is ours and defend it with our lives. We strike first. We do not turn our cheek. We hit back a hundred times harder. Mercy is not in our vocabulary. Only retribution."

A chorus of amens and hallelujahs filled the room. Father said, "On this most powerful occasion the Messiah and I will bless two of the strongest men we know. The men who will help turn this world into the wonderful place it was destined to be.

"Now I ask all of you to bow your heads and offer your prayers to these brave souls. Paul Campbell and Senator Burkhart, please rise and step forward. Take your places before the Lord Almighty and his most benevolent Son.

I turned my head to watch Paul get up from the first pew on the left, the senator from the one on the right. Every seat in the house was taken, people lining the walls, a camera crew in each aisle and one in the balcony— the Christian Network granted special access for their generous support.

Paul, dressed in his brand new black suit, stood tall at the bottom of the sanctuary's steps, his nose once again straight thanks to his plastic surgeon roommate, Teddy. The senator had on a blue suit, red tie, white shirt, the colors of the country he was determined to save.

The senator stepped into the aisle but leaned back in and kissed his wife on the cheek, waved to the three kids sitting on the other side of her.

Father stood at the edge of the sanctuary and waved the men forward, instructed them to kneel on the first step. They obeyed, hands in prayer against their chests, my cue to stand.

The nerves were still there but just barely. More like a sense of excitement, all those eyes looking up to me instead of down on. The likes, the shares, the girls throwing themselves at me. A free one-bedroom apartment, monthly stipend, and all the fringe benefits for simply showing up and filming some messages. Not such a bad gig.

I rarely faced the crowd, preferring to keep the palm print to the wall. When I walked down the steps, the congregation oohed and gasped. At the bottom of the stairs, I turned back to the cross, stepped between Paul and the senator, held my arms out like a T.

Father laid his left hand on Paul's shoulder and said, "All of you know Paul, my second son, the boy born to watch over his brother and document his road to redemption. His dedication and sacrifice are unequal to anyone and he will forever stand at the left hand of the Father."

Father's right hand rested on the senator's shoulder. "Not all of you know this great man, the symbol of strength who represents our wonderful state in the Senate. I have had many conversations with Senator Burkhart about his vision and strategies, and I can assure you they are consistent with the Church of His Son. This man is a believer if ever I saw one."

Hearing Father blatantly lie wasn't as difficult as I thought it would be. Jeremy had given Father the photos. The ones from the night Jeremy and I had taken the good senator to Myrtle Beach where he had a stripper's titty in his mouth, four of his fingers inside her. The senator was so drunk he had no idea what was going on, but I couldn't fathom how Father forgave him.

Father went on and on about what an incredible job Burkhart was doing, what he'd done for the military contractors in our state, strengthening our country by doing so. He brought up the bills Burkhart drafted, thanked him for the funds he'd raised to buy our church, and when it seemed like he couldn't praise him anymore, Father said, "And it is with the utmost pleasure that I am honored to announce that Senator Burkhart is running for, and will become, the next President of the United States."

The church roared with their approval. I couldn't see with my back turned toward them, but it sounded like the four of us upfront were the only ones not clapping.

"Joshua, please place one hand on each of these fine men."

I could've kept my hands up another ten minutes, but I did what he said, Paul flinching at my touch. Father asked me to join him in prayer, so I played along, mouthed the magic words that transformed Paul and the senator into the two most blessed individuals in the world.

✝✝✝

Jeremy arrived at my apartment with his film crew a little after lunch. He told the guys to set up in the living room, we'd use the couch for the main scene, record there while we had the natural light. He turned to me and said, "Nice place. Care to show me the rest?"

"Yeah man, of course."

"I wasn't sure, you know, seeing as how I haven't been invited over before."

I said, "You know how it is," and led him down the hallway, pointed out the bedroom.

"I sure do." He peeked his head in and said, "Damn, black satin sheets. Look at you, Mr. Fancy Pants."

I almost said I didn't pick them but didn't want to bring up his sister.

Jeremy walked around the room, studied the bed from every angle. "We can shoot one scene with you sitting on the edge facing that way. Yeah, this will be excellent."

"Think we'll be able to get it all done today?"

"We have to if we want to get this thing out in time for Christmas."

I asked Jeremy if he had my lines. He walked into the bathroom and said, "Yeah, but most of it is more like talking points. You're gonna have to ad lib a bit."

"You sure that's smart?"

Jeremy craned his neck to look at the mirror. "Sure thing, we'll clean it all up, make it sound awesome." He asked me to stand in front of the sink, my upper body and face filling the mirror. "This is great," he said. "I've got the perfect scene for here."

Having my own documentary was kind of cool and helped bury my initial reaction of wanting to hide my face. Father said it was time to show the world who I really was, scars and all.

Jeremy went back to the bedroom and said, "You mind getting the guys something to drink? I'll be right there, just want to frame this thing."

I got four bottled waters from the kitchen and handed them out. Jeremy returned from the bedroom, double-checked everyone's equipment, and repositioned the camera three times before finally saying he was ready.

I'd been told to wear whatever I wanted, but I felt kind of foolish in basketball shorts and a boring black T-shirt. "Should I change?"

"Nah man, you're straight. Let's do this."

I said I was game and Jeremy set the scene, told me we were going to start with my history, retrace my footsteps.

After a handful of false starts on my end, I got into a rhythm and nailed three sentences in a row, telling them the city and state I grew up in. I had just begun describing the first church inside our garage when the front door opened and killed the recording. Danielle stood frozen in the doorway, key in hand.

I said, "Hey hon, wasn't expecting you until tomorrow."

"What is this? Why is he here?"

Jeremy said, "Nice to see you, too."

I didn't get why she was so upset. "What's wrong? I told you we were planning on doing a documentary."

Danielle stepped inside and slammed the door shut behind her. "You never said anything about filming here."

I knew I had, most likely while she was scrolling through her phone and didn't really hear me. "Well, this is where we decided it'd be best."

"We?"

Having all those eyes on me made it harder to keep my voice down. "What's the big fucking deal? This is my apartment."

Danielle *humphed* and threw her key, nailed me in the chest.

She was halfway out the door when Jeremy said, "Thanks, now would you mind closing that behind you?"

Danielle spun around and launched her purse at his head, shit flying everywhere. "Get the fuck out of here!"

I jumped off the couch and got in front of her, not sure of how Jeremy might react. "Danni, what are you doing?"

The purse lay a foot in front of Jeremy. He kicked it away and laughed. "Holy shit. Nice to see you're off your meds again."

I turned toward Jeremy and said, "Come on."

Danielle ducked under my arm and kicked out the leg of the camera's tripod. Darren, the sound guy, caught it a split second before it smashed on the floor.

Jeremy was no longer laughing. "You stupid cunt! You got any idea how much that cost?"

I stood between them, Danielle's face bright red, an anger I'd never witnessed. She screamed, "You didn't fucking pay for it! And I wouldn't give one shit if you had."

"That's because you're a psycho bitch."

Danielle leapt at Jeremy, her slap only missing because I held her back.

I shouted, "That's enough!"

Jeremy said, "Yeah, get your shit and get out."

Danielle was a hair away from hysterical. "Me? Me! I'm not going anywhere."

I took hold of Danielle's shoulders and led her down the hallway. Hating that I sounded like Father, I said, "Get in the bedroom. Now!"

She tried saying no but I didn't care and closed her in. From the end of the hallway, Jeremy said, "She's got to go. We can't film with her here."

"Dude, we're gonna have to do it another day."

Through the door, Danielle shouted, "Not here!"

"Nice, real fucking nice," Jeremy said. "Charles is going to be pissed."

Only because I didn't think he'd repeat it, I said, "Fuck Charles."

"Nah man, I get fucked enough by his son." Jeremy turned his back and told the guys to grab the gear.

"What do you want me to do?"

He folded the tripod. "The thing is, it doesn't matter what I want. Doesn't matter what anyone wants. It's what you want. You're the Messiah."

I closed the door behind them and went into my bedroom. The pillows and sheets were on the floor, clothes sticking out of the dresser drawers, Danielle bent over, looking under the bed.

"What are you doing? You think he dropped something?"

She stood holding a pillow in hand and glared at me. "Were you with him the entire time?"

"What? You looking for drugs?"

The pillow went flying across the room, knocked the only photo of us off the wall. "No. Forget it."

I was thinking of my stash when I asked, "You think he'd steal from us?"

She hesitated. "I just don't want him over here. How hard is that to understand?"

Her yelling only made me louder. "You're the one always telling me to capitalize on this. What do you think I'm trying to do?"

"What are they paying you? Do you even know? Was it even discussed?"

"For the documentary?"

"Yeah."

I didn't know any details. "That's just one of the things."

"What else? The audiobook? Tell me how much you've been paid for that."

"You see how big we're getting. Father says as soon as we're turning a profit everyone will feast from the table."

"Including the dogs."

I didn't get what she meant.

"You know they pay Jeremy more than they do you."

"They don't pay his rent. Plus, he's the one doing most of the work. All I gotta do is repeat some words."

"You're their low-paid puppet."

If she hadn't said it so sadly I would've snapped and yelled something I'd regret later. I kept my mouth shut and went to the kitchen, opened the cabinet and stood there thinking that Danielle was just telling the truth, pointing out what I needed to admit to myself.

I grabbed a glass and filled it with water, turned to see Danielle sit at the table, wiping away her tears. She said, "I'm sorry. Can you sit down?"

I hated seeing her sad, but my blood was boiling, mad at her, but mostly at myself. I gripped the counter to still my hand and drank half the water. "I'm good."

"Please." Danielle laid her arm across the table, offered her hand. "We need to talk."

I drank the rest of the water and set the glass down. I hadn't officially been dumped before, but this was how they showed it on TV. "Talk or yell?"

"Talk. I said I was sorry."

I left the glass on the counter and took my seat, held her hand when she motioned for it. Her palm was hot and sweaty, her face flushed. "So what's going on? Tuesday you were all pissed off, too."

"I know. I haven't been sleeping much and I feel like crap."

There were dark circles under her eyes, but I'd thought it was from crying. Since Mother, the idea of illness had a new hold on me. "Are you sick?"

She shook her head. "Just stressed out, been doing a lot of thinking."

I didn't want to ask but had to. "About what?"

"Us mainly"

"Good thinking or bad?"

She turned her hand to hold mine with both of hers. "I need to ask you some questions. And I need the truth."

"Of course. I've got nothing to hide."

"When you go out with my brother do you talk to other women?"

"Yeah, but only to be nice."

"And what if they're nice back? What then?"

"Where's this coming from? Did Jeremy say something?"

"Do you ever kiss them or get their phone number?"

"Of course not. I mean, there's been a couple times where they've given me numbers but I just throw them away."

"Right."

I asked her to look at me. "I haven't lied to you. Ever." When she didn't respond, I asked, "Do you believe me?"

She squeezed my hand and nodded, the tears flowing.

"What is it then? What did I do?"

Danielle raised her chin. "You got me pregnant."

Everything stopped, nothing but her fragile face in front of me. Not at all sure about what answer I wanted to hear, I asked, "Are you being serious?"

Her smile was weak, but at least she was trying to look happy. "You're going to be a daddy."

We hadn't ever discussed what would happen if she got pregnant because I assumed she was on birth control. "The doctor told you?"

She watched me closely and said she took the test twice and both came back positive. "I'm sure."

"So what does that mean? What do we do?"

"Well, I guess it's up to you. What do you want to do, Josh? It's your decision, too."

My mouth had dried up. I ran my tongue around it while I searched for the answer. "Honestly?"

Danielle asked, "Do you want me?"

"More than anything."

"Do you want to be a father?"

"I hadn't really thought about it."

"Well, we need to know soon. Do you want to be a father?"

"Yeah, but I've got no idea how."

"And will you ever leave us?"

"No, of course not."

Danielle smiled and sat up straight. "That's what I want, too."

Neither of us had said it before, but I squeezed her hand and said, "I love you."

She held up her free hand and said, "But I won't have the baby here. I can't."

"I'll have them get us a bigger place. They can afford it."

"No, Josh. Not here. Not in South Carolina. Not in this church."

"What are you talking about?"

"Your father scares me. Your brother scares me."

"It's just part of the act."

"This church scares me. The things they have you say scare me."

"Father says some sinners need to be scared."

"I know what he says, but that doesn't make any of it true."

"But everything is building up. We're about to explode."

"Is that what's important to you? To be famous?"

I didn't answer quickly so it seemed like I was considering it. "No."

"You sure about that?"

The answer was easy. "You are. You and the baby."

"Then we have to leave. And we can't tell anyone."

"What about your mother?"

Danielle got up and hugged me tight. "She'll understand."

✝ ✝ ✝

It was three weeks later and I was in the living room holding the last cardboard box while Danielle double-checked we weren't forgetting anything. Someone knocked on the front door, but before I got there, Jeremy had already let himself in.

It didn't look like he noticed all my personal stuff was gone, just the provided furniture remaining, but he said, "Wow, you guys are fast."

I pretended like everything was normal. "Hey, what's up?"

"Not much on my end seeing how you called off. Paul had a lot planned for today, too."

"Yep, had stuff to do." I walked past him in the hopes he would follow me outside. "Just finishing up."

Sounding way too happy, Jeremy said, "There she is."

"Get out," Danielle said from the doorway. "Get out now!"

"Nice of you to help him move. I hope you let him do all the heavy stuff."

Danielle looked to me. I shook my head.

Jeremy turned to me, his eyes all friendly. "You should've told me you were moving. I would've been happy to help."

Danielle said, "What do you want?"

"Damn, you weren't even going to say goodbye. You're cold."

I said, "What are you doing here?"

"That's what I wanted to ask you guys. Charles didn't mention anything about a relocation."

I said, "That's because he doesn't know. Paul either."

"So you're splitting just like that, weren't going to say a word?"

Jeremy was talking to me, but Danielle said, "Just leave. Don't mess this up."

He spun on her. "Me? Me mess things up." Jeremy's laugh was cruel. "That's all you've done from the start."

"Fuck you, Jeremy. I'm a grown woman, right? I can be with whoever the hell I want. Those were your exact words."

Jeremy's smile was big and scary. "Yeah, those were my exact words, in fact I remember what I was talking about. Do you?"

She pleaded, "Stop it."

Jeremy looked like he didn't want to, like he was just itching to blurt it out. "You brought it up."

I got between them and said that was enough, walked Jeremy to the door.

From the porch he shouted, "Can't wait to hear you explain this to Yuri."

I turned to Danielle. "Who's Yuri?"

She ran past me and flew out the door. Jeremy was walking across the small patch of grass when Danielle caught up to him, slamming her hands into his low back, knocking him flat.

Jeremy covered up as he got to his feet and I pulled Danielle to the sidewalk. I said, "What are you thinking? You can't—"

Danielle threw my hand off her, stepped up to Jeremy with just a foot between them. "Why? Why couldn't you just let us go?"

One of Father's town cars had backed into the driveway boxing in my car. The tint was so dark I didn't notice anyone sitting in the front until the passenger door opened. The guy looked about ten years older than me, black hair and a big nose, and not much of a physique.

He looked at Danielle like he hated her. "Who the fuck is this freak?"

I had no idea who he was, but I'd seen all the stares, I'd read all the comments. It didn't matter if Paul 2:41 stated that anyone who took my name in vain or issued any derogatory remark about me or my likeness would burn in hell. There were people who absolutely hated me and this guy was probably one. He clenched his fists and kept shouting, only got louder. "This your boss? This the old bitch you been taking care of?"

Danielle lunged at Jeremy, her nails raking his face. "Asshole!" She brought her arm back but I caught it before she could fire. She screamed at me to let it go, stopped when the guy's fist slammed into the back of her head and dropped her to her knees.

Jeremy shoved the guy back. "What the fuck, Yuri?"

I laid Danielle on the ground so she wouldn't move her head. Neither one of them noticed me get up.

Yuri held his fists by his face, the knuckle on his right one bleeding. He asked Jeremy, "What, you fucking her, too?"

Jeremy was all talk, not about to engage. I had the slightest hesitation because it was a cheap shot, but then I cast my judgment, the fist of God connecting with the side of Yuri's fat face, the crunch of his jaw giving way. Both feet left the ground and he came down hard on the concrete, his body stiff as a board, his right sneaker twitching faster than a dog's tail before dinner.

Jeremy knelt beside Danielle, asked her if she was okay. I kicked him away and said, "Get that piece of shit out of here and stay the fuck out of our lives."

He backed off but remained on a knee. "Is she alright?"

Danielle sat up, one hand over her stomach. "I think so."

"I'm sorry." Jeremy had tears rolling down the side of his face. "I fucked up. I'm sorry."

Danielle said, "What did you expect?"

"I wasn't thinking. I just…" Jeremy shook his head. "I don't have an excuse. I just don't want you to leave me."

Danielle said, "Only because you no longer have a place to stay."

"The church is fucking evil," Jeremy said, his words painted with pain and contempt. "They've fucked us all up. Look at us."

Yuri moaned. Danielle was sitting up on her own so I walked over to the guy, palmed his head with my right hand. I didn't want to know who he was or why he was mad. I wanted to pretend he was just some unfortunate fucker who hit a woman in front of me. I didn't realize how hard I was squeezing his skull until Jeremy grabbed my arm and warned I was going to pop it.

I let go and watched my imprints turn purple. I leaned over Yuri's head and whispered, "I don't care who you are or what you think, but if I ever see you again, I'll fucking crucify you."

Jeremy said, "Okay, okay. We're leaving." He grabbed Yuri around the chest and hauled him to his feet, helped him into the backseat. He opened the driver's door but didn't get in. "Please bring me with you."

I didn't know how mad I should be at him and he seemed really sorry. I said, "I'll talk it over with her. But get him the fuck out now."

Jeremy closed the door and lowered the window, said he'd be waiting, and made a left out of the driveway.

I didn't turn around right away. I didn't want to talk. I didn't want to hear a word.

Danielle was back to crying and called my name.

"Yeah?"

"You said you loved me. Did you mean it?"

I turned around, couldn't stay upset seeing her so torn. "I did."

"I can explain."

"What, that I'm a fucking idiot?"

"I never wanted to lie to you. I didn't have a choice."

"Give me a break, Danielle."

"Yuri was my husband, but I left him. He threatened to kill me if I was ever with another man. That's why I couldn't come around."

I replayed as much of the conversation as I could remember, tried to figure if her story made sense.

She said, "That's why I never filed for divorce. He said he'd slice my face up."

"Why didn't you tell the cops?"

"They wouldn't believe me."

"And Jeremy?"

"We don't talk."

"Do you want to bring him?"

"After what he did?"

"He's your brother. It's your call. Maybe it'd be nice to have some family with us, someone to help with the rent."

Danielle massaged the back of her neck. "If you can forgive me, then I should forgive him."

Thirty minutes later I pulled up their driveway, throwing on the brakes because Jeremy was standing in the middle of it. He had a bulging black trash bag in one hand, his camera gear in the other, a big smile of relief. "You guys are awesome."

I got out and opened the trunk, nodded at the house. "Is he in there?"

Jeremy squished the trash bag into the corner. "Yep, he's passed out."

"Wait, you guys are just going to leave and let that guy live in it?"

Jeremy said, "Thing's worth absolutely nothing. He drained what little equity there was."

Danielle said, "It's nothing but bad memories. We should burn it down."

I said, "Yeah, with that piece of shit in it."

Jeremy looked to see if I was serious. "Dude, are you fucking crazy? They'd come looking for all of us."

"Not if it looks like an accident."

"You got it all figured out. The cops won't want to speak to his roommate. His wife."

I blurted, "Ex," to show I believed her.

The look I'd said something stupid flashed across Jeremy's face. He said, "Or how about the guy who completely fucked up the side of his face? They might want to talk to him."

"No one saw me do anything."

"Holy shit, let's just get out of here," Jeremy said. "Fuck, I don't know who's scarier, you or your father."

I slammed the trunk and shouted, "He's not my father!"

We both looked to the house, but I'm guessing I was the only one wanting that asshole to stumble out and say something he'd regret the rest of his short life.

Danielle waited in the front seat. Jeremy got in the back and said, "Come on, man, make a clean break. Let's put all this shit behind us."

Once we hit the highway, Jeremy said, "So, where we headed?"

Danielle said, "You know damn well where we're headed. You listened to everything!"

"Relax, I was trying to break the tension. Not every day I get to sit behind a killer."

My voice was cold, sounded half dead. "Drop it."

Chapter Twenty

It was five days after I thought I'd be doing it, but it was finally happening. I was going to take my baby girl home from the hospital.

I parked Danielle's shiny red 4Runner that we could barely afford at the green-painted curb across from the hospital's entrance. Afraid I might get a ticket, I walked over to the valet station and asked the guys if that's where I should leave it.

I don't know if it was my grin or the tiny white bear with a halo and angel wings I was carrying, but the skinny one said, "New dad? Yep, that's it."

The NICU was on the fourth floor. Paul sat guard in the waiting room. He'd been in town since the delivery, said he wasn't leaving until he got to hold his niece.

I hadn't believed him, didn't think he would even care, but he'd been sitting on the bench every day, giving me my space, absorbed with his phone.

This was no different and he didn't see me coming, jumped when I said hello. It was a good day, a time to set aside differences. Plus, Paul really never did anything bad, not to me. He was just making the best of his situation.

Paul looked up from his phone with a smile. "Big day."

I said, "Yep," and wanted to leave it at that, but wasn't about to risk bad karma. I doubted that kind of stuff made a difference but ever since Lily had been born not breathing I'd just been waiting for the other shoe to drop. I said, "Been waiting my whole life for it," then gave my name at the intercom. Turning to Paul who was already back on his phone, I said, "It should only be about ten minutes."

The door buzzed open and I entered, washed elbows to fingertips for the full thirty seconds. I dried off my hands and took the stuffed bear toward the third bay on the right. Danielle sat in her rocking chair, hand hiding her face, her back hitching.

I ran over and checked the empty incubator. "Where's Lily? Is she okay?"

She said shush and leaned back to reveal Lily swaddled in her arm. My perfect little angel sound asleep, her skin finally the color it was meant to be, darker than Danielle, her hair just as brown.

Danielle had been so strong, loving, and happy, but it looked as if everything had caught up with her. I asked what was wrong.

She looked up, her eyes red, teeth biting down on her lip. She nodded at the next bay with the five-month-old preemie.

I stood a couple inches higher than the divider. There was a Mexican family huddled together. A white bundle was handed to the old man with glasses. He brought the tiny bundle to his lips and placed the lightest kiss. He said something I couldn't hear and handed it back to the mother.

I took the seat next to Danielle before my legs gave way. There was nothing I could do to make it better. Anything I said would sound like better them than us. I put my hand on Danielle's lower back and rubbed in little circles. My other hand cradled Lily's tiny head.

I knew nothing about being a dad, but swore, "I will never let anything bad happen to you."

A bright-eyed blonde in a light blue smock walked up and said, "Mr. and Mrs. Campbell?"

It was strange to hear our names like that even though we'd made it official the day Danielle's divorce was finalized. I figured the blonde was bringing yet another bill to pay before they released us. "Can I help you?"

She put on a nice smile and stuck out her hand. "I'm Denise with Perfect Portraits."

I said, "We can't do this."

Her smile didn't waver. "It's free. We do it for everyone."

I pointed at the divider. "They just lost their kid."

Denise apologized and left. Danielle thanked me.

I patted the telephone in my pocket. "This thing is nearly full of photos and I'm sure Jeremy will take plenty."

She said she was sure but didn't sound it. Jeremy was splitting rent until he could save up enough for his own place, but resentment ran both ways and I'd yet to see them in the same room for more than a minute.

It'd taken me a bit to get over the lies, especially about their mother being alive, but I couldn't be a hypocrite and think of Jeremy any differently than Paul. Both were trying to survive the best they could. Just like Danielle had.

"So is that it? We can go now?"

"Yeah, just have to tell them."

I made sure she was looking at me. "Are you ready?"

Her eyes were steel blue, hardened but they'd never break. They gave away nothing. "Are you?"

Not even close, but I couldn't say that. I had no idea how to be a father. "As much as I'll ever be."

That got a smile from her. Like we were taking an oath, she said, "We do our best not to screw her up. We don't do what ours did."

"I swear."

She kissed my cheek. "So do I. Let's take her home."

We called the nurse over and she helped us strap Lily into her brown and pink car seat, told Danielle she'd have to be wheeled out. I offered to take Lily, but Danielle placed the car seat on her lap.

Paul walked beside me while the nurse guided the wheelchair through the narrow hallways. In a baby voice Father would slap him for using, Paul gushed over Lily even though he could barely see her.

Outside the front door, I helped Danielle out of the wheelchair, staying close to her side in case she stumbled.

Paul said, "Shoot, I left my briefcase upstairs. You guys go home and get some rest."

I really didn't want to take Danielle out of the car seat, but said, "Don't you want to hold her?"

"Oh I will," he said from the doorway, "but I don't want anyone to take it. The last chapter of the updated *Gospels* is in there."

Jeremy stood to our left by the valet, the light shining on the camera he'd jacked from the Church of His Son. "And here they are, for the very first time. The Campbell family."

I helped turn Danielle to the side and told her to smile.

Jeremy had shaved and even combed his hair. When he smiled there was no doubting it. I'd seen enough fake ones to know the difference. This one was big and pure, like first time we met. "Beautiful, man," he said. "You guys are fucking beautiful."

"Did you get it?" Danielle asked.

"I can't see the princess."

Danielle handed me the car seat and began undoing her straps. I said maybe we should just leave her in, but Danielle ignored me.

Jeremy took a few more photos and came over, laid his finger on Lily's cheek. "Oh my God, she is something else. You guys did great, you really did."

I told him thanks. Danielle had tears in her eyes.

"Okay," he said. "Enough of that. Say something for the camera."

I didn't have anything smart to say and I wanted to get Lily out of the sun. "How about we finish this at home?"

Danielle said that was a good idea and headed for the curb.

I held out the car seat. "Want to put her in?"

Danielle wasn't waiting so I hurried to her side, helped her down the curb. We were halfway across when Jeremy said, "Oh fuck."

I didn't know what was about to happen. I just knew it was going to be bad, so I took hold of Lily and pushed Danielle toward the SUV.

Jeremy shouted, "Behind you!"

I spun around, faced the massive black muscle car barreling down on us. The driver's unyielding eyes locked on mine, both hands on the wheel.

There was no time to move so I held Lily against my chest and dropped onto my side, curled into the tightest little ball. I put my left elbow on my knee, my hand on my head, my forearm her shield. I felt her heart beat and said, "Daddy loves you."

There was no squeal of brakes, no screeching turn. The front tire smacked my foot full speed, five, six, seven bones crunching, each snap distinct.

I felt enormous pressure not pain, all that car crushing my kneecap, my femur, and hip. I stayed in the ball as the tire tore the flesh off my forearm, the weight threatening to burst my body. I pushed with everything I had, everything I was.

Danielle screamed, "Oh my God! My baby!"

† † †

Next thing I know, I was lying flat on a wooden altar, Father's hand resting on my chest, the church ceiling above. Father leaned in, both beard and stubbly hair an ashy gray.

"Shush," he said, "don't try to talk."

"Why?"

Father kept his hand on my chest and brought forth a foot-long diamond-encrusted dagger. "You know why."

I tried to look him in the eyes, but my head wouldn't move. "What are you doing?"

He pushed down hard enough to keep me still. "What I have to."

The light shone off the sharp blade. "What's that for?"

Father pushed the air out of me and raised the knife high. "You have nothing to fear."

The words came out whispers, nothing behind them. "You don't have to. Stop!"

The knife plunged down, hot fire through my chest, brilliant red spiking my eyelids. I couldn't look down to see what he'd done. I gasped, "Why?"

Father pressed harder on my chest and pulled out the knife, blood running down his hand. "It's written."

"You said I'm your son."

"You are. And the Father's. You are the Messiah"

"No I'm not! I'm not the fucking Messiah!"

Father slashed to the side, the blade digging deep in my hip, bouncing off the bone.

A voice on the other side of me said, "Shouldn't say that."

"Jeremy?"

There were three steps then a camera lens filled my face, the reflection a bruised mess I couldn't look at. "Accept it," Jeremy said. "It'll be better for all of us. We'll be rich."

I could barely think through the pain, my words coming out in spurts. "What do you mean?"

The camera stepped out of view, Father's hand and the knife all I could see. Father said, "This is how you save the world."

I screamed no and grabbed hold of his hand, bent it back so hard the knife went flying. I pulled myself up through the pain, kept pressing Father's hand back as far as it'd go.

Jeremy said, "Oh fuck," and kept filming.

I slid off the altar and ran out the door. The soft glow from the moon was my only light as I took off for my corner. Candles burned behind the barn's red curtains, Father's shotgun poking out the middle window, taking aim.

The slug blew through my forearm. Stopping meant death so I leapt over the stone wall, ran until I hit the swamp, dove with no fear.

The water was acid, my skin on fire. I scrambled back to shore, drenched in pain. I heard heavy breathing, but no one was chasing me. A butterfly kite danced in front of the moon.

I kept my eyes on the sky, sidestepping trees, the kite never coming closer. I started to jog and made it two steps before the snapping crunch of Father's bear trap.

My leg was a mess, but I would not stop. I pulled my foot out, skin and tendons bunching up behind the steel jaws, fleshy rivers running through my toes.

I focused on the white bandage holding the butterfly's belly. I followed the string to the middle of the grassy field, the delicate ankle it was wrapped around.

The woman was on her back, her face blocked by the man on top. Frank looked at me and smiled, a bullet hole in the middle of his head. "All you had to do was ask," he said. "I would've told you she wasn't picky."

Jeremy walked up beside me, camera rolling. "Tell me that don't turn you on."

I fell to the floor, buried my face in the leaves. There was nothing. Nothing, but the heavy breathing.

I rolled onto my back and opened my eyes. Light from the cracked door fell on a stack of flashing equipment, the in and out of heavy breathing filling my ears. My first thought was Father captured me, but this ceiling wasn't the church's. It was the same fluorescent tubes and white panels of the NICU.

A shadow shuffled to the left. I tried to say who's there, but it was impossible to talk with my mouth stuffed open, something filling my throat.

A woman in brown scrubs leaned over. "No talking. I'll tell them."

I wanted to grab her, shake her until she said where Danielle and Lily were but I couldn't move.

She held her finger up to her lips. "No, no," she whispered. "I go." She closed the door behind her, everything dark once again.

The bear was back, cloaked in darkness. It kept breathing in and out, in and out. I said, "Is someone there?"

A voice I'd done my best to forget, said, "You retarded? Open your eyes."

I was standing in the middle of a large office, Danielle next to me in her white nursing bra and matching granny panties, Ronnie sitting smug behind a large oak desk.

He was staring at Danielle's engorged boobs but talking to me. "What's up, you big fag?"

"I want my daughter. Where is she?"

"Your daughter's fine."

"Give her to me."

"You still haven't figured out you can't tell me what to do. I'm not scared of you. Look at yourself."

I tried to but my head wouldn't move. The farthest I could look down was at the dingy white Angelbear lying on his desk, plastic tubes taped to the tiny nose.

"Take her," Ronnie said. "She's fine."

I picked up the bear. "This isn't my daughter."

Danielle was crying when she said, "She'll be fine."

I shouted, "Give me my baby."

"That ain't me." Ronnie pointed behind us. "Go talk to that guy."

I had to turn my whole body to see the guy sitting in the chair. I'd almost forgotten his name, but that face never, especially the way his right side bulged too much. His suspenders were leaking water, the puddle under his chair growing inch by inch.

Danielle said, "Who are you?"

Dusty said, "Ask your husband."

"Josh?"

"He's no one."

Dusty raised his knee and looked right at me. "I was." He slammed his foot down, spraying the room, and the floor fell out below us, my heart in my throat as my weight took me down. I shot my hand up and caught hold of the edge, my left hand still holding Angelbear.

There was a bloody hole through the middle of my arm. It grew bigger, widened as the heat from the fire below licked at my feet, the flap of demon wings nearly as loud as the breathing.

I screamed for help as Angel pulled us toward the flames, my fingers sweating on the slick tile.

Danielle was on her hands and knees, her head sticking over the edge. "Everything's going to be okay."

I couldn't last much longer, that hole stretching, my body being pulled apart. She kind of grunted when I said, "You're gonna have to grab her. We got one shot at this."

Danielle pushed back and groaned. "I can't do it without you," she said as her head was jerked to the side by her ponytail, Beth's boss smiling over her shoulder.

I got ready for the throw, not sure if I could do it, but knowing I had to. I was just about to launch Angel when the meathead from the roller coaster appeared where Danielle had been, his face all scrunched up in a grimace.

Bull's hands were on either side of mine, the tattoos ending on his middle knuckle. He asked, "How's it hanging?"

"You have to save my daughter!"

His smirk stretched across his face. "Your daughter? You're joking?"

With everything I had, I flung Angel, her tiny white body soaring toward the edge. Bull snatched my arm and pulled me out, set me beside him.

Shocked he saved me, I ignored he was naked. I kept saying thank you again and again.

When he bent down to pick Angel off the floor, I had a clear shot of Danielle huddled in the corner, Beth's boss controlling her by her pigtails, Yuri towering over her, his head touching the ceiling, but his fist just inches from her face.

Bull blocked my view, said, "Sure thing, not a problem." He handed me Angel and said, "What's that old saying, 'an eye for an eye?'"

I said he was thinking of something else.

He turned around and helped Danielle to her feet, led her to the edge. With the smuggest smile, he said, "Dead wrong."

I saw where this was headed and dropped down a split second before Bull stepped off, Angel in one hand, Danielle pinned to his side with his other. My chest slammed against the floor, my throat bouncing off the edge as I reached out for Angel, grabbed hold of her hand. Bull kept hold of her, too, the rip so loud it shook my whole body.

A hand pushed down my chest. "Don't do that, Joshua. You got to calm down."

I opened my eyes, but they weren't ready for daylight. I blinked away the brightness and saw Danielle standing by my side. The drugs still had hold of me and I couldn't find any words.

"Joshua?" Danielle waved her fingers. "You there?"

My forehead was strapped down so I couldn't nod and something in my throat wouldn't let me speak. When I tried my arm, I felt needles, pinpricks. I blinked three times, the noise from my chest scaring me.

Danielle put her hand against my cheek. "You got to stop moving, baby." It sounded like she was going to lose it, her steel eyes ready to crack. "I know you don't like it, but you have to stop."

I tried to quiet my body, hoped like hell she could read my eyes, tell me everything I wanted to know.

She answered with tears.

I closed my eyes until the crying went away. When I opened them, Paul stood where Danielle had been, black suit, white shirt. He told me I was looking good. "Come on, man, it's time we got the hell out of here."

"I can go?"

"Yeah, I already signed all the paperwork. Just throw on your clothes."

I looked to where he was pointing, so excited I could turn my head, I didn't think much of my red cloak hanging in the closet. I jumped off the bed and got on my black slacks and white button down while Paul told me his plans to build his own bakery franchise, with the first one downtown.

When I put on my right shoe it constricted like a vice. I tried to pry it off, but it only grew tighter.

Paul said, "There, there," but he sounded like a woman. "If you're in pain, just push the button."

I didn't see what button he was talking about, but I didn't care. I shrugged on my cloak and went out the doorway, followed the exit sign, my right foot a throbbing mess.

Paul walked beside me. "So you know what you've got to do, right?"

We were coming up to a pair of closed automatic doors, a small window. I asked, "Does anyone?"

A woman in a black security guard uniform came out of a side room and stood before the door. When Paul walked up and gave her a hug, I saw it was Mother who looked great for being a year in the grave. He told her, "I brought him."

Mother opened the door and said, "Go on."

I tried to follow Paul forward but she stepped in front of me. "I was talking to him."

The door closed and Paul was on the other side, looking at the two of us through the window. "I want to go with Paul."

"Be quiet before someone hears you."

I kept my eyes on Paul. I wouldn't look at her, she wasn't my real mom. "Let me go. I need to get over there."

"I'll tell you what you need."

I glanced behind and saw a pack of surgeons, masks pulled up, knives in hand. "Open the gate. They're gonna kill me."

"You have nothing to worry about. That's what your dad always said."

I pushed past her and pounded on the glass, screamed at the back of Paul's head for him to do something.

Paul turned around, a cotton-candy pink stick of dynamite stuffed in his mouth. I watched the fuse sizzle into an explosion, the window painted red.

A hand touched my face. Danielle said, "It's okay. You there?

I went to nod and found I could just a little.

"You have someone here to see you."

I opened my eyes and looked down, the top of a tiny head resting on my chest, a full head of hair darker than Danielle's.

Danielle kept her hand on my cheek, had her other on the baby's back to keep her in place. She was smiling through her tears and told me to call her name.

I tried to swallow, took in each thump of her racing heartbeat. My throat was raw, my voice scratchy, but I said, "Lily. Lily, baby, is that you?"

Tiny hands crumpled the paper gown, the head slowly rising, the most precious little face. Her dark brown eyes met mine, made me promise I would always protect her.

Chapter Twenty-One

Lily turned three months on my first day home from the hospital. I was propped up on the couch watching the baby monitor, my angel asleep in her crib. Even if the TV were off, the rain from her sound machine made it impossible to hear breathing. I couldn't tell if the blanket was rising. I asked, "She's supposed to be on her back?"

Danielle rocked away, the chair a constant squeak, her eyes never leaving the screen. "You've already asked that. I'll hear her if she cries."

I pulled out a letter from the closest of the three mail bags by my feet. It was addressed to the Fake Messiah, but I opened it anyway. I was a sinner and going to hell. More of the same. I dropped it into the black trash bag.

The next letter was sweet, said I was some kind of hero, someone she'd want her sons looking up to. Whether or not I really was the Messiah, I was a brave man. God watched out for me. I held up the check that came with it. "Got another one."

This time Danielle looked. "How much?"

"Fifty."

She shook her head and went back to her show. She'd lost most of her pregnancy weight thanks to her not eating, but that was taking its toll. I'd never seen her so tired.

I felt like such a liar when I said, "It's gonna be fine."

"How?"

I had no idea so I said, "Just trust me." I reached into the bag and pulled out a long thin box I didn't bother opening. "Another candle."

"Great."

I set it on the coffee table with a dozen others, two regular bibles, three *Lost Gospels*, and a bunch of other religious crap. "We're gonna be fine."

"How, Josh?"

"We'll file bankruptcy if we have to."

"How's that going to help?"

"It'll get rid of the hospital bill and your credit cards."

"What about the apartment? How are we going to make rent? And the car. What about that?"

"I'll start working again as soon as I can move a bit."

"A bit?"

The car had shattered most of my right side, punctured both lungs. I was at everyone's mercy, unable to protect myself or my family. It was going to be a long and painful recovery, but I'd been through that battle before. "I'll get there."

"You broke your neck. You're not bouncing again."

"We'll see. I recover quick. Lucas promised he'd find me something easy and if it comes down to it maybe you'll have to work for a little."

"What can I do? Go find a Waffle House to waitress at?" She poked at her belly. "Look at me. I'm disgusting."

I told her she wasn't and said she needed to calm down.

"I don't need to do anything!"

My first instinct was to yell right back, but I had good reason to stay meek. My broken body was a big part, but the doctor was afraid Danielle was dealing with postpartum depression and I didn't want to say something stupid to set it off. I said I was sorry, I didn't mean to upset her.

Danielle got up with a sigh and went to the kitchen. I opened a letter and dumped a silver crucifix. I tossed it onto the table and wished I hadn't, a blast of pain exploding down my spine.

While I waited for the pain to fade, I picked up the monitor and watched my baby.

Danielle came in with a large glass of water and sat beside me. "Put it down. She's fine."

"Are you?"

She nodded and took a drink. "It's eight o'clock. You sure want to watch it?"

"Of course."

She turned the channel and I pulled the paper from the envelope. It was a photocopied page from Father's updated bible. The first time I'd seen the actual verse. Charles 3:16. Across the page in big black letters, someone had scrawled, DO THE RIGHT THING.

Danielle said, "We don't have to watch it."

I balled up the paper and set it in the trash. "Yeah we do. Rather hear it firsthand, know what people are thinking when they're sending us all this stuff."

The opening credits of the program finished. Danielle set down the remote and put her hand on mine. I must've winced because she said, "Sorry, is this okay?"

I'm not sure if I answered because I was staring at myself on the television, my first time seeing things the way Jeremy did. The tape started with us crossing the street, Jeremy's fuck getting bleeped, me dropping the car seat, grabbing Lily, pushing Danielle to safety, her elbow that always ached denting the 4Runner's side panel.

The camera got shaky, but Jeremy caught the whole thing, the black car barreling forward as I tucked Lily away and fell on my side. Then slow motion as the car smacked my foot, ran up my side, over my head, and smashed into the hospital's waiting room.

"Man saves his newborn daughter. The whole world has seen it, over half a billion hits. Some say it was a miracle. Some say he's the Messiah. Tonight I speak with his father."

The reporter turned toward Father. "Thank you for joining us, Reverend Campbell."

Father was sitting on the other side of the desk, either the makeup or time with Paul's roommate making him look ten years younger. "Thank you for having me on this blessed day."

The reporter looked unsure. "Is today a holy day?"

Father's eyes were wide open, showing he had nothing to hide. Trust me, I'm not crazy. I just want to share a secret, a big one, one that's going to change your life, the life of all your loved ones. The truth.

"Every day I spread the word is blessed."

"First and foremost, I've got to shake your hand and say well done."

Father reached over and shook his hand. "I'm not sure I understand."

"Sure you do. On your amazing success."

"Oh, I'm not the amazing one. Joshua—"

The reporter cut Father off. "I don't know about that. I mean, he's clearly remarkable and my heart goes out to him and his family, but you've done quite a job yourself."

Father thanked him but looked wary.

"Your self-published ebook, *The Book of Charles*, sold fifty thousand copies last week and the hardcover *The Lost Gospels* just made the bestseller list."

"I traveled to news stations all over the country, whoever would have me, whoever would listen."

"It seems to have worked."

Father nodded. "Blessed days."

"I'll say. That's a lot of money."

"I've been preaching this since Joshua was born. We have the largest church in the South and a formidable ministry spanning the globe."

"Seems like a pretty good deal to be Christ's father."

"His return has been a blessing. For all."

"Some people say you're just preying on the weak, that people are so scared with the way China's been acting. They say Americans will believe anything."

Father held up his black leather-bound book, had it turned so we could see the title in red flames. "Have you read it?'

"Yeah, when I was a kid."

Father kind of chuckled, but his eyes didn't. "That was a different book."

"Barely. Not quite as scary."

Father handed him the leather-bound book.

"I feel special. These things go for ninety-nine dollars."

"Plus tax and shipping."

"Of course."

"So why do you think it has done so well, besides the touring?"

"It's the truth. People want to hear it."

"The world needs a messiah."

"They have one. My son."

"A lot of people have questioned whether he's even your son. He's never talked about it and there's not much of a family resemblance."

Father reached inside his suit and brought out a white envelope. "Would you like to see photos? I have his birth certificate in here, too, if you like."

"That's not necessary."

"Then why bring it up?" Father tucked it away and said, "Believe what you will. I know, and my congregation knows. And now, thanks to you, all of America knows who He is. This is His return."

"You expect everyone to just take your word as truth?"

"Joshua has nothing to prove. He's already saved at least three lives, miracles if there ever were."

The guy rolled his eyes. "Well, I don't know if I'd go that far. You're talking about when he worked at the carnival?"

"And the factory. His daughter. And those are just the ones caught on camera."

"He doesn't save everybody though, does he?"

"He will save the just, those that believe in Him, that praise His name."

The photo of Michael, the Vegas banker, filled the screen, nice, clean cut, sharp blue suit, purple power tie, one hand around his wife's waist, the other holding their baby boy. The camera went back to the reporter who asked, "So are you saying this man wasn't just?"

"That is not what I said. I didn't know this man, but all the testimony I read said that he was inebriated, molesting women, and fighting. Doesn't sound like a saint."

"Wow, how Christian."

"That was part of the problem the first time around. The Messiah was weak, didn't want to hurt anyone. But God has always warned not to disbelieve for there will come a day when they stand before my Son. The sinners will pay for what they've done."

"That sounds like a threat."

"Difference between a threat and a promise."

"But that's only if they die after Joshua." He held up the book. "Isn't that right?"

"I don't care if you think I'm crazy. I don't care if ninety percent of your audience does, too, because you've just exposed all those others to the truth, maybe offered them salvation."

"Well then I guess we better end this here before you gain another convert."

Danielle turned it off and tossed the remote onto the pile of candles. "Nice to see it's not just my brother making money off us."

Thanks to all the views of his viral video, Jeremy was bringing in enough to get his own place. I said, "He's still helping with rent. He didn't have to do that."

"How generous."

"He said he'll cover all the rent once his site is big enough. He said all we need is another video."

Meaner than I'd heard her in a long time, she said, "Like of you almost dying."

"That's not going to happen, so relax."

"It's just such bullshit. He sits back and hauls in the money and I sit here taking care of you."

"It's not permanent. I can provide for us."

"How?"

Thinking of Jeremy gave me an idea. "I could make this work for us."

She saw where I was looking. "How we going to live off candles? I'd return them, but we'd get maybe ten or twenty bucks for the lot."

"These people all want my blessing. Just imagine what my blessing and my autograph must be worth. I'd say fifty bucks minimum."

Danielle looked at the bags of mail. For the first time in longer than I remembered, she sounded hopeful, but then returned to her new normal. "But those people sent these things expecting them back."

"Sure, some did, but you know how many enclosed postage for me to return it?"

She didn't guess but was still correct. I told her, "I'm considering all these as donations."

It took a second for her smile to spread. "As long as you promise not to send yourself to hell for stealing their stuff."

"That's more like it. We're going to be fine."

"But how? We get a store? With what money?"

"No, only online, no interaction with anybody."

"You know how to do that stuff?"

"No, but Jeremy does. We'll add our items to his website."

She searched my face. "You really think this could work?"

"Why not? People buy anything. The idiots that bought Father's book will buy them for sure. And with the way Jeremy's website's taking off, I can't see it not."

She said she didn't know, but when I offered to call Jeremy, she shook her head. "I'll call him. I don't want him back in your life."

† † †

Lily was going to turn one in a few days, but I wasn't parked across the street from the gated community to deliver an invitation. The sun beat down on the limousine tint, but air conditioning made it bearable. I was beginning to think maybe I'd better get back home, but then a young kid in a silver BMW pulled up to the front gate.

I gunned it across the street and followed the car in, turned right at the clubhouse, finally seeing why everyone was talking about this part of town.

Jeremy had moved up in the world and quite a few notches. None of the houses were less than 5,000 square feet, nearly half with For Sale signs, but all with immaculate landscapes, beautiful flowers and green grass defying the summer heat.

His house was down the last street to the left, a huge villa with white walls and a red roof. I turned off the car and got slammed with the heat. No one was outside so I hopped over the side wall and darted to the garage, peeked through the window. Parked inside were the white Range Rover I'd seen once before and a full-size Mercedes too new for a license plate.

I crept to the front door and heard the TV. The doorbell rang for ten full seconds. When it stopped chiming, everything went quiet.

I waited for footsteps, but no one was coming. I knocked on the door. "Open up, it's me."

Not a sound.

"I know you're in there."

The sweat dripped down my back and I had to get home before Danielle started freaking out. "Don't make me bust this door down!"

The door looked thick, but I didn't care. Besides some limitations with my neck and right hip, I'd almost fully recovered. I gave him five seconds then slammed my shoulder about two feet above the lock, eliciting a loud crack.

Sounding like he couldn't be more than a few feet from the door, Jeremy said, "What the fuck? Hold on!"

I stepped back and took a deep breath. I blew it out and unclenched my fists.

Jeremy peeked out, his hair all over the place, nothing on but a pair of basketball shorts. "I was going to get it."

I shoved him inside and closed the door behind us.

"What the hell's your problem?"

He reeked of vodka, but I ignored it. "For one, how about you trying to lock me out of your house when I let you live in mine."

"It wasn't your house. You weren't even paying rent!"

I got in his face and backed him into the living room. Two chicks were sixty-nining in silence on his big screen, shiny leather furniture taking up the floor, gaudy paintings plastering the walls. I pushed him down on the couch.

"What's up, Josh?"

"You know what's up. You haven't answered your phone in two weeks."

Jeremy looked at the clock. "Keeping a low profile since the China thing started getting ugly."

"No one worth less than ten million has ever been kidnapped."

"You never know."

"Cut the shit," I said.

"I don't know why you're so pissed."

"You didn't listen to any of the goddamn messages I left? You think I'm that stupid?"

Jeremy grabbed the remote and turned off the TV. "You can't be serious about taking it down."

We were talking about the latest Messiah movie he'd put up on his website. All the things he took out of context from the times he supposedly wasn't recording. A collage of all the pictures beginning with the church sign that'd started it all.

I told him I couldn't be more serious. "Shut it down. Take the whole thing down."

"You're crazy."

"You're greedy."

"Have you seen how many fans we have?"

It was in the millions, at least half of them believers. Way less than Father had but catching up fast. "I don't care. You never should've put it up in the first place."

"I had to. That was the only way to keep the site going. With all that traffic it's not free to run, you know."

"I'm done talking about it. Take it down."

"Why ruin a good thing? You guys are still cashing the checks."

"Yeah, the money made off me."

"Try telling me business hasn't doubled since this video."

"I don't need you to sell them."

Jeremy laughed. "You gonna do it yourself?"

"Danielle's a quick learner."

"I bet."

The way he said it made me stop. "What's that mean?"

"It means she ought to think twice about fucking me over."

What I wanted to do was kick his ass, but I couldn't because of Danielle. "She doesn't even know I'm here."

"I need to call her?"

"Yeah, ask her how scared she is. These people are fucking crazy."

"She's just paranoid."

"You don't think there's anything to worry about?"

"People are full of shit. They're all cowards."

I reached into my pocket and pulled out the envelopes, threw them at his chest.

"What the fuck?"

"Read one."

Jeremy looked down at them then back up at me.

"Pick one up and read it!"

He snatched one up and took the letter out of the envelope, a shiny razorblade falling to the floor.

"Out loud."

In his stupid-ass reporter voice, he said, "'Dear Messiah. My Daddy's dead and Mama's real sick, says she got cancer. Please do the right thing. We can't wait anymore.'"

"I've got bags of that shit."

"It's just some kid."

"For every one like his, I've got ten others threatening to do it for me. It's enough."

Jeremy didn't say a word, wouldn't look me in the eyes.

"Your niece deserves a daddy. I'm not getting killed so you can make money."

His eyes flashed cold, his face rigid. "Talk to my sis. Tell her what I said, then call me back."

"No, I'm telling you now. Shut it down."

"That's a bad move."

I took the envelope from my lawyer out of my other pocket and handed it to him. "It will be for you if you don't do what I say."

✝ ✝ ✝

Lily's hair was down to her shoulders, still curly as ever at two and a half. She had on her fuzzy brown sweats and matching shirt that said *Mommy's Little Monkey*. She was dancing her dolls on the coffee table, making it impossible to finish her ponytails.

I grabbed a handful of hair and started to twist the rubber band around it. "You need to hold still, beautiful."

Lily kept swaying back and forth and the hair came loose.

"Okay," I said. "I guess you don't want to go."

She set down both dolls and put her little fingers in the air, began orchestrating *Itsy Bitsy Spider*.

I said, "That's so sad."

Lily stopped her song and turned to me, her dark eyes so serious. "What sad?"

"I really wanted to go have fun, but I guess we have to say home."

Her lip trembled. "What?"

"If you don't want to stay still so I can fix your ponies we can't go."

"I want to go."

"I do, too, so look straight ahead and hold very still."

She did exactly as I asked and I finished her hair in under a minute, careful not to spray her face when I woke up her curls. "Okay," I said, "let's turn around and see."

Everything good about Danielle was magnified in Lily. So much love in one little girl. A smile that made my heart burst. People always say Lily has my smile, but I must have hers because mine wasn't there before she came along.

Lily had to know how I felt about her, but I never left that to chance. I bent over and kissed her forehead. "What a wonderful little girl."

She grabbed the water bottle when I put it down. "Daddy's turn."

"Just one."

She nodded and sprayed my face.

I went to get the bottle back, but she was already spraying it into her mouth, laughing as it dribbled down her chin. I said, "We'll get you a juice from the kitchen."

Lily got excited and pointed at the ceiling, her eyes big as could be. "Spiderpig."

"I didn't hear a please."

The second Lily's lips started to move, I scooped her up and pressed her over my head so her hands and shoes were on the ceiling. We spiderpigged around the living room, climbed over the drop into the kitchen.

I was just about to yell out to Danielle that we were ready, but she was already waiting for us at the door to the garage, looking pretty in pre-pregnancy jeans and a light blue blouse. I set Lily by the fridge and poured her some juice, didn't bother asking Danielle whether or not she'd already done it. Danielle and I hadn't talked much all morning so I said, "Are you ready for the big day, Mommy?"

When Danielle didn't answer, Lily asked, "Why Mommy cry?"

Danielle had twin lines of mascara down both cheeks, the first time I'd seen any make up in months. "We can't do this."

"Mommy be silly."

I saw she wasn't, but said, "She sure is. Go get me my keys, sweetheart. They're on the table."

Lily ran out of the kitchen and Danielle twisted her hands back and forth. "I'm serious. We can't go."

"Come on, babe. Don't do this."

She shook her head. "We'll do something special here."

"You can't pull this. Not today."

"It's not safe."

"We promised her."

"She's two. She'll forget all about it by tomorrow."

"I won't."

Lily came running back to me. "Daddy, Daddy. No keys."

I put my hand in my pocket and said, "Silly Daddy. Here they are."

Danielle bent down toward Lily. "I'm sorry, baby, but we can't go."

Lily's face melted and she threw herself on the ground. I shushed her and said, "We're going."

Danielle said we couldn't.

I helped Lily to her feet and brushed off her pants. I turned to Danielle and told her Lily and I were going and would very much like her to come.

She asked if I was serious so I picked up Lily and gently moved Danielle to the side so I could enter the garage.

By the time I had Lily strapped into the car seat, Danielle was ready, the mascara washed off her face. Lily squealed in delight and I opened Danielle's door. She hadn't been in it since I installed the bulletproof glass so I tapped on the windshield to remind her. "See? Nothing to worry about."

I opened the garage door and started the car, eased down the driveway. Unlike Jeremy, we didn't have a gate to keep people out. I looked up and down the street, checking for anyone sitting in a driver's seat. Down at the end of the block all the way to my right, there was someone in a gray coupe. I pulled out and headed right for him.

Danielle said, "It's the other way."

I looked back at Lily. "Crazy driver, okay?"

She squealed in happiness and held onto the sides of her car seat. "Oh no! Crazy turns."

Danielle asked what crazy driver was. I floored the gas pedal and streaked past the Honda before the driver sat up. The turn was coming up quick, but I kept my foot on the gas and my voice playful. "Uh-oh. Hold on," I said. "You holding on? Hurry, hurry!"

Lily was hanging on, shaking her body side to side in anticipation.

Danielle sounded worried when she said, "You better not do it."

I did it anyway, spinning the wheel to the right, my tires screeching more than I wanted.

Lily cheered, but Danielle was pissed. "What the hell you think you're doing?"

"It's just a guy from the Network." I made the next right and looked past Danielle, spotted the tip of the Honda. "He's harmless."

Danielle clutched the door handle and put her other hand on the glove box like that would help. "Jesus Christ. Slow down."

We were hauling ass, but it was two o'clock in the middle of summer, a couple cars here and there. "She likes it," I said. "Look at her."

Lily was cracking up. "Again. Again."

I looked at my rearview, didn't see the Honda, just Lily's big brown eyes. "One more?"

She started her shaking and squealed when I whipped the wheel to the left, our house just two houses back the other way.

Danielle turned around in her seat. "Where is he?"

"I lost him. Almost always do. Ain't that right, Lily?"

"Crazy driver!"

Danielle pouted. "None of this is funny."

I made another turn, realized Lily had stopped laughing. I said, "Guess not."

"What? What's that mean?"

I turned on the radio and cranked up *Mary had a Little Lamb*. "Not now."

The mall was only a few songs away, no one bothering to talk the rest of the ride. I parked as close as I could to the side entrance and reassured Danielle we had nothing to worry about.

"You've said that before."

I turned off the engine, but let *Old Mac Donald* play since Lily was singing. "Nothing's going to happen to us."

"What about the kidnappings?"

"Who told you about them?"

"I heard."

I was hoping she meant some friend I'd never met because we'd agreed it wouldn't help her condition to watch TV. It wasn't healthy for her, even when it wasn't about me. "If we had that kind of money, we wouldn't be living here."

Lily had stopped singing, her head turned toward her window. "We're here! We're here!"

I was looking at Danielle when I said, "Yes we are and we're going to have a great time. Right?"

I'm not much of a hat guy and baseball's about as boring a sport as there is, but I was sponsored by the Los Angeles Angels so I put on my cap and added some dark glasses. By the time I got around to the other side of the car, Danielle was getting Lily out of her car seat, arguing over something.

I said, "What's the problem?"

"She wants to take her blankie."

"Is it a big deal?"

"It is if we lose it. Just leave it in the car."

"Daddy!"

Danielle shushed her. "Don't you want to be a big girl?"

Lily said something I couldn't hear.

"Good girl," Danielle said. "You're too big for that."

We crossed at the crosswalk, not far from a group of teenagers sitting along the flower bed, a cloud of cigarette smoke hovering over them. When one said something about the Messiah, everyone turned their phones my way. I told Danielle to carry Lily inside.

A young punk in a bright blue shirt hurried over to me, his hand in the air. The letters I got came from all over the world, from all kinds of people. Most of them didn't include their picture, but even if they did, there'd be too many to memorize. So not knowing who the hell this guy was or what he had in mind, I closed the distance, jammed one hand into his throat, the other his armpit.

The kid bounced back with a loud yip. "What the fuck, man? I was giving a high-five."

I felt bad about it, but said, "I don't know you."

He held up his phone and snapped a picture. He started typing. "Yeah, well I know you."

I urged Danielle to walk faster for the door, head to the indoor play area. The girl at the desk was nice and let Danielle and Lily into the back while I signed the waivers and paid admission. When I got back there, Lily was already at the top of the highest inflatable slide, both arms waving.

She slid down with the biggest smile, ran right by me, and went back to the slide. Danielle asked if everything was fine.

"Yeah, nothing to worry about."

"You sure?"

Lily got to the top of the slide. When she didn't come right down, I said, "What's wrong, baby?"

"What's wrong with her?" Danielle said. "You said she loved this place."

"She does." I walked to the bottom of the slide and called up to her. "Come on, Lily. You know how to do this. You love it."

Lily shook her head and started to cry. The sticker on the bottom of the slide said the weight limit was two hundred pounds, but I went up anyway. When I got up beside her, she curled against my side and said, "Hold me."

"Want me to hold your hand?"

"No! Hold me, please."

I looked down at the row of people standing behind Danielle, half of them aiming their phones at us, the other half typing away on them.

"You don't like them watching? It's okay. Just ignore them."

The punk in the blue shirt started a chant. "Go, go, go!"

Danielle turned around then looked up at us. Her voice trembled when she said my name.

Lily said, "Hold me, Daddy!"

I put Lily on my lap, wrapped both arms around her and kissed her forehead. "Daddy's got you."

Danielle took Lily from me when we reached the bottom. Her eyes were dark with concern and uncertainty. "Honey?"

"Who wants to get a pretzel?"

Lily cheered up a little. "I like sugar."

"Alright, Danielle. Let me talk to these guys. When I wave you ahead, you take her out the front and get her a cinnamon pretzel. I'll be right behind you."

"I told you we shouldn't have come."

"Just do as I say." I pushed back a strand of hair that'd come loose from one of Lily's ponies. "Mommy's going get you a pretzel then we'll come back and play."

Danielle nodded at the pricks behind her. "What about them?"

The group had doubled, more people on the way. "Harmless," I said. "Just wait for the wave."

There was no one who could stand up to me so I walked right up to the punk and raised my hand at the last second. He flinched and jumped back, tripping over the girl in the red movie theater uniform.

"There, now you guys have a clip to show all your friends. I was just going to give you a high five."

The punk got to his feet, didn't look too happy that half the group was laughing at him.

"Now how about you guys get going and let me have some time with my wife and kid."

A couple people walked away, but blue shirt with the red face just stood there staring.

I waved Danielle to walk through the crowd. I waited a few seconds before I started after them. A couple people were making comments. Someone said, "Damn, Miss Messiah still got that fat ass."

I didn't see who said it, but that was for the best. Anything I did to the coward could be caught on tape and used in court.

Danielle and Lily got in line at the pretzel store and I was about to join them when loud moans coming from behind me stopped me in my tracks. I turned and saw blue shirt holding up his phone, something dancing across the screen I couldn't make out. A girl I hadn't thought of in a long time said, "Don't you want to fuck me?"

Lily was within hearing range. I ran up to him and snatched the phone out of his hands.

He said, "What the hell?"

I threw the phone as far as I could, watched it sail across the mall.

"I'm going to sue you."

Danielle and Lily were walking back to me without a pretzel. I pointed them to the electronics store, figured we'd let Lily pick a present and try to salvage the day.

"What was that?" Danielle asked.

I led the way to the back of the store where they kept the kid's games. "It's nothing. Just some jerk trying to earn cool points with his friends."

Danielle looked scared. "I want to go home."

We were walking through an aisle of computers that sprang to life, a bunch of guys cheering. "Is that okay?" a woman said. "You like that?"

It was me on the screen, a firm blonde in a G-string sitting on my lap, her nipples swaying inches from my face, a bunch of guys cheering in the background. "Oh my God," Danielle said. "Is that you?"

My hands were on her waist, but what was I supposed to do. "I didn't do anything wrong. I didn't even want to be there."

"You're smiling! When was this? Who's the whore? No wonder why you don't want me watching anything."

"That was the goddamn bachelor party you made me go to. Jeremy got me pretty drunk, but I didn't do anything, I swear."

Danielle started down the aisle, pulling Lily behind her. "Just great, what are you going to tell your daughter? Think what you just did to her."

An older man in the same blue shirt ran by us, shouting at the punk behind the counter, yelling at him to turn that off.

The video fast forwarded then started to play again as the punk blocked the counter, told the manager he didn't give a fuck he was fired.

Danielle was talking, but her voice came in surround sound, telling me to relax, just relax sweetie, she would take good care of me.

I turned to the computers, Danielle in her nurse getup, her hand pumping my cock, the perfect angle captured by a pro.

Danielle screamed like a banshee, grabbed the closest lap top and slammed it shut.

Another fast forward, another scene, the two of us in the baptismal tub the night I'd lost my mother, the angle capturing all the action, no way it could be dumb luck.

Slam, slam, slam all the way down the aisle, Danielle in berserker mode. Lily crouched into a ball at my feet while Danielle turned to the PCs, ripped free a remote and smashed every screen on the way back to us.

I grabbed hold of Danielle and held her tight, doing my best to keep my voice down, making her look at the computer. "What the fuck is this?"

Her face was a mess of confusion and anger, her voice hysterical when she said, "He swore he got rid of it."

I said, "Who's the whore?"

Those were the same words Danielle had used, but this time they sounded so much worse, the effect immediate and devastating, dropping her to her knees like a shot to the solar plexus.

Chapter Twenty-Two

It was a few months after the mall, the three of us in the living room, the twelve-gauge shotgun over the mantel. Danielle had said we'd be stupid not to have it. She didn't know it wasn't loaded, that I kept two shells on me at all times.

"Daddy?" Lily was on the floor, a puzzle piece in each hand. "You okay?"

She wasn't even three, repeating words she heard too often. "Oh, of course, sweetheart. Daddy was just thinking."

She pointed at the row of puzzles spread across the floor, all but two finished. "I want to show Mommy."

Danielle was laid back in the recliner, mouth open, eyes closed, still adjusting to her increased dosage.

I picked one of the candles off the coffee table and began carving my initials at the bottom. "Why don't you finish your puzzles first? We'll let her rest a little longer."

Lily smiled and said okay. I went back to my candle, taking my time with it because it wasn't already sold, no more playing keep up since we'd parted ways with Jeremy.

I was on my fourth candle when Lily whispered, "Mommy." She stood next to the recliner and said it a little louder.

Danielle blinked awake. "Sorry, baby."

"Look, Mommy. Me do 'em all."

Danielle wiped the drool from the corner of her mouth. "What time is it?"

I told Lily nice job before answering Danielle. "Almost seven."

"Oh, jeez. I bet I look like hell.

"Can I show Grandpa?" Lily asked.

Danielle had seen better days, her eyes lost in an ocean. I said, "You look fine. And don't worry about impressing anyone."

The driveway's motion detector beeped three times. I wasn't ready. Lily was though. She shouted, "Is that him?"

I checked the monitor, my mouth drying as Father walked to the front door.

The doorbell rang and Lily jumped up. "Grandpa!"

"Calm down. You don't even know him."

Danielle said, "You're the one who said he could come."

I told Lily I was sorry and the doorbell rang again. I walked past the mantel, felt the shells inside my pocket. I left the shotgun where it was and opened the door. Father in a brilliant white suit, the finest fitting one I'd ever seen, a bright red package in his hand.

Looking just as young as he did on TV, his hair the blackest of black, Father gave his best smile and spread his arms wide. "Joshua."

I stayed right where I was, my hand on the door. "It's Josh."

He nodded. "Josh. Okay. How about a handshake?"

Danielle said, "Well, go on."

I squeezed Father's hand and looked him in the eyes, wished I knew what he saw before him. Was I just a toy, something to manipulate? Or was I the biggest disappointment?

His hand held strong, but only long enough for me to admire his diamond-encrusted watch. "That's my boy."

I invited him in and saw the two military-type men in crisp black suits standing on either side of the limousine.

"And what a pleasure it is to see you," Father said to Danielle. "A beautiful woman made even more so by becoming a mother."

I locked the door and turned around in time to see Danielle hugging him like he meant something. Father kissed her cheek and stood back. Lily's feet were sticking out from behind the couch, right there for everyone to see, but he put his hand to his forehead and scanned the room. Everything a production, he raised his voice and said, "Oh where is this wonderful little girl I've heard all about. I heard she's an angel, the perfect little sunshine. It's too bad she's not here, because I really wanted to see her."

Lily peeked over the couch's armrest then went back down with a giggle.

"Such a shame," he said. "I guess I'll have to find another girl to give this present to."

Lily popped up and waved her arms. "Me, me. Me here."

I walked to the couch to make Lily feel safe, but she ran right past me and hugged his leg. So quiet we could barely hear, she said, "Grandpa?"

Father held his heart and knelt so they were eye to eye. "You have just made me the luckiest man alive. You have the voice of an angel. Yes you do."

Lily said, "Daddy's angel."

I reminded her, "And Mommy's."

"Well, I guess that makes you everyone's angel," Father said. "And that's exactly what everyone needs—an angel that can take away all their pain and troubles with just one little smile."

Lily was fighting a smile, the corners of her mouth trying to stay down. I said, "Go ahead, sweetheart. Let him see it."

I didn't have to say it again. Her perfect little teeth, her perfect little smile, her brown eyes beaming.

"Oh my. You are going to be a heartbreaker." Father handed her the package and said, "This is for you."

I had a feeling I knew what it was. I patted Danielle's hand and said, "Would you mind getting some drinks?"

She said sure thing, the words running together.

Father helped Lily find an opening and watched her tear off the wrapping. She brought me the cardboard box and said, "What it do?"

I showed her how to open it and pulled out the black leather book. She asked, "Stories?"

"Yeah, stories." I held up the expanded version of *The Lost Gospels*. I flipped to the first page. Copy number one. "Lots of stories, just like all your fairy tale books."

"I like stories."

I ruffled her hair and set the book on the mantel where she couldn't get it and Danielle wouldn't notice. "Some stories are good. These ones aren't for children."

Lily turned to Father who was back standing. "Me big girl."

"And such a big girl. I'm pretty sure you must be at least four or five."

"Me be three on my birthday."

"Do you know when that is?"

Danielle came back with a tray and glasses while Lily shook her head. She said, "We haven't got that far yet. But she knows the entire ABC song. Sing it for Grandpa, baby."

Lily did the whole thing, even slowed LMNOP down to all separate letters. Danielle set the drinks on the coffee table while Father cheered. Two of the drinks splashed onto the tray but Danielle didn't notice, looking at Lily, telling her to show how high she could count.

Lily got to twenty-ten and Father said, "Wow, that really is amazing. You are the smartest thing ever."

That was exactly how I felt about her, like there couldn't be another person out there as perfect. But I also knew how it felt to not live up to those expectations. "We try not to say stuff like that. Don't want to put pressure on her."

Father said he understood. I wiped off the drinks and told him he should have a seat. "Hope water's okay."

He said sure but left his on the tray so he could pull a quarter from behind Lily's ear.

"You're lucky, Lily. I've never seen him play before."

Danielle said my name in a tone that meant *fucking knock it off.*

"I'm just saying she's lucky."

Father took his drink from the table and sat in the loveseat. "I know I wasn't good at some things."

I said, "So?"

"Thanks for letting me come."

"Yeah."

Lily took the box and laid it on its side, stuck her arm in and out, in and out.

Father pointed at the small stack of candles. "How's your business going?"

He must've known it'd gone to shit, but I didn't say a word about that having anything to do with him telling his followers they couldn't support us. I said, "Nothing like your church."

"*Our* church. Nothing can stand in its way."

It was obvious I was being sarcastic when I said, "That's wonderful."

"Why are you acting like this?" he asked as if he genuinely didn't know.

"What do you want?"

"I wanted to see you."

"Why?"

"You're my son."

"Not your real son."

He sighed. "Don't say that."

"It's true and you know it."

"You're being ridiculous. I am your father."

"Look at us."

He looked at me then Lily. "The Lord works in mysterious ways."

"We don't do that. Not in my house."

"Do what?"

"Utter that name. It's brought us nothing but evil."

Father pointed to the large screen TV, the toys spread across the room. "That's not entirely true."

"The evil it brought us is greater than any good that's come of it."

Father looked like he was having a hard time not raising his voice. Finally he said, "I came to ask a favor."

"I figured as much."

Danielle reached out and touched my hand, said, "Honey."

"That's okay, sweetie," Father said. He made sure I was looking at him before he spoke. "I'm opening a church here in Vegas and would like your blessing."

"Why now? You didn't need it for Charlotte," I said referring to the monster of a church Paul was in charge of.

Father's eyes flashed fire, but he kept his voice calm. "You wouldn't talk to me."

Lily was still on the carpet, seeing how far she could get her head in the box. I told her, "Why don't you go play with your toys in the other room? Just for a couple minutes, okay?"

"She's having fun," Danielle said.

Lily really wasn't paying attention to the conversation, but I almost told Danielle to pick her up and stay in the other room. I didn't want Father seeing any part of him in me so I kept cool. "What about the sex tape? It made me a mockery."

"No, it did not. It shows the world you're human. What I saw on that tape between you was real. Some might say love, some might say lust." He pointed at Lily. "And look what it produced."

That wasn't necessarily true because there'd never been a paternity test. And there wasn't a test because it didn't matter. I faced Father and said, "You don't even need me. Why are you here?"

Father rubbed his chin, his face growing cold. "You know what, you're right. I don't need you."

If Danielle had been holding a knife, she might've stabbed me.

I said, "So you just came by to drop off a book? A book that says I need to fucking die!"

Father stood. "Stop it! You will not talk to me like I'm some misguided fool."

The air felt heavy, like it was pushing me down, not allowing me to stand. But my wife was watching, just like my daughter.

There was a foot, maybe two between us. I lowered my voice and said, "If I am the Messiah then I, and I alone, should be the one deciding what I think, who I talk to, and how I speak to them."

Father didn't even blink. "Are you him? Are you the Messiah? Can you finally say it? Finally accept your role?"

Of course I couldn't. I said, "This was a bad idea."

Like he really wanted to know, Father asked, "How in the world could you not know you're Him? How many more miracles need to happen?"

I repeated what I'd told Paul. "Probably about three or four."

His eyes stayed on me like they were trying to burn a hole through my head. "Joshua, you are the Messiah, whether or not you believe it. To millions, you're the Messiah no matter. Give them hope. The world needs hope."

I said, "Even if I could, that's not my job. I never signed up for it."

"Be that as it may, it doesn't change the facts."

"No church has any facts. Except how much money they can rake in."

"Is that it? You need more money? Is that why you both abandoned me? Had I not been taking care of you the best I could?"

He truly believed his version of the truth and suddenly I wasn't so sure mine was right.

"Tell me what I did wrong to deserve that, to have my son abandon me a second time, with not even so much as a goodbye."

Danielle said, "*The Book of Charles*."

"That wasn't released until after. It had to; it's one of the many crosses Joshua has to bear."

I said, "You wrote the whole thing while I was there."

"Have you read it, either one of you?"

We shook our heads.

"Joshua, it absolves you of all wrongdoing because, as a human, you fail, just as we all do. Paul's behind a lot of it. His struggle with your mother's dying, how you couldn't help her."

"It says I have to die. Everyone wants me dead!"

With a smile, like he was delivering the best news ever, he held my shoulders and said, "Don't you get it? You are not accountable for any of the awfulness that consumes this land. You are trying your best and have a pure heart. You are still the Messiah."

"What about all the stuff that's already happened? All that shit I've been blamed for? Am I still guilty of all those crimes you made me watch, every one of those images that flutter through my brain? Never know what's going to pop up next, if it'll be a dead baby, someone jumping out a window, having their fucking head chopped off."

Danielle said, "Language."

"Yeah, I better watch my language with the guy who made me watch snuff films."

Father said, "Not at her age."

I was almost too flustered to speak. "That matters?"

Father opened his mouth, but I cut him off, told Danielle a little too sternly to get Lily out of the room.

Father said, "I know I've made mistakes. We all have."

"That's your apology?"

"You can't look me in my eyes and tell me you are not the Messiah."

I hated he was right. "I don't have to tell you a damn thing."

"You would be doing the world and yourselves a huge favor if you would just acknowledge it."

Danielle asked, "How big of a favor for us? Why should we trust you?"

"I'll give you a new house, men that will protect you with their lives."

She didn't say anything right away. "Any house?"

He nodded. "The church will purchase the house of your choice. Within reason, of course."

Danielle nudged my leg. Our nest egg was shrinking, would disappear within a year if I didn't do something about it. I said, "In exchange for what?"

Father spread his arms. "The world needs a Messiah. Give them something to believe in. Take their mind off the wars, the kidnapping, all the senseless violence."

"Do I have to speak?"

"Yes, but only in your daily message."

We all knew there was more. "And?"

"Let me baptize you. You and Lily. It will be glorious. Let your father wash away all your sins."

"You're out of your mind. Lily is not doing it."

"But you will?"

I hesitated. "When?"

Father eyes were aglow like the glorious vision was before him. "I don't think we rush it. We'll wait until you're ready."

"What if it takes five or ten years?"

"Well, how about we say within three. By then we'll have the Christian Network eating out of our hands, all religions bowing down."

"I suppose I could commit to that."

Father held up his finger. "There's no supposing this time. Are you in or out?"

Only because my back was against a wall I couldn't scale carrying two dependents, I said I was in.

His hug caught me off guard. He squeezed too hard and said, "This is so exciting. You'll bask in the glory that awaits you."

I broke it off so I could breathe and reminded him what the deal was. "This is business."

Looking proud of me for finally catching on, Father smiled. "So help us build it. Let's take things over."

Danielle nudged the back of my foot. I told him, "We're also going to need some money up front. Fifty thousand at least."

Father shook his head. "That's not how you negotiate. Do that part before the deal is made."

I told him we hadn't shaken on it and he said he was just joking. Father reached inside his jacket and pulled out a blank check. He filled it out and handed over the first fifty thousand I'd ever held. "Now we shake."

The agreement was sealed, the appointment over. I had Danielle take Lily to the bathroom and told Father I'd see him out. I felt dirty, like I'd signed a deal with the devil, and didn't want either of my girls around him any longer.

Father didn't complain about not telling them goodbye, and I didn't bother offering an excuse. Both his bodyguards had been facing the street. The dark-skinned driver opened the back door while the white guy with the crew cut met Father at the front of the vehicle. Father introduced him as Troy, said he was the most trustworthy person he knew. He'd been Black Ops in Afghanistan. "This is my family," he told Troy. "You'll protect them with your life."

Troy said he was honored and shook my hand. With enough of a drawl to let me know he'd once been a good old boy, he said, "I won't let you down."

Father slipped inside the car, leaned his head out the window. "Tomorrow we'll go looking for a house, and just wait until you see the new church. And this is only the first step. I won't even tell you the really big news until it's finalized. My vision is soaring higher than the tallest mountain. We are on a path of no return. The entire world will know your name."

† † †

The Vegas church was built just for us with a state-of-the-art studio in the rectory. We had had ourselves a busy morning recording a dozen one-liners for sponsors and two thirty-second pieces. Thanks to all my ums and mumbles, my stutters and slip-ups, what a real actor could have done in one or two hours had taken us five.

Paul, who usually kept quiet during filming, said, "Come on, Josh, we still got one more."

Six months of being back in front of the camera had cured me of lots of my hang-ups, but not having someone like Jeremy to coach my delivery left most of my stuff feeling stiff. Darren, the twenty-something behind the camera, never offered any advice, and kept his comments down to rolling and cut.

This had been about his twelfth cut this scene and even he'd had enough. "What is it, Josh?"

Anything I said around either one of them would go straight back to Father, but I was done caring for the day. "Neither of you thinks it's a little fucked up that I'm giving 5-Halo reviews for places I've never eaten in cities I'd never seen?"

Paul said, "We're done with those for the week. And don't forget they pay our rent."

"And the FEMA camp ad?"

"Did you listen to what you were saying?" Paul asked. "You don't agree they are necessary?"

Darren looked confused. "You don't want stragglers to have a place to live?"

Paul said, "Senator Burkhart and Father share the same view on the Camps. Maybe you don't understand their importance, but that doesn't limit it."

I honestly didn't care about that ad. It was this stupid shit I was filming for the military. I swatted my hand at the two armored tanks filling the screen behind me. "Fuck these guys. They didn't want me before."

Paul said, "You don't mean that. Them not taking you is the best thing that could have happened. You should be grateful for that, and for every man and woman who has volunteered to do the job you couldn't."

I'd gotten used to believers eating up my words, and hated when Paul was right. I told them I was fine and to feed me the lines about sacrifices, true heroes, how a strong military equaled a strong country, how every military member had my ultimate blessing, and that everyone should remember to vote in the preliminary. Twenty minutes later we had it wrapped.

Darren changed the green screen to a doctor's office and wheeled in a black chair with armrests. Paul handed me a bright blue button-down to put on instead of my white one. He dug around his briefcase and said, "Leave off the left sleeve though."

I sat down, set my forearm on the rest. "So why isn't Teddy doing this?"

Paul slipped on a lab coat and buttoned it up. "He's with his mother in Boston. She just had a stroke."

I don't think Paul knew he sounded so sad, but I wasn't about to bring it up. "He showed you how to do it?"

Paul removed a preloaded syringe out of a small metal case. "It's simple." He smacked the middle of my shoulder and said, "I've got a big target."

"But why do I have to do a real shot. I've never gotten one before."

Paul laughed. "You're afraid of a little prick? You've had countless needles jabbed in you."

I thought it was a stupid idea, but said, "Fine, but I'm not redoing this. Get it right on the first take."

Darren promised they would.

"So do I just sit here? What do I say?"

Paul said, "We'll film the injection first, your lines right after."

I asked them if they already got their shots. Over the past few weeks we'd recorded a couple clips promoting the vaccine, but I hadn't been following the story very closely, just knew the vaccine was free and the flu one more thing to fear. "Are they making it mandatory?"

Paul said, "They tried, but the President vetoed it."

Darren said, "They're predicting this as the absolute worst ever. I got mine soon as I heard."

Paul and Darren did their thing getting ready and I did mine, deep breaths through the nose to calm my mind. This was all just part of my paycheck, a little sting to remind me everything came with a price.

The needle punched through with a pinch, the brownish-yellow liquid a cold push.

Paul began to pull out the needle when the loudest bang made us jump. My first thought was gunfire and I hit the ground, Paul and Darren following suit. I crawled to the door to lock it, but it burst open, the edge flying by just inches from my face.

Father's cheeks were beet red, his eyes aflame. He yelled, "What in the name of hell are you doing?"

I got to my feet. "It sounded like a shotgun blast."

"And this is how we react?" Father shook his head, didn't hide his disgust. "Good thing we have guards."

I had no reason to say sorry, but still did. Paul and Darren both played it smart staying quiet behind me.

Father pointed at the broken needle sticking out of my shoulder. "Want to do something about that?"

Paul rushed over with a napkin, apologized as he picked the needle out with his fingernails. He asked Father what was wrong. "They didn't accept the plans?"

"Those heathens laughed in my face." Father's fists were clenched like he was strangling someone. "I gave them a verbal lashing they won't forget. They'll cower before us when they see our power. We will have the grandest church of all, one fit for the Messiah, and no one will stand in our way."

† † †

We hadn't left the house in nearly a month. Nevada had officially lifted their State of Emergency four days before and now the three of us were squished in the back seat, me on the left, Danielle the right, our hands clasped, an extra seatbelt for Lily who was asleep in her Wonder Woman car seat.

Troy's crew cut stuck out above the second row captain's seat in front of Danielle. No more trips without a guard by my side every moment. I'd requested both guards sit up front so we could pretend to have some privacy, like a normal family, but Father refused, said to leave the protecting to the professionals.

Lily had fallen asleep a few minutes into the ride, her chubby little cheek leaning on the headrest, the softest snore barely audible over the wheels. From what I read online, most kids started cutting out naps around her age, but Lily didn't get enough solid sleep at night.

I hadn't wanted Danielle or Lily coming with me, but not because I was worried about our safety. Danielle said no way, they were going with me wherever I went. I didn't argue because I understood. All my life I'd seen death, been blamed for it, too, but never on such an unprecedented scale.

Danielle was staring out her window, the Strip deserted except for the security guards and cops roaming to prevent looters. It was more of the same on my side of the street, but I tried to look on the bright side, thankful we weren't like 90% of the country whose streets were littered with corpses.

The smart ones were burning their bodies and doing it quick. Boston had made the mistake of mass graves, the blood seeping into the rivers and creating a red coast. Vegas had shut down first out of fear, but even when we realized the flu had skipped us, there was no point reopening the casinos. With initial estimates listing a quarter of the country dead and most states on mandatory lockdown, tourist season was officially over, no sign it'd ever come back. It'd been six days without a death from infection, but the death toll was rising every day from the overburdened and unmanned healthcare systems, riots and crime rampant with most law enforcement agencies crippled.

Johnny hit a speed bump and Lily threw herself against her straps, eyes wide and panicked. "Daddy! Daddy!"

Danielle took Lily's hands and I held her face. "It's okay, baby. Daddy's here, everything's okay."

Tears ran down her cheeks, her brown eyes piercing mine. So sad, like she knew it was true, she said, "You died."

"No, honey, it was a nightmare. You were asleep. I'm okay."

We'd had this conversation too many times, my fucking nightmares seemingly hereditary. It killed me to hear Lily say she was sorry. I put my lips to her forehead and held them there, breathed in her sweet strawberry shampoo. I broke it off with a kiss and lied to her. "I'll never leave you."

Danielle patted her chest. "And neither will I." Saying it like she really wanted to believe it, she said, "We'll all going to grow old together."

I wiped away Lily's tears and told her to smile. "As soon as I'm finished with work, the three of us will have a picnic and play at the park."

Danielle asked, "You think that's safe?"

I pointed out her window. "Couldn't see it being any safer."

Danielle nodded and had Lily look at her. "But we're only going if you can be a good girl. We have to be quiet."

Lily said, "I be good."

Troy turned around and said, "You can cut the audio to your room, but still let her watch."

I ignored him and said, "I don't want you guys in there today. You guys can stay in the car."

Lily said no. Danielle said, "She's going to be crying for you the whole time."

"No you won't, will you, sweetie?"

Her eyes were magnets pulling me in. "I want to watch."

I couldn't say why I didn't want them with me because Troy answered to Father. "I'm afraid not. I need you two to go with Troy and pick up the stuff for the picnic. I bet I'll be done by the time you get back."

Before Lily could say no, I said, "We'll have more time for the park." To Danielle, I mouthed, "Trust me. Please."

Troy turned around again. "I have orders to follow, sir."

I reminded him the church was closed to the public, this mass only to be witnessed by Darren and his lackeys. A special message to assure our members that everything is okay, the worst is over, and to welcome the National Guard and military to come in and restore order.

"There's plenty of men to watch over me. I want you to take care of my family."

"This is my job, sir."

"And I promise you'll always have it if you obey me. Father will not overturn my wishes."

Johnny pulled into the church's driveway and stopped at the gate. Troy hemmed and hawed a bit, but made his decision by the time it rolled back. "You won't tell him?"

"As far as I know you'll be making rounds outside." To Johnny I said, "Please take me to the rectory."

The car rolled to a stop and Troy stepped outside, said it was all clear.

I kissed Danielle and said I loved her, something I'd been trying to do more often, especially in front of Lily, who only let me go after our fifth kiss.

Dwight opened the rectory door and stepped aside to let me in, his smile falling flat, his voice just as dull when he said I was early.

I didn't know Dwight very well, but he seemed like a good guy, always going out of his way to make Lily smile. I asked, "Everything okay?"

With empty eyes, he said, "All my family was in Dallas."

"Shit. I'm so sorry."

The words didn't have any visible impact, but he thanked me anyway. "Charles is in the studio warming up."

"Don't tell him I'm here yet. I've got some warming up of my own to do."

Dwight said he understood and would be walking the perimeter if anyone needed him.

The studio was down the hall to the right, the sacristy straight ahead. I left my cloak on the hook and suppressed the urge to throw Father's chalice at the window knowing it'd only bounce right back. I parted the satin curtains and walked across the stage, entered the room we'd built into that side like a regular mother's room, only instead of four rows of chairs there was just my throne and a seat on either side. The windows could withstand a .50 caliber shot and the enhanced lock on the only door had turned it into a temporary safe room.

The throne was padded, the opposite of my childhood. The entire church was hard-wired with high-speed connections. I pulled out my phone and typed in flu.

Messianic Flu was the top result. Messianic Flu Kills Millions, the number rising each article, the latest count up to 70 million.

I switched from news to images; piles and piles of bodies, loved ones and strangers rotting as one.

From images to videos. I clicked the top result which was purple from already watching it. Darren had filmed a close-up of Father's face. His eyes hadn't been so sparkly and crazed with joy since the last time I'd nearly died, his voice as passionate. "This was written. It was spoken. It was preached. And nearly no one took note."

It looked like a lie when Father said he wished it weren't true. "But I'd told all of you a disaster would strike this year, nonbelievers falling in numbers untold. And what happened?"

The screen turned to a map of the US, all of it sprinkled red, with only a few spots remaining virgin white. A triangle inside Nevada, and a strip stretching from South Carolina to Washington D.C., and around each of our military bases.

"The only areas untouched by the Messianic Flu are the holiest of areas blessed by my son, the Second Son. He did not want all this death, just as he doesn't want nonbelievers to burn in hell. Joshua is a kind and just man, but he is the Messiah, and as the Messiah he must cast judgment.

"It tears me up inside to see such a massive waste of life, but at least now we have proof, we have hope. We can all join forces and believe, pray that the Lord Almighty is done teaching us."

A door opened then closed, probably the rectory as I had a clear view of the church's entrance from where I was sitting. I figured it was Dwight and went back to the news, forced myself to read the latest prediction, which cities would recover, and which would never bounce back.

A door slammed followed by shouts, one of them Father's. There was a thud and more shouts, a bang in the sacristy. Something crashed, perhaps a cabinet. Dwight ran down the center aisle and flew up the stairs as the sacristy's curtain blew open, Paul and Father grabbing at the other's black suit, tumbling toward the altar.

Dwight grabbed them a split second before the collision and pushed them apart. Paul didn't let go of Father's jacket, a loud rip as the lapel tore off in his hand.

I couldn't see Father's face, but I could hear his fury. He pointed to the door. "Dwight, leave us. Now! And no one comes in!"

Dwight said, "Yes, sir," and left, the front door clunking shutting behind him.

Paul wiped blood from the corner of his mouth, his eyes red, nostrils flaring in and out. He started to speak, but Father cut him off, shouted, "You got what you wanted!"

Paul said, "You killed Teddy!"

Father closed the gap, smacked Paul upside his head, knocked him to his knees.

Paul got back up, held his cheek. Father hit him even harder, knocked him back down, stood close enough to let Paul know he better stay where he was.

"I did nothing that you didn't do yourself. We both knew there'd be casualties. And if your cocksucking little boyfriend—"

Paul shot back up and shouted, "He's not—" but Father slammed him down, warned him to stay there.

"You got a choice to make, right now, Paulie. You're free to go. But you will not reap any of the rewards. I won't stop you."

Paul stayed on one knee.

Father said, "You say we don't need Joshua. I say we don't need you."

Paul said something I couldn't make out.

Father told him to speak up.

His voice trembled as he said, "I'm sorry."

Chapter Twenty-Three

All of Father's town cars were upgraded after the shooting at President Burkhart's inauguration. Now our only means of travel was in full-size SUVs, same bulletproof windows, airless tires, and armored frames nearly thick as a tank's. The glaring difference was that they'd turned around the second row of seats so the bodyguard could always face me.

Of course I never told him out loud, but Troy reminded me of one of those green army men forever locked in the same position, his body just as stiff, his face giving nothing away. His nose had been broken, there were a couple small scars on his forehead, and his cold eyes said he'd taken lives and wouldn't hesitate to take more. And he still looked like a fucking model compared to me.

Father liked to say Troy was part of our family, but even though I spent more time with him than anyone else, I barely knew a thing about him. Troy never talked about the war and I never asked. He never spoke about the rest of his life either; every conversation never adding a word, but always listening.

I still felt guilty for when Troy got reprimanded by Father, but I needed him to break the rules once again. When Greg pulled up to the gated community's guardhouse and rolled down the window to give my name, I asked Troy, "Do you believe I'm the Messiah?"

It was the first time I'd ever asked him or any of the other guards. I assumed most of them thought it was bullshit and just considered it a job, so I was fairly shocked when Troy said, "Of course I do. You are His Second Son."

"Really?"

"Oh yes. Every day I protect you is an honor."

Greg rolled up his window and drove past the raised gate. In case he was eavesdropping, I kept my voice low, "Then don't you think it might be a good idea to listen to me instead of Father?"

"Last time—"

"Last time was unlucky. This time he's not here." I nodded toward Greg and said, "And he'll go along with whatever you tell him."

"What do you want?"

"Just stay in the car. No one knows we're here. We're fine."

Greg turned down the last street and parked in front of Jeremy's house, almost two years since the one time I'd visited.

I patted the .40 caliber Glock holstered on my hip. "I can handle myself from here to there. But if it makes you feel better, you can walk me to the front door."

Troy, who had taught me how to shoot, opened the door, made a show of looking up and down the deserted street before stepping aside. "Not a word to your father."

I darted to the door and rang the doorbell, didn't recognize the older guy in black fatigues who answered it.

In the same no-nonsense tone Troy had, the guy asked my name and I gave it. He told me to turn around for a pat down and I asked if he was serious.

"Sorry, pal, cost of the ride."

I told him about the gun. He removed it from my holster and set it inside a black lock box. I didn't care for the fondling but appreciated his precaution.

Jeremy walked down the hallway, looking about the same, a little heavier around the waist. "And all your electronics, too."

I pulled out my phone, thought about how we talked a couple times, all but the last call coming from him. Him saying sorry. Him saying he missed us. Him begging for forgiveness, for us to let him see Lily. I said, "You don't trust me?"

"Dude, you work for The Church."

He had a point. I put the phone beside my gun.

"Hank, you got any idea who this is?"

Hank locked the box and handed me the key. Speaking to Jeremy, he said, "Your two o'clock meeting. Joshua Campbell."

"True. But he's also the most famous motherfucker in the world right now." He turned to me and said, "You just passed one billion followers."

"I thought we were still in third."

"Well, nothing like the worst catastrophe ever to bring in the sheep. But don't get too cocky. The only thing the chick two spots behind you accomplished is sucking the right singer's dick."

Hank excused himself, took my box to his desk with the large computer monitor. The screen was broken down into 16 sections, capturing what must've been the entire inside and outside of the house.

I nodded toward the surveillance. "When did all this start?"

"When the person wanting me dead became President."

"Burkhart?"

Jeremy's eyes asked if I was really that stupid. "He was trashed that night, but he remembered who he'd been with. He knows it was me that took the photos."

"He saw them?"

"Why else would I have taken them?"

"Father said it was just in case."

Jeremy brought his hand up to my repaired cheek and I flinched away. He stopped and said sorry. "They did a great job. Can I?"

I nodded thinking he'd just touch the bullet groove. Instead, Jeremy took the tip of his finger and ran it from the start beside my eyes to the end an inch behind my ear. He gave the edge a few flicks and said in his sexiest voice, "Oh yeah, baby, you feel nice."

I slapped his hand away, laughed as I called him an asshole.

"I can't believe they put it on every channel, the first live televised execution in nearly a hundred years. I expected to see you in the front row cheering next to Charles."

"I was still in the hospital. Turned it off when the nurse put it on."

"Well they sure showed that fucker and the rest of the world what happens when you mess with the Messiah."

"Doesn't help Dwight any."

Jeremy got serious. "Sorry, man, just trying to make light of some heavy shit. Talk about close calls. It can't get much closer."

"I don't know. Close is how it's gone all my life. I shouldn't even be here."

He knew I wasn't talking about his house. "Well, I'm glad you are. You were the one who said my niece deserved a daddy."

I wasn't going to bring it up but there was no way to keep it in. I managed to keep my voice playful and said, "Yeah, and then you decided to show the world my cock."

Jeremy looked all out of apologies, a sheepish grin on his face like he couldn't help himself either. He spread his fingers about four inches apart and said, "True, but not all of it."

"You know what, dude, I don't even care about that shit anymore." I was sure the assassination attempts were part of the reason I had moved on, but I was over holding grudges. I got why he did what he did, how he lashed out at his loved ones when he was hurt. But I left all that unsaid and told him, "But I do need to talk with you."

"Shoot."

I nodded at Hank who was watching the monitors. Jeremy headed for the hallway and told me to follow. He paused at the last room on the left, punched a series of numbers on the keypad. The metal door slid into the wall and we walked inside the large room, the right half a fancy office, a bed and bathroom on the other.

Jeremy pressed a button and the door slid shut. "Nothing's getting through that and we got enough food and booze in here to make it through the winter."

"Good to know but they're expecting me for dinner."

He walked around the black marble desk and eased into his chair, poured himself a large Grey Goose on the rocks. He raised his glass toward the seat across from him. "Come and join me."

I said I was fine.

"So how's Lily?" I could hear the old hurt when he said, "She start school yet?"

"One more year before kindergarten, but I'm guessing she'll be home-schooled." I hoped he knew it was Danielle who cut him off. "She's getting big."

He took a swig and said, "I bet."

There were three movie posters on the wall. *Mounted by the Messiah, The Messiah Always Cums Twice,* and *The Power and the Glory-hole.*

Jeremy saw where I was looking and opened a drawer, handed me three DVD cases. On the back of *Mounted* there were stills including a giant baptismal tub, a hot nurse, and a strip club. He said, "I would've asked you to take the starring role if you weren't married to my sister."

I turned over the other two and took it all in. "And I might've said yes."

Jeremy put the cases away and said, "So what's up? Why you here?" He smiled to show he was joking when he said, "Not another letter from your lawyer?"

"Fuck, I don't know where to start."

"You need money?"

"Why'd you think that?"

"That's usually why strangers reappear."

"If I'm right I'd need a lot more money than you could lend us, and I'd never be able to pay it back."

"Why don't you just ask Charles? Have you seen how much your little city is costing the Church? They say it's going to be complete by Christmas, in time for your baptism."

"That's what they say."

Jeremy held up a finger. "Hold on, right about what? Spit it out."

I wasn't sure how much I could trust him, but figured I didn't have much to lose. "What do you know about the church?"

"Know-know, like everything?"

Jeremy had often hinted at things, referred to them evil more than once. I said, "Yeah, I need to know what I'm part of."

We both knew he could've made a sarcastic remark about it taking so fucking long for me to ask, but he just said, "You've got to sit then." He topped off his drink and poured one for me. "You'll want this."

Jeremy woke his computer and asked, "So is there something specific you're looking for? You only want facts?"

I sipped the vodka and forced myself to sit back. "Everything. I want to hear what you know."

"You mean like that Charles is one scary son-of-a-bitch? That he would do absolutely anything to spread his religion?"

"Yeah. Like that."

Jeremy clicked away. "I've got so much shit on here. I'm guessing the beginning is probably the best place."

I took another sip, waited for him to begin.

"I had my suspicions about him before I even met you, just like everyone else when someone starts saying crazy things. But then I met you and you gave us that sign. I thought maybe I could see why he believed what he did, even if it was pretty nuts."

"What were you suspicious of?"

Jeremy turned the screen so I could see, a mugshot of Paul as a teenager, his nose leaning left. "Your brother's juvie record which didn't come cheap." He pointed at the text. "Arrested for stealing a cross. This one's vandalism of a church's rectory."

"You think Father made him?"

"Of course he did. This kind of shit had been happening around our area as far back as I can remember. Broken windows, nails in tires, sugar in gas tanks, crosses cut down. I'd bet my ass Charles was behind nearly all of it."

I didn't realize I'd had another drink until I set down my empty glass.

A new image popped on the screen. "You remember this guy?"

I couldn't place the guy at first, but I'd seen those eyes locked on mine, focused not fearful. "From the hospital."

"Killed in County the next night even though he had a guard at the door."

"You feel sorry for him?"

"Did anyone ever tell you he was a member of the Charlotte church?"

I shook my head, didn't like where this was headed.

A video clicked on of an attack on our Hartsville church that had gone viral, none of the men in black ever arrested. Jeremy pointed to the third guy on the left. "That's him right there."

"Who? The driver?"

"Yep."

"How can you tell?"

"Because I filmed it."

"Are you serious?"

"Charles said it wasn't hurting anyone but ourselves and if the government could use false flags then why shouldn't we." Jeremy saw I wasn't getting it and said, "It was just a ploy to raise sympathy and draw attention. But that dude was there. He was a believer."

"You think he was just following Charles 3:16 when he hit me?"

"That I don't know, but I bet they put him up to it. That's what happened to the guy who rushed you leaving the church."

"But Paul was there, too."

"Yeah, he sure was. You weren't surprised how brave Paul was standing up to a guy with a machete? You thought I just got lucky capturing the right angle?"

"Why didn't you tell me?"

"It was my job. They wanted it to be a natural reaction. No one ever expected you'd kill the guy, but I bet that's what would've happened to him anyhow, just like the other fuckface."

The words sounded ridiculous coming out of my mouth. "You think they tried to kill me?"

"Well, definitely not that first time. That was just promotion." Jeremy turned to the computer, put on a clip of my assassination attempt, pausing it a second before the gunman took aim. "And I don't think you were ever the real target on this. You just ducked into that bullet."

"That's crazy."

The gun was aimed at Dwight's face, never wavering before the bullet blasted through his brain. Jeremy said, "One guess what church he belonged to."

"That would've been all over the news."

Jeremy shook his head. "Who do you think controls the news?"

"But why try with the car but not the other times? Why Dwight?"

"You were a liability before, but now you're the golden boy, doing what you're told. I got no idea about Dwight, but I'm guessing he pissed off the wrong person."

"Or saw the wrong thing."

Jeremy filled both our glasses, took a big swig, and said, "And people think I'm the sick fuck."

Everything felt kind of numb, but not from the booze.

"Hey, you alright?"

I finally knew something Jeremy didn't, but I was too ashamed to tell him. I'd been sitting on the information for nearly a month. "You know anything about the flu?"

Jeremy sat up. "Like what?"

"Like who was behind it."

"You're shitting me."

"I wish I was." I took the papers from my back pocket, hated my hand was shaking when I unfolded them.

Jeremy laid the papers on his desk. "What's this?"

"Proof. A proposal I found on Father's computer."

"These numbers?"

"That row is estimates in life. Entirely way too low across the board."

"And this?"

"The revenue to be collected. I have no way of knowing what the real numbers turned out to be."

"Holy shit." Jeremy collapsed in his chair, finished his drink.

I did the same. "The news made the government look like the good guys, clearing all the bodies and taking over the housing. The inheritance law alone must've already brought in billions."

"There's no way." Jeremy's fingers flew across his keypad. "As much as I hate him, I also respect his intelligence, but there's no way he could pull it off."

"With Burkhart in his pocket?"

Jeremy shook his head. "He wasn't President yet."

"This is what handed it to him. Every liberal state was wiped out."

"But how?"

"No idea. But I heard Paul call Father a killer, watched Father beat him down until he said he was sorry."

"Oh shit." Jeremy double-clicked a photo. "Recognize this guy?"

"Burkhart's buddy at Myrtle Beach."

"Yeah. He's also the Secretary of Health."

I took a big breath and blew it out. "You see why I need money."

"I see why you can't ask Charles."

"Jeremy, I'm fucking scared. We all are. We need to get out."

"Have you thought of when and where?"

"No, we need the how first. It has to be enough so we never have to come back."

He thought about it for a second. "Alright, this shouldn't be hard. Any famous motherfucker can make money." Jeremy closed his eyes, steepled his fingers, bowed his head, and lightly tapped forehead to fingertips again and again. After a minute or so his eyes popped open. "I think I got it. It's going to be this Christmas's number 1 wish list item."

"What is it?"

He asked how my hands were and mumbled something about me doing a little wet work.

"I thought you were all against that."

"Why would I care?"

Whispering in case someone had found a way to listen in, I said, "Wet work's killing someone, right?"

"Wood," he said slowly. "Wood work."

I said, "Oh, yeah, that should be no problem."

Jeremy said, "Let me figure this out. Give me a week."

It only took Jeremy five days to figure everything out, but it took me ten to convince Danielle this was our best option and that we were running out of time. She hadn't said a word the whole ride to the north side of town. Which wasn't surprising with Troy sitting across from me, his eyes constantly shifting from one window to the other.

Troy caught me staring, sounded curious when he asked what we had planned.

Danielle looked beautiful, her hair tied back tight in a ponytail, bright red lipstick to match her blouse. She acted like it hadn't been three years since she spoke to Jeremy and said, "Oh, we're going to film something with my brother."

He looked at the rows of warehouses on either side. "Why not in the White room?" Making it sound less like an interrogation, he said, "Doing some outdoor scenes?"

I said, "I'm not sure what he has in mind. Just that it's top secret."

Troy gave his two-second courtesy chuckle and held his ear piece. "Roger that."

We slowed and made a left into a parking lot that was empty except for Jeremy's Humvee and a sleek lime-green sportscar. Twenty yards from the building, we came to a stop, the car idling. Danielle squeezed my hand hard enough to hurt.

"He's not one of ours," Troy said. "That his man?"

He wasn't asking me, but I looked out and saw Hank standing a few feet from the warehouse's front door, his hand on the butt of his holstered pistol. "Yep. He's one of Jeremy's."

Troy spoke into his cuff mic and rogered something else. "Air support says there's a guy on the rooftop with an AR-15."

I said, "It's fine. He's Jeremy's."

Troy glanced at me. "You can't even see him."

"Well, I'm guessing if it was a bad guy, him and Hank would've been shooting it out by now."

Troy told Randall to pull up close to the door and the others to keep an eye on the roof. Randall got out the front, spoke with Hank, and then opened our door. Troy joined him and leaned back in to say it was all clear like we couldn't have figured that out.

Hank assured Troy everything was under control and told them they were welcome to wait in the car. He opened the warehouse door for us and said Jeremy was inside.

The lobby was nothing like I'd expected, everything white and sparkly, a purple neon JL Productions sign on the wall behind the counter. Trying to cheer Hank up, I said, "What, no pat down? Getting sloppy."

His smile unnerved me. "Against my wishes. Boss said you are to be completely trusted."

"Hold on," Jeremy said from the doorway, his foot propping the door open. "I didn't say her."

Hank apologized and asked Danielle to turn around. Right before her tears let loose, Jeremy said, "I'm just fucking around. Glad to see you, sis."

Danielle kind of smiled. "Good to see you, too."

"I didn't think you'd be joining us."

It didn't sound like it was going to be a problem, but I didn't want her saying the wrong thing and causing an argument. I said, "We both felt better about it."

She said, "Figure we're in this thing together. 'Til death do us part and all that."

"Where's Lily? Please tell me you didn't bring her, too."

Danielle said, "Janet's watching her."

"Is she a guard?"

Danielle said, "Lily loves her."

I said, "Because she lets her watch TV and play her electronics."

Jeremy studied me when he asked, "You trust her with your daughter?"

I hadn't told Danielle all the stuff I'd learned because it would've paralyzed her with fear. So he'd drop it, I said, "Janet's great."

"Trained killers do make for some wonderful friends. Ain't that right, Hank?"

Hank grunted and Jeremy held the door all the way open. "Then let's do this. We've got an exit plan to finance."

The warehouse was huge, storage and props lining the outside walls, three small movie sets in the middle. Hospital room with a bed. Office with a desk and couch. Bathroom with a sink, a stall, and holes in the wall.

Jeremy said, "When we started we didn't have any of the fancy stuff. Hell, we had to roll the one bed from set to set."

Danielle said, "Eww."

"We changed the sheets."

I asked him if he owned the building.

"Cost next to nothing." Jeremy saw where I was looking. "Yeah, it goes all the way back. We've got another three sets facing that way."

Danielle asked, "What will you do with it?"

We turned the corner. I spotted the baptismal tub against the wall and was glad when Jeremy distracted Danielle by pointing toward the last set. "That's ours. As far as this place, I'd probably sell what I can then torch the rest."

I said, "Seems a little extreme."

Jeremy stopped at the last set. "I'll make sure everyone's out."

"Hi there," a voice cracked from the set.

It looked like a teenage girl's bedroom, the blonde on the bed in the pink G-string looking way more like a mom, her fake tits lumped up like she'd stuffed them full of rocks. Making a point of staring at my body, she licked her lips and said, "Wow."

"Easy, tiger," Jeremy told her. "Why don't you slip on your outfit while I go over some things with them." To me, Jeremy said, "Please tell me you brought them?"

"Three of them. Didn't know what color or size would look best."

Danielle opened her oversized purse and pulled a 12-inch long black mahogany crucifix, a 9-inch rosewood, and 6-inch ash. Each of their bases had been smoothed down into dildos, my initials etched deep.

Jeremy inspected them and kissed the round tip of the red one. "I love it." He gave Danielle a sly look and said, "You didn't use these, did you?"

Her expression didn't change, her eyes on the blonde slipping on the scarlet robe. "Let's not do this today."

I told Jeremy I was a little worried about how long it was going to take to finish the entire order. "I don't know how the hell Charles does it. He used to carve all the time and never complained but I just did these three and had to take four aspirin to take away the ache in both hands."

"Probably the type of wood. Regardless of what we use in this, we'll put in the fine print, they'll get whatever we have, selections starting with highest bidders to lowest."

Danielle said, "I don't like this."

I followed her gaze to the blonde stretched out on the bed, the gown bunched up so we could see she'd already ditched the G-string. "I don't think any of us do, but we're talking a thousand for each one."

"That's just the starting bid," Jeremy reminded us. "We do a good job here and I bet we'll average five times as much."

Danielle's head kept slowly shaking. So soft that I had to lean in to hear, she said, "No. Not with her. She's gross."

Jeremy still overheard. "No, we already agreed. She's gotta do. I shut the place down for this. I couldn't find anyone better for our timeframe. This is it."

I said, "I'm not even going to touch her." I looked to Jeremy, "Right?"

"Totally. You're just gonna stand there. I mean maybe rest your hand on her."

"You said—"

Danielle cut me off. "I'll do it."

No one said a word.

She was serious, her face set. "I'll be better than that whore."

Jeremy said, "No way. Craig's paying for the commercial, not your crosses. This commercial is what'll make these bad boys worth so much."

"Exactly," Danielle said. "You want people thinking they are going to catch syphilis with these things? That's what I'd be thinking."

Jeremy said, "You're just being jealous."

"I don't know, man. Maybe she's got a point. I'll be way more natural if I can be next to her."

"I don't want to film you."

Danielle chuckled. "What's happened to you? This place give you morals?"

Jeremy said, "We were planning on running two versions. R and X."

Her face didn't waver. "That's what brought us together." She looked at me and said, "I'll do whatever it takes to keep it that way."

Jeremy said, "Fine, we'll try. One hour. If we can't get it done, we bring her back in. Agreed?"

I said I'd do anything Danielle wanted. She told me to get changed, and for Jeremy to get rid of the skank.

He asked, "You think that robe will fit you alright?"

"Yuck. I'm not trying. Don't worry, just give me the script and five minutes."

I walked Danielle to the bathroom while Jeremy went over to the blonde. Her frown turned into a smile and she slid off the bed, gave him a huge hug, and headed for the front.

I asked Jeremy what he told her.

"Where I keep my coke." Jeremy walked around the set's wall and came back with a black cloak that looked identical to the one I wore for church. He handed it over and said, "Might be tight. You saw the dude that played you."

"You wash it?"

"It's fine." Jeremy arranged the crucifixes on the night stand. "Just don't wear it anywhere near a black light."

I started to slide it over my head, but he stopped me and said, "Take off your shirt, we don't want anything showing at the collar."

The cloak was snug across my shoulders, tight against my chest.

Jeremy said, "Fuck yeah, that looks even cooler."

I pretended I wasn't shaking inside and walked onto the set, stood beside the bed. "This good?"

Jeremy was giving me a thumbs up when Danielle came around the corner, walking with a purpose wearing nothing but a purple negligee I'd never seen. He said, "Oh shit."

Danielle said, "Not a word, Jeremy. Just record. Don't make a sound."

He nodded and got behind the camera, its red light blinking.

I stayed where I was, didn't know what to say. Our sex life had been all but eradicated after Lily's birth, our love making more of a monthly chore done in the dark, sexy negligees never playing a part.

Danielle stepped onto the set and took my hands, looked up at me. "Just go with it," she said. "This is for us."

I said I'd do my best. She turned me so we both faced the camera. With one hand on my shoulder, the other on my chest, Danielle spoke to the camera in her sexiest voice. "Ladies, let's not lie. We've all wondered what it's like pleasured by a god."

Danielle turned me so my back was to the camera and eased off my cloak, letting it fall to the floor. Her right hand traced my tattooed cross while her left hand made a cross over her chest, subtly undoing her negligee and letting it fall. "But only one of us knows what it's really like to be filled with the power and the glory of the Messiah."

My hard on was pushing out the front of my jeans and I prayed she wouldn't turn me back around.

Danielle ran a hand down my stomach and undid my top button, her eyes on the camera, her nipples just as hard as me. "The only problem is that the Messiah can't be home all day. What's a girl to do?"

Keeping her hand on my jeans, Danielle crawled onto the bed completely naked and pulled me so my leg was up against it. She popped another button free and said, "When I can't have the real thing, there's only one substitute." She reached across the bed and picked up the rosewood crucifix, held it up for the camera.

She freed the third button, my hard on begging to be touched, her thigh pushing against my hand as she spread her legs. I wrapped my hand around the inside of her leg to keep it in place, impressed she could remember the sales pitch.

My last button popped open and Danielle wrapped her hand around me, made the sexiest purr as she accepted the crucifix. Her hands maintained a slow rhythm that matched her voice when she said just as there was only one Messiah, there was only one dildo approved by Him. Sounding completely natural and letting the *oohs* and *ooos* punctuate her speech, Danielle said, "This is a once in a lifetime opportunity. Only a limited number of blessed crucifixes, inscribed by the Second Son, will be auctioned off."

Danielle pulled the crucifix from her, showed why she hadn't needed any lube.

Knowing that was the end of the scene, I leaned over and placed a gentle kiss on her lips. "You were great."

The crucifix went back to the night stand, her hand still wrapped around me. "Come here."

It sounded just like she said it when she wanted to fuck, but that was crazy with her brother there. I stalled. "I need Jeremy to help me film one last thing. I want to tell the world what I really think."

She opened her leg even further and put it behind my back, used it to turn me toward the bed. With her arms around my neck, she pulled me closer and said, "Okay, but after. I need you."

I turned to the camera, the red light off, Jeremy nowhere to be seen.

✝ ✝ ✝

It was two weeks from Christmas and the day Father had planned my rebirth, a glorious baptism that would put me in the minds of every person on earth. But we had different plans. The four of us were getting on a private airplane in less than ten hours, the commercial set to air another ten after we landed safely in Barcelona.

Back when we thought I'd fly right through the crucifixes, Craig said we should release the commercial early, we were sitting on a gold mine. Thinking about how much an extra week could potentially increase the bids made me consider it, but I couldn't risk deviating from the plan.

I was in the office, sitting at my desk, gripping the black walnut crucifix so I could etch my initials into the fattest part of the rounded base. Getting started was the hardest part, the tip of the knife pressing just hard enough to indent the wood. The long stroke down, curved at the bottom. The line across the top to finish the J. The small curve of the C. My hands a little jittery from all the coffee and lack of sleep.

An inch below my initials, I carved a nine, then an eight. I was finishing the two when a blob of sweat splashed off the crucifix and the knife jumped, digging a line across my nail and biting into the quick.

"Goddamn it! It's like ninety degrees in here. Can someone turn that down?"

I held my hand and wrapped my finger with a rag. There was blood on the crucifix, but I didn't bother wiping it off. I rubbed it into the number. Liking the way it looked, I undid the towel and stained nine more crucifixes, placing tiny drops of blood instead of checkmarks on my master sheet.

The bleeding stopped on its own. Eighteen more to go. Three more hours if I rushed. Only problem was the pain in my right palm, the arthritis a spear through my impalement, pulsing like the hole had never closed.

I put each of the anointed crosses in individual bubble wrap sleeves and set them in the box next to my chair. I was shaking out my hands, flexing my fingers when Troy spoke on the intercom. "Excuse me, sir. I have a caller on line one."

I opened the blind to let in some fresh light. From this side of the house, I could see down the hill, three separate Charles 3:16s painted on top of neighboring roofs in large white letters.

To the right was our circular driveway with the fountain in the middle, a massive gate that could only be opened with the correct code or approval from the guest house where Troy sat behind the desk.

When I picked up the handset, I noticed he'd only paged the office. "Did they give a name?"

"Said his name is Craig. Wouldn't say who he was with, but said he's a partner of yours."

I looked at the remaining crucifixes. "Did you tell him I was in?"

"No, sir. Said I would check. Want me to get rid of him?"

I thought about it a second then told Troy I'd get it. I pressed line one and said, "You shouldn't be calling this number."

"Well, you should answer your cell."

"It'll be ready just like I said."

"Not like you originally said. That was last week."

"I'm practically done. Eighteen to go."

"Good. They'll have to be mailed the second the bidding's over or they're going to be some angry people with nothing under their Christmas tree. Your delay cost us a fortune."

"I went as fast as I could. They'll be ready."

"You thought any more about what I said?"

I looked at the stacks of giant mail bags in front of the bookcase, proof of how screwed up the world had become. "Nope, this is it," I said, loving how true those words felt, hanging up to make them final.

The crucifixes had to be finished, but I needed a break. I picked up the stack of letters, not many left. I almost hit the intercom, but a terrible thought stopped me. I didn't touch a thing and just said, "Hey, Troy."

Troy looked to his left, where they kept all the monitors. He didn't talk so I spoke again.

"Can you hear me?"

He looked over and nodded. It was hard to read his expression.

I picked up the phone and pressed his extension.

"Sorry about that," Troy said. "That feature isn't supposed to be activated. Someone must've hit it by mistake."

"Why's that feature even there?"

"In case a client needs assistance, but can't reach a phone. Some people insist on it."

"I always got my phone on me so do me a favor and keep it off."

"Yes, sir. Anything else?"

I didn't want it looking like I had just called to give him a hard time. "Has the mail been sorted yet?"

"I got it a little while ago, but I'll have it to you within the half-hour."

"That'd be great. I'd appreciate it if you can bring in whatever you have, hate mail as well."

"Threat assessment team has most of it, but I'll bring what I can."

I hung up the phone, my stomach tied in a knot. I wondered just how long that button had been pressed. I replayed all the conversations Danielle and I had whispered. All the ones we hadn't been as careful with.

It was too late to worry about it. I took out the first letter and set the stack next to my knife. The first was all death, the second one, too, both in the shredder before I finished reading. The third said they pitied me, only wished me the best. The fourth said he, too, had a daughter.

There was movement behind me. Everything slowed and I spun around ready to attack.

Lily laughed as she pointed. "Got you. Made you jump."

I swallowed my reaction to yell out of embarrassment. "You got me, but remember, honey, you've got to be careful sneaking up on Daddy." I pretended to bop her head and said, "I might've turned around and bonked you."

She reached for the letters. "I want to help."

I grabbed Lily's hand and put it by her side. "Remember what I said about Daddy's office. There's sharp stuff in here. It's not a place to play."

Lily's hand went back to the letters that were just inches from the knife. I slapped it away before she cut herself. "Lily! What did I say?"

She lowered her head. "Sorry."

I hadn't hit her hard, but I hated myself for doing what I swore I never would. "Shouldn't you be taking a nap?"

"I'm having a hard time sleeping."

"Well, I'm working so I can't play right now."

"I want to go to the park."

"It's too cold, sweetie."

"I want to go."

"Then go ask Janet." The stress and lack of sleep was making me a grouch. "Why isn't she playing with you?"

"Getting lunch from outside."

I pulled back the blind. Janet was talking to Raymond outside the guesthouse. Lily got on her tip toes, could just barely see over the sill. She said, "Janet said I was silly."

I closed the blind. "And I agree."

"Cuz I hide all my clothes."

I looked at Lily, found it hard to breathe. "Wait, what?"

"She said I was silly. All my drawers are empty."

I didn't say fuck, but I was screaming it. We'd packed ahead of time, figured it was safer than someone walking in on us packing.

"Did she say anything else?"

"We played treasure hunt."

"No, no, about the clothes. Did she say anything about the clothes?"

Lily got a huge smile. "You're silly. That's what I said. A treasure hunt. We found them in the closet."

I picked up Lily and hugged her tight so she couldn't see my face. "Oh, I am silly."

Danielle appeared in the doorway and said, "So are we going to the park?"

I knew how nervous Danielle had to be, but she was hiding it well. If I told her what Lily had just said, I feared she would lose it. "You really want to go?"

Danielle looked lighter, like some of that worry had been lifted. She said, "It'll be fun."

I pointed at the stack of crucifixes. "I've got to finish all these in the next six hours."

"You've been working nonstop," Danielle said. "How about a little break? For all of us. And honestly, he won't cancel payment if you're a few short."

I couldn't see it mattering at this point. If we went out for a little playdate it'd only ease suspicions. Who cared if we'd packed a bunch of clothes? "We'll need a driver."

"I already took care of it. Troy said he'd have someone here in ten minutes."

I picked up number 983. "Okay. Let me get one more."

Lily cheered. "Yeah, Daddy."

Danielle said, "You'll probably want to change."

I finished the J and was starting the C when my hand slipped and I grazed my thumb. I sounded just like Father when I said, "We'll go when I'm done."

Danielle took Lily's hand. "Come with me, sweetheart. We need to get dressed."

I finished the crucifix and checked it off when Lily called from the hallway.

"We're ready!" Lily had on her pink snow pants and matching cap, bopping a giant red balloon in the air.

I turned back and noticed movement on the monitor, a car at the front gate. I waited for either a phone call or the car to be sent away. When the front gate opened, Troy gave the driver of the small Toyota his practiced nod.

The car drove forward out of sight, just the trunk visible on the driveway camera. I figured it was a delivery and got up from my desk, set the knife high.

The doorbell rang and from upstairs. Danielle said, "I got it."

I took my sweatshirt off the back of the door and put it on. "Troy didn't call."

Danielle's shoes clicked down the stairs. "It's probably the driver."

"No, he isn't one of theirs."

The doorbell rang again and Lily sang, "Ding-dong, ding-dong!"

I put on my boots as Danielle opened the door, her body between me and the bearded man, a gust of cold wind blowing past them.

"Afternoon, ma'am," the man said, no question he was from the Deep South. "Is your husband in?"

I locked the office door and started down the hallway.

Lily said, "Daddy, can we go?"

I wanted her out of the way so I pointed to the shoe cubby to the left of the door. "Yeah, go get your shoes on."

Lily did as I said and Danielle showed the man inside.

The guy's face was fat at the bottom and narrow up top, bald except for a couple clumps of hair slicked over. He gave a crooked smile and closed the door behind him. "Thanks so much. It's awful cold out there."

His face registered, the eyes crazed with joy, the scribbled signature scrawled below his Polaroid. His warning it'd be the last face I'd see.

I ran down the hallway. "Run, Lily! Run!"

Lily was down on her bottom, struggling with her shoe. "One minute."

Danielle backed up a step.

The man shed his thick jacket and said, "Forgive me Father for I have sinned."

I was nearly to them, the high table my last chance. I shouted at my girls to get down and grabbed hold of the table, held it in front of me as I leapt toward Lily.

Everything flashed white, then went black.

Chapter Twenty-Four

The strip is all headlights and torches, a hundred thousand flashing phones. All the casinos north of us turned their lights off out of respect, possibly fear of retribution. Some might not consider retaliation a Christian virtue, but only those that haven't read *The Lost Gospels*.

It's too dark to see the cemetery anymore, but I have the memory from this morning. Danielle already heard the speech, but I wanted to practice. I read it to her and Lily, trying so hard to keep it together, picturing what little remains of my baby girl piled on top of her mother, ignoring the paparazzi outside the gates with their cameras, people yelling at me to save them, stop being a selfish bastard. One motherfucker even pegged the back of my head with a rock.

I swivel my throne around and face the empty church, Jeremy waiting out in the hall with the first group. Up on the screen is a live newscast. They're calling it an unofficial report, but trusted sources are telling them the Messiah vote is nearly tied, too close to say which way it will go. They even included the phone number at the bottom.

The special report goes back to our program, Father and Paul standing tall in front of the church's main entrance, Troy holding the handle. I give the command and Troy opens the door, escorts them in after Jeremy hurries through with the camera.

Jeremy backs down the aisle ahead of the dynamic duo with their matching black suits and powerful strides. They'd already been instructed what to do, but Troy takes no chances and ushers them into the first pew in the middle. The only one that Father hand carved. The one that came from the tree that almost killed me.

Darren, who's helping Jeremy with the filming, comes in from the side entrance, his camera capturing Father's smile as he slides into the pew.

Jeremy says, "The Messiah requests everyone kneel."

They get down on the kneeler, Father's grimace making me a little giddy. I bet he wants to ask why we removed the cushions, but he's a smart guy. I'm sure he'll figure out that what's good enough for the Messiah is good enough for them.

The screen switches to an outside shot, the sound of fire crackling, electric flames reaching halfway up the building. It won't be long now.

Jeremy gives Troy a nod at the bottom of the staircase and heads up. His camera's off and by his side, no one filming him, but he's walking with a purpose, a professional taking this moment seriously.

All those crucifixes and the money we would've made were lost with the lives, but instead of saving his own ass and getting on the plane, Jeremy stayed by my side. The four months I was in the hospital, he provided his own guard to watch over me, keeping a close eye on Father's guards to make sure they didn't try anything. Since my release three weeks ago, I've been living at his house, both of us waiting for a drone strike or some kind of attack. If I can't trust Jeremy, I can't trust anyone.

On the right armrest there are three buttons. I press the first and tell Jeremy the door's unlocked. He comes in, closes it behind him. I hit the second button that turns off the audio, cutting us off from the people on the other side of the glass.

Jeremy sets the camera on the edge of the altar, probably not even thinking how much it must piss Father off. He reaches into his suit and says, "I've got something for you."

I say, "Me, too," and pour him a drink, set it on top of Father's bible, then fill mine back up.

Father and Paul are the only ones looking our way, but they can't see the massive silver revolver Jeremy's cradling like a baby. He says, "It's a 44 Magnum. Six hollow points. Bought and loaded them myself."

"Perfect."

Jeremy sets the gun on the altar between the remote and the bible. "Dude, how much you had to drink?"

"What's it matter?"

"We want to get this shit right, don't we?"

"We will."

"So you're cool?"

"Super." I nod at his glass. "Come on. One drink won't kill you."

Jeremy says I'm right, clinks my glass, holds it high. "Here's to you."

"And to you."

I set mine down after a sip but Jeremy keeps going. His glass comes down empty, his eyes so goddamn sad. He says, "No sappy bullshit, right?"

"That was our rule."

He takes a deep breath and rolls his neck in a full circle before blowing it out. "Okay, let's do this."

Jeremy picks up the camera and turns it on, radios Hank who's hanging out in the back. "Only play the video. Starting in five, four."

The camera is zoomed in on the gun, the 6-inch barrel running the length of the screen, flames crackling in the background, a mounting roar pouring through the speakers, the chants recharged.

Jeremy says, "Josh, stand and put your hands on the altar." He beats me to my question and says, "Just grip the edge."

My equilibrium's a bit off, but it seems most of my pain's gone. "Like this?"

"Fuck yeah." He zooms out and the gun's just inches from either hand, the masses screaming their approval.

The screen switches to Darren's feed, Father and Paul, excited eyes glued to the screen above them.

Jeremy says, "Go ahead and pick it up."

I don't carry mine anymore, no longer see the point. I used to think a gun might save my life, but even if it could, that'd just be one more reason not to have one. Jeremy asks again so I grip the black handle, raise it, thinking it's heavy, then remembering I'm just so goddamn weak.

"Go ahead and have a seat, but hold it over your heart, barrel up by your shoulder."

I'm glad to sit, wonder if Jeremy sees me shaking.

"Here," Jeremy says, handing me my drink. He backs up a bit, looks through his viewfinder. "Nice. This is awesome. Hank, in ten seconds cut back to me."

Jeremy snaps his fingers. "Alright, here we go. Sit up straight."

I'm tired and just want to get this over with. I don't really move much.

"You're not some pussy Messiah. Sit up. Let's show these fuckers who's boss."

It hurts a bit, but I spread my shoulders, stick out my chest, hold my head high. His red light pops on, the screen showing the bible and bottle on top of the altar. The camera creeps up and zooms out, shows me in all my glory. A body and mind that's been through hell, supposedly preparing me for Heaven.

Again the crazy yells, the shrieks, the calls for me to fucking do it. I ask, "Can we cut that?"

Jeremy hits a button and the screen jumps back to Father with his worried look that only I know is complete bullshit. Jeremy pulls out his phone and starts setting the camera on the altar.

I scream, "No!" and leap from the throne, knock the camera at him.

Jeremy nearly drops it and says, "What the fuck?"

The pain hits hard, rips through my whole body. I grimace, nod at the tiny remote he almost crushed.

His face loses some color, but he forces a laugh. Looking back at me, Jeremy says, "Shit, you okay?"

I want to answer but can't. He slides around the altar and helps me back on my throne. He says, "Take your time."

The back of my hand wipes away the tears that crept through. I say I'm okay and Jeremy shows me his phone, flips through each of our accounts, pointing out all the likes, shares, and followers. He pats my shoulder. "No pressure, but we've got the entire world watching. This is fucking history. There ain't a kid in the world that's ever gonna forget this."

I say good like I really mean it and switch to channel 3, which shows Charles 3:16 now past ninety-nine percent. He faces the screen and smiles. "I'd say our trusted sources are paying off."

"Wait." I switch to channel 4, can't believe my eyes. "Holy shit, it's more than doubled since I last checked."

Jeremy just stands there, mouth open. "That's in dollars?"

"Well, it ain't fucking pesos, amigo."

That gets another smile. Jeremy radios Hank. "Take us outside for a minute but play the music."

The flames are licking the arms of the blinding cross, the outline of my face emerging from the fire.

I use the armrests to get up. I look Jeremy dead in the eyes. "Thank you. For this. For everything."

Jeremy wraps both arms around me and squeezes tight. "Messiah or not, you were always my brother."

Neither of us say the word love but I know it's there. I break off the hug and say, "I'd feel better if you left."

He shakes his head. "Well, tough titty said the kitty. You can't make me, and I'm not leaving."

I sit back on my throne. "Fair enough. Then I guess it's about time to bring in the others."

Jeremy passes the message to Hank and readies his camera, steps outside the door to film the nine individuals walking down the main aisle in three rows of three. I can't see that far and turn to the screen, six black suits and three red shirts headed our way. The black suits are Father's guards, one on each side of our special guests in the red button-downs with their hands behind their backs.

Of the guards, Janet, Darryl, and Raymond are the ones I dealt with the most, but all six have been entrusted with my safety. I'm paying them each five times their hourly rate for an unarmed assignment and a guarantee of permanent employment if Father doesn't agree with what I ask of them.

If I didn't know who our guests were, I'm not so sure I'd recognize them. Part of it's my memory, part of it's the bruises. Part of it's the white gags tied around their head and spreading their cheeks back in a distorted, painful smile.

Yuri's first, and the least banged up, falling for Jeremy's promise he'd have all the fame and money he'd ever want if he accepted my apology in Vegas. Raymond and Kent direct Yuri into the second row, shuffling him down so his handcuffs don't show as they walk in the pew directly behind him.

Rick, my old boss from Arizona, had put up a fight and gotten both eyes battered shut. Darryl and Greg each have an arm looped inside his, staying that way as all three of them scoot down the pew until Greg is beside Yuri.

Last up is William and Janet setting Tommy at the end of the pew. I hadn't known Tommy's name until yesterday, but I'll always remember his coked-up eyes when he bent Beth over his desk, gun aimed at my face, me on my knees. Now his eyes are just burning with rage, his gag the only thing keeping him smiling.

Jeremy suggested the gags so there wouldn't be any problems with our audio, but I had agreed to them so I wouldn't snap. I don't care if it was a curse or an apology, if I heard a word from any of them I'd erase their brain with a bullet.

My screen's synced with theirs, the cross a brilliant white diamond slicing through the flames. My face morphs in and out of the fire, faster and faster before it solidifies, the shouts from outside coming through the glass.

Jeremy motions for Darren to take over filming below and comes back in the sanctuary, camera on me. He asks, "You ready?"

I nod, my focus on Father and Paul who are only sort of kneeling, their butts propped on the pew's seat. The command is for everyone, but I stand and stare directly at them. The face on the building is live, Jeremy's program making my voice even deeper and darker as it's amplified inside the church and across the city. "Everyone on your knees. Kneel before your Messiah."

Paul looks shocked, Father furious, but they both fix their posture. The second row stays seated until Darryl and Greg link arms with all three prisoners, bringing them onto the kneeler that is nothing more than a strip of metal, both the cushion and wood removed. Raymond moves into the aisle and kneels beside Yuri, places a hand on his shoulder. Janet does the same on the other end with Tommy.

I don't know if he heard something or saw Darren's concern, but Father glances behind him. He shouts at the guards that used to be his, "What is going on?"

No one says a word, so he spins back around, his hand on the front of the pew. "Joshua! What is the meaning of this?"

The screen cuts to the crowd outside, the majority on their knees, the fire crackling louder than before. Keeping it so only the people inside could hear, I say, "It's a lesson you taught me. Watch and you'll be proud."

There's that flicker of faith, that light that's kept him bouncing back from all the disappointments. My face burns on the building, but I redirect my eyes, stare in the lens. I tell Jeremy, "Let's do it."

He gives me the go ahead and I begin. "I was born dead thirty years ago and have been giving death the middle finger ever since. Some say it's because I have a higher purpose. Some say it's so I can fulfill my destiny, so I can save the world when all seems lost.

"Many believe that today is the day. This is the day the Messiah finally accepts his role. The day I cast judgment, on both the living and the dead."

I pause to catch my breath, reel in the anger. Insane screams fill the air outside.

"I've had one true teacher in my life and today he kneels before me. Charles Campbell."

I intentionally left off the Almighty and all the other names he'd made for himself, but even without it, the crowd roars for him. Three cheers for the puppet master.

"Charles knew I was the Messiah the moment he heard me scream from the grave. When no one would listen, he would only preach louder, demanding attention and risking ridicule. He dedicated his life to his message because he had a world to save.

"This is the man who built a church out of our garage and turned it into this. Jesus with his bread is nothing compared to a handful of followers multiplied into a billion. A feat never heard of, fueled by faith, believing in me when I wasn't able to."

I need a drink, so Hank takes us inside, Father beaming bright, the first time he's ever heard my praise.

"Charles taught me three important lessons preparing me for this moment: When someone wrongs you, you cast judgment. Search for the absolute worst in a person and judge them by that. The safest form of vengeance is hurting others before they can hurt you."

It looks like everyone inside and out is loving the speech except the three unlucky fuckers in the second row. Darren's feed zooms in on them and I say, "Today there are sinners in my midst. Individuals who have committed crimes against me, but more importantly, crimes against humanity."

Darren remains on the red shirts, the stone-faced guards surrounding them.

"I have judged them, and they will face the same ending as me."

The roar outside sounds like bloodthirsty lions. Hank lowers our volume while Tommy shrugs off Janet's hand and tries to stand. William grabs his shirt and shoves him down on the kneeler, his howl finding a way through his gag.

"It is a shame though seeing how most are probably only guilty of the same thing I was. Being tricked by a slick-tongued snake who's read too much Stephen King, and his son, the serpent whispering in his ear."

Father shoots up. "How dare you!"

Troy steps forward, about ten feet and the pew between them. "Sit down."

"What! You sit down!"

Troy aims his .357 at his Father's chest. "I won't tell you again."

Jeremy takes the camera off me and steps out of the sanctuary, Hank switching to his feed because Darren's is jumping all over.

Raymond stands. "What is this?" He steps toward Troy. "I didn't agree to—"

Troy's bullet punches through Raymond's forehead, the big fucker thumping on the carpet before the rest of them know what's happened.

Everyone disappears beneath their pews. Janet scrambles for the main entrance. No one stops her because it's locked.

Jeremy yells at Darren, "Get the fuck up and film!"

All I see of him is the tip of one shoe sticking out from the fifth row. Troy says, "Do it. Now!"

The camera raises like a white flag.

Jeremy says, "You film these fuckers or you're next. Understand?"

Darren aims his camera, nods over and over.

Hank switches to show us his work. Jeremy sighs. "You better breathe and calm the fuck down."

Darren takes a deep, ragged breath, and Jeremy says, "Not so goddamn loud."

We knew someone was bound to get blasted so we're prepared. Jeremy zooms in on Raymond, the carpet staining dark around his head. I'm glad it was Raymond. He was the first one Troy gave up after pulling me from the rubble.

"Look upon this man and look closely," I say. "This is how we all end up, a pile of meat rotting on the floor. The sinners in this church will meet that end tonight."

Father breaks his silence. "Joshua, stop this. You cannot kill innocent men."

My laugh scares me. "'No killing innocent men' says the tyrant responsible for killing half this country."

Father shrieks, "You've gone insane!"

"Quiet!" My echo continues, an effect Jeremy built into my mic for anything over a certain decibel. "This is not a discussion. This is my turn to speak. I may not know the extent of the crimes committed by everyone here, but I do know yours. And even if some are innocent, you must remember your words: 'There are casualties in every war.'"

Only Father, Darren, and Janet cowering by the back entrance are visible. I say, "Everyone on your knees. Troy, execute anyone who does not obey."

Everyone listens. Jeremy says, "Not you, Darren."

Darren's feed stabilizes and Jeremy steps back in the sanctuary, a nasty smile behind his camera.

To the whole world, I say, "So listen to my message, realize your sinful ways. You put your faith in a man who conspired with the President of the United States to deliver tainted vaccines designed to kill."

Father shouts, "That's a lie!"

Troy fires a bullet into the wood a few inches from Father's hand. Tommy goes for it, takes off down the aisle, makes it five feet before a bullet smacks his shoulder, knocks him face first on the carpet. Hands behind his back, he's not going anywhere. But his screams are cutting through his gag until Troy walks up and shoots him in the back of his head.

Hank puts clickable links on the screen. I say, "Everything's documented. See the proof. Your President is a criminal. Charles Campbell is a criminal."

I've no doubt Father wants to hurl a string of obscenities, to grab me by the throat and squeeze until the jugular pops, but Troy's back at his spot, his gun aimed right at Father's face. I continue, "You have all been compliant in your unquestioning support of an evil man. As have I. I am just as guilty, if not more so."

Someone shouts stop and messes up my train of thought. Paul stands, tears streaming down his face. "I'm sorry! I'm so sorry! I beg forgiveness!"

Father pushes Paul out of the aisle. "Judas!"

Troy orders Father back down with his gun, showing restraint because I want Father alive as long as possible. This show is for him more than anyone else. He has to see this crumble.

Paul gets to his feet in the aisle, bows his head. "Please, Joshua. I accept my fate, but please grant me forgiveness."

I ask, "Why should I?" and hate I've even given him that much.

"Because you're my brother."

"Not good enough."

"I didn't know about the bomb."

I don't say anything because we hadn't confirmed his involvement either way.

Jeremy says, "Fuck him."

I agree but I also know Paul would've never wanted any of this if he hadn't suffered the same father I did.

Troy takes a step to the side, but keeps his gun on Paul. "Joshua?"

To me, Jeremy says, "Don't let him."

I pull the remote closer, put the gun where I can pick it right up. I say, "Go ahead, but only to the door."

Paul comes up, head bowed, Troy's gun swiveling back and forth. Jeremy backs into the corner to my right to get a straight shot of the door. Paul steps on the boundary and Jeremy tells him, "That's far enough."

I reach for the gun because Paul's leaping for it, his nails digging into my hand.

I pull back my bleeding hand, not the gun. Paul aims at me, but Jeremy swings the camera like a baseball bat smack in his face. Paul's eyes go blank, his body falling, the gun exploding like a cannon.

Jeremy clutches his stomach and drops the camera, goes to his knees. He says, "Oh fuck," with barely any breath behind it.

My ears are ringing so loud I can't tell whether Troy fired another shot. I look up and see Troy crumpled on the stairs, Father scrambling out of the pew with a gun he must've snuck in.

Father runs past Troy and up the stairs. My gun is on the other side of the altar, not likely I'd make it before Father reaches the door. I grab the remote and plan to negotiate, but Father doesn't waste words, firing from the doorway. The first bullet flies a few feet to my left, the second, over my head. The third and fourth blow by my face.

Father stops, glances at the gun then at me, raises it slowly. "Hold still, you backstabbing little bastard." His eyes are scarier than any demon's. The eyes of my every nightmare. Spit flies from his lip, "You thought I would trust you? You think I'd let you sabotage my dreams?"

Up on the screen is an odd-angled shot of Father from the waist up, his arms shaking. Father turns to see what I'm smiling at then whips back around and steps toward Jeremy huddled in the corner, the camera balanced on his hip, his waist sopping wet with blood.

Jeremy doesn't look away. He stares down the gun. "Go ahead, Charles. Show the world who you really are."

The boom makes me jump, the bullet shattering the camera. Father tells Jeremy, "No, I say we keep it between us."

I consider saying I'm mic'd, but it doesn't matter. Father fires, Jeremy screams, holds his knee.

I had forgotten what I was holding, that I wasn't powerless. I yell, "Stop!"

Father glares at me, says, "You don't talk!"

I hold up the remote, my thumb an inch above the button. It's hard to think over the noise Jeremy's making, but I say, "You know what this is?"

Father checks over his shoulder. The screen shows Kent with Troy's gun, obvious whose side he's on. Father tells him, "No one else comes in here."

I point out, "Doesn't look like anyone was planning on it."

Father looks at me like I'm an idiot. "Did Paul look like he was planning on doing what he did?"

I lower my thumb just a bit, enough to make Father blink and step back to the doorway. "Do I look like I'm going to do what I'm about to?"

Father says, "It's a bluff." Keeping his eyes on me, he shouts over his shoulder, "William, get the authorities. Greg make sure this level's clear."

I don't mention him forgetting the paramedics for Paul and say, "All the doors are locked, the elevators disabled."

Father yells for them to hurry and they answer back exactly as I knew they would. I tell Father, "I don't need to lie."

Father raises his gun and a blast blows him forward. He crashes into the altar, knocking *The Lost Gospels* to the floor not far from his gun. Both his hands are on the altar. He tries to push up but can't, his blood pooling around him.

There's a half-dollar sized hole in his upper-right back, his blood dribbling onto the carpet. I hadn't heard a second shot, but Kent's lying on the floor, a massive exit wound where he'd once had a face. I don't see my savior, but say, "Thank you, Hank Spencer."

I kneel beside Jeremy who's barely breathing, his face scrunched up in agony. He tells me, "Nice job. But how about we call it a wrap?"

I lean over and kiss his forehead. "And thank you, Jeremy Ludlow."

I gather both guns and set them beside my throne, Paul still knocked out cold and Father not going anywhere. I say, "Darren, get up here. But not past the door."

Darren jogs up the stairs, does exactly what I say like he might still have a chance.

Father's eyes are closed so I give him a little slap, turn his head so he has to watch my final performance. I say, "And lastly, I'd like to thank those of you who voted in my favor, the few who acted as decent human beings."

That quiets the crowd but only for a second, followed by chants of 3:16 sounding from every direction.

The plan was to give a speech about Wrath and Judgment and warn the people down below, but now it's my turn to say fuck them. I take Father's face so he knows what I have to say is aimed at him. "All my life I've wanted so desperately to tell you I ain't no Messiah. I never have been. Never will be. But the truth is that there's only one way to find out for sure."

I hold up the remote so Darren can zoom in on it. "Before I press this button, let it be known that I, and I alone, am responsible for this. Don't let anyone tell you it was terrorists. No, this wasn't China or Russia or some

Islamic group. There's no conspiracy theory here. Don't go looking for some bad guy who blew me up. This is my decision. This is my wrath."

Hank switches the feed to the crowd, at the base of the building. I say, "It took my team of twelve most of the day to lace the thermite. If you don't want to be caught up in the explosion, I suggest you all run. NOW."

The chants abruptly stop, but there's a new kind of scream. Panic as everyone pushes back from the building, trampling one another.

Father reaches out his hand, too weak to hold it up. "Don't, Joshua."

Jeremy whispers, "Do it."

I say, "Goodbye," and press the button.

Nothing happens so I hit it again and again. One tremendous boom after another rocks the building, knocking me off my feet and onto my throne.

The booms keep coming, closer and closer, a thousand cracks run through the glass roof, everything as planned. There's a huge jolt and my world starts to tilt instead of freefalling.

I hold the edge of the altar to get out of the throne. The church and the rest of Building 7 are going straight down in the controlled demolition, but I'm still too high, falling away, the elevator breaking off, something we'd never considered.

Oh shit, we're picking up speed, my feet standing on the throne as I scramble on the altar, ashamed to be holding on for my life beside Father who's facing the window, screaming the whole way.

My throne breaks off the floor and knocks out the bullet-riddled window. There's water below us, but we're fucking flying, my feet hanging in the air, the altar breaking loose.

We're going to hit and I hope this is it, but I hold tight, letting go at the last second. I slice through the water, my feet shattering on the lake's concrete bottom. My body rises to the surface despite my best efforts, my wish for something like the altar to pin me down. I don't want to come up. I don't want to breathe. But I have no choice.

Fuck. Maybe I am the Messiah.

The End

Book 2 in the Tales of the Blessed and Broken series scheduled for 2024.

Horror

90 Short Stories

Download Your Free Copy

Includes the first two chapters and one death scene
from each of the first seven books in the Try Not to Die series.

Time for a Decision

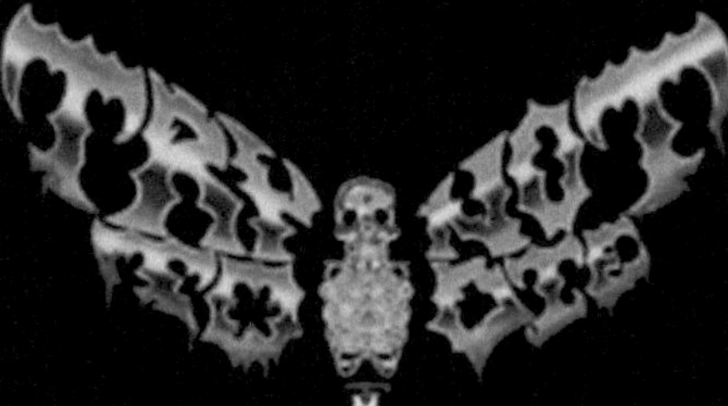

Which books do you want to die in?

Listen to the Books

You can listen to several books in the Try Not to Die series, short horror stories , suspense novels, or nonfiction. Find your next listen at your favorite retailer or www.MarkTullius.com

DETHFEST

FLAMETHROWER   OMNES MORIMUR
DETHROS

An Interactive Adventure

You've got tickets to the metal festival of the year. Get ready to rock. And try not to die.

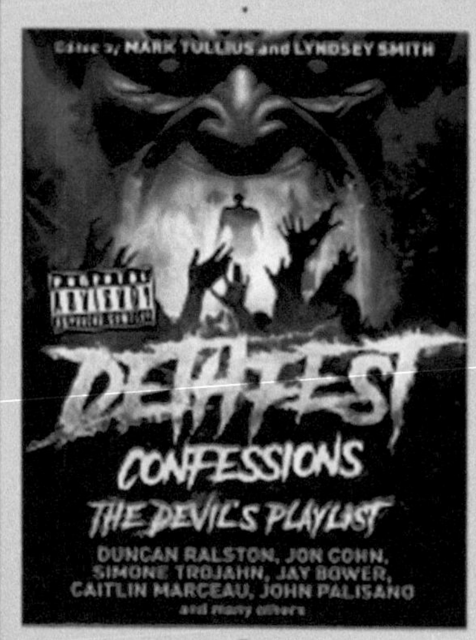

An Anthology

15 Horror Stories about each of the bands that played the Dethfest tragedy.

Nonfiction

MMA

Exploring the
Motivations of Fighters
100 gyms
23 states
400 interviews

Brain Health

Facing fears of
dementia from
repetitive blows to
the head.

Jiu Jitsu

Current Project
A coffee table book
featuring Mark and
his family training
around the world.

Connect with Mark

Mark enjoys sharing his
passions on social media.
Check him out on IG at
https://geni.us/TulliusIG

In addition to Instagram,
you can also check him out on
Tik Tok at
https://geni.us/TulliusTikTok

And on Facebook find him at
https://geni.us/TulliusFB

To watch Derek the Demon, book reviews,
podcast clips and more.
https://geni.us/TulliusYouTube

www.ingramcontent.com/pod-product-compliance
Lightning Source LLC
Chambersburg PA
CBHW051242210726
48287CB00002B/352